MOUNT WEATHER
ZOMBIE RULES BOOK 5

DAVID ACHORD

SEVERED PRESS
HOBART

MOUNT WEATHER

PREVIOUSLY IN THE ZOMBIE RULES SERIES

At the beginning of the Zombie Rules series, Zachariah Gunderson is a skinny know-it-all, struggling through his sophomore year in high school. At the time, he is infected with a common teenage malady known as puppy love.

His sweetheart, Macie Kingsley, does not have the same feelings and dumps him. Unfortunately, his grandmother dies, which also happens to be the same day as his sixteenth birthday. If all of this was not bad enough, Macie's new boyfriend and his buddies beat him up and vandalized his house.

Zach is consoled by his friend and boss, Rick Sanders. A grizzled old Vietnam vet with a drinking problem, Rick convinces Zach the apocalypse is occurring and the two of them should ride it out at the homestead of the farm they work at.

Rick dies on Christmas Eve of the first year. Zach is lonely and depressed, but presses on. He meets his future wife, Julie Frierson, and they eventually have two children. He also meets Fred McCoy, a man who becomes a father figure to Zach and is a pivotal character in the series.

Zach is shot in book one. It's only a grazing wound to the side of the head, but there are strange side effects.

He also meets a man by the name of Charles Ward, who prefers to be called The Captain and has a crew of people who share their leader's vision of grandeur.

In Z14, book two of the series, the relationship with The Captain starts as a friendship but quickly turns sour. At one point, he attacks Zach and takes a knife to him. Zach is saved by Andie Ward, The Captain's own niece, whom he had been sexually abusing.

Book two is also when Fred, burdened with guilt, decides he must go to Los Angeles to find his only daughter. Along the way, he meets Major Sarah Fowkes, a pilot stationed at Tinker air base in Oklahoma.

Book three, Zfinity, hammers home the reality of living in a post-apocalyptic world. Zach and his group meet a Marine contingent who is travelling the countryside, conducting blood tests on survivors. Amazingly, they discover Zach has an immunity to the zombie virus.

It all sounds good, but the demented Marine colonel decides to abduct Zach and his children and conduct tests on them. Oh, and he orders the murder of several of Zach's loved ones, including Fred, Julie, and others. Even the dogs.

Destiny, which is book four in the series, starts with Zach in a state of depression. His wife is dead, his kids are missing. His only saving grace is

Kelly, who found Zach after he had escaped from captivity. He discovers an encrypted note, written by a female Marine who had befriended Zach during his captivity, indicating his children have been relocated to the CDC in Atlanta, Georgia.

He and Kelly plan to go to the CDC in Atlanta in hopes of rescuing them, but, much to his surprise, a few Marines show up in Nolensville with his kids in tow. They beg Zach's forgiveness for their part in the abduction. Zach is tempted to kill them on the spot, but in the end, he finds forgiveness in his heart.

Colonel Coltrane isn't finished though. He has become obsessed with finding Zach and eventually returns to the Nolensville community. Karma catches up with the colonel though. Janet, Zach's mother-in-law, slits the colonel's throat.

With the help of new friends, Zach organizes a rendezvous, a method of bringing together other survivors for the purpose of meeting each other and bartering. It proves to be a success.

During the rendezvous, everyone is surprised when radio contact is made with the president. He later sends a delegation to Nolensville whereupon they invite Zach and his friends up to Mount Weather. At first, Zach is dead set against it, but one night he has a dream…

The Characters

Zach – When the apocalypse began, Zach was a smart but naïve teenager. Now, he's a nineteen-year-old man, wise beyond his years, but troubled with the lingering effects of PTSD.

Kelly – Four years older than Zach, she admits to have been smitten with him from the moment she first met him, even though he was married to another woman at the time. Taller than your average woman with long dark hair and even longer legs, Zach thinks she's beautiful. They fell into each other's arms after the massacre and have been together ever since.

Frederick Zachariah Gunderson – Named after Fred McCoy, Zach's two-year-old son is described as a rambunctious kid who gets into everything.

Macie Marie Gunderson – Zach's one-year-old daughter loves attention and loves her adopted mother. She has Zach's blond hair and brilliant blue eyes. She was named after Zach's first love.

The Nolensville Crew – Ten other people from the Nolensville community travel to Mount Weather with Zach (not counting the Mount Weather delegation). But, there might be one late arrival…

The Citizens of Mount Weather – There are a total of one hundred and thirty people at Mount Weather, give or take, consisting of the president, politicians, support staff, a few military, and other various sundry personnel.

CHAPTER 1 – PASSIN' THROUGH

Riley tried to remain still, but she couldn't help herself. She'd not shaved in almost three years, and for some crazy reason, she decided to last night. Everything below the waist was fine, but her armpits itched like crazy. At least she wasn't scratching her crotch every few minutes.

She wasn't sure why she did it. Maybe it had to do with the group from Nashville that had passed through last week. There were a few single men with them, and she'd caught at least a couple of them eyeing her frequently. But, they didn't stick around.

With the exception of her brother, the men in her group were all old. Much older than her. Lately though, she'd started having notions about Ben. He turned fifty the day before. He was a handsome man, trim, salt-and-pepper hair, and nice teeth. He was a successful businessman back before, with a beautiful wife and two kids in college, who were now dead. Whenever he saw Riley, he'd smile and give her a wink.

At his birthday party, Riley caught him alone and kissed him. He turned red, mumbled something unintelligible, and hurried back to the crowd.

Riley fumed at the memory. She'd never been with a man before and wanted Ben to be her first. She had it all planned out, but those plans went to hell the moment he ran off.

While she stood there, fuming and red with embarrassment, her older brother had walked by and made fun of her hairy legs sticking out of her cutoff shorts. She retorted with a snide comment of her own, but she also wondered if it was the reason Ben was frightened off. Maybe he wasn't frightened, maybe he simply found her unattractive.

That night, she found a disposable razor and went to town. The next time Ben saw her wearing short shorts, and she was going to wear them until he did, he was going to regret not kissing her back.

Riley scratched herself again as she sat in her makeshift sniper pit. She hated guard duty. Sitting in a hole in the ground, sweating, getting bitten by mosquitos, not her idea of fun. Well, with the exception of getting to shoot zombies when they came wandering through.

She peered through the rifle scope down at her dad. He was sitting under one of those big umbrellas beside their van, fanning himself with a fly swatter. Riley gritted her teeth. Why couldn't she be the one who sat in the shade waiting for prospective customers to come along? Besides, if any cute guys came through, how was she going to attract them like this?

She didn't know why they kept up with this trading post nonsense. Nobody had come through since those people from Tennessee, and that was four days back. The only bright moment happened a few hours ago when she spotted two zombies slowly walking up the interstate.

Both of them were adolescents, a boy and girl somewhere around Riley's age. They looked like they'd recently turned. Neither of them bore the scarring and blackened skin of old zombies. No, these two still had festering wounds and nasty bite marks. The boy's face and neck had been chewed up pretty good. No surprise there. Once those nasty things got ahold of you, they went crazy.

The girl was odd looking. She was wearing camouflage shorts, hiking boots, and nothing else. In addition to multiple bite marks on both arms, her breasts no longer existed. It looked like they'd been torn off. Her face was still mostly intact though. She would have been a pretty blonde at one time.

She found it strange. If they were freshly turned, they couldn't have travelled far, yet Riley did not recognize either one of them.

It didn't matter though. They were infected, and there was only one thing to do about it: Kill them. Riley waited until they had lined up in her sights and fired. The bullet entered the right eye of the girl, exited out of the back of her skull, and entered the cheek of her male companion, lodging itself in the C1 vertebrae. Both of them slumped to the roadway without making a sound. Grinning, she turned her scope back on her father. He signed to her to leave them both lying in the roadway.

She settled back, thinking about maybe taking a nap, but her thoughts were interrupted by the rhythmic sound of hoof beats. She turned slowly and peered through the camouflage down the opposite side of the interstate. A man on horseback was making his way down the road. He barely glanced at the two fresh zombie kills as he rode by.

Riley remained perfectly still. She was hidden well enough, she was sure of it. After being spotted by the cute blue-eyed boy, Zach was his name, she took a lot of ribbing from her brother about it. She worked hard on her new sniper pit after that. Nobody could spot her now.

She sat motionless as the man on horseback casually rode up. Much to her consternation, he stopped on the road no more than ten feet away from where she was hidden. The horse looked in her direction and snorted. The man on the horse looked down the interstate at her father, took his hat off momentarily, and wiped his brow.

"Excuse me, miss," he said as he put his hat back on. "I'm wondering if you people could spare some clean water for my horse."

2

"How did you spot me?" Riley demanded.

"I didn't," the stranger replied. "My horse did."

Riley stared at him, wondering if he was joking with her. She glanced over at her father who was smiling good-naturedly.

The stranger was older than her father by a few years. Tall and lanky, he had a deeply weathered face, most of which was covered by a thick beard. His eyes were cold, strained, belying the fact he'd had a hard few years. He was pretty stiff when he got off his horse and a momentary expression of pain had flashed across his face, making her wonder what'd happened to him.

"Your horse didn't know I was a girl," Riley argued.

"Sure he did," he said, and offered a small, forced smile.

"What brings you around these parts?" her father asked.

"Just passin' through," the man answered. It was a vague answer, as were all of his responses. When Big Joe introduced themselves, he nodded pleasantly and said he was pleased to meet them, but he didn't bother offering his own name. Father and daughter exchanged glances, but they didn't push it.

Joe looked over at the man's horse, which was picketed under a nearby black locust tree. He had a saddle, a rifle in a scabbard, saddlebags, and a tarp rolled up and tied to the back of the saddle. Joe also noticed the six-shooter holstered to his waist. The leather holster looked well broken in. For some reason, Joe had no doubt the old man knew how to use that pistol.

"You look like you're travelling light," Joe commented.

"Yes, I am. I'm afraid I don't have anything to trade."

"No matter," Joe said as he looked over at his daughter. "We were about to take a break for lunch when you came riding up, would you like to join us?"

"I'd be most appreciative," the stranger replied quietly.

"He didn't have much to say," Riley said as she and her father watched him ride away.

"Nope," Joe replied.

"He didn't even tell us his name," she said.

"I guess he thought it wasn't necessary."

"We could've killed him and taken his stuff."

Joe looked down at his daughter. "We don't do that anymore."

CHAPTER 2 – MOUNT WEATHER

They were everywhere. I was alone in the guard shack and down to my last magazine. I'd killed dozens, but there were hundreds more.

"Someone bring me more ammo!" I yelled, but somehow I knew nobody was left alive. Shooter and his brother were lying outside of the guard shack, currently being chewed on by several zombies.

I fired my last round at one of the things who had managed to crawl up and into the guard shack. Pulling out my machete, I began swinging wildly as they came pouring in. One of them, an ugly gaunt-faced male of indeterminable age, grabbed me in a bear hug. I tried to push him away, but his face moved inexorably toward mine, his teeth gnashing. I could even smell his hot, rank breath. He then stuck his tongue out and licked me.

I jerked awake sometime during the second or third time Zoe licked my face. When she saw my eyes open, her tail started thumping against the floor, which caused Callahan to jump up on the bed and give my face a lick as well. I guess they needed to go outside and were telling me they'd be most appreciative if I got my butt out of bed.

I reached out and acknowledged them both with a head pat, rubbed the sleep out of my eyes, and tried to calm myself from the nightmare. Kelly stirred beside me.

"What time is it?" she murmured.

I glanced at the luminescent dials on my watch. "Almost five."

Kelly voiced her displeasure with a groan of irritation. I gave her a kiss on the cheek, ignoring her morning breath.

"Go back to sleep. I'm going to walk the dogs."

Upon our arrival at Mount Weather the evening before, we were greeted with open arms, more or less. Even President Richmond gave a welcoming speech. We were fed MREs, which I never liked but didn't complain, and then were assigned to rooms that were located underground in the famous top-secret bunker. I found out the private rooms were reserved for the VIPs, and the rest of the personnel were relegated to either small, single rooms or the dormitory. So, so far we'd been treated wonderfully.

4

Sammy Hunter, our recently adopted ten-year-old kid (almost eleven, he was quick to point out), was sleeping on a cot in the den, but when I entered, he was instantly awake.

"What are you doing?" he asked sleepily.

"I'm going to take them for a walk," I said, gesturing at the dogs. "Do you want to go with me?"

He readily agreed and began dressing.

The elevator hummed smoothly as we ascended to the surface.

"How do they have electricity?" Sammy asked.

"According to Seth, it comes from a dam that's located about two hundred miles from here." I saw Sammy looking at me in puzzlement.

"The dam supplies hydroelectric energy," I explained.

"What's that?" he asked. I gave him a look.

"It's when water is used to create electricity. We're going to have to get you enrolled in school."

Sammy made a face. "Can't you teach me?"

I smiled and gave his shoulder a squeeze. "Sure I can, but I want you to be smart."

"You're smart. Everyone says so."

"I want you smarter than me," I said.

The elevator door opened. Zoe and Callahan ran ahead and waited anxiously at the main entry door.

"Where's everyone at?" Sammy asked as we watched Zoe sniff around before finding a suitable spot. She'd grown a lot since she was given to us by a gentleman who called himself Hillbilly, but there was still a lot of puppy in her. I made a mental note to ask if there was a veterinarian here.

"I guess they're all still asleep," I replied.

It was a humid gray morning. It felt like rain was on the way. I looked around at what I could see of Mount Weather. I'd read about it once on the internet, and I got the impression it was a massive fortress-like facility. So, I was a little surprised when we got here. There were multiple buildings, all built without seeming regard to symmetry or efficiency. I was told they were all connected by tunnels, but I had not had a chance to get that far, yet.

There were a lot of things present that I'm sure were added after. Greenhouses, a couple of barns, someone had even built a small smoker. And lots of clotheslines. I'd seen the laundry room down below, but I guess some people felt like energy conservation was important.

The fencing looked like it had been reinforced several times. I could see the original fencing and then there was additional fencing, added posts, and concertina wire, lots of concertina wire. It was full of trash. I guess keeping it clean was not a high priority. There was a guard shack down at the main entrance. It was supposed to be manned twenty-four hours a day.

"Let's go say hello to the guards."

The main guard shack had been constructed sometime within the first or second year. It was at the northern edge of the property where State Route 601 and Old Blue Ridge Mountain Road intersected. They'd erected large concrete barricades with a heavily fortified steel gate. The guard shack was surrounded by Hesco barriers, like the military uses. For added protection, a couple of those bad ass Strykers were parked at angles on either side of the roadway with machine guns mounted.

They also had a decontamination station set up outside of the gate which consisted of a water tank and a gas-operated pressure washer. When we'd arrived yesterday evening, a gentleman dutifully washed down our vehicles while we disinfected our hands and shoes.

I pointed at the Strykers. "Those are awesome, aren't they?"

Sammy nodded. "I want to learn how to operate them."

I smiled. "Me too, buddy. Maybe we can get Seth to train us."

I could see two men manning the post. One was reading a book, the other one had his chin propped on his chest, snoring heavily.

"Good morning," I said as we walked up.

The one reading the book jerked and looked up, startled. "Don't do that, man," he said. "You scared the shit out of me."

I gave an apologetic shrug. So much for diligent guarding of the compound. I hoped it wasn't this lax all of the time.

He closed his book, stood, and stepped out of the guard post. "You're the new people, right?" he asked. He was in his mid-twenties, lean, sandy-brown hair, scruffy face. I noticed he was wearing Marine combat utilities.

"Yes, we are," I said. "My name's Zach, and this is my partner, Sammy." I then pointed. "Those are our dogs, Zoe and Callahan. Callahan never met a human who wasn't a friend; Zoe is mostly the same. Mostly."

"Good to know," he said. "Oh, I'm Conway, Bret Conway, and Sleeping Beauty here is called Joker," he said as he slapped the side of the shack. Joker went from a deep snore to instantly coming awake. His eyes darted around and settled on us. He was also wearing Marine combat utilities, but he had maybe a weeks' worth of beard growth and long hair.

"These are the new people," Bret informed him and introduced us.

Joker stood and stretched. "Yeah, good to meet you," he said rather indifferently as he scratched his crotch.

"What are you guys up to?" Bret asked.

"We woke up early and had to let the dogs out, so we thought we'd look around." I glanced around. "Are you two the only guards on duty?"

Bret hooked a thumb behind him. "There's another four guard shacks posted around the perimeter of the compound, and when we have the manpower, we have roving guards. It's probably not enough, but it's worked so far." He looked at his watch. "Speaking of which, it's time to call in and let the OD know we're still alive."

"OD?" Sammy asked.

"Officer of the Day," Bret replied and gave Sammy a grin. "When you're in the military, you use acronyms whenever possible."

"Oh."

I pointed out their clothing. "Those look like Marine combat utilities."

"Yep, we're Marines," Joker said with a scoff. "But it's not too much to brag about these days."

They certainly didn't look like Marines. Both men were in their twenties with scruffy faces, long hair, and sloppy-looking uniforms. No, they certainly didn't have the military bearing like Justin, Ruth, and Seth had. Even Grant shaved every day.

Joker continued. "Yeah, nowadays we sit in guard shacks, mop floors, clean toilets, and haul trash."

I frowned in puzzlement. "I would have thought there'd be no lack of combat work for you soldiers."

"If you mean action in the way of zeds or other hostiles, the answer is no," Bret answered after he got off of the field phone. "When we first set this place up, we had a kickass captain. We'd go out on regular patrols and hunt down zeds."

"We did a good job too," Joker added.

"Yeah, we did such a good job, we've been relegated to bullshit work," Bret finished.

"Every once in a while, we'll get a few zeds wandering in," Joker said. "But, we've killed most of them off around here."

"What about hostiles?" I asked.

Bret shook his head. "Back in the beginning, we had some attempted incursions, but we had superior firepower on our side. There were more than a few idiots who thought they were Rambo and tried to attack us. They died needlessly. To be honest, I don't think anyone within a hundred miles lives around here anymore."

"There definitely ain't any women," Joker lamented. "None worth having."

"Do you do any patrolling?" I asked, hoping I could get in on the action.

Conway shook his head. "Maybe one a month. They decided the fuel could best be used for other things. Like the delegations."

"Too bad," I said. "Who's your CO?"

Both men gave a look like I asked them if they had pierced nipples and liked to dress up in drag on Saturday nights.

"We used to have a squared-away captain by the name of Jones," Bret said. "He wasn't big on formalities, everyone called him Jonesy. He was a good man, but he got sick and died. The docs said it was dysentery."

"He shit himself to death," Joker said. "Now we have this Navy ensign." He scoffed and spit on the ground. I guess that meant Joker didn't like him too much. He scratched himself again, and snapped his fingers.

"Hey, somebody said you guys had a couple of Marines with you."

"Yep," I replied. "Major Grant Parsons, Lieutenant Justin Smithson, and Corporal Ruth Bullington." I was surprised they hadn't introduced themselves to the Marines already. Maybe that was planned for today.

"Bullington is a girl?" Joker asked. "How's she look?"

"She looks pregnant with Justin's child," I said.

Bret chuckled in understanding.

"Aren't there any single women?" Joker asked.

"A couple, but don't count on me to play matchmaker." I looked around. "I've never been in the military, but it seems to me this place can't be too easy to guard."

Bret frowned. "You got that right. Let me tell you about this place."

Joker groaned. "Here we go."

Bret ignored him. "It started out as a weather station, which is the reason for the name, I guess. During World War Two, it was set up for conscientious objectors to do some kind of work rather than going to war, but at some point, they decided this would be a good place to hide Congress if DC was attacked. At that time, there were only two buildings: the dormitory and a lab. In the fifties, they built the underground bunker. You know, the Cold War and all of that shit. Since then, they've added all kinds of buildings, and any idiot could see there was no strategic planning done when they were laying shit out. We got buildings scattered everywhere, making it a tactical nightmare to defend. The whole place is about four hundred and thirty acres, and we only have thirteen Marines."

"How many soldiers in total?" I asked.

"Well, let's see, if you include all of the officers, nineteen."

I furrowed my brow. "Doesn't seem like very many to protect this place."

Joker grunted in agreement. "And most of these civilians don't know squat about soldiering. If a large number of marauders raid this place, we'd be in trouble."

Bret glanced over at him. "I'm not so sure about that, but a well-trained recon team could easily infiltrate this place." He pointed around. "Don't get me wrong, we've made improvements." He pointed at the guard post.

8

"Like this, for instance," he said. "And we've reinforced the perimeter with wire and additional guard posts, but it isn't enough."

"Hey, where did they put you guys up?" Joker asked.

"A suite of rooms on the habitation level."

Joker cussed. "They *still* have us living in the dormitory, even though there are spare rooms, sitting empty."

"Have you looked around in the bunker?" Bret asked. I shook my head.

"Well now, the bunker is what sets this place apart from any other place. There's a hospital down there, dining and recreation areas, a water reservoir, an emergency power plant, and a television studio which has been wired in to communicate with all of those satellites up there," he said, pointing skyward.

Yeah, Seth told me about the satellite feeds. The nation's leaders sat in the comfort and safety of their bunker watching their country implode, and being impotent to do anything about it.

"There's even a crematorium down there," Joker said, interrupting my thoughts.

Bret nodded, and then gestured around in the growing dawn at all of the buildings.

"All of them are interconnected by a tunnel system, it's all pretty complex. But, unless you have a special access card, you won't be able to get in them tunnels."

"How about sewage?" I asked.

"There's an on-site sewage treatment plant, but we still have to haul off the trash. Food scraps go to a nearby hog farm and all other trash is burnt and dumped in a nearby landfill, along with any zombies we kill."

"It's a big place," I remarked.

Bret nodded. "When it was at full capacity, this place had around nine hundred personnel, give or take."

"And now?" I asked.

Bret's brow furrowed. "Oh, about a hundred and thirty, give or take. When it went bad, the place went on lockdown. A lot of folks didn't make it inside before they sealed up the bunker. Did you see the entry door?"

"That big blast door at the entrance?" I asked. "It's hard to miss."

"Yeah," Brett replied. "That thing weighs thirty-four tons. It takes ten minutes to shut and secure it."

"So, you've been here since the beginning?" I asked.

Bret nodded. "Yeah, both of us. We were at DC and escorted a group of senators here."

"We stayed in lockdown for thirty days," Joker said. "Someone finally got the idea to send us Marines outside to check things out." He shook his head at the memory and spit.

"I'd sure like to hear about it," I prompted.

"It was about what you'd expect," Bret said. "Utter chaos. We lost a lot of people during that fiasco."

"It took us weeks to clean up the bodies," Joker added. "They insisted on shutting that big blast door every evening. Finally, I guess about the second year, a decision was made to leave it open and only close in the event of an emergency."

"This place was specifically designed for Armageddon, but even so, it took everyone by surprise. Even with the FEMA gurus, it took a while before we got it sorted out," Bret said. "The biggest problem was all of the politicians think they know everything and they'd debate every little decision. It took three full months to convince all of them to let us outside and do what we were trained for."

"We must have killed thousands," Joker said. He offhandedly pointed toward the north and east. "The zeds came wandering out of the big cities."

"The first year we had a mild December, so they were active. A cold snap rolled in the first week of January." He frowned at the memory. "Man it was cold, and it snowed like crazy. The good thing is, the zeds froze, and it gave us time to work on hardening this place up. We were also able to go into towns and load up with supplies. But the first year was the roughest." He looked over at his friend. "I'd say we lost fifty percent the first year, right?"

"Yeah," Joker answered. "Sounds about right. A lot of them know-it-all government pukes did stupid stuff. They got themselves killed and other people who were trying to protect them killed." He grinned suddenly and chuckled at a memory.

"There was this one senator. Where was he from, Vermont?" he asked. Bret nodded. "Yeah, Vermont. Old white-headed dude. He and his entourage of butt sniffers went into DC one day, when was that, May?"

"Yeah," Bret said. "May of the first year. They got it in their heads it was safe to go into their offices and retrieve all of their important paperwork or something. They never came back." He made a sour face and shook his head.

"We lost our only two MRAPs and the four Marines who were ordered to go with them."

"What are MRAPs?" Sammy asked.

"They're military vehicles," Joker said. "They're designed to protect soldiers from roadside bombs and rocket-propelled grenades, but they also turned out to be exceptionally good anti-zed vehicles."

"Oh," Sammy said.

Bret continued. "The president sent us on a recon a couple of days later. We got into the outskirts of DC and saw thousands and thousands of Zeds. Jonesy ordered us to abort and we headed back."

10

Joker then gave me a look. "Hey, why don't you give us the four-one-one on those Marines?"

"The three of them were with the CIBRF," I answered.

"What the hell is that?" Joker asked. Conway glanced at him.

"The Chemical Biological Incident Response Force," he said.

"Oh," Joker replied.

"Yeah, Major Parsons is a pathologist. He's more of a doctor than anything else. Justin and Ruth are squared-away Marines. They're good people."

"Well, we certainly need the people," Joker muttered.

We talked some more before putting the dogs up in one of the kennels and making our way to the cafeteria. There were some lights on, but the main dining area was still empty. I heard movement in the back, on the other side of some double doors, which I assumed was the kitchen and walked back there. As we were about to walk through the doors, we were almost run over by a man pushing a cart bearing one of those large stainless steel coffee urns and a stack of cups.

"Good morning," he greeted with a pleasant smile. "I'm Jim Hassburg."

"I'm Zach Gunderson, and this is Sammy."

He gave us both fist bumps, and then motioned for us to follow him as he pushed the cart.

"Yeah, everyone knows who you people are. When Seth sent the message all of you were coming, it's all we've been talking about." He maneuvered the cart into a spot between buffet servers and locked the wheels.

"Coffee?" he asked.

"Absolutely," I replied. Sammy wanted to fit in, so he nodded. Jim poured two cups.

"I hope you like it black, cream and sugar are somewhat of a rare luxury, but we have enough freeze dried coffee to last for the next hundred years," he said with a chuckle. "Breakfast won't be ready for about an hour, but you're welcome to hang out."

"Not a problem," I said agreeably. "Are you the designated chef?"

Jim laughed. "We rotate duty assignments. This week it's my crew. Monotony is a mind killer, so we swap things up, unless you have a specialized skill."

"Sounds interesting," I said, as I sipped the coffee that could best be described as one grade lower than truck stop quality.

"Yeah, get ready for that. I imagine Lydia already has some kind of work detail lined up for all of you. My advice, don't tell her anything will do. Think of something you'll enjoy doing and insist on it."

"Thanks for the heads up," I said.

He then cleared his throat. "Um, the seating arrangements around here are kind of funny."

"In what way?" I asked.

"Certain groups of people have staked claims to certain tables," he said with an apologetic smile and pointed. "Those four tables over there are unclaimed."

"Sounds like grade school," I replied. "Or prison."

"Yeah, people can be peculiar about trivial things," he said. "Anyway, I have to get back to work. Welcome to Mount Weather." He smiled and hustled back into the kitchen.

"I guess we need to stake out a table," I said to Sammy, who nodded uncertainly. We picked one Jim had declared available and sat quietly as people started filtering in. Some said hello, some either had their mind on other things or they were simply rude.

The first of our group to walk in was Josue Garcia. He never told anyone his true age, but I suspected he was in his late fifties. He was maybe five-eight, wiry but fit, and a jack-of-all-trades. He wasn't a talkative guy, but he always seemed to be in a good mood and had a dry sense of humor. He gave me a nod, Sammy a wink, and made a beeline to the coffee urn.

His adult children, Jorge and Maria, were close behind him. They greeted us quietly and sat. Maria, a naturally shy woman, had been melancholy since she lost her son back in March. Both Josue and Jorge worried over her constantly.

Major Sarah Fowkes and her girlfriend, Sergeant Rachel Benoit, soon came through the door, along with Grant Parsons, Ruth, and Justin. All of them were wearing freshly cleaned uniforms.

"Big day today," Grant said with his own grin. "We get to have a sit-down with the Secretary of Defense."

"Hello, newcomers," a voice said behind me. I looked around to see a man who could have been forty-five or sixty-five. He had a smooth, tanned face, pearly white teeth, and his brown hair was perfectly groomed. Not a single gray strand. He was freshly showered and clean-shaven, and it was impossible to look at him and believe the world had gone to shit.

"I'm Conrad Nelson, may I join you for a minute?" he asked.

"Of course," I said.

Raymond had been kind enough to show me a file on his laptop during the trip up here. It had a brief biography of everyone at Mount Weather. I made a point of reading and rereading everyone's biography until I had it memorized.

Conrad Nelson was a senator from Florida, a position he'd held for two consecutive terms. Before that, he was the mayor of Pensacola. A graduate of Florida State University, he'd started his career as a lawyer before the lure of politics took hold. On the ride up, Raymond had mentioned the good senator was suggesting a presidential election needed to be held and he was going to run.

I gave him a friendly smile and introduced him to everyone who was present. His pleasantries actually seemed genuine, but he was a career politician, so it came naturally to him. He looked up as the cafeteria door opened and his grin grew in size. I looked over to see Kelly and Janet walking in, my two kids in tow.

Kelly's long dark hair was still wet, and it glistened in the fluorescent lighting. Conrad's quartz green eyes sparkled as I introduced him to my wife and monster-in-law.

"If I had known the women in Tennessee were so beautiful, I would have abandoned my constituency and moved," he said with a friendly chuckle at his own coquetry.

Kelly smiled politely and then ignored him as she kissed me and set Macie on my lap before sitting on the opposite side of the table away from the senator. Janet did the same, but I could still see her making lingering eye contact. Suddenly, he grabbed me by the shoulder.

"Say, Zach, you look like an athletic guy. Are you any good at volleyball?"

"I haven't played in a while. Why?"

"Our league is about to start up a new season. The Marines are undefeated; we'd like to change that."

"You have sports competitions?" I asked.

"Oh, yes," he said enthusiastically. "We have various recreational leagues. Volleyball, badminton, ping-pong, chess, of which I'm the reigning champion, by the way. No contact sports though."

We talked some more and he was about to leave when Kate and Kyra joined us. The idiot brothers, Cutter and Shooter, were close behind. When the sisters failed to respond to Senator Conrad's subtle flirtations, he stood.

"It's been a wonderful meeting all of you," he said with the same smile. "I hope we all can become good friends." He gave Kelly a wink before walking off.

"Oh, be still, my quivering heart," Kelly said and rolled her eyes.

Everyone was in a good mood, even sourpuss Janet, and we were enjoying meeting and talking to the Mount Weather people. They were an interesting, diverse group. Most of them seemed to have been government employees in their past lives, and whether that was a good thing or a bad thing remained to be seen.

Breakfast was rather uninspiring but filling, and the multiple ongoing conversations were a challenge to keep up with. Here is where my excitement started to wane.

I hadn't gotten more than a couple of bites of food in me when I felt a presence behind me. Turning, I saw Seth, formally known as Captain Seth Kitchens of the United States Army. Standing beside him was Raymond Easting, one of the civilian members of the delegation, and a woman I had not yet met.

"Good morning everyone," Seth said.

"Back at you," I replied with a grin. "Do y'all want to join us?"

"I'm afraid we can't," Seth said. "We've got work to do."

"That's too bad," Kyra said, and gave Seth a lingering look.

Kyra and her sister were attractive women in their late twenties. Both of them had a sultry look, enhanced by their Native American features. Kate was the dumb one. She had to be, because she'd hooked up with Shooter.

Kyra recently lost her boyfriend out on the road somewhere in Oklahoma, and since then, she'd been rather aloof toward men, but even I saw the chemistry developing between her and Seth.

Seth was momentarily distracted as the two of them stared at each other for a couple of seconds, realized everyone was looking at him, and cleared his throat.

"Unfortunately, you guys are part of the work." He looked over at the far end of the table. "All military personnel are to come with me, after you've eaten, of course."

"Aye, sir," Justin answered.

"Do you have any idea what will be on the agenda?" Sarah asked.

"The standard meet and greet, a debriefing, and job assignments." He paused and gave Justin a grin. "Oh, that thing we talked about, all I can say is be careful what you wish for."

"He's going to be put in charge of the Marines?" I asked.

"Oh, I wouldn't know," Seth said, but continued grinning and then gestured at Raymond.

"There will be a separate debriefing for the civilians."

Raymond smiled tentatively. "I have convinced them only one person needs to be present for the debriefing, so guess who's been nominated," he said while eyeing me.

"Wonderful," I said.

Kelly nudged me in the ribs, tacitly telling me to behave myself. The woman standing beside Raymond had remained quiet, but now she cleared her throat and looked pointedly at Raymond. She was a rather plain-looking woman in her early forties, wearing wire-framed glasses and a nondescript pants outfit.

14

"Oh, where are my manners. This is Lydia Creamer. She will be taking down information from the rest of you and assigning work duties."

"Work duties?" Shooter asked.

Lydia nodded curtly. "Correct, work duties. Nobody slides by for free." She spoke with a tight, toneless voice. I had an instant disliking of her but didn't show it. She spotted an open seat beside Kelly.

"May I?" she asked.

Kelly smiled warmly. "Of course."

Lydia had already seated herself before Kelly's mouth had closed and opened a computer tablet. "We'll need to start with your names, and then I'll need you to tell me about yourselves, tell me your specific skills, otherwise, I'll put you where I see fit."

Shooter made a derisive snort. Lydia frowned at him. "Is there a problem, mister…?"

"They call me Shooter. You got any work involving shooting, I'm your man. If you expect me to be on a work detail cleaning toilets and mopping floors, you can take your fancy computer and stick it where the sun don't shine."

Lydia's face tightened and she gave him a withering stare.

Cutter spoke up. "That's my brother."

"I'm terribly sorry for you," Lydia said.

"Yeah, tact isn't his strong point, but let me ask you something." Cutter briefly pointed toward the far end of the cafeteria. "Those look like a bunch of politicians, am I right?"

Lydia glanced over to where Cutter was pointing. "What's your point?" she asked.

"My point is this. When I got my coffee just now, I asked for sugar. The gentleman told me there was no sugar." He wagged a finger back at the table full of politicians. "And yet, I'm looking over at that table full of people, and I'm seeing people putting sugar in their coffee. Why is it they have sugar and we don't, Lydia?"

Lydia did not answer and continued giving him a cold stare through her glasses. Everyone else at the table was now staring questioningly at her.

Cutter continued and gestured at the Garcias. "Let me guess, you're going to make Maria a maid and have Jorge and Josue cut grass."

"Everyone shares in the work assignments," Lydia proclaimed.

Cutter suddenly reached across the table and grabbed Lydia's hand. He rubbed her palm before she snatched it away.

"What do you think you're doing?" she asked angrily.

Cutter sat back in his chair. "I was checking your hands for callouses, but it's as smooth as a baby's butt." He pointed at Lydia and the table full of politicians. "You people don't do manual labor, go ahead and admit it."

Lydia, who was now absently rubbing her hand, began stammering. "I, I most certainly do."

Shooter scoffed. "Yeah, right."

Lydia slowly gathered her items and stood. "I'm sure the trip here must have been hard on you. I'll come back when you've gotten settled in."

Shooter cackled as she walked away. "You sure set her straight, little brother."

Josue shrugged. "I like cutting grass."

I couldn't help but chuckle. I handed Macie back to Kelly and gave them both a kiss. Kelly pulled me close and whispered in my ear.

"Be nice in the debriefing, and watch your temper."

"I'll try my best," I whispered back, gave her another kiss, and gave everyone a small wave.

"Y'all have fun," I said and followed Raymond out of the cafeteria.

Raymond and I were sitting in a conference room promptly at eight. There was nobody else present. Raymond had his laptop in front of him and had a formatted word document opened with the title of today's briefing. He saw me looking.

"Paper is limited, but everyone has a computer of some sort and we have power, so, we document everything on the computer. Oh, we have a local internet as well. I'll get you set up with a username and password."

"Wow, impressive," I said and meant it. I glanced at the report again. "The date is wrong," I said.

He looked at it with a frown, and there was a brief moment of deep pain in his expression.

"Thank you," he muttered as he backspaced and corrected the date.

"No offense," I said, wondering what the heck I did.

He shook his head quickly. "Oh, I'm sorry, I was just thinking about something."

I looked at him thoughtfully. Raymond Easting and I first met when the delegation, which he was a part of, came to Nolensville. He was a slender, foppish man in his early thirties, a product of a wealthy family and the accompanying highbrow upbringing. Back before, he was a career bureaucrat working for the State Department. He had the gift of gab and persuasion, the kind of guy who could probably sell a sandwich to a zombie. Overall, I liked him, but even so, we both knew that back before we would have never run in the same social circles.

Something was nagging him. I had no idea what, so I kept quiet.

He cleared his throat. "August 5th is my son's birthday, or it was. He would have been four today." He smiled now, but it wasn't a happy smile. More like one of those rueful smiles when you're thinking of a painful memory.

"He was something else. He was always smiling, and he was very loud," he said with a chuckle. "My wife was three months pregnant with our second child when the plague roared through Maryland. That's where we were living."

"I'm sorry," I said.

He emitted something between a laugh and a sob. "It's okay. My only hope is, with your help, a cure will be found so nobody else will wake up one day and find their family had turned into monsters."

"I hope so too," I said. We sat there in silence for several minutes while Raymond busied himself with typing. Finally, I couldn't stand it anymore.

"Where is everyone?" I asked.

He shrugged.

"Why are we doing this? Haven't you guys already told them everything about us?" I asked.

"We've submitted reports, yes," he answered. "But, you know how people are who think they're important, they want to conduct their own inquiry."

He paused a moment, I could tell by the expression on his face he was searching for the right words. "You're going to be peppered with a lot of questions that you may find…"

"Inane, idiotic, condescending, naïve?"

Raymond laughed. "Yeah, something like that. You remember what Seth and I said about these people before, right?"

I remembered. These people were out of touch. They only had a peripheral understanding of how difficult post-apocalyptic America actually was.

Raymond laughed again. "Inane, idiotic, condescending, naïve. You certainly have a large vocabulary. Remind me never to play against you in the Scrabble tournament."

Our conversation ceased when people finally started trickling into the conference room. Raymond smiled and greeted each of them by name, or title, depending on who it was. One of them walked up to me with a politician's smile and an outstretched hand.

"Hello, Mister Gunderson, I'm Senator Bob Duckworth, from the great state of Utah."

He was a fit, polished man in his forties. Clean-shaven with a haircut similar to Senator Nelson's. He had on a pressed white button-down shirt and gray slacks. I remembered from reading his bio, Senator Duckworth was a successful dot-com entrepreneur before the allure of politics beckoned him. And, as Cutter had observed with Lydia earlier, the senator's hand was as smooth as a baby's butt. Not a single callous.

"Is there anything left of Utah?" I asked.

His smile faltered. "Truth be told, nobody is sure. As you're aware, we're diligently trying to reestablish our once great society."

"A noble effort," I responded, wondering if I meant it.

His smile returned. "We've heard an awful lot about your group. I must say, most impressive."

"That's great," I said. "So, there's no need for this meeting."

He looked blankly for a moment, and then realized I was being sarcastic. He laughed casually.

"A necessary evil, I'm afraid. Please bear with us." He turned and walked over to a group of people I recognized as various politicians.

And so, three hours later, I was still sitting at the same conference table while being peppered with questions by no less than forty different people. It started pleasantly enough. There was a formal opening of the meeting followed by an invocation, confirming my belief that politicians loved their ceremonies and rituals as much as any other radical group. When the preamble was finally dispensed with, we got down to business.

"Mister Gunderson," Senator Duckworth said. "Would you please start by telling us of how you and your people have survived this pandemic for," he paused a moment as he looked heavenward. "Oh, my, it's been almost four years now." There were some murmurs of agreement, followed by someone making a stupid quip of how time flies.

He repeated his question. "Could you tell us how you've survived the past four years?"

I expected the question and had a prepared response. I started by telling them about my friend and mentor, Rick Sanders, and how the crazy old man had it pegged from the beginning, and then I spent the next forty-five minutes or so describing the events in our lives up to the point when the delegation arrived.

I didn't go over every minute detail. There were a lot of things these people didn't need to know about. They certainly didn't need to know about who all I'd killed. Would they understand if I tried to explain the circumstances of how I killed my first person? Doubt it.

How would they react if I told them of the time I ran over a woman who was trying to set me up for an ambush? Would they call it an act of survival or would they accuse me of murder?

Like I said, there were a lot of things they didn't need to know about.

When I was finished, there was a five-minute break, and when everyone got seated, ten minutes later, the barrage of questions resumed. I thought I'd been thorough enough to satisfy them, but I was mistaken.

"Have you ever killed anyone, Mister Gunderson?" a woman asked. I would've known her even without reading her bio. She was Senator Esther Polacek and, back before, she was an outspoken far-left liberal; a feminist and gun-control advocate. She'd been a senator since before I was born, and it showed. Her political beliefs were of no concern to me, but I'm sure they influenced what she thought of me. After all, I was a white, southern, gun totin' redneck, the antithesis of what she believed in.

"I have," I replied.

I knew the question was going to be asked. It was simply a matter of when and by whom. As Fred would've said, always get to know the lay of the land. Well, I'd read all of these people's bios before coming up here, and I had a pretty good idea of who would be friends and who wouldn't.

"More than once?" another asked. I didn't answer.

"Why?" Senator Polacek pressed. "Why did you feel the need to kill?"

"Survival," I answered. "We didn't have an underground bunker to hide in, nor did we have any police or military to protect us, so we had to do what it took in order to survive." I leaned forward in my chair. "You see, Senator, when society collapsed, morality seemed to go out of the window with it. People would kill you simply for the sake of stealing the can of pinto beans in your backpack, and I won't even go into all of the other atrocities I've personally witnessed."

Her demeanor was stoic, yet she was staring at me pointedly. "How many have you killed?" she asked.

I stared back at her. She remained expressionless, but I knew she was trying to get a read on me.

"I'm not going to answer you," I said.

"Why not?"

"Because it's none of your business. It's nobody's business."

"I must disagree, Mister Gunderson," she continued. "Part of this debriefing is an attempt to determine if we have inadvertently allowed undesirables, or even murderers into our fold."

"And what assurances can you give me there aren't murderers already present?" I countered.

She looked back at me with a mildly surprised expression.

"You see, ma'am, it's a two-way street. My friends and I have been fighting for our lives every day since the world went to hell, while you people have been holed up here, protected by a thick steel door and a bunch of soldiers. Now, don't get me wrong, if it were offered to me back in the day, I would've been right here with you, but that's neither here nor there. What I am saying is some people believe successful politicians are nothing more than high-functioning sociopaths. How do I know there aren't any sociopaths among you?"

There was a long moment of silence before a small smile formed on her lips.

"Touché," she said and nodded at a man sitting beside her, who began tapping away on his computer tablet.

"Could you perhaps give us the scenario in which you were forced to take a person's life so that we could better understand?" Senator Duckworth asked. "Perhaps you can explain what led you to kill a Marine. Let's see," he paused and looked at his own computer tablet. "On the night of September 16th, you killed a Marine and escaped custody."

"Yes, I was illegally being held prisoner. Do those notes you have tell you my children were also illegally abducted and several of my loved ones were murdered?"

He looked at me plainly. "Not in those exact words."

"No, not in those exact words," I said. "Let me fill in some of the blanks." I then recounted the details of my abduction and subsequent escape.

When I had finished, a solid three minutes passed while people took notes or whispered among themselves. I wondered what they were discussing. Perhaps they thought I should be arrested for murder or something. Finally, Senator Duckworth spoke up.

"If you would, give us your recounting of the brutal murder of Colonel Almose Coltrane."

"Colonel Coltrane had committed various atrocities, including murder, kidnapping, and authorizing the illegal experimentation to two small children. When the two children were rescued and brought back to me, Colonel Coltrane pursued them and announced his intention of retaking them and conducting further harm upon them. It was evident the man had gone insane. He was killed by the children's grandmother in order to protect them."

"Mister Gunderson…"

"Call me Zach."

He smiled. "Thank you. Zach, it's my understanding she slit his throat."

"Yeah, she didn't know a sniper was targeting him and was about to blow his fucking brains out, but no matter, it worked out in the end."

"And you don't believe this was an act of murder?" Senator Polacek asked.

"What would you have done?" I retorted.

"Well, I most certainly would not have committed murder," she replied.

"Yes ma'am, I believe that. But my question is, what would you have done?"

She stared at me as she worked her mouth. I held a hand up.

"Let me help you with the answer. You have no idea what you would've done because you don't know what it's like out there. You either fight for your survival, or you bend over and hope they're gentle with you."

There were a couple of chuckles. The senator's face turned a scarlet red.

While she glowered at me, my stomach rumbled. I glanced at my watch and confirmed it was well past my lunchtime.

"Senator Duckworth, let me ask you a question."

"By all means," he said.

Before I could ask, I was interrupted.

"You don't ask the questions here, Mister Gunderson." The person who said it put a derogatory emphasis on the mister. I scanned the room and found him.

He was an older, prune face man with an authoritative scowl. He had to be in his sixties, and it looked like he was fighting a losing battle with a receding hairline. I did not recall meeting him when we arrived, but I noticed he'd been squirming around and scowling during the entire debriefing, kind of like his hemorrhoids were acting up, or maybe he had pinworms.

Now you can see why I was irritated. On the one hand, I felt obligated to help out in any way I could, but on the other hand, I was wondering why I was allowing idiots like prune face to treat me like a child. If he noticed I was getting pissed, he didn't show it.

"We are not through with our investigation of the murder of Amos Coltrane."

"It's Almose," I said.

"What?" he asked.

"His name was Almose, you called him Amos, and I've already discussed the incident. Either move on to another topic or I'm going to lunch."

"Well now, young man, if I say we're going to discuss it that is exactly what we're going to do."

"We have a saying down south, Senator. We don't chew our cabbage twice."

He frowned at me over his bifocals. "You're not making any sense."

"It's called a colloquialism; it means I don't care to repeat myself." The man obviously had never watched Ernest T. Bass in action. I leaned forward in my chair.

"You people are focusing too much on stuff that doesn't matter. Coltrane's death is in the past. What are you going to do, put Janet on trial? I bet you don't even have a judicial system in place. And what if you do? Are you going to send her to prison if you find her guilty? Have you even thought this through?" I looked around the room to emphasize my point.

"You need to be focusing on the future, and everyone sitting around doing nothing but engaging in endless prattle is not the answer."

"Alright, Zach, I'll bite," Senator Duckworth said. "What do you believe we should be focusing on?"

I made a conscious effort not to grit my teeth. Kelly said it was a dead giveaway that I was getting mad or frustrated because my jaw muscles flexed and a vein popped up along the side of my neck. I looked around the room and then focused on Senator Duckworth.

"I'm not sure exactly what you people have been doing the last four years, but if this morning is any indication, I'd say not much. Now, the delegation, and others like it, is a positive step, but I think you people are missing something important."

"And what might that be?" Senator Duckworth asked.

"The zombies," I answered.

"We are well aware of the zombies, Mister Gunderson," hemorrhoid man retorted. "We have them well under control."

I found myself shaking my head. "All of you listen carefully: these things are changing. They're thinking again, they're working together. They're planning, coordinating. In short, although they're numbers have diminished somewhat, they're far more dangerous now."

"Again, we're aware of all of this, Mister Gunderson," Senator Polacek said this time. "In fact, our scientists expected this type of behavior from the surviving zombies. It is nothing more than primitive behavior."

"There is one other thing I don't believe you people know about." Before I could speak further, Senator Polacek interrupted.

"Oh, let me guess, they're communicating telepathically."

"Yes," I said.

She laughed out loud now, as did several others.

"Oh, come now, Mister Gunderson," she said. "I must admit, you have an active imagination, but that is all it is, the overactive imagination of a naïve young man."

Now, I felt myself clenching my jaw and was about to tell them all to go fuck themselves, but, I didn't want to embarrass Kelly, so I took a deep breath and nodded in acquiescence. A hand raised up from the back row. It was an older man, and he didn't look like a politician. He saw me looking at him.

"Mister Gunderson…"

"Call me Zach," I said.

"Thank you. Zach, I would like to hear why you believe they are now communicating telepathically."

"I've personally witnessed it."

That stopped the guffaws, but I still saw a lot of skepticism.

"Could you describe those instances, please, Zach?" the man asked.

"During the second year, I was out hunting them one day and witnessed them communicating through guttural noises."

"You were hunting them?" he asked.

"Yes."

His brow creased. "By yourself?"

"Yes."

"Why?"

"For much the same reason you people have utilized the Marines to eradicate the zombie population around here," I said.

Now, Seth piped up. "Zach, we had a whole contingent of Marines to do that."

"I understand, safety in numbers and all that. And we did follow that line of thought, when feasible. For instance, we all got together on Christmas Eve of the second year and killed off a sizeable amount, over a thousand, but we didn't totally eradicate them. So, sometimes I liked to get out and do some hunting."

This statement caused a man to whisper fervently into Senator Polacek's ear. She arched an eyebrow.

"Are you saying you enjoy going out alone and murdering infected people?"

"Yep, but it's not murder."

"What is it then?" she pressed.

"It's more of an act of mercy." And, it's fun, but I knew better than to say that out loud.

"Alright," the man said. "Getting back to the telepathy, tell me about the telepathy you personally witnessed."

"On April 22nd, a group of zombies were led by a singular zombie and planned a deliberate and simultaneous ambush on two of the houses we were living in." I paused a moment to let it sink in.

"It could have been verbal communication along with simple, basic teamwork, I can't say one way or another, but that kind of an operation takes training, rehearsals, communication. The first time I saw an actual telepathic communication was September 29th of the second year. Kelly and I were hiding out in the semi we came here in. We were parked near some railroad tracks. There were thousands of zombies walking together along the tracks. We believe they were migrating toward other food sources, but that's irrelevant right now. The relevant point, all of a sudden, they stopped in tandem and turned their heads toward us. As you can imagine, it was unnerving."

"They might have heard something," somebody suggested.

"I disagree," I said.

"Please continue," the older man said.

"There are other, small examples, but I think the most telling example is the sophisticated attack on the CDC. I would recommend reading Lieutenant Smithson's report. In short, there is no way fifty thousand zombies could be coordinated into a massive attack using only grunts and clicks."

I was getting antsy and shifted in my chair. "In addition to their bodies healing, their brains are functioning different now. That makes them a stronger adversary, and therefore, they need to be studied."

The man nodded thoughtfully and then turned his head toward another older man sitting beside him. This one looked over his bifocals at me.

"Did you create a network of people down in Nolensville, Mister Gunderson?"

"On a small scale, yes. If you'd read the report prepared by the delegation, you would know we started what was called a rendezvous. It wasn't large, but it was successful."

"Interesting," he said. "And, did you get any manufacturing facilities up and running?"

"No," I replied. He gave me a look over his bifocals like he was saying, you should practice what you preach.

"I take it you ran into obstacles?" he asked.

"Yes, you could say that."

"How about a power grid?" he pressed.

"Our home was run on solar power with generators for backup power."

He continued gazing at me a moment with that same expression before focusing on something on his laptop.

"Let me see. It says on the delegation's report there is a lady still living in Nolensville by the name of Tonya Lee."

"Yes."

"She is a nuclear engineer, correct?" he asked.

"Yes. She's a smart lady." And, a tee-total bitch, I thought.

"Her resume is impressive," the secretary said. "It looks like she has the capability of restoring the power grid down there in Nolensville, yet, she has not done so. Why?"

"She built a small scale steam power plant at the elementary school they live at, but I don't believe she had any inclination of going any further with it."

"Yes, I've read that. If my fact sheet is correct, there are twenty-nine hydroelectric dams in Tennessee, would you know if that number is correct?"

"I believe that's correct. None of them are in the Nashville area though," I said. I'd read that the Percy Priest dam was hydroelectric, but a high school friend's father worked for the TVA and he had said it wasn't.

"Have you visited any of them to see if they are still operational?" he asked.

"No," I replied. He made a good point. I should have at least made an effort to visit one of those dams. I had no idea how to operate one, but I should have at least made an effort to check.

"I also read where you jury-rigged a system to tap into a fuel reservoir."

"Yes. It was somewhat successful until downtown Nashville flooded and put the reservoir under water."

"Ah, yes. You speculated the Wolf River dam had collapsed."

I nodded. "Yes, based on the amount of flood water."

"But, you did not make any attempts at confirming this particular catastrophe," he said.

"I'm sorry, I never did get your name," I said.

"Parvis Anderson," he said.

Senator Polacek spoke up. "We refer to Parvis and his colleagues as the secretaries," she said. "They are employees of Mount Weather." She gestured at Parvis. "Parvis, why don't you explain?"

The older man cleared his throat again and smiled pleasantly.

"Our duties were to keep Mount Weather running as well as creating and enacting various scenarios. Those would include wartime situations as well as post-apocalyptic scenarios."

"I see."

"Back to my original question…"

I cut him off. "Parvis, I want you to understand something. From the time the sun came up until well after dark, all of us worked. Anything from farming, scavenging, hunting, killing zombies, defending ourselves against marauders, you name it. We simply did not have the time nor the manpower to send out long-range surveying parties."

"That's too bad," he said under his breath and began typing on his laptop. He paused a minute and looked up. "Have you ever heard of Ergon, West Virginia?"

"No, I can't say that I have," I replied and then pursed my lips. "The fuel reservoir I mentioned was owned by Ergon Petroleum, are they related?"

Parvis gave a small smile, but didn't respond. There was yet another lull in questioning. Everyone else was either looking at their laptops or whispering amongst themselves. I took my cue and stood.

"What are you doing?" hemorrhoid man asked.

"Ladies and gentlemen, this has been, well, I would say interesting, but I'd be lying. I'm sure you'll think up more questions and I'll be glad to answer them, but only if you'll first read the damn report Raymond and the others spent so much time preparing. In the meantime, I'm done here."

"You'll be done when we say you're done," hemorrhoid man said with an air of indignation. "Sit back down."

I gave him a long hard look. I could feel my teeth clenching this time. "Wrong answer," I said before walking out.

CHAPTER 3 – CHANGE OF COMMAND

The meet and greet with the military personnel was far different from what Zach was having to endure. The commanding officer of the military arm of Mount Weather was the Secretary of the Defense who had never served a single minute of military service. Abraham Stark was a career government service employee who apparently knew the right people. Although he was only fifty-two, he'd held various top-level government positions over the years, and I guess he was okay at his job because he kept his job after the election.

His right-hand man was a four-star general by the name of Harlan Fosswell, a fifty-eight-year-old career soldier who maintained a fastidious flattop haircut to go along with his fit physique. His military bearing was so pronounced, he could've been wearing bib overalls and he'd still look like a soldier. He was the Chief of Staff of the Army when the plague broke out. He was standing immediately outside of the office door at parade rest when they approached.

"Good morning," he said perfunctorily and held the door open for them, something a general never did for subordinate officers. Secretary Stark was sitting at a conference table talking to two people when they walked in. He nodded, but didn't bother standing. After brief introductions were made, he got down to business.

"We have a lot to go over, but the first order of business concerns a mission that has been in the planning stages for far too long," he said.

"It has been delayed due to a shortage of military personnel and more importantly, someone who is well versed in a combat role," General Fosswell said. "That would be you, Lieutenant Smithson." He swiveled his laptop so Justin could see the monitor. He hurriedly looked it over.

"Captain Kitchens has written up a glowing report on you, Lieutenant, and we believe it's time for a little change in the status quo of our Marine contingent," Secretary Stark said.

"Currently, we have thirteen Marines," General Fosswell said.

Justin looked surprised. "That's all, sir? I mean, I thought there'd be at least a company-sized unit present."

General Fosswell's face tightened. "At one time, we did, but we've suffered a substantial amount of attrition through casualties and desertion."

"Our current OIC for the Marine contingent is Ensign Boner," Secretary Stark said.

"Ensign Lawrence Boner," Fosswell added with a small twitch below his right eye. "He was fresh out of the Naval Academy and his uncle happened to be the Chief of Staff of Naval Operations. That would have been Admiral Jackson Walker. Admiral Walker had Ensign Boner assigned to him as an aide. Unfortunately, Admiral Walker became infected shortly after his arrival here. Ensign Boner is the one who ended up killing his uncle. Suffice it to say, it was rather traumatic for him." Fosswell paused a moment, forming the words in his head before speaking again.

"Sometimes, I'm a little too blunt, so I'll say this with as much tact as I can. Ensign Boner has no practical combat training and has shown no real desire to learn or assume a leadership role."

Now General Fosswell stared pointedly at Justin. "Our contingent of Marines has been suffering since the loss of their original CO. They need a Marine to lead them. A Marine with leadership ability and combat experience under his belt."

Captain Kitchens even joined in now. "Your prior position with the CIBRF also makes you uniquely qualified for the next mission."

"I'm your man, sirs," Justin said without hesitation. He wasn't sure if the two men were aware of it, but Captain Kitchens had already given him the heads up on this course of action and he was ready.

Secretary Stark smiled and General Fosswell gave a small nod.

"Excellent," Fosswell said. "I've already sent word. Your Marines should be formed up in the parking lot right outside. Perhaps you and your corporal better get moving. Report back to Captain Kitchens when you've gotten things squared away."

Justin and Ruth came to attention. "Aye, sir," they both said in unison and then rendered crisp salutes before leaving the office.

After the door had shut, the two men turned their attention to the other new arrivals.

"Major Fowkes, Major Parsons, let's now focus on integrating the two of you into our chain-of-command. Major Parsons, as a doctor, your mission is clear."

"Uh, sir, I think I need to make a clarification, if I could," Grant said.

"Go on," Fosswell replied.

"I became a de facto medical doctor after the outbreak. Colonel Coltrane had taken to referring to me as such and it stuck. My original discipline is pathology; I have a doctorate in it, but I never attended medical school."

"I see," Secretary Starks said, gazed steadily at Grant for a moment, and then focused on Sarah.

"Major Fowkes, since we have no operational aircraft, your job here would seem to be a little more problematic."

"Sergeant Benoit and I both have ample combat experience under our belts, sir, and if I may be frank, the Marines will need the two of us on this upcoming mission."

Sarah could see both men frowning and held up a hand. "I believe I know what you're thinking." She pulled a notepad out of her breast pocket. "Captain Kitchens has already given me an overview of the upcoming mission. Justin and I, excuse me, Lieutenant Smithson and I put together something."

All of them at the table now listened in rapt attention as Sarah began reciting a mission order.

Justin and Ruth walked by the conference room and paused long enough to glance through the little window. Zach's back was to them and they could hear him describing his list of rules. They stood by the door and listened a moment.

"I wonder how long it'll take before he tells them where to go," he said.

Ruth snickered as the two of them walked off and made their way outside. They paused outside the door and watched as the small contingent of Marines slowly gathered in a loose formation. He made a headcount of twelve; one missing. Two if you count Ensign Boner.

"There doesn't seem to be much of a sense of urgency with them," he muttered. Ruth nodded in agreement. He was about to give her a pat on the butt before catching himself. "Alright, let's get this started. Go on and join them."

Ruth grinned as she came to attention and saluted her lover before jogging over to the other Marines. She bid them good morning and stood at the rear of the formation. The other Marines looked her over casually and then went back to their private conversations. Justin approached them in a purposeful walk, came to a stop in front of them, and called them to a position of attention in that unique Marine lingo.

They all came to attention, but not with the precision Marines were normally noted for. They were sloppy, Justin thought. Zach would've used a big word like lackadaisical. They stared at Justin indifferently, perhaps even with a hint of insolence.

Justin wasn't intimidated and returned their stares. A tardy Marine rounded a corner of one of the buildings and casually strolled over to the formation. Justin stared daggers at him as the soldier worked his way into formation and scratched himself as he stood at attention.

"Where the hell is your CO?" he finally demanded. There were a few guffaws, including one from a soldier in the front rank. Justin immediately walked up and stood in his face.

"What's so funny?" Justin growled. The laughter stopped, but the soldier returned Justin's stare. One of the older soldiers, Justin thought, who looked around twenty-seven or so, cleared his throat.

"You'd be referring to Ensign Boner," he said. "He ain't here – sir." There was a long pause before he said sir, which emitted a chuckle in the back ranks.

Justin looked at his nametag and rank. He had three stripes, a bottom rocker, and the crossed rifles. An E-6. That meant this man was a lifer, a career man. He was a lean, dark-skinned soldier, standing a little over six feet tall and was staring back at Justin impassively.

"Crumby, is it?"

"Yes, sir, Sergeant Jeremiah Crumby. I'm the squad leader for first squad, such as it is." He pointed behind with his thumb to a soldier standing directly behind him.

"That there is Corporal Conway; he's the squad leader for second squad, such as it is."

"Sergeant?"

"Yes, sir?"

"Where do you think Ensign Boner may be?" Justin asked in a harsh voice barely above a whisper.

Sergeant Crumby gave an apathetic shrug. "Well, sir, he comes and goes. To be honest, I didn't see him at breakfast. He has a habit of sleeping in sometimes."

Justin eyed Sergeant Crumby a long minute before he resumed his place at the front of the formation and began speaking.

"Alright everyone, listen up. My name is Justin Smithson. I was a Gunnery Sergeant in my beloved Corps until recently when the president himself promoted me to lieutenant. I am now in charge of you people."

"Uh, sir, have you cleared this with command?" Sergeant Crumby asked. Before Justin could answer, another Marine spoke.

"Incoming," he said under his breath.

"Sir," Sergeant Crumby said in almost a whisper and a nod of his head. "Here comes Ensign Boner."

Everyone turned toward the sergeant's head nod. A beefy man with a pink face still puffy from sleep was strolling toward them. His uniform was a digital camouflage pattern as well, but it was distinctly different from the Marine's uniforms. He stopped in front of Justin and stared at him askance.

"Who are you?" he demanded.

"Smithson, Lieutenant Smithson. I'm taking charge of these Marines and am hereby relieving you of duty."

"The hell you are," he growled.

Justin stared at him for a long five seconds before looking around. His gaze wandered to a spot across the parking. He looked at it a moment before returning his stare to Ensign Boner.

"Sergeant Crumby, what is going on over there?" he asked as he pointed to a patch of ground that appeared to have been recently tilled.

"Well, sir, I believe Senator Hassburg tilled that patch up just yesterday."

"He's going to plant cabbage and Brussel sprouts there," one of the other Marines added.

"Has he sowed it yet?" Justin asked.

"No, sir. He'd planned on doing it today," the same Marine responded, but didn't tell Justin he had volunteered to help the senator.

"Perfect," Justin said and turned toward Ensign Boner. "In Parris Island, we have sand pits for training young recruits. Sometimes they served other purposes, would that be correct, Sergeant Crumby?"

"Yes, sir. Sometimes those pits came in handy when Marines needed to settle a difference of opinion."

Justin nodded and gestured. "Ensign Boner, I believe we have a difference of opinion that needs to be settled off the books." He gestured at the dirt patch. "It's not a sand pit, but it'll have to do." He turned and walked toward it without waiting for a response.

Ensign Boner stared at the back of Lieutenant Justin Smithson in irritated confusion before turning toward Sergeant Crumby.

"What the hell is that idiot talking about, Sergeant?" he demanded.

"He's challenging you to a fight, sir."

"You've got to be kidding," he said as he watched Justin remove his utility blouse. His taut T-shirt barely hid a lean but muscular torso. "I outweigh him by twenty or thirty pounds, at least."

"Then you should have no problem, sir," Sergeant Crumby replied gleefully. There was some derisive remarks in the back ranks now, followed by a couple of them surprisingly urging Ensign Boner on. Boner made a show out of removing his blouse and flexing a heavily muscled torso, indicating he spent a lot of time in the weight room.

"He's about to learn the hard way I played linebacker in college," Boner growled with arrogance. He smirked at the Marines, and then casually walked over to where Justin was standing.

"You Marines pay attention," Ruth said from behind them. A couple of them turned and looked back at her.

"You don't seem too concerned that your boy is about to get his ass whipped," one of them remarked.

Ruth snickered. "Boner ain't my boy."

When Boner got to within ten feet, he immediately lowered his head and charged Justin like an angry bull. He got to within a hair's breadth of tackling him when Justin sprawled his legs out while simultaneously wrapping an arm around Boner's head and snaking his forearm under the big man's chin. He grabbed his wrist with his other hand and used muscle and leverage to cinch his arm down around the big man's neck.

Boner grunted when Justin started squeezing and quickly realized he was in a predicament. He started throwing punches into Justin's gut, ribs, and groin, but Justin didn't relent, worked his legs, and maneuvered around to Boner's back. He kept his forearm under Boner's chin and held on tightly. It took maybe thirty seconds. Boner flailed around ineffectively before slowly going limp.

Justin held on tightly for another fifteen seconds or so before releasing him. As everyone watched, Justin stood erect and admired his handiwork a moment before casually brushing the dirt off of him and putting his blouse back on. Walking back to the group of Marines, he came to attention and barked a command.

"Marines, atten-hut!"

There was no delay now; the soldiers responded quickly and snapped their heels together in unison.

"Open ranks, march!" he barked. The front rank walked forward two steps.

"At close intervals, dress right, dress!" When the Marines had the proper intervals, Justin barked out a third order.

"Ready, front!"

Justin then approached and began closely inspecting them and their weapons one by one, emitting occasional grunts of dissatisfaction. When he was finished, he marched back to the front of them and ordered them to close ranks.

"At ease," he said in a tone of disgust. "I'm afraid it's even worse than I thought; all of you look like a bunch of slack-jawed hippies, and your weapons are filthy. Would you agree, Sergeant Crumby?"

"Well, sir, we've been stuck here for a while, and we operate under a more relaxed atmosphere."

"Sounds like a bunch of BS, Sergeant," Justin retorted. He shook his head in disgust. "You people look like shit, but fear not, God has answered your prayers and sent me here to square you away."

"Lieutenant?" one of the Marines from the back rank asked tentatively.

"Yes, Marine?"

"No disrespect intended, but my enlistment ran out almost a year ago. Now I don't mind helping out and pulling my weight, but I'm not so sure I want to continue taking orders and all the other bullshit that goes along with it."

There were some immediate murmurs of agreement.

Justin thought for a moment before responding. "Alright, I believe I understand your point. There are probably more than a few of you who feel the same way."

The Marines responded with some grumblings of assent. Justin nodded in understanding.

"I'm sure all of you are aware we came up here with a group from Tennessee. But do you know why?" Justin paused, but there was no response. "They had a nice set up down there. So why did they decide to come here? For that matter, why did you people stay here and not simply pack up and leave?"

"Some of them did," one of the Marines lamented.

"But you people didn't," Justin replied quickly. "Why not? I'll tell you why not. Deep down, all of you know this is the starting point for the rebirth of America. Down in Tennessee, I became friends with a man named Zach Gunderson. When you first meet him, you'll see a rangy, hard-looking man who's not yet twenty years old, but don't let his looks fool you; he's a smart one. We had many talks about the history of mankind, how societies emerged, and more importantly, how some societies became great while others died out. What do you think the common denominator those great societies had?"

"Free Wi-Fi?" one of them said. There were a few chuckles. Even Justin smiled.

"Let me guess, you're the one they call Joker."

The Marine who made the facetious comment, the same one who was late, grinned proudly. Justin knew this one was going to be a wise-ass, no matter the circumstances.

"As I was saying, the common denominator was, each of those successful societies understood the need to have an elite fighting unit who were instilled with a sense of honor, duty, and integrity. These elite units protected their society and, more importantly, they protected the weak against an enemy who was stronger than them." He paused and looked at them pointedly.

"That's us, Marines. These people need us, now more than ever. And I mean lean, mean, fighting Marines, not a bunch of slack-jawed pussies."

Joker spoke up. "No disrespect, sir, but lately we ain't been treated too well. We've worked our asses off around here killing off every zombified critter within miles, and these people treat us like we're nothing more than a necessary evil." Joker finished his diatribe and spit. One of his fellow Marines gave him a pat on the back.

Justin nodded in understanding. "I've no doubt you're on point, but that's all about to change. I'll make you Marines three promises. First promise: I will treat you like a Marine, no more, no less. Second promise: anyone outside of our chain-of-command who gives you a rash of shit will have to answer to me, and I will guarantee they will not like the outcome."

"So, what's that third promise?" Corporal Conway asked. Justin eyeballed them all.

"If any of you ever have a problem with me, we'll find us a cabbage patch and work it out." He made a subtle gesture toward Ensign Boner, who was still face down in the dirt. They were quiet now, even Joker.

"So, there it is, my fellow Marines, those are my promises. All I ask is you give me two weeks. Give me two weeks and see how you like it with me as your CO. If, at the end of two weeks you feel like a real Marine again, don't give your term of enlistment a second thought. We'll be Marines for life, a family. We'll take care of each other, and we'll take pride in devoting ourselves to duty."

"And if we don't, sir?" the Joker asked.

"If you don't, you will be formally released from active duty." There were now some loud murmurs of elation, but Justin cut them short.

"But, you will leave. You will leave this society we are attempting to rebuild and never come back." Everyone was silent now. Justin continued. "You can't have your cake and eat it too, people. You're either a Marine, shining like a beacon on a dark stormy night, or you're a limp-wristed civilian who has no business here. We've already got too many of those."

He waited for any type of rebuttal, but there was none.

"Alright, two weeks it is. The first thing we're going to start with is make you shipshape again, and we're going to start with haircuts."

"We have no clippers, sir," Sergeant Crumby said.

"You may not have clippers, but Corporal Bullington does, and speaking from personal experience, she is an excellent barber. She also has a razor and a strop for those of you who believe it is acceptable for a Marine to have a scruffy beard. Sergeant Crumby!"

"Sir?"

"See to it."

"Aye, sir," Sergeant Crumby answered and began barking out orders.

Justin watched in satisfaction as his Marines lined up. That's how he thought of them now, *his* Marines. They began talking excitedly now and peppered Ruth with questions. He then looked around and saw there was a small crowd of people watching. There were also a handful of people staring out of some windows. It was Secretary Stark, General Fosswell,

Seth, Sarah, Rachel, and Grant. Most of them were grinning. General Fosswell gave him an approving nod.

Justin walked back over to Boner, who was conscious now and sitting up. He had that dazed and confused look most people had after they'd regained consciousness.

"Would you like a hand?" Justin asked and reached down to help the Ensign. Boner glared at him, slapped Justin's hand away, and worked himself to a standing position. He marched off on wobbly legs without saying a word. Justin withheld comment and walked back over to Sergeant Crumby.

"I don't think you two are going to be friends anytime soon, sir," Sergeant Crumby said.

Justin snorted. "No big loss."

The sergeant noticed him wincing. "You okay, sir?"

"He hits pretty hard," Justin answered. "I think he might've broken a rib. Good thing I wore a cup." He paused a moment. "So, what's your story, Sergeant?"

Sergeant Crumby shrugged. "Not much to tell. I was stationed at Eighth, and I got assigned to the White House about a month before it went bad. Been here ever since. Good speech, by the way."

"Yep, Corporal Bullington wrote it and made me rehearse it a dozen times."

"Sounds like you two are a good match."

"I noticed we don't have any female Marines," Justin remarked.

"We had a few when we were at company level strength. Some died, some bugged out. This is all that's left."

"Anybody hooked up with any of the women around here?"

"Just me," Sergeant Crumby replied. "I was lucky enough to charm the pants off of a congressional aide. The rest are single. I'm pretty sure Conway is gay, but he ain't telling and I ain't asking."

"If anyone's giving him a hard time about it, let them know; I won't put up with it."

"You don't have to worry about that, sir. He's a good Marine. Everyone likes him."

"Good."

Lieutenant Smithson and Sergeant Crumby watched a few minutes as Ruth cut hair.

"Sir? I get the feeling something's about to happen," Sergeant Crumby said.

Justin smiled. "You'd be correct, Sergeant. We have a mission briefing in two hours."

"Is it going to be bad, sir?"

"Well, Sergeant, it's not going to be a walk in the park." He glanced at Sergeant Crumby briefly before looking back at the group. "You men are already starting to look like real Marines again."

CHAPTER 4 – MELVIN

The sky was blanketed in dark thunderclouds when Melvin made it to the outskirts of Oak Ridge. Actually, it was a small area known as Elza, which was on the Oak Ridge Turnpike. He spotted a few businesses at the Melton Lake Road intersection. He stopped and killed the truck's engine.

"One of these might do," he muttered, got out, and softly closed his door. He looked around before walking to the front of his truck where Peggy was sitting. Opening her visor, he gave her a light tap on the nose.

"Smell anything?" he asked in a low voice, almost a whisper. Peggy only looked at him.

"Me neither," he said. With the exception of the wind, it was dead quiet. Not even any birds chirping. Melvin looked up and watched as the dark, ominous storm clouds moved across the sky from the east. There was a lot of lightning in the background, and now he could hear distant thunder. He grunted and looked at his Casio watch.

"Sixteen hundred, that's four o'clock in the afternoon to you civilian pukes," he said. Peggy stared at him in silence. "We made better time than I thought."

He'd departed two days ago from Mount Weather. Normally, the trip would've only been a few hours, but zombies, bad roads, and abandoned cars slowed him considerably, which was the norm these days.

His mission was rather simple in design, but was going to be a little more complicated when put into action. It was a twofold recon mission. The location of part one was a building down the road less than a quarter-mile away containing the Office of Scientific and Technical Information, which was run by the Department of Energy. The second location was the famous, or infamous if you will, Y-12 facility. It was south of the city.

But, one step at a time, he told himself. He retrieved his tools of the trade for searching buildings; an M4 assault rifle with a light attachment and three-point sling, his Glock model 21 holstered on the left side of his hip, a tactical vest with a trauma plate which also held a knife and spare magazines, and his favorite toy, a Chinese Da Dao war sword, which he had slung over his shoulder. He carried a Dewalt canvas tool bag, which held various tools for building entry, reasoning he could simply drop it if he had to fight or run.

He started with a building identified as an Army Reserve Center. As soon as he tapped on the front door, two zombies, still wearing military uniforms, suddenly appeared, and tried desperately to force themselves through the same broken-out glass door. Melvin dropped the tool bag and readied his war sword. He had no problem severing the necks of the two zombie-soldiers with the razor-sharp edge.

There was nothing else of consequence inside the building; everything had been pillaged long ago. The same went for the rest of the buildings within the intersection. There was a standalone building containing a law office and some other business, and further down was a five-bay auto mechanic's business with a detail shop next door.

He carefully went from building to building, using the same protocol each time. He'd give a gentle knock before making entry. Then he'd whistle, which sometimes elicited the response of feral dogs looking for a meal. Finally, he'd call out, just in case there was a real live human inside.

He only shot if he had to, for obvious reasons.

Clearing each building was slow, meticulous work, but Melvin planned on being here a couple of days. So, it went without saying that he wanted the area to be zombie free.

He made an assessment and chose the detail shop for his OP. It was a concrete block building with a single garage bay, which was empty, and the view allowed him to observe the intersection. He backed his truck into the solitary bay, and as quietly as he could, pulled down the bay door.

There wasn't much to the business. In addition to the garage, the building had a front office, a back room with a separate entry door, and a restroom. The back room had a cot and the back door was fixed with three heavy-duty deadbolts.

The front window was still intact, but the main door had been pried open at one time. That was no problem; he already figured a way of securing it. Overall, it suited him. If any scavengers or marauders were to wander into the area, this would be one of the last places they'd look.

If anyone had thermal imaging equipment, well, they'd easily spot his heat signature, but there wasn't much he could do about that.

He walked over to Peggy and looked at her to see if she had an opinion on the matter, but she merely glared at him.

"Yeah, this'll do," he muttered. He got his binoculars out of the truck and sat in a chair in the front office. With the exception of a few stray pieces of trash being blown by the wind, there was nothing moving outside. Nor did he see any artificial lighting or telltale smoke, sure indicators there were humans around. It was going better than expected, although Melvin knew from experience it could all change within minutes.

He checked his watch again: 1730 hours. It was dark now, with the exception of bolts of lightning. The corresponding reports of thunder told Melvin the storm was getting closer.

"Just a few more minutes," he told himself. He stood, went back to his truck, and drank some water from a canteen. Looking at Peggy, he took her helmet off, grabbed a handful of her hair, and pulled her head back. She gagged a little as he poured some water in her mouth, but she swallowed a couple of times.

"Good girl," he said quietly. "I'm going to be gone for a little while, so don't go wandering off." He'd used the same line many times, but it still brought a sardonic grin to his face as he patted her head.

Her hair used to be blonde, but now it was dark and matted. He tried to brush it out one time, but she kept trying to bite him, so he never attempted it again. She looked a lot different from back when he first met her. Back then, she could've passed for Pamela Anderson's little sister. Now, her face was covered in scar tissue, her blue eyes were now a milky black, a common side effect of the infection, and her teeth looked like they belonged in the mouth of a meth addict.

She still had her tits. Big, fake, beautiful 34DDs. They stuck out like ripe melons. Melvin had loved them at one time. He started to give one a playful squeeze, but decided against it.

He moved to the back of the truck and unloaded a carbon frame mountain bike. He'd found it fastened to a bike rack on the back of a wrecked SUV on the interstate outside of Richmond. It was quiet, didn't use any gas, and was easily maneuverable.

He made another equipment check and transferred the Da Dao sword to a scabbard on the bike. He'd found the sword the same day as the bike. The specifics were a bit of a blur on account of the bottle of tequila he found two hours before the sword.

What he did remember, sort of, was how he went buck wild when he found it. He was so excited, he began running down the streets of the city, screaming like a rabid drunken samurai. He chopped off a few heads before rounding a corner and coming head on with well over a dozen zombies. A moment of lucidity struck, and he hightailed it back to the safety of his truck. He was still uncertain what was worse the next morning, the raging hangover or the memory of how stupidly suicidal he had behaved.

A bolt of lightning streaked across the sky and there was an almost immediate clap of thunder. Within seconds, a torrent of rain descended. It was loud and thick.

"Alright, here we go," he said and peddled the bike out of the front door. As he neared the Department of Energy building, a bolt of lightning struck a telephone pole not more than a hundred feet from him. The flash momentarily blinded him and the clap of thunder sounded like an explosion.

"Fuck me," Melvin mumbled, but kept pedaling. He reached the building in question and rode around it. This evening was about assessing the building itself. Was it still intact? Was it occupied? If so, by whom?

A lone zombie emerged from between two cars about twenty yards away and began loping toward him. Melvin pulled the sword out, aimed his bicycle, and decapitated him as he rode by.

"Olé, shit bag," Melvin growled. Another one emerged, and then another. Melvin dismounted and made quick work of them, six in all. When the last one fell, he waited in silence while focusing on breath control. Nobody else wanted to play, so Melvin got back on his bike and pedaled over to the first objective, a government building housing the Office of Scientific and Technical Information.

The building was dark, silent, maybe even a little foreboding. He began checking doors and windows, finding an unlocked door on the back of the building, but did not dare go in. It was too dark. All he had was the light on the end of his M4, and the thing about lights, even though it allowed you to see in the dark, it also gave away your position. And, it was easy to get disoriented in a large, dark building. He'd done it once in an office building in the nearby city of Sterling. It wasn't fun. Hell, it took him almost twenty minutes of fevered searching before he found the exit.

No, he was going to wait until tomorrow to explore the inside. He made a mental bookmark of the location of the door on the building and then looked around until he found a rock weighing about ten pounds. Heavy enough to prevent a gust of wind from moving it. He put it in front of the unlocked door. If it was moved when he came back in the morning, he would know there was someone around.

He continued reconnoitering the nearby area. The lightning had abated slightly, but there was still a heavy downpour, which Melvin liked. The diminished visibility effectively masked his movements if anyone were watching.

There wasn't much of interest. In fact, the things he was seeing were commonplace now; abandoned cars with flat tires and open gas caps, doors left open, broken windows, dead corpses, mostly decomposed down to skeletons hidden in rags that used to be clothing, broken windows, the shells of buildings that had been ravaged by fire. Melvin had seen it everywhere, and he imagined the rest of the world looked much the same.

He checked his watch. Time to head back. He carried his bike inside and secured it back in the bed of the truck.

"Did you miss me, honey?" he asked facetiously. She responded with a guttural growl. He ignored her and found one of his soda cans which he'd rigged to hold a candle. He lit it, set it beside his truck, and rigged some rope to hang his wet clothes. Satisfied, he stripped, hung his clothes, and used a towel to dry himself off. He held off on putting on fresh clothes; his intention was to wash up, but he was going to eat first.

Dinner consisted of an MRE. While he ate, he spotted a stack of shop rags. Some of them still looked fairly clean. He grabbed a couple and disturbed a nest of baby mice. The mother scurried off, leaving her babies helpless. Melvin's first instinct was to kill them, but then he left them alone and used the two rags he'd grabbed and wiped down his weapons while the momma mouse squeaked at him in protest.

He normally slept in his truck. He'd grown used to it, but tonight he thought he'd take advantage of the cot. It'd be nice to be able to stretch out, he thought. His knees wouldn't be stiff when he got up in the morning. He unloaded some blankets, a pillow, and some mosquito netting and fixed it all up.

He checked out of the back door. It was pitch black outside. He took a chance and shone his flashlight for a half of a second, hoping it resembled a flash of lightning if anyone saw it. There was nothing back there. Looking out the front door again, he saw a broken gutter where a stream of water flowed out. It gave him an idea. He went to his truck, retrieved a bucket, and put it under the streaming water. It filled quickly.

He then went back to his truck and assembled his most important find since it all went bad: a Berkey brand water filtering system. This one was the plastic version. It consisted of two cylinders. They were both about nine inches in diameter, and when assembled, a little over two feet tall.

He grabbed the bucket and poured the water into the upper cylinder. The filters went to work, and within seconds, clean water began dripping down into the lower cylinder.

He was about to set out his noise alarms and turn in for the night when he heard an unusual sound, like something had bumped into one of the abandoned cars out in the street. He worked his way to the front office and peered out of the window. The lightning strikes illuminated the roadway in a strobe light effect. He could see zombies running down the roadway, and as he watched, one of them jumped onto the hood of a car, almost slipped off, and then scrambled up onto the roof. When it started kicking at the zombies, Melvin realized it had to be a human.

He didn't think twice. He grabbed the war sword and flashlight, and yanked on the door. He forgot he'd already secured it, spent a few long seconds unwrapping the chain he'd used, and sprinted out.

Melvin still had his mil-spec flashlight from his days in the Army. It was nine hundred lumens of blinding light, and Melvin had learned a neat trick with it when hunting zombies. He switched it to the strobe function and jogged up to the nearest zombie, a haggard-looking woman wearing jeans and a heavily soiled orange Polo shirt with a college logo over her breast.

He made a backhanded swing with the sword, burying it in the left side of her head at the top of her ear. His actions got the attention of the taller one, an adult male, who made a beeline toward him.

Melvin activated his light. The blinding strobe froze the zombie in place. Melvin pulled the sword out of the female's head, raised it high, and brought it down. It made a satisfying crunching sound as it split the male's skull open and traveled downward, stopping right about where the zombie's nose formed nostrils.

The third one, he looked like a teenaged male, charged Melvin. He reacted instantly and lashed out with a snap kick to his chest, sending him barreling backwards. He cast a quick glance at the person on top of the car as he worked the blade out of the dead zombie's skull. He couldn't see much; he was small framed with long hair, probably a kid, and he was breathing heavily.

Melvin freed up the sword and used the flashlight trick again as the teen came toward him. This time, he got the blade into the neck and made a clean separation. His head came off with little difficulty and gnashed its teeth impotently as it lay on the asphalt.

Melvin then focused the strobe light on the smallest one of the bunch. It was a child, probably no older than eleven or twelve. He stared at Melvin, or rather the bright strobe light, in a kind of hypnotic zombie trance. Melvin almost felt pity, but it didn't stop him. The kid's head hit the asphalt a split second before the rest of its torso.

Melvin crouched in a fighting position and pivoted in a circle, utilizing the lightning strikes to search out other potential threats. Seeing none, he focused on the boy standing on top of the car.

"Who the hell are you?" Melvin growled. The boy didn't answer. Melvin risked it, changed the setting on the flashlight to a steady stream, and pointed it at the boy.

Only, it wasn't a boy: it was a girl.

CHAPTER 5 – POTUS

"Hold up, Zach."

I turned at the sound of my name as I was walking down the hall. It was Raymond hurrying to catch up. I reluctantly stopped and waited for him.

I stabbed a finger back down the hallway. "What's wrong with those people?" I asked him.

"Ah, well, it's hard to explain their behavior sometimes."

"That one who looked like a prune with hemorrhoids, who is he?"

Raymond frowned. "That would be Senator William Rhinehart from Ohio. A staunch conservative." From the tone of Raymond's voice, it was apparent he didn't like the good senator either.

"Well, I'm done with these silly debriefings. There's got to be more productive things to do around here than sitting around gabbing all day."

"True," he replied, and looked at his watch. "It's too early for lunch, but I bet there's coffee."

"Yeah, sounds good," I said.

It must have been bad mojo or something, because no sooner had we sat down in the cafeteria than Raymond's radio barked.

"What's your twenty?" the disembodied female voice asked him.

"I'm in the cafeteria," he replied. "What's up?"

"See if you can round up Zach and bring him to the range. POTUS is requesting."

He replied with a ten-four and looked at me. "I believe POTUS wants to meet with you." He stood. "C'mon, I've got a golf cart parked outside, we'll ride over." He paused. "Um, you're not armed, are you? You're not allowed to be armed in his presence."

"Nope. All of my weapons are stored in my truck." I had my hideout gun, a three-eighty caliber semi, stuffed in my crotch, but I didn't let him know it. I wanted to keep at least one assault rifle in the room, but my son's insatiable curiosity prevented it.

"Okay, good."

We got in one of the golf carts lined up in front of the building, and Raymond took off toward the exit before making a hard left at a helicopter-landing pad. There was a small group of people there. I recognized Earl and Sheila Hunter, a married couple who were part of the delegation. Sheila grinned and waved as we drove up.

There were a couple of Army soldiers, both armed with assault rifles, and there was POTUS, President Harrison Richmond. He was a boisterous billionaire businessman who, with no experience in politics whatsoever, managed to become elected. Gloom and doom had been predicted by the idiots in the media, but he seemed to be doing okay, up until it all went bad.

Currently, he was hitting golf balls. And Callahan was chasing them.

We got off of the cart and watched in silence as he addressed the ball. He brought the driver back and then struck the ball as hard as he could with a loud grunt. The ball travelled about a hundred yards before it began fading to the right. He frowned in consternation as Callahan took off at a full run. He chased down the golf ball, ran it back, and dropped it at the president's feet. The president patted him on the head and was about to tee up again when Earl whispered something to him. He looked up and saw me.

"Good morning, Mister Gunderson," he said.

"Good morning, Mister President."

"Do you play?" he asked, gesturing with his golf club.

"No, sir, never have," I replied.

"It's a wonderful game, isn't that right, Earl?"

"Yes, sir, it certainly is," Earl replied. Callahan barked impatiently and crouched. The president grinned as he teed up the ball and took a practice swing.

"One of our goals for this year is to rehabilitate a golf course that's located a couple of miles from here. There've been a lot of obstacles, but maybe now with the extra manpower, we can finally get it accomplished."

I hastened a glance at Raymond as if to say, what the hell? He made brief eye contact with me before looking away.

"What do you think of the idea, Zach?" he asked.

"Sir, if you had been with us at the debriefing, you would know my diplomatic skills are nonexistent. If you don't want my honest opinion, it would be best if you don't ask the question."

"Oh, I was there, Zach."

I looked at him in puzzlement. I'd made a point of looking at everyone in the room and he was not present.

"The conference room has cameras," he explained. "I watched you on a monitor in another room."

"Oh."

He explained. "Sometimes I can get a better read of a person when I'm not around; a person's demeanor is sometimes different when they're in the presence of the President of the United States."

"I see," I said. "I suppose it makes sense."

"Indeed," he said. He addressed the ball with his driver. "You said a few things I found somewhat intriguing."

"Um, thank you?"

He chuckled. "There were several things you didn't say as well, Mister Gunderson."

"Call me Zach, please."

A wry grin spread on his face. "Zach, what's your opinion on building a golf course?"

I thought a moment before responding and watched him hit the ball. This one had more distance than the previous one, but it still had a fade on it.

"A little more rotation in the hips, I think," Earl said in a quiet voice. The president acknowledged the advice with a slight frown and then looked at me, waiting for my answer.

I cleared my throat. "I know people require some kind of recreational outlet, and I don't know a whole lot about golf, but, if I understand correctly, a golf course requires an enormous amount of maintenance."

"I suppose it does," the president conceded.

"Well then, I think it'd be a waste of resources and labor," I answered bluntly.

Earl looked startled, but to my surprise, the president laughed. "Did you hear that, Earl? The young man doesn't mince words."

"No, sir, he certainly doesn't."

President Richmond looked at me thoughtfully a moment before teeing up and hitting another drive. This one went straight and fairly long. He watched it long after it hit the ground.

"Yeah, more rotation. How far do you think, Earl?"

"That one had to be pretty close to three hundred, sir," Earl replied.

I looked at him sharply. My range estimation skills were spot on, if I do say so myself, and I would have bet a New York Strip the ball travelled no more than two hundred yards, and that was after it rolled a good twenty. I was about to say something, but I caught sight of Raymond as he gave me a subtle, singular shake of his head. I got the hint. The president stopped talking and continued hitting balls. I guess the conversation was over.

"Sir, I'll let you get back to your balls, um, I mean, your golf."

He hit another shot and began speaking to me as he continued watching the ball.

"You believe these things are now communicating telepathically," he stated.

"Yes, sir, I do."

"Interesting," he said. He paused in thought and then turned to Raymond. "Have Mister Gunderson in the TOC after lunch for the mission briefings." He then summarily dismissed us and went back to his balls.

"Well, that was an odd meeting," I said to Raymond as we rode back to the main area.

"He was getting a feel for you," Raymond said. "You must have passed muster."

"How so?" I asked.

"Only a limited number of people have access to the tactical operations center. Most people here have no idea of what goes on in there." He thought a minute; I guess he was thinking about how much he could tell me.

I looked at him thoughtfully as we rode. "I'm sensing a tenseness though."

He stopped the cart and thought a minute. "Zach, we did not tell a single lie back when we recruited you people to come up here."

I narrowed my eyes at him. "But you didn't tell us everything, did you?"

"What I'm about to tell you isn't public knowledge."

"Okay," I said.

"Surprisingly, only ten percent of the satellites have gone offline. We still have access to most of the others. They give us some fairly decent intel of what is going on around the world."

"Okay, I'm all ears, what are you guys seeing?"

"All major cities are totally overrun. It also appears there have been at least four nuclear events." He held up a hand and displayed four fingers as he spoke. "Mumbai, Delhi, Peshawar, and Islamabad."

"That sounds like India and Pakistan went to war with each other."

Raymond nodded. "Yes, it appears so." He looked solemn now. "We've had intermittent contact with other government entities. POTUS is getting the impression some countries are going to use nuclear devices in densely populated cities in an effort to eradicate the plague."

"Raymond, tell me if I'm wrong, but won't nuclear explosions screw up the earth's climate?"

"If there are enough detonations, yes, without a doubt. The world leaders, what's left of them, have held off, but there is a growing tension."

"How so?" I asked.

"It'll be discussed more during the meeting, but the human race is in danger of becoming extinct. Some of the leaders feel there is no other alternative than to go nuclear. The president believes if we can show proof we've manufactured an effective vaccine, it will keep them from doing so."

"Sounds simple enough," I said. "But, I'm sensing a problem."

"There is an inner power struggle going on between the president and a couple of his political adversaries. We've been doing well, but some people are clamoring for an election."

"I thought we were still under Martial Law," I asked.

"Oh, the Constitution and every other law is now only something to talk about and not something to abide by. There have been many challenges. Now, here is where you come into play."

"I think I've already figured it out. You need my continued cooperation, at least until an effective vaccine is produced."

"Yes."

I chuckled now. "Sure, Raymond. All I ask is honesty and to shoot straight."

Raymond agreed and began driving again. I glanced over the parking lot where our truck and trailer were parked. The back door of the trailer was open and I saw someone crawling in.

"Stop the cart," I ordered.

CHAPTER 6 – SAVANNAH

"Who the hell are you?" Melvin demanded again.

"Savannah," she croaked. She continued standing on top of the car, anxiously staring down at him.

Melvin couldn't see much in the dark, but he did notice one thing, she was keeping her hands together, like she was hiding something. Melvin sprang suddenly, grabbed one of her feet, and pulled her off of the car. She hit the ground with a thud and an exhalation of breath. He swung his sword, slinging goo off of the blade, and then brought it down, stopping it a millimeter from her neck.

"Bring your hands up very, very slowly," he growled. "And they better be empty."

She struggled to catch her breath. Her face was fixed in mortal fear as she slowly held her hands up. "I'm handcuffed," she said.

Melvin frowned in consternation. He used the flashlight and pointed it. The metal of the cuffs reflected the light. She wasn't lying, he thought.

"Why are you cuffed?" he asked.

"I was being held prisoner," she said and continued looking at Melvin anxiously.

Melvin wasn't sure what to make of it, but he didn't let his guard down. He squatted and put his knee against her chest. She let out a fearful moan as he put his weight against her.

"Quiet," Melvin admonished and began searching her. There was no sexual motive to his actions. On one of his tours in Afghanistan, a Taliban prisoner had a small pocketknife hidden, and it was missed during a cursory search. The SOB came damn close to cutting Melvin's throat. But, even so, when she whimpered, he felt a stab of guilt for treating her so roughly.

Finding nothing, he stood up. She lay there looking up at him, raindrops hitting her frightened face. She looked like a drowned cat. A starving drowned cat. He looked around before focusing on her with the flashlight. She wasn't much to look at. A ragged pair of jeans, a gaudy plaid long-sleeved shirt that was soaking wet and clinging to her. When he brought the light to her face, there was a look of utter despair.

48

"Are you going to rape me?" she asked.

Melvin looked at her in surprise. "What? Why do you think that?"

"Because you're..." She didn't finish. She didn't have to.

Melvin suddenly understood. He was totally nude, splattered with zombie goo, and standing over her wielding a war sword. He imagined he looked like a raving lunatic. He took a deep, calming breath.

"C'mon," he said and helped her to her feet. She felt light as a feather, causing Melvin wonder when she'd eaten last. "Can you walk?"

"I think so," she rasped.

"What's wrong with your voice?" he asked. "You sound like you've been eating rock salt."

"I'm thirsty," she responded.

As Melvin stood there looking at her, she started swooning. Melvin caught her before she did a face plant and cradled her in his arms. She whimpered again and he could feel her whole body shaking uncontrollably.

"Relax, I'm not going to hurt you."

She looked up at Melvin, wild-eyed fear etched on her face. When a nearby lightning bolt cracked, she jerked violently.

"Easy now," he soothed and looked around. "Let's get out of this rain."

He carried her back to the auto detail garage, walked inside, and set her down in a chair.

"Wait here," he said.

He hurried back to the bay and went directly to his truck. He dried off with a towel and then picked some dry clothes out of a duffel bag in the back seat. He slung the towel over his shoulder, and then grabbed an assortment of items. Picking up the candle in the soda can, he walked back in the main room. He expected her to have run out of the front door as soon as he walked out of sight, but surprisingly, she was still sitting in the chair.

"Alright, let's get those cuffs off. Hold your hands out," he directed. He had a key ring of various gadgets, a handcuff key being one of them. When she held out her hands, they were shaking uncontrollably, making it a little difficult to work the key into the locking mechanisms, but after a minute, he had the cuffs open. He looked at them before putting them in his pocket. After all, he might put them back on her later.

"Thank you," she mumbled and tenderly rubbed her wrists. "May I have some water now?" she asked.

"Oh, yeah," Melvin said and handed her the canteen.

She took it tentatively, unscrewed the top, and turned it up. Water ran down her face as she slaked it down. Melvin reached out and pulled it out of her hands. She jerked back, as if expecting Melvin to give her a slap for some perceived transgression.

"Easy," he admonished. "If you drink too fast, you'll get cramps and throw up." He handed the canteen back. "Take slow sips."

She nodded worriedly and did as Melvin instructed. He watched her and let her take several sips before speaking.

"What'd you say your name is?" he asked.

"Savannah," she replied, her voice clearer now, and continued sipping.

"Who else is with you?"

Savannah shook her head, causing more water to dribble down her chin. "Nobody, I'm alone."

"What're you doing wandering out here alone, and in handcuffs?"

"I was being held captive," she said. "But I got away."

Melvin narrowed his eyes. "From whom?" he asked.

"They call themselves the Blackjacks. I was one of their..."

Her voice cracked a little and she didn't finish. She didn't have to, Melvin knew all about the Blackjacks. He'd bumped into them not too long ago. They were not nice people, which caused him sudden concern. The last thing he wanted was to bump into any of them by accident.

"Are they somewhere around here?" he asked.

Savannah shrugged. "I don't know. I escaped two nights ago. I don't even know where I am."

"You've been running around for two days while handcuffed?" he asked in surprise.

"Yes, sir," she answered.

"Without food or water?"

She nodded. "When it started raining, I got some in my mouth, but not much."

"Damned impressive," he said, got up, and wrapped a blanket around her.

"Thank you," she said and pulled it tight.

The water seemed to have helped a little; her tone was no longer raspy. Now it was soft, wobbly. She stared at the floor and would only cast short quick glances at him. He tried to be nonfrightening, avuncular.

"I bet you're hungry too."

She gave a slow nod as she stole another look at him. Melvin nodded back at her, picked up an MRE package, and read the label.

"Ah, this is a good one, chicken with rice, and it has a fudge brownie in it." He cut it open and handed it to her. She ineptly fumbled with the individual packages.

"Here," he said and tore them open for her. "Alright, remember to eat slowly."

"Okay."

She started with the fudge brownie and devoured it in seconds.

"Go slow," he admonished again.

She nodded as she licked her fingers clean, then started in on the chicken. He watched her in silence as the storm raged outside. The speed at which she ate began to slow. After a minute, she stopped.

"I don't think I can eat anymore," she apologized.

"No problem," Melvin said and took it from her. He looked over the leftover food and gauged her intake. It wasn't much.

"Your stomach has shrunk," he said. "You'll get your appetite back in no time, but don't try to force it; you'll only mess yourself up." He hated to see food go to waste, especially these days, and began eating the rest of it.

Savannah adjusted the blanket. She was still shaking.

"You should get out of those wet clothes," he said.

"I'm okay," she muttered, and as Melvin watched, her eyelids fluttered and her chin slowly dropped to her chest. He caught her before she did a face plant.

"Damn it," he muttered, thought about it a moment, and then carried her to the cot in the back room. She was still shaking as he laid her down. The wet clothes weren't helping.

"Damn it," he muttered again and began taking them off. When she was nude, he used the flashlight to inspect her. She looked rough, emaciated, bruised, scratched up, and battered, but there weren't any bite marks, which he took as a good sign. He covered her with the blanket and adjusted the mosquito netting.

"Guess I'm not sleeping on the cot tonight," he mumbled to himself.

When he was finished, he straightened and looked at her in the dark. If she was a captive of the Blackjacks, there was only one reason why they kept her alive. The land was filled with lawless heathens nowadays and a young girl like Savannah was easy pickings. It was a shame. He could only imagine what she'd been through. Rape, abuse, degradation, you name it. He doubted she'd ever be the same. He'd been diagnosed with PTSD, courtesy of his last mission in Afghanistan, but he couldn't even fathom the torment she'd gone through.

He secured the front door as best he could and then retrieved a couple of trash bags out of the back of the truck. Both of them were full of used plastic water bottles. They were a good rudimentary alarm system. He spread them around the floor. If anyone came in during the night, it'd be nearly impossible for them not to step on one or two. The noise of crinkling plastic would, in theory, wake him, alerting him to an unwelcome intruder.

Satisfied, he got into his truck and put the seat back. It wasn't the most comfortable position in the world, but he'd gotten used to it.

CHAPTER 7 – THIEVERY

"What is it, Zach?" Raymond asked.

"Somebody's in my trailer," I replied as I jumped out of the cart and ran toward the trailer. I slowed down as I got close and moved in as quietly as I could.

I could hear at least two of them talking to each other and rummaging around. One part of my brain was saying there might be a perfectly logical explanation, but the other half was telling me to pull my hideout gun and shoot on sight.

I stopped at the side, out of sight of whoever was inside and collected my thoughts. Who was inside the trailer? I spotted the padlock; it was lying on the ground and had been cut. It was the confirmation I needed. Somebody was stealing from me. The rage built inside me as I watched articles were being thrown out and landing on the ground. I heard Raymond jogging up.

"Who is it?" he whispered.

"I'm about to find out," I growled and walked around to the open doors.

The first one saw me as he was crouching to jump out of the trailer. His expression was one of surprise, and then he gave a challenging stare. I didn't say a word as I grabbed him by the wrist and yanked him out. He hit the asphalt with a thud and an exhalation of air. Blood flew as the toe of my boot impacted with his nose. He groaned in pain, and I was about to kick him again, but didn't get a chance.

I'd stupidly turned my back to the open door, which the second one took advantage of. He jumped on my back, wrapped his legs around me, and began hammering me with rabbit punches to the side of the head. But, the punches were soft, not a person who was accustomed to fighting. I quick-stepped backwards and slammed his back against the lower edge of the trailer. He gasped in pain, and his leg lock around my torso slackened. Working one of his legs loose, I grabbed an arm and twisted sharply, flipping him onto the asphalt beside his buddy. Raising my boot, I was about to stomp his face into oblivion when I realized it wasn't a man, but a woman.

She glared at me in a mixture of pain and anger. Now, back before, an honorable man would never hit a woman. But, this wasn't before. This was after, and stealing someone's property was a serious offense.

Even so, I hesitated. She stood awkwardly, rubbing the small of her back and trying to get her breath. She was rather attractive with short hair the color of cinnamon and a nicely shaped physique. I found myself starting to ask her if she was okay, and then she attempted to kick me in the groin. I deftly sidestepped and put a hammer fist to the side of her neck. Her eyes rolled back as she slumped to the ground, dazed and confused.

My first instinct was to continue stomping both of them until there was no life left. And, in fact, I'd started to raise a foot but caught sight of a couple of people watching me. The look on their faces stopped me. I took a few deep breaths, trying to regain control of the raw hostility coursing through my veins.

"Zach," Raymond cried in exasperation.

I looked at him angrily. "I just caught these two little shits breaking into my trailer," I declared.

"Uh, yeah, okay," Raymond replied. He looked puzzled, conflicted.

"Alright, I suppose you people lock criminals up around here. Get on your radio and call for the police." I didn't wait for a response, jumped in the trailer, and found a roll of five-fifty cord. Jumping back to the ground, I tied their wrists tightly behind their backs. Standing, I stared at them. I turned to Raymond, who continued standing there, unmoved.

"What's wrong?" I asked.

"We don't have any police here, Zach. No jail either."

I stared at him. "No jail?"

He shook his head.

No police, no jail. I sighed angrily.

"Then I'm going to kill them," I said as I opened my lock-blade knife. The girl, who'd regained some of her senses, paled in fear.

Raymond stepped closer. "As much as I understand the sentiment, I don't think you should kill them," he said in a quiet steadying voice. He pointed at the two thieves. "Those two are the son and daughter of Senator Rhinehart from Ohio. You kill them, there'll be repercussions."

My stare turned to a hard glare. Raymond's expression was serious, somber. I didn't like it, but I understood what he was saying. He was right. I knew it.

"Yeah, I believe you," I said. "It's total bullshit, if you ask me."

He shrugged again. I looked around, and spotted a tree a few feet away.

"I believe I have an idea though. Keep an eye on them, will you?" I asked and walked over to the tree. Inspecting it for a moment, I found a suitable branch, cut it off, and skinned the leaves. Some people saw it as nothing more than a branch I'd skinned with my knife; others would have correctly induced it was a switch.

I whipped it through the air a couple of times, letting it make that all too familiar sound as I approached the two miscreants. They were both conscious now, and were staring at me angrily. But, they couldn't hide the fear in their eyes. I gave a small, hard smile.

"Raymond here has told me nothing much is going to happen to you two," I said.

The man spit blood. "Oh, you got that right, but I can't wait to see what happens to you when our father finds out what you've done."

"Yeah, I bet. Well, if this happened anywhere else, you'd already be dead."

"That'd be the biggest mistake you ever made," he declaimed.

"You're probably right," I said, all the while keeping my smile. "But, you two are going to remember this day for a long time."

I then twisted him around, grabbed a handful of his belt and lifted him off of the ground. He howled in pain as I put the switch to his backside, and when it was sister's turn, she screamed even louder. I could have whipped them all day, but stopped after a minute. When I was finished, I looked over at Raymond, who was nervously grinning from ear to ear.

"Holy moly," he exclaimed. His grin disappeared when he saw a golf cart approach.

"Here comes the father," he said with concern.

I recognized him immediately. Senator William Rhinehart. Hemorrhoid man.

"What is the meaning of this?" he shouted as he walked over to the boy and began trying to untie him. I grabbed him roughly and jerked him away. He glared at me, like he was not a man to be trifled with. He took a step toward me, and I responded by readying my switch. He froze.

"Zach has caught your children breaking into his trailer," Raymond said.

I nodded at his statement and noticed several people were joining us now. Some were pointing and grinning, while others frowned and looked concerned.

I gestured toward them with the switch. "I don't know how things work around here, but when I catch someone stealing from me, don't expect much mercy."

The boy and girl were lying there, writhing in agony, and glaring at me with hatred in their eyes, but they were too afraid to voice any objection.

"They're lucky I didn't cut their fucking heads off and stick them on a pole," I growled.

"My children are not criminals," the senator said with an air of contempt.

"You'd be incorrect, Senator," Raymond said. "They've been caught red-handed." He looked around at the crowd of people. "We've had a rash of things being stolen lately, right? I think we've found the culprits."

"Stay out of this, Raymond," the senator admonished.

"If you'll take the time to look, you'll see a pair of bolt cutters and a cut padlock," I said.

"We didn't do it, Dad," the male thief said. "That padlock was already cut." His sister readily nodded in agreement.

The senator, Daddy, looked at me to say, see, I told you so. I shook my head.

"Even if that were true, which it isn't, but even if it was, I caught them inside my trailer and taking things out. They're nothing more than common criminals. Scumbags."

He glowered at me long and hard, probably trying to think of a caustic comeback. I guessed him to be in his sixties, which told me he had his kids later in life, probably from a younger wife.

"You seem to be confused, young man," he said with the same contemptuous tone. "Once you brought that trailer into this compound, it became community property."

"Well then, why don't you climb up in there and help yourself?" I suggested as I whipped the switch through the air. He narrowed his eyes. I gestured at the trailer. "Go ahead, what're you waiting for?"

He didn't move and continued glaring at me. I stepped closer to him and lowered my voice.

"You know you're full of shit. There is no community property rule here."

"There most certainly is," he responded haughtily.

"Well, then, remove your clothes," I ordered, my voice loud enough so everyone could hear.

Now, his glare faltered. "What?"

"I didn't stutter. If everything here is community property, I want to use your clothes. Take 'em off."

Raymond laughed in spite of himself, as did a few others in the crowd.

"He got you there, Willie," someone in the crowd said.

"You're a Republican, correct?"

"I most certainly am," he replied haughtily.

"Community property is a socialist value, correct?"

From the expression on his face, I believe my rhetorical question did not seem to sit well with him.

"You're not going to fit in here, I'm thinking, Mister Gunderson," he finally said.

I nodded. "Well, now, I believe I can agree with you on that one." I pointed at his children with the switch. "When I catch two miscreants committing a crime and your only response is to blame me, yeah, I'm not sure I'm going to fit in either." I stared hard. They were in their early twenties, not much older than me, snobby, self-absorbed, the kind of people who didn't think the rules applied to them because they were privileged.

Dropping the switch, I reached down and roughly cut their bindings.

"Take your kids," I said. "If you're as good a parent as you seem to believe you are, you might want to sit them down and have a long talk with them."

"Those two won't be sitting for a while," someone in the crowd said. "Not after that ass whipping." There was now a chorus of laughter.

The girl turned and glared petulantly at me as she rubbed her ass before following her father and getting on the golf cart.

CHAPTER 8 – BURT

To say I was pissed would be an understatement. Raymond watched as I put everything back in the trailer and slammed the doors shut.

"I'm only here a day and already I'm dealing with a couple of common thieves," I growled under my breath. I didn't have another padlock handy, so I did the next best thing and put my switch in the hole on the hasp where the padlock would have gone. I hoped once the story got out, the message would be clear: fuck with my property, and there was going to be an ass-whipping coming to you.

"I'm sorry, Zach," Raymond said.

"Not your fault, Raymond, not your fault." I leaned against the truck and forced myself to calm down. It took a minute or two before I looked over at him.

"What a bunch of bullshit," I lamented. Raymond nodded. I sighed and brushed my hands off.

"What do you say we go eat some lunch?" Raymond suggested.

I nodded in agreement and the two of us got back on the golf cart.

By the time the two of us got to the cafeteria, it was full and there was a lot of chatter going on. Raymond excused himself and made a beeline toward a table full of senators. I got more than a few looks as I filled my plate and sat at what I guess was now going to be our table. Not seeing Kelly, I sat beside Sarah.

"So, I don't know how your briefing went, but mine sucked."

She shrugged. "Most of it concerned Tinker Air Base. They wanted to know all about it."

"Do they have planes here?" I asked as I scooped a big helping of potatoes in my mouth.

"Yes," Sarah answered. "In a manner of speaking. Dulles is thirty-two miles away. Lots of planes but no fuel. We're working up a mission plan. I told them about how you guys tapped the fuel reservoirs. They mentioned an oil refinery not far from here, but no specifics. I think they have some future mission planned, but they wouldn't discuss it."

I wondered what they were up to and shrugged it off. If they wanted us to know, they'd tell us. "Where's Kelly?" I asked.

"All of the moms and kids are having some sort of get together. Janet insisted on going with them."

Rachel laughed. "I wonder how long it'll take before she starts critiquing everyone's parenting skills."

I groaned. Between me and Janet, we were probably going to be invited to leave before the week was over.

Sarah continued. "She said to tell you it's supposed to last all day, but she'll be done by dinner."

"Okay." I looked over at Sammy. "Why aren't you with them?"

He made a face. "Hang out with a bunch of little kids? No way." His response drew some laughter.

Josue gave him a friendly nudge. "I like you hanging out with us," he said.

"When is your birthday?" Rachel asked.

"August thirtieth," Sammy answered. "I'll be eleven."

"Well, we'll have to throw you a party of some kind," Rachel said with a grin.

An older man walked up and slapped his tray on the table beside me before doffing a well-worn Resistol cowboy hat.

"Ladies," he said politely before sitting down. "I heard about it, but I'm not so sure I believe it," he said. "Did you just take a switch to those idiot Rhinehart kids?" he asked.

I looked him over, trying to get a read on him. He was about sixty, lanky, white hair as short as mine, and his face looked like he'd spent many years outside in the sun and weather. He reminded me a little of Fred.

"I did," I replied. "I caught them stealing. Do you have a problem with it?"

He nodded, as if he already knew why. "People are also telling me you've done some farming and you know your way around a cow, is that true?"

"True on both counts," I said.

"Hot damn!" he exclaimed loudly as he slapped the table. "Don't that beat all!"

"Burt, settle down," a woman admonished from a nearby table. Burt waved a dismissive hand at her.

"That's my wife, Anne. Don't mind her."

I peered over Burt's shoulder to see a woman approximately the same age as him boring holes in the back of his head. Burt knew what she was doing, but it didn't seem to bother him in the least.

"The name's Burt," he said, holding out a hand. "Burt Cartwright, and I am sure glad to meet you."

I tentatively reached out and shook his hand. "Zach Gunderson," I said.

58

"Now look here, I'm going to put in a word with Lydia and get you assigned on a work detail with me. To tell you the truth, I need help. These people," he barked, "are a bunch of candy-asses."

"You have a cattle operation?" I asked.

"Yes, sir. We have a five-hundred acre spread a couple of miles down the road full of beautiful, fat, Black Angus. That's where I've been all day. Let me tell you, good help is hard to find. This past spring, I had to do all of the castratin' by myself and one of them damn baby bulls kicked me in the head."

"And he's still brain dead," his wife commented glibly. He waved another dismissive hand behind him amid some laughter.

"What do you say?" he asked.

"Yeah, it sounds good to me."

"Burt, get over here and let them eat in peace," his wife ordered. Burt glanced back at his wife, and then looked at us with an annoyed expression.

"That woman is a royal pain in my posterior. I'll catch up with you later." He stood and moved his tray over to his wife's table, whereupon they traded one or two barbs.

Burt caught up with me after lunch as I was walking Zoe.

"You want to go see the farms?" he asked.

"Sure."

We got into his truck and headed down Blue Ridge Mountain Road, took a gravel road, and after five minutes, we emerged from the woods out into farmland. He waved a hand at one field.

"Alright, let's see if you're a real farm boy. What kind of corn do we have out there?"

I looked at Burt, who was eyeing me with a challenging grin.

"Field corn," I said. "Looks like dent corn. I'd say it'll be ready for harvesting about the last week of September. Stop the truck, if you don't mind."

Burt did so and I looked over the field with a discerning eye. "I'm going to say the yield is going to be twenty thousand ears per acre. A little low, but that's how it is these days."

Burt slapped his thigh. "I love you, man." He began slowly driving again, scaring some crows.

"We need to kill off these crows before they eat it all, though. Did you know a group of crows is called a murder of crows?"

I chuckled. "Yeah, I've heard that."

He pointed out different crops as he drove. "We've only been farming the last two years, so I think we're doing okay. I turned those fields this past spring and let some cows graze. We'll try potatoes in that field next year and I think we should plant an extra acre of sweet corn." He gestured back over his shoulder.

"Back before it all went bad, there was an active wine vineyard north of here. The grape vines are doing nicely, so we have ample grape juice and wine."

"Have you tried anything like exotic fruits or coffee beans?"

"We've had some limited success. We had a healthy orange crop growing last year in one of the greenhouses, but the knucklehead who was in charge of them let them freeze one night."

He spit out of the window. "Lots of dummies around here."

CHAPTER 9 – COLD SHOWERS

Melvin awoke early the next morning. He stifled a groan as he got out of the truck and worked the stiffness out. He spent a long minute stretching and doing some deep knee bends before he worked his way around the plastic water bottles and peered out the front window. It wasn't quite sunup and the sky was a thick, dull gray. More rain was coming. The most important thing though, they weren't surrounded by a horde that'd snuck up on them during the night.

He went outside, relieved himself, and then walked over to the dead zombies. It was a man and woman somewhere close to his age, a teenage boy, and the younger boy. They looked like a family. Melvin peered at them closer and inspected the scant amount of decay of their features.

"You people haven't been zombies long," he concluded in a whisper, the statement meant only for himself.

He then looked them over for anything useful. The man had a Leatherman multipurpose tool sheathed on his belt and an empty gun holster. The boys were wearing backpacks and had empty canteen holders attached to web belts. Melvin started with the man and snaked his belt off so he could get the Leatherman and its sheath.

"I know someone who could use it," he explained to the dead man.

He then checked out the backpacks. They smelled with the rankness of zombie essence, making him wonder if they could be washed and reused. Looking inside, he saw a number of goodies. The young man had one of those fancy straw filters, a hunting knife with a small whetstone in the sheath, a mostly full container of bug spray, a pill bottle containing Q-tips, a well-used toothbrush with an almost empty tube of toothpaste, dental floss, fingernail clippers, a can of spray paint, a couple of bungee cords, a poncho, extra pairs of socks and underwear stuffed in a plastic trash bag, a small rocket stove, and a small first aid kit. The little boy's backpack had similar items, along with a small tarp and five-fifty cord.

"You raised a family of survivors," Melvin said quietly to the dead father. All four of them were dressed for the outdoors, sensible hiking boots, jeans, and neutral-colored shirts. The mom had her hair pulled back in a bandanna and was wearing a loose-fitting long sleeve shirt, possibly to hide her femininity. Smart thinking.

From the amount of bite marks, it looked like they were attacked by a horde of somewhere around five or ten. The mom's entire left side of her face had been torn off, and one of the dad's arms looked like he was a training dummy for a police department's K-9 team.

"I bet you guys fought to the end, eh, Dad? Too bad, we could've used you at Weather."

Melvin did a sniff test and decided the teenager's backpack was the least smelly one. He loaded it up with his findings and jogged back to the building.

He dumped the contents on the lone desk and set the backpack under the broken gutter, hoping the approaching rain would wash some of the stink off. He stuck his head in the back room and checked on Savannah. She'd moved the blankets aside, exposing her breasts. Even though he was the one who stripped her, he instantly felt like a peeping Tom and backed out of the room. He'd hung up her clothes the night before, but when he checked them, they were still a little damp.

As he finished off the remainder of the MRE from last night, the rain returned in force. With so much rain, Melvin surmised there must have been a hurricane out in the Atlantic before moving inland. Soon, the broken gutter was once again streaming with water. He knew it was going to be a little chilly, but he needed to bathe.

He hastened a quick peek in the back room to ensure Savannah was still asleep, got his toilet kit, a couple of towels, and walked outside. He stripped and stepped under the miniature waterfall. It was colder than he expected and he was quickly covered in goosebumps. He soaked himself, soaped up, and rinsed off quickly.

Grabbing the towels, he stepped back inside to see Savannah sitting in a chair, watching him. He hurriedly wrapped one around his waist.

"How're you feeling?" he asked as he used the other towel to dry off.

"A little better," she said and looked at her clothes hanging from bungee cords. "Did you take them off of me?"

"I did. Even though it's warm out, you had a little bit of hypothermia going on last night. It was the only way to get you warmed up."

"Oh." Her tone was quiet, meek. She stared at him in silence as she watched him as he put a pair of underwear on under the towel and then put some jeans on.

Melvin had a lean but hard physique, typical of a Special Forces operative, which he once was. Standing at a hair or two under six feet, he weighed somewhere in the neighborhood of one-eighty, all of it muscle.

He had a couple of scars here and there, nothing major. His back had a few pockmarks, courtesy of shrapnel from an IED in Afghanistan. He earned a Purple Heart for it, but other than a bad case of jock itch during basic training, that was his only injury.

Melvin pointed at the stream of water. "You should get yourself cleaned up. I got soap here, and I think I got something you can wear until your clothes are dry."

"I'm fine," she said, somewhat defensively.

"Negative," Melvin rejoined as he put a shirt on. "You smell like a monkey's ass on a hot summer day."

"I do not."

Melvin chuckled. "Oh, yes you do."

"It's too cold. I saw you shivering and your dick even shrink up."

Melvin gave her a frown. "Have you seen yourself in a mirror lately? Quit arguing and get yourself cleaned up."

She looked down at the ground, causing Melvin to regret his tone.

"Are you going to watch?" she finally asked.

"Nope. Have at it." He tossed her the towels and walked to the garage. Searching through his duffel bag of clothing, he found a football jersey and some socks. It'd have to do. He set them on the table immediately inside the door and glanced at her briefly. She'd soaped herself up, much like he did and was now rinsing off. He ducked back into the garage bay before she caught him looking and made himself busy.

"It's a little big."

He looked toward the doorway. Savannah was standing there, wearing the jersey. It hung loosely and came down to her knees.

"Yeah, well, maybe you'll grow into it one day," he said and chuckled at his own joke. She didn't laugh. "Well, alright, it'll keep you warm until your clothes dry out. Do you need to go to the bathroom or anything?" he asked.

She shook her head. Although the sky was dull, it was lighter now and he got a better look at her. Her hair was a wild mess of light amber brown surrounding an oval sunburnt face with a pert nose and brown doe eyes. In spite of how skinny she was, it wasn't hard to see a cute teenage girl under the mess.

Melvin reached into his pocket and retrieved his comb.

"Here," he said, handing it to her. "There's a mirror in the restroom."

She subconsciously ran fingers through her hair before disappearing into the restroom and reemerged fifteen minutes later and looked at Melvin expectantly.

"Much better," he said.

"I don't smell like a monkey's ass anymore?"

Melvin pantomimed sniffing and smiled slightly. "Nope. You smell like fresh petunias."

He waited to see if she laughed, or at least smiled, but she merely stared at him.

"Alright, let's eat something." He led her to the table and tore open an MRE.

She sat and looked at the contents before choosing a food item. She nibbled at it and slurped water from the canteen.

"Oh, here, I made something for you." He used one of the shop rags and took a canteen cup off of his rocket stove. "Drink some of this."

Savannah looked in the cup. "What is it?"

"Pine needle tea, it's rich in vitamin C. Oh, wait, you're not pregnant are you?"

Savannah stared at him. "No."

"Good. Here," he said and handed it to her.

Savannah took a small, tentative sip and made a sour face.

Melvin chuckled. "Oh, I forgot to tell you, it doesn't taste that great."

She gave him a look. "You think?"

"I know, but you're malnourished. Drink as much as you can stand, it'll be good for you."

She hunched forward in the chair and watched Melvin as she took small sips.

"Um, can I ask you a question?"

Melvin glanced at her. "Sure."

"What's with the zombie taped down to a chair on the front of your truck?"

"That's Peggy, my wife, or what's left of her."

Savannah looked sideways at him, as if he was playing some kind of twisted prank.

"And you keep her with you?" she asked.

"Yep."

"Why?"

"It's a long story," Melvin said. "But, the main reason is when there're other zombies around, she can somehow sense them and she'll start snarling like crazy. It's a good alarm system."

"But, she's a zombie," Savannah said.

"Yep."

"Kind of creepy," she remarked.

Melvin didn't respond.

"Why were you naked last night?"

Melvin felt a little uncomfortable now. "Oh, well, I'd been out in the rain and got soaked, so I took my clothes off and hung them up to dry. When I spotted you and your friends, I didn't realize you weren't a zombie at the time, and I didn't want to get another pair of clothes wet and dirty."

"So, you ran out naked so you wouldn't get your clothes dirty."

"Yeah, I'm sure it looked weird."

"A little," she said. "I thought you were some kind of crazy pervert."

"Anyway, they had some decent gear on them and one of the backpacks is still in pretty good shape. I created a kit for you and your clothes should be dry in another hour or two. Then you can get going."

She stopped in mid-bite and looked at Melvin with sudden anxiousness. "What do you mean, get going? You're getting rid of me?"

"Yeah, well, I mean I'm sure you want to get moving along. There's plenty of cars around here, maybe I can get one of them running for you, if you want."

She sat motionlessly, staring at him with her big brown eyes.

"What?" he asked.

"Can't I stay with you?"

"Don't you want to get back to your family?"

Savannah's features darkened. Her eyes started watering up again, but she quickly wiped them with the back of her hand. "My family's dead," she replied. "The Blackjacks killed them. I don't have anywhere to go."

"Oh, I'm sorry to hear that," he said.

She remained quiet and sat there, staring at the table.

"Tell me about it," he prodded.

He didn't think she was going to answer at first, but after a moment, she emitted a heavy sigh.

"Oh, not much to tell. I was living with my aunt and uncle near a bump in the road called Crozier. Have you heard of it?"

"I believe so."

"Yeah, well, Mom and Dad split up when I was thirteen and I went to live with Uncle Ray and Aunt Pat." She let out another sigh. "It's a long story, but anyway, I liked them. They were good to me. They had a small farm and we had chickens, and cows, and I even had a pet goat. Her name was Daffy."

"Sounds nice," Melvin remarked.

"It was. Aunt Pat liked gardening and canning. So, when it all went bad, we were actually doing okay. Oh, and we had some neighbors next door who helped out a lot." She gave a small, sad smile.

"Suzie was my cousin, but we acted more like sisters. We even shared the same boyfriend, Bobby. He was dumb as all get out, but he was cute and nice, and there weren't any other boys around."

"So, what happened?" Melvin asked quietly.

"Toothpaste," Savannah said, her voice cracking slightly. "We'd run out of toothpaste and some other stuff. We bitched and complained, so Uncle Roy decided to do something about it. He and Bobby and Bobby's father went into Richmond for supplies. Taz, that's one of the Blackjacks, told me later they caught them coming out of a pharmacy. They tortured Bobby's father until Bobby told them where we lived. Then they killed them."

Her face was full of misery while she talked about it. Melvin had heard similar stories the past couple of years, but it still got to him.

"Anyway, I guess you can figure out what happened next. They came and killed everyone. Aunt Pat hid me and Suzie in the basement, but it didn't do any good. They found us, took us prisoner, and threw us in a trailer with four other girls. The first night was the worst. They passed me and Suzie around like we were rag dolls." Savannah tried to tell the rest, but was too choked up.

"How long ago was that?" Melvin asked.

She wiped her eyes again and took a deep breath. "I'm not real sure, about a month or two, I guess. They kept us locked up most of the time in one of those little travel campers. You know what I mean?"

"I think so."

"The only time they let us out was to do chores or when they wanted – you know."

"Yeah. How'd you escape?"

"One day, they'd found like a couple of cases of booze and meth. I don't know the circumstances; I can only guess they killed someone. So, anyway, they all started smoking that stuff and drinking and getting rowdy. They let us join in, but whenever we were let out, they handcuffed us. Anyway, everyone was fucked up and having themselves a good old time. After it got dark, they built a big bonfire like they didn't have a care in the world. That's probably what attracted them, the fire and all of the noise. Taz was sitting next to me when those things came out of nowhere. One of them ran up from behind us and latched onto his neck."

"Are you sure they were zombies?" Melvin asked.

"Oh, hell yeah. I started screaming, and then Suzie and a couple of the other girls started screaming, and it was, I don't know what you'd call it…"

"Chaos?" Melvin asked.

"Yeah, I guess that's a good word. Chaos. It was chaos everywhere. Somebody started shooting, but there were a bunch of them, they were everywhere. I panicked and ran. I didn't know what else to do, so I started running and kept going."

Melvin thought it all over.

"Do you know where you were when you escaped?" he asked.

"No idea. I ran most of the night down some road. The next day, I was down there near a gas station," she said as she pointed down the road. "There's a cop car parked there and I was trying to get in it to see if I could find a handcuff key. Before I could even get in the car, those things were on me. I took off running again, but I didn't have any energy left. I was barely able to get on top of that car I was on when you found me."

Melvin listened as he thought of the Blackjacks. If they were still nearby, it could be problematic, he thought. He stared out of the window, wondering where they were. She interrupted his thoughts.

"Yesterday, I found a saw and kind of tried to cut one of my hands off, but I lost my nerve."

Melvin stared at her now, wondering what he would do if he were in the same predicament.

"Do you think your cousin got away?" he asked.

"I don't think so. When I was running, I heard her scream, and it was one of those blood-curdling screams, you know what I mean?"

"Yeah," Melvin answered. "Tell me about them. The Blackjacks. How many of them are there nowadays?"

She paused and looked at him. "Do you know them?"

"I bumped into a couple of them a few months ago, but I haven't seen them in a while. Is Lonnie still their leader?"

"Yeah, and he's scary as shit. One day, they caught some people and one of the men made some kind of smart-assed comment. Within like a microsecond, Lonnie grabbed the man, threw him on the ground, and pounded his head on the asphalt until there was blood and brains all over. It was awful. Taz said he used to be a pro wrestler."

Melvin had heard something like that as well. The man was huge, Melvin gave him that; well over six feet tall, almost three hundred pounds and mostly muscle.

"Is Snake still around?" he asked. Snake was Lonnie's de facto second-in-command. He was a little guy, but that didn't make him any less dangerous.

Savannah shuddered. "Yeah. He's like the opposite of Lonnie, but just as mean. Lonnie's big and loud, Snake is small and quiet. And he had a forked tongued, like a snake. One day, they'd caught a man. They tied him down, and Snake spent the rest of the day skinning him alive. It was sickening."

Yeah, Melvin thought, he could see that. Back when he'd bumped into the Blackjacks, Melvin and Lonnie struck up a friendship immediately, but Snake merely stared at Melvin the whole time and never said a word. If Melvin ever encountered him alone, he knew he'd need to kill the little dude immediately.

"I don't think I met all of them. Who're the others?" he asked.

She paused and thought a minute. "Let's see, besides Snake, there's Pig, Taz, Dizzy, Tank, Hot-Shot, Crank, Topsy, Mako, Crash, Scooter, and Freak."

"They sure love nicknames," Melvin commented. It reminded him of street gangs. Nobody went by their real name; they had to create an alternate identity for themselves. Create a new persona, or something.

"Yeah, Taz told me one day there used to be more of them, but a few days before they found me and Suzie, they got into a big shootout with some people up in Staunton and some of them were killed. He said they were cops."

"Cops?" Melvin asked in surprise.

"Yeah, they had a compound or something. Lonnie thought it'd be easy pickings."

Melvin grunted. There was a headquarters office for the Virginia State Troopers in Staunton. He wondered if it was them and made a mental note to pay them a friendly visit sometime soon.

"What about the women?" he asked. "You said there were four more of them?"

"Yeah. The girls are Sunshine, Dimple, Fanny, and Leah."

"How'd you get along with them, the women, how'd you get along with the women?"

Savannah made a face. "Fanny was the favorite, but that was only because they had a vote one night and decided she gave the best blowjob."

She paused to make a gagging impression. "The rest of us got along okay, but sometimes they'd make us fight for food. It wasn't fun."

Judging from her emaciated appearance, Melvin guessed she seldom won any of those fights. They sat in silence for several minutes while Melvin thought over everything she said.

Apparently, Savannah interpreted the silence as rejection to her earlier request. She slowly stood.

"Thank you for everything, Melvin. You truly saved my life." She walked away and Melvin watched as she went into the front lobby. He got up and followed her. She took her pants off of the bungee cord and began putting them on.

"They're still damp," Melvin said.

"It's okay," she said and began putting her socks and shoes on.

"Hey look, you don't have to go."

"No, it's okay, Melvin. You've been nice to me, but I can tell you don't want me around here."

She started to walk past him, but he stopped her by grabbing her by the shoulders. She jerked back, a hint of fear flashing across her face. He quickly pulled his hands back.

"Listen, it's not that. I'm not much of a social person these days, but you're welcome to stay here." He cleared his throat. "I want you to stay," he found himself saying.

She stared at him a long moment with her big brown eyes. "Are you sure?" she finally asked.

"Of course I'm sure."

She stared at him, like any second now he was going to say, "Just kidding!"

After a few seconds, she realized he was being sincere. "You won't regret it," she said. "I promise."

"Okay," he said. "No need to get all gushy."

Savannah didn't make it much past breakfast before falling asleep. Still weak from the lingering effects of malnutrition and running for her life for the past two days, she'd lain her head on the desk after only eating a few bites and was out of it. He picked her up gently, put her back on the cot, and left a note for her in case he was gone when she woke up.

He hoped there weren't underlying health issues with her and she was going to die in her sleep, but there was nothing he could do about it. He geared up, got the bike out, and headed back to the government building.

It was a one-story brick building and the unlocked door was located in the back. The rock had not been moved, which was seemingly a good sign. He parked his bike and opened the door.

He was immediately struck by the orderliness. Most buildings he'd entered were trashed, in disarray, and often there were and abundance of vermin. Things were often broken or vandalized. Not this one. Melvin interpreted it as a sign someone was caring for this building. He searched it in his deliberate, methodical procedure. The labs were dusty but otherwise clean, but there were no signs of life. The computer system was still intact. Melvin tried a few light switches. No power.

It took him three hours in total. The entire time he found himself continuously asking himself what he should do with Savannah. She wasn't a plant or a spy, he was sure of it. She looked like death warmed over. If she were healthy, he'd be suspicious. So, it came down to two choices; kick her loose or take her back with him when the mission was finished?

The Mount Weather people, the originals, the ones who'd had it rather easy the last three years, could be rather snarky to newcomers. Not physically, no. Those people were passive-aggressive types; they were cowards at heart after all. Instead of telling someone outright they were not liked, they'd act snotty, make snide remarks, and talk about them behind their backs.

Melvin knew it was especially going to be true when it came to Savannah. The girl looked like a concentration camp survivor, it was obvious her formal education was limited, and it was doubtful she had any special skills that would ingratiate herself with the community.

When he emerged outside, it was raining again. It was going to push his plan forward for part two of his mission: to check out the national laboratory.

Melvin peddled back to the auto detail business, once again soaking wet from the rain. He'd tried riding with a poncho once, but it got in the way.

"Hey," Melvin said when he walked inside. There was no answer. He walked in the backroom and found Savannah huddled in the bathroom. She looked frightened, anxious.

"What's wrong?" he asked.

"You were gone," she exclaimed.

"Yeah, I had something I needed to do. I left a note, didn't you see it?"

She nodded, but it didn't seem to help. "I didn't think you were coming back."

"My truck is still here," Melvin responded as he gestured toward the garage bay. "I'm not going anywhere without it. Okay?"

She looked uncertain, but finally nodded her head.

"Come on out," he said. "Maybe you can eat a little bit."

She looked at him uncertainly. He held out a hand and helped her up.

"Okay." Her tone was still tentative, frazzled, but she willingly let Melvin lead her to the front office. He pointed at the open MRE.

"If you're not hungry don't eat, but if you think you can, try a bite or two."

"Where did you go?" she asked after she'd eaten a cracker with some peanut butter on it.

"I had to go check out a building," Melvin answered.

"Why?"

"That's my job," he said.

"What do you mean?" Savannah asked.

"I'm from Mount Weather and I do missions for them."

"Mount Weather, what's that?" she asked.

"Back in the day, it was the FEMA command center. When it went bad, they relocated the majority of the executive and legislative branch there."

"Why?"

"Because they have an underground bunker and housing," Melvin said.

"Okay, but why? We don't have a government anymore," she replied.

Melvin grunted and didn't explain. He was tired of talking.

"Anyway, I've got to send them a message."

Savannah watched as Melvin set up a military-looking radio and attached a satellite antenna. He prepared a message and sent it on burst mode. He left it on for several minutes as he ate lunch. Savannah listened in silence.

After ten minutes, he received an incoming message. He went through the decryption and listened. So did Savannah.

"You're going to check out the lab? Isn't that where they build nuclear bombs or something?"

"Sort of," Melvin said. "There's no actual bombs stored there, but there is nuclear material and a supercomputer there. We have reason to believe it's occupied, so I'm going to check it out."

"A supercomputer? What's so special about a computer?" Savannah asked.

"Smart people can do all kinds of things with it," Melvin replied. He thought about the two computer geeks back at Weather. Garret and Grace. They were twins. They took him to a section in the east tunnel and showed him Mount Weather's Cray supercomputer. They said it was close to the same model as the Titan, the name of the Oak Ridge computer, and went on and on about its capabilities. They dazzled him with numbers and the computer's performance.

Most of it went over Melvin's head. The only thing he got out of it was the Titan was too large for him to dismantle and load up on the back of his truck. The politicians were adamant the computer didn't fall into the wrong hands. If worse came to worse, he had some C-4 to deal with the issue.

"Alright," Melvin said. "I'm going to be gone the rest of the day. You'll be okay here."

He looked and saw Savannah's big brown eyes starting to water up.

"Can't I go with you?" she implored.

Melvin thought about it and found himself shaking his head. "I can't guarantee your safety. I don't know if there's anyone there or what."

"I'll be okay," she countered and her voice dropped to barely above a whisper. "I don't want to be left alone."

Melvin sighed. "Yeah, alright," he said. "But, you have to do exactly what I say. If I tell you to run, you don't ask me to explain, you do it. If I tell you to shut up, you don't ask why or back talk, you stop talking. It's not that I'm bossy or like ordering people around, it's a matter of life and death. I've survived on my own for a long time now, partly because I didn't have someone with me doing stupid things and endangering my life."

"Okay," Savannah said.

Melvin gave her a hard stare for a long minute. "Alright then," he finally said. "Let's get loaded up."

CHAPTER 10 – THE MISSION

Raymond appeared right when I was about to get a second helping of powdered eggs.

"Good morning, everyone," he said with mock cheerfulness. "I need Zach, Major Parsons, and Major Fowkes to come with me." Without waiting for a response, he motioned us to follow him.

We walked to the bunker entrance and waited at the elevators. I waited for him to explain what we were about to get into. He saw me looking and grinned.

"I think we're going to be in for a lot of rain today," he said. "There was a hurricane that formed in the Atlantic and hit landfall a couple of days ago."

"That's nice," I said. "So, what are we doing?"

Raymond grinned again. "Patience, Zach, patience."

We went down at least two floors below the living quarters, and the elevator opened up into a rather large room with several tables of computers and yet another conference table. There were also unmarked doors in the back of the room, which lead to I don't know where.

"The situation room," Raymond informed us. It was impressive. There were multiple computer terminals, large flat screens mounted on the walls, and I even saw a soundproof room that looked like a recording studio.

"We use it as command and control for the away missions," President Richmond said. He had emerged from a side room, holding a steaming cup of coffee, and sat at the head of a conference table. Soon, others started trickling in and taking what I assumed was their reserved seats. Justin along with a couple of his Marines came in, and there were a couple of those secretaries I saw at the debriefing. Raymond gestured for Justin and me to sit together.

"What's going on?" I whispered to him.

He grinned at me. "Big mission," he said, but wouldn't elaborate.

Raymond walked over to the president and whispered in his ear before sitting. POTUS nodded and stood.

"It appears most everyone is here, so why don't we get started." He gestured at me. "Did something happen after our initial meeting, Mister Gunderson?"

"Yes, sir," I answered. "I caught two people breaking into my trailer and stealing stuff out of it. I was told they are the adult children of Senator Rhinehart."

He furrowed his brow, which seemed more of an act rather than genuine concern. "I will have to address that issue immediately," he declared.

"No need, sir. I took care of it." I looked at all of them. I noticed one of those secretaries was trying hard not to grin. He must have heard the details of how I took care of it. I couldn't help but throw in one last barb.

"I don't know why an SOP isn't already in place to deal with criminal behavior. It seems rather odd for a group of supposedly enlightened people."

I heard Justin give a quiet guffaw, but the rest of the room was quiet.

"Yes, you make a valid point," President Richmond said. "We'll look into it. In the meantime, let me show all of you the purpose of this meeting." He nodded at Seth, who stood.

"The previous forty-five months have been bad, but all of you know that." He gestured toward one of two people who was sitting in front of a computer console.

"This is Garret and Grace Anderson. If you haven't figured it out, they're twins."

"Fraternal," Garret quickly said.

The woman gave a cheerful wave. Both of them were pale, skinny, mousy brown hair, and looked like they were in their mid-twenties. The woman's hair was longer and she was wearing nerd glasses, but otherwise, there was no mistaking they were brother and sister.

The man began clicking his mouse and the flat screens came to life. It was a scene of chaos, people attacking each other, soldiers shooting people, people attacking soldiers. I recognized the location from a news video.

"Cairo, Egypt," Seth said. "We are reasonably certain Cairo was ground zero. The origin is still unknown, but what is known is how quickly the pathogen spread." The image changed to a world map and a graphical overlay of red lines began forming. The lines would start in one city and move to other cities, and wherever the lines stopped, the cities would turn red.

"The model has been sped up, but I'm sure all of you know the entire world was infected within two weeks."

Seth gave a running commentary as the images on the screens changed. The next series showed video feeds of military bases, naval ships, missile silos, and other fortified facilities I could not identify.

"Because the pathogen was so contagious, it infiltrated most of our military personnel before we were even aware of its presence."

The images were interspersed with what looked like closed-circuit TV cameras, surveillance cameras perhaps. They showed the same thing over and over again. Normal people getting attacked by infected people. I looked over at the president.

"Am I correct to assume you watched these events while sitting here in relative safety?"

President Richmond gazed steadily at me. "Yes, Mister Gunderson, we all did." He took a moment to make direct eye contact with all of the recent arrivals.

"We did not sit idly by, Mister Gunderson," Secretary Stark said. "There were multiple actions taken, but the virus had delivered a knockout blow before we even knew we were in a fight."

"We were lucky to get it contained here before all of us got infected," General Fosswell added.

"And there are other survivors you've been in contact with, sir?" Sarah asked.

"Yes, Major," the president said. "I am happy to report that as of this date, we've made contact with over twenty pockets of survivors within the United States. The largest group we have been in contact with is sixty-five."

"Sixty-five? That's a decent-sized number. Where are they at?" Sarah asked.

"Kansas," he answered. Now, he leaned forward slightly in his chair. "There is a possible issue we have identified though."

We all waited. President Richmond took his time and finished his tea before responding.

"The human population is in peril," he declared in a somber voice. "This zombie virus has created a chain of events which threaten our very existence."

He then nodded at Seth.

"Famine, pestilence, disease, a lack of health care, violence, and even nuclear events are taking their toll," Seth said and looked at Grace. She took her cue and clicked her mouse.

The next screen was raw numbers of the population of each major city and the projected infection rate. The last number was the predicted number of initial deaths, and annual deaths each year after. There was a cross reference of the birth rate, which had declined to practically zero within a couple of years.

"If you will note, the projections show the human population steadily declining. The extinction event is projected to occur within the next fifty years."

Everyone was quiet now. The members of Mount Weather were watching us newcomers with somber amusement. I looked around and tentatively raised my hand.

Seth looked at me. "Yes, Zach?"

"How many people became infected while locked up in here?" I asked.

"Thirteen," a man answered. He'd been quiet during the entire presentation, but I noticed he'd been watching me the entire time. "And, all of them were tested prior to being admitted into Mount Weather."

Seth spoke up. "This is Doctor Kincaid, and his colleague there is Doctor Smeltzer. At the time of the outbreak, the two doctors were assigned to USAMRIID, which is the United States Army Research Institute of Infectious Diseases, and based out of Fort Detrick, Maryland."

I looked at them thoughtfully. The two men looked like mad scientists straight out of a low-budget movie. Both were in their mid-to-late sixties, disheveled white hair that hadn't been on the receiving end of an experienced barber in a while, identical furry eyebrows, and both were wearing horn-rimmed glasses. Kincaid looked a little bit heavier and had a larger, rounder face, but that was about it.

Seth continued. "In early December, during the first year of the outbreak, Doctors Kincaid, Smeltzer, and a third virologist, Doctor Mayo Craddock were at Fort Detrick. Unfortunately, the infection spread throughout the facility within a matter of hours. The three doctors were trapped and had to be rescued." He gestured toward the screens. "For the first two years, Fort Detrick was swarming with thousands of infected. This is a live satellite feed of it now."

Fort Detrick appeared to be a neatly arranged conglomeration of buildings. There was nothing I saw that would indicate anything amazing or horrifying. The screen went to a close-up and the image was frozen into a still-shot. There were two abandoned military vehicles with maybe a hundred zombie corpses lying around.

"One hundred and seventy-seven," Garret said. He must have seen me trying to make a count. I nodded in thanks.

"Fort Detrick is forty-four miles from here. Seven days ago, we sent a task force to the location in order to neutralize all hostile threats and secure the facility. Doctor Craddock insisted on going with them. The contingent used those two Strykers parked in front of the main lab. We lost contact with them ninety minutes after their arrival." Seth paused a moment to let us newcomers digest it. I started to raise my hand, but Seth cut me off.

"I believe you are about to ask if we know what happened to them," he said. "Short answer, we don't know." Seth looked over at one of the computer geeks. "Garret was monitoring the live feed at that time. Garret?"

Garret clicked his mouse a couple of times. The image on the screens changed once again.

"They arrived at Detrick with no issues and checked in accordingly," he said and pointed at the screens with a miniature laser light. "You can see them unloading from the Strykers and forming a defensive perimeter." He sat back in his chair while we watched a team of soldiers entering one of the buildings while another team maintained security outside. Garret then sat up and clicked something with his mouse.

"Fourteen minutes after their arrival is when they had their first contact."

We watched as a horde of around twenty infected approached them at what can best be described as a slow jog. The soldiers had no problem taking care of business and made short work of them.

"Now watch," Garret said. Another horde, this one about fifty in size, came around a building from behind and began running toward the soldiers. One of the soldiers that was manning the machine gun from the Stryker was guarding the rear. He opened up and appeared to have killed off at least half of them by himself before the rest joined in. As we watched, this happened three more times.

"They're timing is off," Justin whispered. I nodded in agreement. If it was a planned attack, the waves should have been overlapping and not at intervals.

"So, I'm sitting here, watching the whole thing and listening to them talk to each other on the radio," Garret said. "The team inside had no contact, and they were going to come back out and assist the soldiers outside, but Sergeant Rivera told them not to worry about it, they had it under control." He looked at us. "I mean, they sounded like they were having a good time. Everyone was joking and they were having a competition to see who could kill the most."

"I take it something happened," Justin said.

"That would be affirmative, Lieutenant," Garret said.

Seth cleared his throat. "Show the eighty-eight-minute mark, please, Garret." He waited until the appropriate image was now on the screen. It showed the soldiers still maintaining a defensive perimeter, and there was one soldier in the middle. Seth used his pointer and put a small red dot on the soldier.

"That's Sergeant Rivera. Now listen."

We listened to the audio of Sergeant Rivera having a one-sided conversation. From what I could tell, he was speaking with the people inside the building and they were requesting assistance. And then, the screens once again became nothing but snow.

"We've confirmed solar flares during this time period, although we're not ruling out the signal being jammed," Seth said. "In any event, we had no signal for a little over seven minutes, and then we have this." He pointed with the laser. What we saw were the dead zombies, the two Strykers, and nothing else.

Seth spoke up. "In order for these esteemed doctors to manufacture a vaccine, they will need access to that specific building. That's where the labs are. And here is the mission."

We listened as Seth outlined the mission in the military format. In short, the Marines were going to attempt to secure Fort Detrick. Sarah was going to lead a contingent that would act as a rear guard and, if needed, a reactionary force in case the Marines needed help.

Doctor Kincaid explained. "Virus research was never the mission for Mount Weather, so, it doesn't have the necessary equipment, nor does it have the proper containment protocols. In a word, our only hope lies with Fort Detrick."

"We're going back," Seth said plainly. "We have to secure the facility so the two doctors here can successfully create a vaccine."

"And that's where you come in, Zach," Doctor Kincaid said.

"How so?" I asked warily.

"Securing the lab is the first step," Seth explained. "The second step is getting the lab or labs up and running again. The third step is you. The two doctors will need you in order to create the vaccine."

"Okay," I said. "Count me in. When do we leave?"

"You will not be going to Fort Detrick," Stark said.

I looked at him and back at Seth. "What gives?"

"Until the doctors can create a suitable vaccine, we are under orders to not use you in any high-risk mission," he said.

I frowned. "Whose orders?"

"Mine," President Richmond said plainly.

I tried in vain to form a plausible argument which would allow me to join the mission. And I voiced a few of them, but the president was adamant. The bottom line, I was grounded.

"Alright," I said in surrender. "But I'd like to believe I can help out in some way."

"Oh, there is, Zach," Doctor Smeltzer said. "You see, you are far more unique than you realize. We've reviewed the tests performed by Major Parsons. The results of the testing were somewhat remarkable. We know of only one other person like you, but sadly they've died."

"The woman in Kentucky," I said.

Doctor Smeltzer nodded. "Was she a relative of yours?"

"I don't know of any of my relatives living in America."

"All the more reason to protect you," Seth said.

I looked at Doctor Smeltzer. "So, what do you need from me?"

The two docs smiled broadly. "A few vials of blood should do it," Doctor Smeltzer said. Doctor Kincaid nodded in agreement.

"Excellent," Stark said. "Now, with the president's permission, why don't we check in with Sergeant Clark?"

President Richmond gave a silent nod. He seemed more interested in his cup of tea at the moment.

Grace took the cue, and we watched as the satellite's image began moving in a southeasterly direction. Soon, it zoomed in a building that looked like a gas station.

"Sergeant Clark's current location," Grace said.

I tentatively raised my hand. Seth nodded at me.

"Who is Sergeant Clark?"

"Do you remember encountering a gentleman outside of Roanoke?" Seth asked.

"I do," I answered. "A crazy dude with his zombie wife mounted on the front of his truck."

Grace giggled.

"Yes," General Fosswell said. "That's Sergeant Melvin Clark. Prior to the pandemic, he was an operator on a Special Forces A-team."

"His rank was E-7, sergeant first class," Seth added. "He's had personal issues, but he is a damn good soldier. In fact, at one time General Fosswell had submitted his name to receive the Congressional Medal of Honor."

"Oh, yeah?" Sarah asked.

Seth nodded. "His entire team was wiped out in Afghanistan in an ambush by the equivalent of two company size units of Taliban. Melvin held them off for over thirty hours, calling in air strikes on them while under heavy fire. When reinforcements finally arrived, Melvin was surrounded by dead Taliban. He'd killed several of them in hand-to-hand combat."

"Wow," I said.

"Yes," General Fosswell said. "He has some personal issues, but he's one of a kind. Over the course of the last two years, he has conducted several long-range reconnaissance missions on behalf of Mount Weather."

Grace stood and pointed at a solitary building displayed on one of the monitors. "He checked in last night and gave grid coordinates to that building. He's out there all by himself," she said, her voice trailing off.

Garret made a face. "She has a crush on him."

"You do," she quickly retorted.

Seth looked at his watch. "In fact, we should be receiving a message from him at any minute."

"What is his mission?" Sarah asked. Seth nodded at Garret, who was grinning broadly.

"Oak Ridge has power," he said.

"They're not mind readers, Garret. Explain," President Richmond admonished.

Garret's grin faltered slightly. Grace jumped in.

"My brother loves to play with the satellites," she said. "Two nights ago, he was looking over the country and found a significant amount of lights at the Oak Ridge Laboratory known as Y-12, which is located in east Tennessee."

"But they only stayed on a few minutes, and then they went dark again," Garret added.

"Melvin's mission is to go to the lab and attempt to make contact with whoever is there. If he deems them to be hostile, he is directed to take necessary action."

"He's going to take them out?" I asked.

"Only if it's necessary," Seth replied.

"He must be one hell of a badass," one of the Marines muttered.

"He's very capable," General Fosswell said, and then made pointed eye contact with the Marine. "And expendable, just like you."

"Point taken, sir," Justin said and cut his eyes at the Marine, subtly warning him not to argue about it.

"Oh, we have an incoming message," Grace said as she looked at a console.

"Put it on audio, please, Grace," President Richmond said.

"Mike Whiskey, Mike Whiskey, this is Mad Dog Forty. Objective reached. The first location is unoccupied but has indications of human upkeep. I will proceed to objective two in one mike and will attempt contact. Mad Dog Forty, out."

CHAPTER 11 — NUT SACKS

Lieutenant Justin Smithson was standing at parade rest when the rest of the Marines sauntered outside.

"Good afternoon, Marines," he'd said when they'd formed up and he ensured all were present. "I hope lunch was enjoyable."

There were some murmurs of assent, but he hushed them with his next statement.

"Well, now. You men *look* like Marines again, but now I need to see what kind of shape you're in, so I think we're going to go for a little run around the perimeter."

The grumbles of protest were loud now, causing Justin to suppress a grin.

"Sir?"

It was Joker. Justin acknowledged him with a slight nod.

"We just ate and we ain't got running shoes on."

Justin scoffed. "Well, now. I imagine if you ever run into a pack of zombies, tell them you can't run on a full stomach. I'm sure they'll understand."

"I don't see Corporal Bullington joining in," another one remarked.

"That is because Corporal Bullington is pregnant. Are you pregnant, Marine?"

The Marine had nothing to reply.

"Do we at least get to stretch, sir?" Joker asked.

"You already should have," Justin replied. "You're Marines. You should always be ready for action." With that asseveration, he barked a few commands, and in short order had them running at a double time.

It wasn't until the third time around the perimeter when the first Marine ran off to the side and puked. Justin smiled inwardly and kept them running. By the time they'd made it to lap number six, everyone except Justin and Sergeant Crumby had tossed their lunch. Justin finally relented, and for the last lap, he slowed them to a walk.

When he'd marched them back in front of the main building, he halted them and ordered them to stand at ease.

"Not bad, but there's a lot of room for improvement," Justin said. He was about to speak again when Joker raised his hand.

"Speak," Justin ordered.

"Sir, I'm willing to give all of this stuff a chance, but so far, I ain't happy."

"Oh, my. You poor thing. What would make you happy, Private Joker?"

"Hell, I don't know. We've been cooped up in here for months. Why don't we go out on some patrols or something?"

"Yeah, let's go kill some zeds," another one said. Justin glanced over at Sergeant Crumby.

"Be careful what you wish for," Crumby said. "We're going out on a mission tomorrow morning."

There was at least one whoop of joy and a lot of grins.

"Alright, listen up." Justin spent the next thirty minutes giving the mission order. As he spoke, he could see looks of anticipation. He liked it; they'd already forgotten about how he'd forced them to puke no more than thirty minutes ago.

"Alright, Marines. Head to the chow hall and see if they'll let you men get a snack. We're going to need two weeks of water and rations. Corporal Conway, that's your responsibility."

"Aye, sir."

"Sergeant Crumby?"

"Sir?"

"They're going to let us use two Strykers. Make sure they're squared away."

Sergeant Crumby responded with a silent nod.

"I'll be in the armory. After you get a bite to eat, come and draw your weapons." He looked at his watch. "I'll see you there in thirty minutes."

When Justin walked into the armory, he found Ensign Boner sitting with his feet propped up, bright red Beats headphones covering his ears, eyes closed, listening to who knows what. Justin slapped the side of the open door to get his attention.

Boner opened his eyes slowly, wondering why someone was annoying him. When he saw Justin, he put his feet down and removed the earphones.

"What do you want?" he asked.

"We're going to be drawing weapons for the mission, and I wanted to get a look at them, make sure they're battle worthy."

Boner's eyes narrowed. "Mission? I haven't heard of any mission."

Justin gave a somber nod, like he was surprised and concerned nobody had informed him of the upcoming mission. In fact, he knew Ensign Boner had been intentionally left out of the loop.

"Look, I don't know what your history is, and I don't know what you've done to get on the bad side of General Fosswell. I'm just a Marine and I follow orders. You know what my first order was when I arrived here, right?"

Boner continued staring at Justin for a long minute. "So, what's the mission?" he asked.

"We're to escort Smeltzer and Kincaid to Fort Detrick, secure a lab, and protect them while they attempt to create a vaccine."

Boner made a face and shook his head. "They already tried it once and it failed. The whole contingent disappeared. It's a suicide mission."

"Those are my orders," Justin replied.

Joker and two other Marines walked into the armory while the two men were staring at each other.

"We're here, sir," Joker said.

Boner scoffed and sat back down. "Have at it," he said. "It's your funeral."

Justin faced them. "Alright, let's take a look at the weapons."

Justin pulled each individual weapon off of the rack and inspected them carefully.

"They're dirty," he muttered.

Boner gave an apathetic shrug. "We have a shortage of cleaning products."

"Steam," Justin said.

"What's that, sir?" Joker asked.

"Do we have anything around here like a steam cleaner?"

"Yeah, I mean, yes, sir," one of the Marines said.

Justin gazed at him. "Jenkins, right?"

"Yes, sir. Jenkins. Kirby Jenkins."

"Alright, Jenkins. Round up that steam cleaner and set us up a cleaning station. We're going to have these weapons good to go before we head out tomorrow."

"You can't do that," Boner contended. "They'll rust."

"Not if we lubricate them," Justin rejoined.

"We have maybe one ounce of Hoppe's lubricant left," Boner rejoined.

Justin sighed and turned to his Marines. "Joker, go find Zach. I happen to know he has a case or two of 5W30 synthetic motor oil stored in his trailer. Tell him what we're doing and I would be most grateful if he let us borrow a quart."

"Aye, sir," Joker said and started to walk out.

"Oh, Joker."

Joker stopped and turned.

"Zach is particular about some things, so don't go in that trailer until you get his permission, unless you're ready for a fight."

Joker chuckled. "He and I are cool, sir."

After Joker and Kirby walked out, Justin turned his attention to the remaining Marine.

"Private Merritt Burns, you were a sergeant once, correct?"

"Yes, sir."

"What happened?"

"Dirty piss," he replied. "They'd already busted me down in rank and I was about to be discharged. You know the rest."

"Well, there are no more piss tests, aren't you the lucky one," Justin said with a small grin.

"And you better believe I've smoked since then," Burns said. "They have a pretty good supply here."

"They got marijuana here?" Justin asked in surprise.

"Oh, yeah," Boner answered. "They had a hydroponics lab going the first week."

Justin chuckled. "Go figure. Alright, back to business. Burns, your job is the ammo. For the sake of simplicity, all of the weapons we'll be carrying will be one caliber. M4s, M16s, and two M249s. Standard load, but I want the 249 gunners to have a minimum of five nut sacks each."

"Five nut sacks? Sounds pretty kinky."

They looked around at the voice to see Rachel and Sarah walking in. Rachel acted like she was confused and continued.

"A Marine with five nut sacks? I'm calling bullshit, I'll need to see proof," she demanded.

"Uh, it's a slang term for the ammunition holders for the M249 light machine gun," Burns said.

Rachel gave a sly grin. "You'll still need to show us your nut sack."

"Knock it off," Sarah said.

Rachel kept grinning and changed the subject. "Are you big tough Marines going to share any weapons and ammunition for us?"

Justin cleared his throat. "Major, have you chosen your personnel?"

"Briscoe and Stallings," Sarah replied. "They're both electricians."

"Can they shoot?" Justin asked, and then remembered there were others listening. "Can they shoot, ma'am?"

"They say they can," Sarah replied.

Burns cleared his throat. Justin gave him a questioning look.

"We've had some target practice lessons in the past with the civilians. They did okay, sir."

Justin nodded and looked back at Sarah questioningly. She gave a halfhearted, dismissive shrug.

"They'll have to do. None of those so-called secretaries are interested in going. Apparently, they're immune to being voluntold."

"You got that right," Boner said. He'd been sitting in his chair, silently listening to their conversation.

"What's the story on them, Lawrence?" Rachel asked.

Boner shrugged like it was old news. "There's eleven of them, all are supposedly geniuses. Ten of them are married to each other. Only Parvis Anderson is single. Not only do they run the place, they're a pseudo think tank for the president. They're the ones who keep the power grid up, the sewage plant working, pretty much everything."

"It sounds like they don't even need the president or senators," Rachel said.

"Secretary Stark is their de facto supervisor," Boner said. "And President Richmond is in charge of Secretary Stark, so there you have it. Things are getting tense around here though, it might all change soon."

"How so?" Justin asked.

Boner was silent now and leaned back in his chair.

Rachel walked over and started massaging Boner's shoulders. "C'mon Lawrence, don't be the strong silent type. Tell us what's going on."

"That feels damn good," he muttered, his eyes partially closing.

"You know you want to tell me," she cooed and grinned at the others.

"There's an internal power struggle going on," he said. "Some of the senators want Richmond out and are pushing for a presidential election." He chuckled. "It won't do any good though."

"Why not?" Rachel asked.

"Because they're all power hungry and they don't even realize how impotent they are."

Rachel squeezed his shoulders one final time before stopping. He looked back at her questioningly. She responded with a wink.

He sighed, stood, and stretched. "That felt wonderful, but I've got to make my rounds." He then looked pointedly at Justin. "You're responsible for the armory until I get back."

They all watched him leave.

"I wonder what's really going on," Rachel said.

"That is the question," Justin replied, and then changed the subject. "Alright, let's get to work."

CHAPTER 12 – BLOOD

They took no less than twelve vials of blood, all the while gabbing on like teenage nerds seeing their first set of breasts. As they chatted, I looked around at their lab. It held the usual pieces of equipment you'd find in a lab and was fastidiously neat with the exception of several pieces of paper hung on the wall with thumbtacks. They were black and white photographs printed out on regular paper.

Doctor Smeltzer saw me looking. "Those are what are called micrographs."

"Ah, okay. What are they?"

"They are images of the zombie virus taken from an electron microscope," he said. "Have you ever seen anything like that?"

"The only pictures I've seen of a virus were on the internet, and they looked like prickly pears." I pointed. "Those look more like icicles."

"Indeed they do," Doctor Smeltzer said. "That's one of the many things that makes this virus so damned interesting."

I nodded, but I wasn't sure interesting would be the definitive word I would use. The infection had effectively caused billions of casualties. But, whatever.

"There's a few things I'd like to ask," I said. They looked at me expectantly.

"This virus, that's what it is, a virus, correct?"

"Indeed it is," Doctor Kincaid answered.

"What is the incubation time?"

"Anywhere from a few minutes to several hours," Doctor Smeltzer answered. "It varies, depending on the person. The longest recorded instance is approximately twenty-four hours, give or take a few minutes."

"And you don't know where it came from?" I asked. "I mean, other than the fact you guys believe Cairo is ground zero, where the heck did it come from?"

"The simple answer is, we do not know," Doctor Kincaid replied and gave a patient smile. "We've never encountered this viral family before."

"It could have come from the ocean, perhaps spewed out of the earth as a result of an earthquake or a volcano; there's even speculation that meteors entering the atmosphere have the capability of carrying alien viruses."

I arched an eyebrow. "Has that ever been proven?"

"Merely speculation," Kincaid said.

"How many viruses are there?" I asked. "I've read different numbers."

Doctor Kincaid gave a patient smile. "The exact number is somewhat elusive. One of the last studies on the topic hypothesized there are at least 320,000 unknown viruses that infect mammals. Now, that particular number was derived from a computational projection, and the study was based on only nine known viral families, so the number could be exponentially higher.

"At one time, it was believed a virus can only infect cells that have specific receptors that allow it to gain entry."

"And then, along came the West Nile virus," Doctor Smeltzer said. "There are several viruses that use different receptors and infect different species."

Doctor Kincaid nodded in agreement.

"A virus is an incredible piece of work," he said. "It is the fastest evolving life form on earth. Quite frankly, it's a wonder something like this hasn't happened eons sooner."

"We could easily spend a lifetime studying it," Doctor Smeltzer said. "We were in the beginning stages of sequencing it to determine its DNA code at Fort Detrick when it all went bad. The CDC personnel had made some amazing headway before they became overrun."

"What about them evolving?" I asked. "Does this virus cause a mutation in the brain or something?"

"Now that is a fascinating observation on your part, Zach," Doctor Kincaid said while tapping his temple with his forehead and then grinned. "But, incorrect. In order for something to evolve it must replicate."

"Like a human giving birth," Smeltzer added.

"Oh."

Kincaid nodded. "The virus would not cause the brain itself to mutate. However, we believe the virus itself mutates, which in turn may cause different outcomes in an infected person, depending on their genetics."

"Which still makes your rule valid, in a manner of speaking," Doctor Smeltzer added. "We believe, now this is only a hypothesis, but we believe these Rule 14 zombies you refer to have brains that have been altered by the virus in a way we cannot yet explain. It appears there are two different phenotypes, both that completely alter the brain, but the Rule 14 zombies appear to have developed different brain functions activated by the virus."

"But they're doing some unusual things," I said. "Things that a normal human can't do."

"You're referring to your belief that they are communicating telepathically," Doctor Smeltzer said, almost like an accusation.

"Yes." Among other things, I thought.

He nodded. "Yes, well, more research will need to be conducted on that matter."

"That's not much of an answer," I said.

"Yes, well, we haven't been up close and personal with them as you have," Doctor Smeltzer said. "I'm the first to admit we've been rather sheltered here."

"When did you first learn of your immunity?" Doctor Kincaid asked.

"I was made aware of it by Major Parsons," I answered and nodded toward Grant, who was sitting at a nearby desk reading something. When I began explaining our first encounter, he looked up briefly and smiled before burying himself back in the thick file in front of him.

"We initially believed I became exposed when I was attacked by a zombie, but there had to have been something that happened earlier." I then briefly explained my possible first exposure.

"The man shot me," I said, pointing at the scar on my head. "It didn't kill me, but I don't have much recollection of what happened for several hours after that. I was told I was in close proximity to several zombies, so there could have been some type of exposure." I'm sure they'd already read Grant's report, but they wanted to hear all about it firsthand.

"Fascinating," Doctor Smeltzer said under his breath, reached for his tablet, and began typing some notes.

"But, as you know, my kids are immune as well, so the incident where I was attacked by the one zombie was not what made me immune."

The two men glanced at each other before Doctor Kincaid spoke. "Yeah, I'm afraid you may have been misled a bit."

I looked at them in puzzlement. "How so?" I asked.

"Your children have the same antibodies, this is true, but we don't believe they're immune."

"Just as you aren't totally immune," Doctor Smeltzer added.

Now, even Grant stopped reading whatever was so fascinating and looked up.

"Alright, you two have definitely confused me," I admitted.

"Let me explain," Doctor Smeltzer said. "Think of other, similar virus infections, like the mumps or chicken pox. Once you've had either one, the risk of getting the disease again is extremely low."

"But, it can happen," Doctor Kincaid said. "Now, in regards to your children, think of it like this. Let's say you caught the chicken pox when you were a kid."

"Yep, I did."

"Okay, now you have an antibody in your system. If we were to test your children for that particular antibody, we'd probably find residuals of it, but that doesn't mean they are immune to chicken pox."

"While it has not happened with any of the children here in Mount Weather, it's entirely possible children born out there," Doctor Smeltzer made a waving gesture, "are developing antibodies as a result of prenatal exposure by their mothers."

I slowly digested what they said. "Let me ask you guys something. This virus, how far has it gone as far as infecting other species?" I asked.

"Hmm, how best to answer," Doctor Smeltzer said with a small frown. "How'd you do in high school biology?"

"I aced it," I answered. "Obviously, I don't have the level of formal education the two of you have, but I catch on pretty quick."

Doctor Smeltzer nodded. "Very well, as I'm sure you remember, life forms are identified through scientific classification. Humans are part of the Animalia kingdom, and fall into the primate order. The virus has not spread beyond primates, as far as we know."

"If you don't mind me speculating with my limited education, but it seems to me that that would be an indicator the virus could possibly be genetically engineered, no?"

The two doctors exchanged a glance before Doctor Smeltzer answered. "There is that possibility," he said, and after a moment, spoke again. "But, there are other viruses that have not crossed over into other species. Mumps is a good example."

"West Nile virus did though, correct?" I asked. Both doctors nodded.

"Getting back to the zombie virus, there is possible evidence of a synthetic genesis," Doctor Kincaid said. "But, once it enters a human, it quickly mutates and takes on similar characteristics of other viruses."

They exchanged another glance and he continued. "At one time, this was considered top secret information, but I suppose it doesn't matter these days. Anyway, there was a lot of debate on the topic, but *we*," he said it while waving his finger between the two of them, "believe it's manmade."

"I guess that begs the question, who made it?" I asked.

The two doctors shrugged in unison. "The virus first presented in Egypt and spread quicker than anything we'd ever seen," Kincaid said. "One could induce either the Egyptians accidentally exposed their own people or it was an enemy of Egypt. Perhaps the Jews."

Doctor Smeltzer scoffed. "It wasn't the Jews."

Doctor Kincaid made a face. "They have the wall, they can seal off their entire country, and as far as we know, they're still intact."

It sounded like they'd had this argument before, so I redirected. "So, it hasn't crossed over into other orders or higher?"

"We've found no evidence of any species crossover. However, I must make a caveat to that answer; we've lost contact with other research facilities long ago and have no idea what they may have discovered."

I nodded thoughtfully as I digested what they said. "Okay, I have some information for you two that might change your premise."

The two docs eyed me. "Yes?" Doctor Smeltzer asked.

"Back in Nolensville, we had a kid who was eaten by a snake, a Burmese Python to be specific. When we found the snake, it was acting funny, and the kid had either become infected prior to being eaten, or the snake infected him."

"How do you know the child was infected?" Doctor Kincaid asked.

"After we killed the snake, we cut it open. The kid was infected. We had to kill him too. Now, I can't tell you if the snake was infected, all I can say is it was acting funny. Was the kid infected when the snake ate him and that's why it was acting funny, or was the snake infected when he ate the kid and it caused the kid to become infected? I don't have an answer for you."

"Fascinating," Doctor Smeltzer said and quickly notated it on his tablet. "Tell me, have you done anything like that with any other animals?"

"Not so much with animals, but I've cut open several zombies."

Now the two of them looked at me as if I'd just told them I'd discovered a permanent cure to erectile dysfunction.

"You've been cutting them open?" Kincaid asked.

"Yeah."

"How many?"

"Twenty-two," I replied. "At first, I was fascinated by them. Then, I mostly stopped, but sometimes I'd see one of them that looked a little different and would decide to have a look inside."

"Did you find anything?"

"Most of the time, they all looked the same, but there were some of them that had unique characteristics. The ones I cut open recently, they're digesting what they're eating. I'm sure you two have studied people when they first became infected, they'd eat and eat and eat, but their stomachs weren't working, they'd just walk around all bloated and everything. A lot of them seemed to have eventually died off, but the ones who lived changed somehow."

"Yes, we believe it is the phenotypes at work," Doctor Kincaid said. "Different phenotypes, different reactions to the infection."

"What did you find when you cut those particular zombies open?" Doctor Smeltzer asked.

"The only thing that stood out was their intestinal tract. The organs are not a healthy pink, they're a blackish color, and the bile is a black syrupy goo, and let me tell you, it smells awful." I paused a moment and then snapped my fingers.

"You know, I'd totally forgotten about it, but a while back, I found a journal kept by a jailer who did experiments on live zombies."

They stared at me in rapt attention now. "Yeah, he and a co-worker did all kinds of things."

"Like what?" Kincaid asked.

"They put one in boiling water, they froze one, they injected poisons, set one on fire, oh, and they even cut open the brain of one of them."

"You're kidding?" Kincaid said in disbelief.

"Nope. They also conducted testing of their senses with various stimuli. It was an interesting read."

"Do you happen to still have the journal?" he asked.

"No, it was destroyed, but I can rewrite it for you if you'd like."

Grant cleared his throat. "He's never been tested, but young Zach probably has a photographic memory."

I shook my head. "I used to. Back before I took this bullet," I said, pointing at the scar again. "But it's still pretty good. I won't be able to rewrite it word-for-word, but I can come close."

Oh, yeah, they were giving me that look again. Now, in addition to my erectile dysfunction cure, they were looking at me like I'd also told them I could make it grow a few more inches.

"We would be most appreciative if you would, Zach," Smeltzer said, his voice quaking a little.

"Certainly," I answered.

"Paper is at a premium around here," Doctor Kincaid said. "Would you happen to have a computer? A laptop or tablet, perhaps?"

"I do," I said. "And Raymond got me access to the local internet."

"Excellent," Doctor Kincaid said and sat down in front of his own laptop.

"By the way, what kind of server do you guys have?"

"We have a Cray computer," he said, like it was nothing special.

"A Cray?" I asked. "A Cray supercomputer?"

Kincaid grinned. "Yes indeed."

"Holy shit," I said, wondering how much access to all of the files I would have.

I watched as Doctor Kincaid finished typing and looked up at me. "Alright, I created a file folder for you in the medical section of the cloud. If you don't mind, when you write up the journal, store it there so we can review it."

"Will do."

"If we can get power back online at Fort Detrick, one of our goals is to upload all of the files at Detrick onto the Mount Weather cloud. It should help in our research," Smeltzer said.

"This is awesome," I said. "I hope I'll at least have read-only access."

"Indeed you do," Kincaid said.

"So, since I can't go with y'all, what's the procedure going to be?"

"A lot has already been accomplished at the CDC," Kincaid said. "Major Parsons has a lot of data on file. We've been spending hours going over it and comparing it to our data."

"Fort Detrick has state-of-the-art equipment, including electron microscopes. The first thing we'll do is use one of them to observe your blood with the virus."

"And then we'll introduce the virus and observe it," Doctor Smeltzer said. "It's going to be fascinating to watch your leukocytes in action."

They continued talking about the process of creating a vaccine, but even I had a hard time keeping up. I smiled at myself, remembering how smart I used to think I was.

"This is going to be the most intriguing work I've ever done," Doctor Smeltzer said and then gave me a questioning look. "You still have your spleen, correct?"

"Yep," I answered.

"Excellent. The spleen makes lymphocytes…"

"Lymphocytes identify foreign substances such as a virus and then creates antibodies to fight them," I finished. The two doctors looked at me in surprise.

"Yes, exactly," Smeltzer said. "You seem to know your white blood cells."

"Grant tutored me a little bit on the subject," I said.

"The ultimate goal, of course, is to be able to create a vaccine," Smeltzer said.

"And possibly even an antidote to administer to someone who has become infected," Kincaid added.

"Were you guys able to achieve any results when you were at Detrick?" I asked.

Doctor Smeltzer shook his head. "Sadly, we were only beginning to make headway when disaster struck."

"You're looking at two of the only three known survivors," Doctor Kincaid said.

"What happened?"

"They are excellent facilities," Smeltzer said. "We even had a level four containment lab."

"I'm guessing that's a good thing," I said.

"It's the highest level containment protocol there is," Kincaid said. "Very complex."

"And expensive," Smeltzer added with a dry chuckle. "But well worth it." He sighed then. I looked questioningly at the two men.

"I should preface my next statement with this," Smeltzer said. "The scientific personnel assembled at Fort Detrick were some of the smartest in the world."

"And yet," Kincaid rejoined, "an act of incredible stupidity was shared by most, if not all of us."

"How so?" I asked.

"A refrigeration unit that was used to store pathogens, including the zombie virus, went on the fritz, so a brilliant decision was made to put all of the samples into picnic coolers until the unit could be fixed or replaced. The coolers were then stacked in a hallway."

"An unsecured hallway," Kincaid added. "An unsecured hallway which had a lot of foot traffic."

"So, what happened?" I asked.

"Oh, the specifics of what happened has been lost to the memories of those no longer with us, I'm afraid," Kincaid said. "It could have been a defective cooler, or perhaps an unintentional bump by a person who was in a hurry. It may have even been an intentional act of sabotage. Suffice it to say, the containment was compromised."

"The entire facility was infected within a few hours," Smeltzer said sadly.

"Except for the three of you," I remarked. The two men nodded. "How'd that happen?"

"Remember me mentioning the level four containment lab?" Smeltzer asked but did not wait for a response. "The three of us were in the lab, suited up, oblivious to the disaster unraveling around us." He smiled. "We would wear diapers when we were suited up so we could stay in the lab longer without having to take restroom breaks."

"So, there we are, engrossed in our work, and the alarm sounded," Kincaid said. "There are, were, almost eight hundred people on the grounds at that time, over a hundred in the secure part of the facility. We don't know how, but when we emerged from the level four lab, everyone was either infected or getting attacked by the infected."

"Our containment suits actually saved us," Smeltzer said. His expression reflected the memory. "The suits are hooked up to an air hose while in the lab, but there is also the option of attaching an oxygen tank."

"It's only for emergency purposes," Kincaid said. "In case the air filtration system goes on the blink. If that happens, you simply help each other hook up an oxygen tank, secure anything you've been working on, and exit the lab. There is a decontamination procedure and then you could go back to the outside."

"You two knew something was wrong," I guessed.

"Yep. A couple of our co-workers were in the main room. We watched through the glass partition as one of them turned and attacked the other."

"What did you do?" I asked.

"We came up with a plan," Doctor Smeltzer said. "When we exited the lab, Doctor Kincaid and I kept our two infected friends occupied while Doctor Craddock bashed their heads in with his oxygen tank."

I tried to imagine the scenario, two nerds trying to ward off an attack while a third nerd swung an oxygen tank.

"What did you do then?" I asked.

"We secured the door, turned the lights off, and hid. The observation room had respirator masks. We managed to get our protective head gear off and the respirators on without becoming infected, and then spent the next twenty-four hours hiding in there."

"Cowering in fear, to be specific," Kincaid said, "and crapping in our diapers."

"And yet, somehow, the three of you made it out alive," I remarked, wondering exactly how they did make it out if everyone else was infected

"Doctor Craddock and General Fosswell were good friends," Kincaid said. "They went to the same church and Mayo was even the godfather to Captain Fosswell. He got on his cell phone and called. The general mounted a rescue operation. He sent some soldiers in those armored vehicles and brought us here."

"For some reason, Mayo insisted on going with the first task force last week," Kincaid said. "They were only supposed to secure the facility, and then a second group of Marines was going to ferry us up there so we could restart our work."

"We wanted everything ready for your arrival," Smeltzer said.

I made a mental calculation and realized they'd been preparing for my arrival before I'd even made a decision. It was either optimistic of them to think I'd say yes, or they had a contingency plan in case I said no. I hoped the former was the correct answer.

"We're going to exercise a much higher level of caution this time," Kincaid said.

"How so?" I asked.

"For one, everyone will be fully suited up in protective gear and will stay that way until testing has been done to determine if Detrick is a hot zone."

"I didn't think it's airborne," I said.

"We don't believe it is either, but we're not taking any chances." He shook his head ruefully. "One would think that after three years any residual contamination would be long gone, but with the mysterious disappearance of the prior task force…"

He didn't finish, and for once, his counterpart had nothing to add.

The next morning, we watched them leave. Several of us had gathered and waved at them, wishing them luck. Especially me.

"When are they coming back?" Kelly asked me.

"Two to five days," I answered. "That's for Sarah and her crew. Justin and his unit are going to stay until those two scientists are able to formulate a vaccine."

Josue was standing beside me and I heard him emit a sigh. "There goes all of our músculo," he said, and then interpreted. "Muscle. All our muscle, there they go."

He was right. Sarah and Rachel had two civilian personnel in their Humvee, but Justin had all of the Marines with him. I hoped there was not going to be any trouble while they were gone. I had no idea about how these civilians would react if we were attacked.

"No training," he muttered. I looked at him.

"Say again?" I asked.

"No training," he said in a louder voice.

I nodded in understanding. Although we'd only been here three days, the duty assignments for the rest of the week were posted online for everyone to see. There was not a single kind of training session on the itinerary.

"Yeah, you're right. Seems odd. I'll ask Seth about it."

"Maybe everybody is already trained up," Jorge suggested.

It was possible, I thought, but judging by my first impressions of these people after the type of questions asked during my debriefing, I wasn't sure they were up to snuff. I saw Josue looking at me. He must have been reading my thoughts because he slowly shook his head.

CHAPTER 13 – OAK RIDGE

Melvin stopped on Scarboro Road near a water reservoir. He put the truck in park, turned it off, and listened as he looked around.

"What are we stopping for?" Savannah asked.

He held up a finger and pointed at Peggy. After a couple of minutes, he got out and motioned for Savannah to do the same.

"Okay, I don't believe there're any zombies around at the moment. Come with me," he ordered.

Without waiting for her to follow, Melvin grabbed a tattered-looking rucksack and a similar-looking rifle case and jogged to some trees near the water tank. Looking around, he found a spot, set the gear down, and covered it with branches and leaves.

"Take a good look around so you can find this place in the dark, if you have to," he told her.

Savannah did as he directed before focusing back on Melvin.

"Got it?" he asked.

She nodded her head. "Could you explain what we're doing?"

"Yeah, come on." He motioned toward the truck and explained while he drove.

"Alright, so here's what we know. This place we're going to is occupied. What we don't know is if they're good guys or bad guys. So, always have a contingency plan," he said.

"It might go bad when we get there and we might have to make a run for it. If that happens, make your way back to that water tower and to that rucksack. It has food and water in it, and there's a shotgun with ammo in that rifle case." The rucksack weighed somewhere around sixty pounds. An easily manageable weight for him, definitely too much for her. She'd figure it out, if it came down to that.

"Where do I go?" Savannah asked.

Melvin thought about it. "Make your way back to that auto detail shop. If I don't show up in three days, you bug out."

"Bug out where?" she lamented. "I don't have anywhere else to go, I'll die."

"Don't say that. You'll be okay," Melvin assured her. "If I'm not around and you have to bug out, try to make your way to Mount Weather. If not, you find your own way. You're not helpless; you're a survivor. No more of this self-pity nonsense. I don't know of anyone who could've gone through what you did and survived. You're tougher than you think. Okay?"

He glanced over at her as he drove. Her lower lip was quivering, but she didn't argue.

As he approached the Bear Creek Road intersection, he caught sight of a slight difference in the vegetation in the wood line. He drove slow and avoided staring straight at it as he turned onto Bear Creek Road.

"Alright, they know we're here," Melvin said.

"How can you tell?" Savannah asked.

"We just drove past an OP, an observation post. I'll show it to you when we leave." He handed her a cell phone. "Here."

She looked at him funny. "What am I going to do with this?"

"Take pictures," he said. "But don't let anyone see you doing it."

They rode for no more than a quarter of a mile before they came upon a manned roadblock. It was a preexisting roadblock, built back before, but it'd been heavily modified. There were sandbags, a machinegun port, and the shoulders of the roadway were blocked with old tires that'd been repurposed into defensive barriers. They were stacked about five feet high. He couldn't see how, but it looked like the tires were fastened together somehow and then filled with earth. Another thing Melvin noticed: everything was neat and orderly. There wasn't even any scrap of plastic stuck in the barbed wire.

He looked toward the main compound and noticed several of the buildings surrounded by similar barriers. Melvin stopped several feet away and waved. There were two men standing behind the barricade, both wearing combat utilities and both were armed. Neither waved, but one of them gave a slow nod of the head. Melvin took it as an encouraging sign.

"Alright, you wait here. If they do something like shoot me, get in the driver's seat and haul ass out of here." He pulled his Glock out of the holster and handed it to her. "Only use this if your life is in danger. If you have to dump the truck, remember that water reservoir and make your way to it. Got it?" he asked. Savannah nodded nervously. He lowered his voice.

"I suspect they're friendly enough, I usually get a vibe when they aren't. Even so, keep your eyes open and don't let them see you taking pictures. Be sneaky, okay?"

Savannah nodded again, all the while wondering if Melvin was about to get the two of them in deep doo-doo. Melvin gave her a reassuring wink and began walking toward the barricade.

"Good morning. Who has coffee?" Melvin asked loudly as he walked up. The two men stared hard at Melvin and then looked at each other. Melvin stopped a few feet from the barricade and kept his hands visible. He noticed both men make direct eye contact with his empty holster.

"I left my gun back in the truck, so no need getting nervous."

Melvin waited for a reply, but they remained silent. He kept talking.

"You guys sure are a sight for sore eyes; we haven't seen any other humans in a few days now. How're you men doing?"

"We're alright," one of them finally answered. "Who're you?"

"The name's Melvin, Melvin Clark." He hooked a thumb back behind him. "That's Savannah sitting there. She's got scabies and a mild case of explosive diarrhea, so I made her stay in the truck."

They continued staring hard at Melvin, and after a couple of seconds, one of them pointed at Peggy. "What the hell's that?"

"That's my lovely wife," Melvin replied. "She doesn't care much for coffee, but I sure do."

They looked at each other again briefly in a mixture of confusion and bewilderment. It was exactly what Melvin hoped for.

"What brings you to Oak Ridge, Melvin?" one of them asked.

"I'm glad you asked. I've been sent here by POTUS. That would be the President of the United States."

The two men continued staring oddly at Melvin, pausing only long enough to exchange another glance.

"Right, buddy," one of them drawled out sarcastically. "And I'm Batman."

Melvin laughed. "Good one. You don't suppose I could speak with your CO, could I?"

The one who proclaimed himself Batman grimaced. "I'm not so sure the boss man would find the humor in some crazy dude coming up here claiming the president sent him."

"Well, sir, you're certainly entitled to your opinion, but I can assure you POTUS is alive and well." Melvin paused, pulled a small notepad out of his breast pocket, and thumbed through it until he found the page he was looking for.

"Thirty-six hours ago at approximately twenty-two hundred hours UTC, give or take a few seconds, there was an event in which several lights were activated on the premises of the Y-12 facility," Melvin paused and pointed. "I believe that'd be that mess of buildings right over there. Anyway, where was I? Oh, yeah. The premises were lit for thirteen minutes and eleven seconds before all lighting was turned off. This incident was recorded by Mount Weather personnel via a satellite and then shown to POTUS the next day shortly after his morning crap."

Melvin finished, put his notepad away, and looked at the two men expectantly. "What happened? Someone's kid go wandering off or something?"

They glanced at each other in concern, making Melvin wonder if he'd guessed correctly.

"I'll get on the radio," one of the men said.

"Thanks, Batman," Melvin replied. "Now, how about that coffee?"

Melvin waited and listened as Batman explained, more than once, about Melvin. For some reason, the person at the other end of the radio was having a difficult time understanding. Finally, he got his point across, and the other voice advised they'd send someone out. While they waited, Melvin took the opportunity to get to know the two men.

"You two have a military bearing about you," he suggested.

"Close," Sergeant Bastone said. "Police."

Melvin nodded. "Cops had it rough when it went bad. They were expected to protect the civilians from all of them zombies."

"Yep, and it got a lot of good people killed," Sergeant Bastone said. He gestured toward the truck. "Have you two been wandering around out here by yourselves?"

"More or less," Melvin said. The other one grunted.

"That's a good way to get yourselves killed these days."

"Yes, sir," Melvin replied. "But we're careful. I ran into a few zeds yesterday, up on the turnpike, but I took care of them."

"How many?" Sergeant Bastone asked.

Melvin shrugged. "Ten, or so."

Bastone swore. "We make frequent sweeps, and every time we think we've killed all of them, more show up."

"Like cockroaches," the other one remarked. "By the way, we don't have any coffee. Ran out about a year ago."

"That's too bad," Melvin said.

Directly, a contingent of people exited a building and rode up in ATVs. There were six of them. They killed the engines and eyed Melvin before getting off and walking up.

"Sergeant Bastone advised you're an envoy sent by the president," one of them said. He was a lean, older man, silver gray hair, dressed in jeans, a blue golf shirt, and a khaki vest. Melvin noticed he wasn't armed, which either meant the others were bodyguards or he had a hideout weapon. He also noticed the man was clean-shaven and his clothes were clean.

"Sergeant Melvin Clark at your service," Melvin replied. "And, Sergeant Bastone is correct."

"My name's Kries. Around here they call me Doc. And what message are you to deliver on behalf of the president?" he asked.

"I'm glad you asked. We are making a concerted effort to reestablish communication with the organized survivors in an effort to rebuild America. I've been sent to give you people a formal invitation to join in."

The man looked at Melvin for a long moment with the disguised expression of a professional poker player. He then turned and motioned toward one of the men in the entourage. He was a younger version of Doc, fit, serious-looking, and armed with a Heckler and Koch MP5.

"Walk with me," he directed to Melvin and the young man.

"This is my son," he explained as they walked down the roadway away from the rest of the crowd. The young man followed behind. "If he sees something suspicious, he'll kill you."

"Fair enough," Melvin said.

After a moment, he made a slow, sweeping gesture with his hand.

"We've worked hard to make this place what it is today. We are totally self-sufficient and frankly, we don't need POTUS, or anyone else. What do you think about that?"

"I can certainly understand. But, there is an issue that should be addressed."

"And what is that?" Kries asked.

"You have the Titan computer and nuclear material," Melvin said. The man didn't answer. Melvin continued.

"It'll only be a matter of time before a hostile nation with their shit together will attempt an incursion. My guess will be Russia, although China is also a viable threat."

"And how might that concern us?" he asked.

"Y-12 will be a viable target. I think you already know that."

Melvin waited for a response, but the man was quiet. He was staring at something at the far end of the compound, seemingly lost in thought.

"How many survivors are at Mount Weather?" he finally asked.

"A little over a hundred," Melvin replied. "The VP didn't make it. We have several politicians and their staff, personnel who worked at Weather, and we've picked up a few survivors along the way." Melvin snapped his fingers.

"Dang, I almost forgot. One of those survivors is a young man from the Nashville area. Apparently, he's immune. He agreed to relocate his people to Weather, and the scientists we have are working on creating a vaccine."

"That's certainly encouraging news," Kries said. He absently rubbed his hands together.

"What's in it for us?" he asked.

"For the next year or so, absolutely nothing." Melvin looked at him pointedly. "You seem like an intelligent man. Hell, if you're the leader here, you have to be. You know exactly what the POTUS is trying to achieve." Melvin fixed him with a serious stare. "Let me ask you, how much longer do you expect to live?"

Kries fixed him with a hard stare. "That's a rather odd question," he said.

"It's mostly rhetorical," Melvin replied. "Me, I'm thirty-nine. If I'm lucky, I'll live to see sixty. So, what do I do for the next twenty-one years? Men like you and me have to create a model for the future. For your son, for your son's kids, and for your great grandkids. Wouldn't you agree?"

Doc grunted. "Perhaps."

Melvin gestured toward the buildings. "I haven't even been inside, but I can tell you people have done a lot of work, but what happens in the next ten years? Are you going to continue to be an autonomous society?"

He didn't answer. Melvin was undeterred and continued.

"Up there at Mount Weather, we have some of those what you call smart people. I suspect you have some as well. Now then, our smart people got together one day and did a bunch of calculations with their own super computer. Do you know what they figured out?"

Doc looked at Melvin. "What's that?"

"They figured out unless something drastic changes, the human race is going to die out."

"Do you have any kids, Sergeant?" he finally asked.

Melvin shook his head. "No, I don't. Maybe I'll hook up with someone one day and we'll have a family. Maybe."

"Then why are *you* doing this?" Kries asked.

"Because it's the right thing to do," Melvin said without hesitation. "I'm a soldier, sir. Soldiers have to have a mission in order to feel as though they have a purpose."

The older man grunted. If it was a sign that he agreed, Melvin couldn't say, but at least the man was listening.

"How is it at Mount Weather?" he asked.

"In spite of the politician's best efforts, we're doing okay."

Now, the older man chuckled. "Sergeant, you may not realize it, but you've just identified why we would like to remain autonomous."

"The politicians?" Melvin asked. Doc Kries nodded. "Yeah, they can be a tremendous pain in the ass, but even so, we've made progress. I'm a good example. We've been sending people out to find survivors, interview and assess them, recruit them."

"Have you come upon any undesirables?" Doc asked.

"Yep, a few. I've managed to keep my hair, so far."

Doc Kries paused a long moment. "Have there been any nuclear events?"

"It's my understanding Pakistan and India glow in the dark nowadays."

He nodded in understanding. "Figures. Is POTUS in contact with other countries?"

"Yeah, a few," Melvin replied. "Canada, Germany, Russia, a few others he hasn't bothered telling me about."

Doc Kries continued staring in the distance for a minute more before turning and walking back toward the barricade. When they approached Melvin's truck, he glanced over at Peggy.

"Nice trophy," he remarked.

"She was my wife, back in the day," Melvin replied. Kries stared at him oddly a moment and then glanced in the truck at Savannah. He appraised her for a moment, gave a small nod of his head, and turned back to Melvin.

"You've given me a lot to think about," he finally said.

Melvin pulled out his notepad again and tore off a piece of paper.

"Radio frequencies and call signs," he explained. "If you have anyone who knows Morse code, even better."

"I'll discuss it with my people," he said. "If you're waiting on me to invite you into our compound, it's not going to happen. There are too many risks."

"Understandable."

"You need any food or anything?" he finally asked.

"No coffee around here?" Melvin asked.

Doc smiled and shook his head. "How about a picnic basket of some fresh food for the road?"

"That'd be wonderful," Melvin said. "I'm tired of MREs."

Doc gave a nod. "I'll see to it. If you'll excuse me, I have a pressing matter to attend to."

"Certainly. Is there any message you'd like for me to deliver to POTUS?" Melvin asked.

Doc had started to walk back to his people, but hesitated.

"Tell him I didn't vote for him."

Melvin watched the man walk back to his people before getting in his truck.

"Is that it?" Savannah asked.

"Yeah, they're suspicious of outsiders, so they aren't going to roll out the red carpet for us." He started the truck and turned around. "It's okay though. The next time I roll through here, it'll be a warmer reception. You get any pictures?"

Savannah nodded. "Lots."

"Atta girl. Let's go pick up my cache and go home."

CHAPTER 14 – REMINISCING

The rain had relented for only about six hours before returning. It was okay with Melvin; he liked the rain. He seemed to recall a poem describing a sky dreary and gray, but he couldn't remember the exact words. The only thing he didn't like was if it got any gloomier, he was going to have to use the headlights to see where he was going.

"You put on a show," Savannah said, interrupting his thoughts.

"What?" he asked as he glanced over at her.

"Back at the Oak Ridge place. You put on a show. You come off like your crazy, but then when you have everyone believing it, you hit them with a haymaker. They never see it coming."

"Yeah, I suppose." He slowed to a crawl as he maneuvered several potholes.

"Let me get this straight, you go out on your own and scout places out?" she asked.

Melvin nodded. "Yeah, something like that. There are survivors out there, and we're trying to reach out to the good guys and form networks. Not all are good guys though, but I guess you already know that."

"Aren't you scared being out here, all alone?"

"I've had some scary moments a time or two," he admitted.

"Why are you a scout? Are you like a Navy Seal or something?"

"Nope, not a Seal. I was in Special Forces back in the day though."

Savannah's eyes widened. "Really?"

"Yep."

"Special Forces, that's Army, right?"

"Yep. I was a career soldier, but it didn't end well for me."

"Why not?" she asked.

Melvin grimaced and pointed at Peggy. "Because of that crazy, psycho, bitch."

Savannah arched her eyebrows. "Oh, you've got to tell me the story."

"Oh, not much to tell. She and I got into a fight one night. She had me arrested on a domestic violence charge, which is a big no-no in the military. So, I got kicked out."

Melvin didn't bother with the rest. It didn't seem to matter anymore.

"You don't seem the type," Savannah said.

He glanced at her. "What kind of type?"

"The type of man who would beat a woman."

"It was more of mutual combat, but like the judge said, that's irrelevant. It's not something I'm proud of."

"Why do you still keep her around?"

Melvin found it hard to answer and squirmed a little in his seat. "Well, um, a couple of reasons."

"Like what?" she asked.

"Well, she makes a good zombie alarm," he finally said. "If there are any zombies close, she can somehow sense them and she starts snarling and carrying on."

He thought a moment. "And, she makes a good prop."

Savannah looked at him in puzzlement before understanding crossed her face. "When you put on your routine and people see her, it adds to your bat shit crazy act."

"Yep, exactly," Melvin said with a nod.

"Okay, I have one more question."

"What's that?"

"Are you still fucking her?" she asked with an arched eyebrow and a wry grin.

"No, smartass."

"Okay," she drawled. "I mean, if you are and you're feeling the need, just let me know and I can give you two some privacy."

"I'm not having sex with her," Melvin asserted, a little louder than he intended. "Change the subject."

"Sure, what do you want to talk about?"

Melvin thought about it. "Okay, I've been thinking. When we get back to Mount Weather, people will naturally be curious. They're going to ask you all about yourself. You know, where you're from, what happened to you, things like that. I don't think you should tell them about the Blackjacks."

"You don't think?"

"No," he said, choosing to ignore the sarcasm in her tone and explained his thoughts. "Not anyone. Even in these times, people can be cruel and judgmental."

"You haven't," she countered.

"Yeah, well, I've got my own demons."

Savannah frowned for a moment. "Okay, I can tell them I'm your long lost daughter and call you daddy," she said with a smirk.

Melvin responded with a curt shake of his head. "No."

"Okay, we'll tell everyone I'm your new squeeze," she said lightheartedly, but then she saw the consternation in his face.

"What? Is that not a good idea either? Oh wait, let me guess, you already have a girlfriend." She snapped her fingers. "Oh, I know, you're gay. Is that it?"

Melvin ignored her.

"C'mon, you can tell me. Do you have a boyfriend? I've heard about you soldier boys."

"I'm not gay."

"So, you do have a girlfriend."

Melvin didn't answer. In fact, a couple of months ago, he'd hooked up with a frisky young filly back at Weather. She apparently was not getting enough attention from her older husband and caught Melvin in a weak moment one night when the two of them had guard duty together. He regretted it, but not enough to keep going back for seconds, thirds, and fourths, and maybe a few more.

Finally, guilt had gotten the best of him, and he told her they were through. The conversation quickly disintegrated and he'd walked off while she was still yelling at him. That was the day before he left Weather on his latest mission. He wondered if there was going to be any drama awaiting him when he returned.

"Alright, we'll tell everyone my relatives were killed by marauders and you found me after I had escaped and was hiding. It's the truth."

"Yeah," Melvin found himself saying. "That's what we'll go with. And nothing else. When they press for details, act like it's too terrible to talk about." Which most likely is, he thought.

"Let's just hope your girlfriend is satisfied," she said. "Is she cool with you banging Miss Piggy?"

"I don't have a girlfriend, and I'm not banging Peggy," he finally said. Savannah started to say something, but he shushed her.

"Look, I loved her at one time. She ruined my life, but I loved her."

"Do you still love her?" Savannah asked.

"I don't think so," Melvin reluctantly answered.

"She's dead you know. The old Peggy, she's dead."

"About ninety-nine percent is, yeah, but there's still a little bit of Peggy in there."

Savannah looked at her curiously now. "How is she still alive? I mean, don't they die off after a while?"

"If they don't eat, but I feed her."

Now Savannah's eyes widened. "You do?"

"Yep."

Savannah kept staring. "Does she pee and poop?"

"Yep. She didn't for most of the first year, but one day I was putting on some fresh duct tape and got a whiff."

"What'd you do?"

He pointed toward Peggy. "I cut a hole in the bottom of the chair and cut the seat out of her pants. Every once in a while, I throw a bucket of water on her to clean her off."

Savannah looked at him incredulously now. "That's not only weird, it's like Walmart weird."

Melvin glanced at her. "Walmart weird?"

"Yeah," she said. "You know way back when and you'd go shopping in Walmart and you'd always see one or two people that looked like they came from another planet and people would sneak pictures of them and post them on the internet. That kind of weird."

"Yeah, well, she saved my life when I ran into Lonnie. He had Pig and Snake with him, and one of the girls. I don't know which one."

Savannah stared at him questioningly. Melvin continued.

"I'd come out of a building about the time they turned down the street. Jumping in my truck and trying to out run them would've showed weakness. They had me outgunned, so they probably could've chased me and got close enough to kill me."

"What did you do?" Savannah asked.

"Instead of running, I stood by Peggy and waved cheerfully. They thought I was bona fide loco."

"Wow, who would've thought that?" she asked. Melvin ignored her facetious response and continued.

"So, there I am, with my arm around Peggy, waving to them like I've got a screw loose. They stop and Lonnie gets out. When he walked up to me, I start my spiel."

"And he didn't kill you and take everything you own?" she asked. "That's unreal. The man's a psychopath."

"Yes, he is."

"How long ago was that?" she asked.

"About five months ago. It was down near Richmond, so it was probably a short time before you came into contact with him."

Savannah arched an eye at him. "Okay, so how'd you keep him from killing you?" she asked.

"Lonnie and I struck up a conversation. I told him I was an armorer and told them I travelled around the countryside fixing people's guns for trade. He had a Colt Anaconda with a busted firing pin. I happened to have had a spare and fixed it for him. He showed his appreciation by inviting me to have a go with the girl."

"What'd you do?"

"I declined and asked him if he wanted to have a go with Peggy. The two of us laughed like hell and ended up getting drunk together."

She looked at Melvin coldly. "So, you two are friends."

Melvin shook his head. "He may think so, but we're not. All I was doing was using my wits to keep from getting killed."

Savannah was quiet now. Melvin didn't know if she was finally out of questions or she was digesting the fact that he was seemingly on good terms with the Blackjacks.

"Describe the girl," she asked.

"Hard to tell her age, maybe twenty-five or so. Big fake breasts, like Peggy's."

"It had to be Fanny. He probably had her out giving them BJs while they rode around."

Melvin drove slowly. It wasn't wise to drive fast and hit an exceptionally deep pothole or some other hazard. He slowed down as they approached an RV and looked it over as they drove past. He pulled to the side and stopped.

"What are we doing?" Savannah asked. Melvin got out and looked around. Savannah got out, walked around the truck, and stood beside him. He pointed.

"Look at that," he said.

Savannah looked at the RV. "It's one of those fancy campers, so what?"

"Technically, it's called a recreational vehicle, or RV for short."

"No shit," she said.

He pointed again. "So, Miss Smartass, this is a nice one, a Winnebago. It's like a home on wheels, but with the roads the way they are these days, I imagines it's a little difficult driving it around."

Savannah nodded at his explanation, but couldn't keep the confusion from her face. "So, why did we stop?"

"Alright," Melvin said. "How many cars, trucks, buses, vans, and RVs do you think are out there on the roads?" he asked as he watched a solitary zombie ambling toward them.

"I don't know, thousands?" Savannah replied.

He nodded. The zombie was small framed, probably a woman or a young teenager at one time.

"Yeah, something like that. Most likely tens of thousands. So, look down the road," Melvin said. "A man, or a woman, could spend hours upon hours searching through cars that've already been searched. You know what that means, right?"

"Uh, no," she replied.

"It means, you'll waste precious time and energy searching empty vehicles, and at the end of the day, you won't have much of anything to show for it."

"Okay," Savannah said. She stared at him uncertainly, wondering where he was going with this.

"Hold on a minute," he said, pointed at the zombie, and got his war sword. He started to walk up to it, but Savannah stopped him.

"Can I do it?" she asked.

He looked at her. "Are you serious?"

She nodded. He could see she was nervous, but she obviously wanted to prove herself.

"Okay," he said and handed her the sword. "It's razor sharp, but your strike still has to be true, otherwise you'll either have a glancing blow or you'll miss altogether. Their motor skills are messed up, so when they get close, sidestep and then strike at the head. Got it?"

"Sidestep and strike," she said.

"And put your weight into it," he directed and motioned her toward the zombie. He fell in step behind her, his lock-blade knife in his hand, just in case.

He could see her shaking, but she didn't waver. She walked purposely toward the zombie, the sword cocked back. When she got within five feet, she jumped to her left and swung the sword like a baseball bat with all of her might. The blade made a sick wet noise as it buried itself slightly above the bridge of the nose. It reminded Melvin of the time he watched a Gurkha soldier bury his knife in a cow's neck as part of a ritual sacrifice.

Savannah had a death grip on the sword. The zombie fell to the roadway, pulling Savannah down with it. She cried out as she scrambled back to her feet. Melvin stepped forward.

"Watch," he said, put his boot against the zombie's head, and wrenched the sword free.

"Not bad," he said and wiped the blade against the zombie's clothing, which appeared to be leather chaps over blue jeans and a canvass type of jacket. She even had fingerless leather gloves on. Some biker chick, he guessed.

Melvin pointed at the RV again. "Okay, like I was saying, you have to be able to have an eye for something that's worth stopping and searching. So, tell me, what do you see?"

Savannah focused on the RV, trying to figure out what her crazy savior was trying to show her. She looked it over slowly, wondering what little clue caused Melvin to stop. It was dirty, and the front right tire was missing, propped up on a jack and some big rocks.

"Uh, it doesn't have a tire," she said. "Whoever was driving it knocked the dog shit out of something and got a flat, so they took the tire off and, I don't know, went looking for a replacement?" She phrased it in the form of a question.

"Yep, I'd say you're right. How long ago, do you reckon?" he asked.

Savannah could see a little gleam in his eye, so she knew it was a trick question. She refocused on the RV. It took her almost two minutes, but she finally saw it. She pointed excitedly.

"The fucking front windshield!" she proclaimed loudly.

"Shh," Melvin chastised. "Don't be loud."

Savannah closed her mouth and her lips tightened.

"Okay, don't get all out of sorts. Now, what about the windshield?" Melvin asked.

"It's cleaner where the windshield wipers swiped across the windows."

"And what does that tell you?" Melvin challenged.

"The wipers have been used recently. It's been raining a lot the past couple of days, so it hasn't been here very long."

Melvin nodded and held up his hand. "Fist bump," he said. Savannah made a fist and bumped it with Melvin's. He noticed she was grinning. It was the first time he'd seen that since he'd met her.

"You need to learn these things if you're going to hang out with me," he said.

"I will."

"Alright, let's give it a look-see." He drew his handgun and opened the side door. They were immediately overcome with the stench of putrefaction. Savannah gagged and coughed.

"Gross," she said when she saw the source of the odor. There were two small children in the back, still strapped in their booster seats. Melvin assessed the decomposition and it jived with his estimate the RV had only been there a few days.

"What the fuck happened?" she asked. "Where are the parents?"

"If I had to guess," Melvin replied. "I'd say they went off looking for a tire and got themselves killed somehow."

"That's fucked up," she said.

Melvin nodded in agreement. "It's a messed-up world these days. You can't dwell on it; otherwise, it'll drive you crazy."

"I guess you've seen a lot," Savannah said. He wasn't sure if she was being sarcastic or not.

"You might say that," Melvin answered. "Alright, I'll get the kids out to help with the smell. You do the searching, top to bottom, and don't forget to look for hidden compartments."

Melvin was careful unhooking the safety seats and gently carried them outside. He'd seen a decomposed body bursting open one time when one of the Mount Weather Marines got a little too rough moving it. It was nasty.

He set them off to the side, and while Savannah searched, he looked over the dead female zombie. She had a wallet attached to a chain in the back pocket of her soiled jeans. There was maybe fifty dollars in it, along with some credit cards and a driver's license. All worthless artifacts of a dead civilization. Her other pockets were empty. He knew a biker chick once who kept a knife hidden in her crotch. He wasn't going to bother checking this one.

Savannah's efforts rewarded them with several cans of spam and a fifth of Jack Daniels. She handed the bottle of whiskey to Melvin and inspected the cans.

"They expired over a year ago," she said.

"Are the cans dented or swollen?" he asked. Savannah inspected both and shook her head.

"Canned spam is like fruit cake, it doesn't expire," he said. "Try one out."

Savannah opened one of the cans and dug her finger into the meat. She chewed on it for a few seconds and swallowed.

"It'll probably give me the raging shits," she said as she got some more and handed it to Melvin.

Melvin gave a short guffaw and pointed up at dark clouds. "If that happens, at least we'll have plenty of rain to wash up."

"Do they have hot water at Mount Weather?" she asked.

"Hot water, indoor plumbing, electricity, even hot food."

Savannah looked at him like he was lying. "Bullshit."

He chuckled again as he took another sip of whiskey. "You'll find out when we get there."

Melvin looked over the Winnebago. "Anything else in there?"

"Yeah. There's a big toolbox. It's too heavy for me to lift, and there's four or five bottles of water. Oh, and a couple of used toothbrushes and some dirty clothes. That's it."

Melvin thought about it a moment. He had plenty of tools, but he hauled the toolbox out anyway and put it in the back of the truck. He explained his thoughts to Savannah.

"I've got plenty of tools, and there's more tools than we know what to do with back at Weather, but we're taking these anyway. Do you know why?"

"For trade?" she asked.

"Exactly." He gestured back at the RV. "We'll leave the water and clothes; somebody'll come along who'll need it."

"Okay."

"Alright, let's get moving," he said and the two of them got back in their truck. Melvin continued to lecture as he drove.

"Scavenging is a unique talent these days. Not only do you constantly have to be on the lookout for zombies and bad guys, you have to be able to search places that've already been searched in hopes of finding something the other people missed. And, you always think repurposing. A washing machine, for example. Pretty worthless without water and electricity, right?"

"Yeah," Savannah answered uncertainly.

"You'd think so, but if you know what you're doing, a washing machine motor can be repurposed as a generator."

Melvin paused and nodded smugly at his knowledge. "I think we're going to do a little bit on our way back. It may add a day or two, but we still have plenty of food, water, and fuel left. Besides, this route hasn't been scouted in a while."

"Do I get to help?" Savannah asked.

"Of course. Consider it on the job training."

"Fuck yeah," she exclaimed.

They were silent for several minutes now before Melvin broke the silence.

"Alright, let's talk about another issue."

"What?"

"Your language and manners."

"What about my language and manners?" Savannah asked.

"The people at Weather can be rather persnickety."

"Persnickety? What the fuck does that mean?" she asked.

"It's a word used to describe people who are snotty and place too much emphasis on minor issues, like clean language. Your overuse of the word fuck, for example."

"Well, fuck that," Savannah said.

Melvin sighed. "I just want you to fit in."

"Persnickety?" she asked.

"Yeah."

"Where did you learn a word like that?"

Melvin shrugged. "I don't know, college maybe."

"You went to college?" she asked. Melvin nodded. "Did you graduate?"

"I did. I have a Master's in Military History, not that it matters anymore."

Savannah stared at him thoughtfully. Finally, she gave her own sigh.

"Okay, I'll work on it. What else?"

"Do you know how to shoot?"

"Uncle Ray taught me with a twenty-two rifle a little bit. I got to where I could shoot rabbits if they weren't too far away – and standing still."

"Okay," Melvin said, pointing toward his assault rifle. "That's a military issue M4. It's kind of like a twenty-two on steroids, but I think you can handle it. When we get a chance, I'll give you a quick lesson. We'll do some serious training when we get back to Weather."

"Can we shoot it?" she asked.

"Not now, we don't want to make any noise. We'll shoot it later." He took another swallow of whiskey.

"Do you drink a lot?"

"Probably."

"Lonnie drinks a lot. He's mean when he's drunk."

He gave her a glance. "I'm not Lonnie."

"You're right. I'm sorry."

He glanced at her again, wondering if she was being sincere.

"So, what happens when we get to Mount Weather?" she asked.

"I've been thinking about it, and you've got a few options."

"Is staying with you one of those options?" Savannah asked.

He glanced at her again. She was staring out of the window and the look on her face was of – apprehension. Melvin realized she was afraid he was going to dump her at his first opportunity.

"I think that'd be the best option," he said. "Now, I'm not telling you what to do. You can go off on your own if you want, and I'll help you get set up, but I think you should stick with me, at least for now."

"Okay," she said.

If she was pleased, she didn't show it. But then, she surprised him by reaching over and gently squeezing his arm.

"What's that for?" Melvin asked.

"I don't know."

"Oh."

"I mean, you've been nice to me, Melvin. When I first saw you, I thought, here we go, I'm about to be beaten and raped again. But you…"

She didn't finish. Melvin glanced over and saw she was quietly crying. He reached over, found her hand, and gave it a gentle squeeze.

"What's that for?" she asked.

"I don't know," he mimicked. She gave a short laugh as she cried. Melvin handed her the bottle of Jack Daniels.

Savannah had taken all of three swallows. Ten minutes later, she put the seat back and passed out. He drove slowly through Bristol, wondering if they were going to encounter those people he'd met before, but he only saw zombies. Some got close enough to bump into the truck, most simply stared as they drove by.

The rain held off until they reached the outskirts of a city named Abingdon. Melvin spotted an airport off of I-81 and took an exit. His intention was to park in one of the plane hangars, but there was a Presbyterian church on Route 11 that had a drive-thru carport. It was perfect.

While Savannah slept, he parked under it and searched the church. There was a solitary corpse slumped over in the front row. A revolver was grasped in his decomposed hand, and Melvin saw the white collar affixed to his shirt.

"You gave up, huh, Preacher-Man?" Melvin murmured. He worked the gun out of the pastor's hand and opened the cylinder. It only had two cartridges and one of them had been fired. He wondered if the second bullet was meant for somebody else. He stuffed it in his backpack and carried a folding metal chair outside.

Obtaining water was a never-ending job. Melvin could get by on a gallon a day if he didn't do anything too strenuous, but now he had Savannah to worry about. After taking another long look around at his surroundings, he placed a bucket out in the rain and set up the water filter. He then unfolded the metal chair and sat beside Peggy. Cradling the M4 in his lap, he took a long swallow from the bottle.

"Oh, yeah, good stuff," he said and looked at Peggy. He saw the helmet turn toward him, so he got up and raised her visor.

"That better?" he asked facetiously, sat back down, and looked thoughtfully at the bottle.

"You know, I believe I was drinking the same flavor the night I met you."

He gazed out toward the airport as he drank. The rain was a steady, dreary, a slate-colored curtain. He wondered how the fall crops were doing back at Weather. Too much rain could cause problems.

The bucket filled quickly. He poured the water in the Berkey, set the bucket back out in the rain, and watched the filters start to drip clean water into the bottom container.

Drip, drip, drip.

He watched for a moment more, took a swallow, and then his gaze wandered back to Peggy.

"Reminds me of the time you came down with that nasty yeast infection," he said. There was a muffled snarl from beneath the helmet.

"Yeah, I remember. You blamed that on me. You blamed everything on me," he muttered and took another long drink.

Melvin had been going on a four-year bout of depression. As he drank, he thought about the tumultuous relationship he had with his beloved wife, starting the first time he saw her. It was at a strip club. Peggy was on stage when he and his buddies walked in. She was a twenty-three-year-old version of that petite blonde bombshell, Pamela Anderson. They could've passed for sisters, complete with the tight ass and enormous breasts. When she left the stage, Melvin immediately asked for a lap dance. The both of them were smitten before the song ended. He went home with her that night and the two of them were married a month later.

Melvin had no idea what kind of person Miss Anderson was, but Peggy was an emotional rollercoaster who had a proclivity for drugs. Cocaine mostly, but she wasn't particular.

"Remember the plans we'd made?" he asked her.

Melvin had eighteen years in the Army when he met her, thirteen of them serving on a Special Forces A-team. He only needed two more years to get a full pension. He was going to retire at the ripe age of thirty-eight.

She'd kept working at the club after they'd married. Melvin didn't like it, but the money was good. One night, he was hanging out there and Peggy introduced him to one of the regulars, a five-hundred-pound fat man that had more money than he knew what to do with.

When he found out Melvin was in the Special Forces, he became enamored. He'd buy drinks all night, all the while begging Melvin to tell him war stories. Melvin tolerated him. After all, the alcohol was free. One night, Melvin told him of his retirement plans. The jolly fat man immediately volunteered to bankroll him.

Opening a gun store, that was Melvin's post-retirement dream. During most of his military career, he'd been the team's light weapons specialist and had a thorough understanding of all firearms. Place a weapon in front of him, any weapon, he could completely disassemble it and put it back together while you watched. He loved them. He loved working on them and shooting them. He loved the smell of gunpowder, gun oil, even cordite. It was like aromatherapy. Opening his gun store was all he thought about.

And then, it all changed.

He took a drink and stared at his wife. Yeah, she'd done an excellent job of messing his life up. He scoffed at himself, knowing he was equally to blame.

Their relationship was passionate, fevered, but not without many episodes of intense arguments. One time, a buddy told him she was his kryptonite and he should run far, far away. Melvin didn't listen. The arguments always led to freaky makeup sex, and that made it worth it, he contended.

Unfortunately, they'd gotten into one of those heated arguments one night and it didn't end well. Melvin's emotions were fueled by whiskey, Peggy's by crack, and the neighbors called the cops. She claimed Melvin hit her, which he had, but only after she attacked him and tried to claw his eyes out. Long story short, he went to jail, and later, got kicked out of the Army with a general discharge.

Goodbye pension.

His jolly fat friend lost interest too, moved to Florida, and bought a strip club with the money he was going to finance Melvin's dream with.

Goodbye gun store.

He was lucky enough to know people and got a job at Mount Weather. Not as their armorer though. He was the caretaker for the grounds, a fancy way of saying he was the guy who cut the grass, trimmed the bushes, and picked up trash.

It was dark now. Melvin looked at the bottle. Grudgingly, he put the top back on. He stood, stretched, and looked at his Casio. It was only nineteen hundred hours. He wasn't tired. He grabbed his sword and hopped on his bicycle.

CHAPTER 15 – FORT DETRICK

Justin had his Marine contingent split up into the two armored Strykers. He would have preferred a couple of MRAPs, but Mount Weather did not have any. The Strykers were incredible vehicles, but they were full of computerized equipment. Justin knew from experience, the more complex the piece of equipment, the easier it was for it to break.

But, you went to war with the equipment you have.

He was in the lead vehicle, followed by the second Stryker commanded by Sergeant Crumby. Major Fowkes followed in a Humvee occupied by Sergeant Benoit and the two civilian electricians, Briscoe and Stallings.

They travelled in tandem and would have made good time, but each vehicle was towing an item they were going to need. His Stryker was towing a trailer full of decontamination equipment. The second Stryker had a four-hundred-gallon water tank, and Sarah's Humvee was towing a tanker of diesel earmarked for one of the lab's generators.

Eventually, they exited the freeway and soon came to Porter Street where they had to stop suddenly.

"Well, this wasn't on the satellite feeds," Justin muttered. Standing in the road and in the surrounding parking lots were zombies. A lot of them. Justin estimated at least four hundred.

"Alright," he said. "Here we go."

The Marines crowded into the open hatches and began firing. As planned, Justin had the Strykers drive in circles, the Marines shooting at everything that moved while the drivers ran over zombies who were too stupid to get out of the way. With eight large heavy-duty tires, there was little risk of damage to the vehicles.

Rachel had stopped the Humvee, and while Briscoe and Stallings watched from the backseat, she and Sarah casually picked off targets of opportunity with their M4 assault rifles.

It took slightly over an hour to kill them all. Some of them seemed to sense they were in a losing battle and loped off, avoiding being shot by zigzagging between abandoned cars. Justin ordered a cease-fire and reached for the microphone.

"Sergeant, is the drone ready?"

"Aye, sir," Sergeant Crumby responded. Seconds later, Privates Kirby and Jenkins exited the rear Stryker. It took them a minute to assemble the drone and then launched it.

The cameras on the drone were patched in to the monitors on the Strykers and were also linked up to Mount Weather. They navigated the drone with the ease of experts. It circled the perimeter of Fort Detrick and then was navigated until it hovered over the USAMRIID labs.

There were a scant number of zombies wandering around. When the drone would fly over them, they stopped whatever they were doing and stared stupidly at the drone.

"Alright, I'm not seeing any major obstacles," Justin said. "Would you agree, Major?"

"I counted seventeen zeds," Sarah replied. "Nothing we can't handle."

"Recall the drone," Justin ordered.

They repacked the drone and loaded it up, assuring Justin and Sarah they could unpack it and reassemble it in under five minutes once they got to the labs. The next order he gave got him more than a few sour looks.

"Alright everyone, we've already discussed it. Get suited up. MOPP level four."

Once everyone was fully suited up and had their respirators on, the three vehicles got in line and headed toward the first security gate into Fort Detrick. It was open, but manned by four zeds in uniform. Justin made quick work of them as their convoy drove past.

"About what I expected," Sergeant Crumby commented over the radio.

"Everyone double-check your weapons," Justin directed. "I have no doubt there's more."

The USAMRIID building was a one-story structure with a basement. Justin tried his best to memorize the floor plans before leaving, but had the blueprints downloaded in their onboard computer as well. Even so, it was bigger than he thought it'd be. North of it was a newer building with additional labs. It housed the National Biodefense Analysis and Countermeasures Center. That was their contingency if the first building was somehow destroyed or untenable.

Justin radioed for them to stop on Porter Street. He stood up in the open hatch and looked over the two abandoned Strykers parked in front of the main entrance. They were both surrounded by multiple zombie corpses, but there were no soldiers, or any other live humans.

The bulky protective clothing, cumbersome rubber gloves, and the gas mask made them all feel overly clumsy. Breathing through the filters also stifled his sense of hearing. He gave the signal to kill the engines, took a deep breath, and held it as long as he could. All was quiet.

He reached down, grabbed the radio's microphone, and held it up to the voicemitter outlet valve on his mask.

"Each of you perform one more equipment check, please, and check your buddies," he ordered. He wasn't taking any chances. He watched as each Marine performed a breath check on their respirators and then giving the okay sign. Sergeant Crumby gave a click with his mike to indicate the Marines in the second Stryker were ready.

"Dismount," he ordered. By predesign, the drivers would remain buttoned-up inside the Strykers and provide security. Joker and two other Marines dismounted and jogged over to the unoccupied Strykers. The rear hatches stood open silently. Joker led with his M4 and peered inside one of them. After a moment, the abandon Stryker's engine roared to life. Joker opened the command hatch, gave Justin the "all clear" hand signal, followed by, "wait one," and ducked inside the second Stryker. Justin waited. Soon, Joker reemerged and ran over to his lieutenant.

"Both are empty," he said loudly through his respirator. "No blood. Each has about three-quarters of a tank. The engines are good and the onboard equipment looks undamaged. It's like they just shut 'em down and walked away from them."

Justin felt himself frowning under his respirator. The soldiers would not have simply abandoned the Strykers. Would they? If they decided to strike out on their own, no pun intended, they would have taken one or both armored vehicles with them. Why wouldn't they? He stared at them as he thought. They were the ultimate post-apocalyptic, anti-zombie vehicle. There were only a few weapons or weapons platforms capable of taking them out. A tank or a hellfire missile could kill it. Nothing a zombie was capable of handling. Their only drawbacks were the individual cost of them, several million each, and that issue was no longer relevant, and the gas mileage wasn't the best in the world.

It was damned odd.

He turned toward the two doctors who were still sitting inside and pointed at the rear hatch. They exited the armored vehicle, walked several feet away, and began methodically collecting and testing air samples. Justin watched as they performed the tests, even at one point taking what looked like an elongated Q-tips and rubbing them along various surfaces, including the vehicles. After several minutes, Doctor Smeltzer took his respirator off and made a show of inhaling deeply. Doctor Kincaid immediately held a finger up, tacitly telling the others not to be so quick in taking their respective masks off. The two doctors stood close and spoke to each other for several minutes before Doctor Kincaid slowly followed suit.

Justin dismounted from his Stryker, and the other Marines formed a defensive perimeter. He took his respirator off and directed the others to do the same.

"Definitely no airborne contagions," Doctor Smeltzer said. "At least, not anymore. Outside is fine. Inside may be another story. We'll need to do the same testing once we go in. It goes without saying: we should put our masks back on before going in."

Justin nodded and looked over at Sarah, who responded with a small nod of her own.

"Alright, you two," she said, looking over at Briscoe and Stallings. "Let's get on that generator."

There were two of them, both located behind the building. The two men unloaded their toolkits and opened the service door to the first one. They made their assessment in less than five minutes.

"They're still good," Briscoe said. "But, the fuel is bad."

Stallings pointed at the fuel tanker behind the Humvee. "Back it up right about here and drop it. We'll clean out the fuel system, run a line from the tanker directly to the generator, and we'll have power."

"How long?" Sarah asked.

Stallings shrugged. "A couple of hours." He waited expectantly and Sarah nodded. They got to work.

Once they'd unhooked the tanker from the Humvee, Sarah and Rachel stood around, watching the two men. Verbal communication between the two of them was minimal, but it was not necessary; they worked well together. When Sarah and Rachel attempted to help, they shooed them away.

"I'm bored," Rachel said.

"Yeah," Sarah answered. "C'mon."

Rachel followed Sarah back to the front of the building where the Marines were preparing themselves to go into the lab.

"Have you got it covered?" she asked Justin.

"Yes, ma'am. Sergeant Crumby's team is going to provide security, the rest of us are going in." He looked at her a moment. "Do you want to join in, ma'am?"

"Negative. Sergeant Benoit and I are going to reconnoiter the rest of Fort Detrick."

"Aye, ma'am," Justin said.

"Reconnoiter?" Rachel asked when they'd gotten inside the Humvee.

Sarah looked at her and grinned. "Whatever you want to call it, let's go exploring, maybe kill a few zeds."

"Ooh, you're making me wet," Rachel said with a giggle.

The reception area, administrative offices, and conference rooms were all in front, and the labs were through a set of thick security doors and down at the end of a hallway. Justin and the Marines methodically cleared every square inch. The exertion in the hot unventilated building was hard enough, but doing it while in the MOPP suits had them quickly soaked in sweat.

Justin had them divided into two teams. When the lead team reached the doors, the point man stopped and motioned Justin forward. He pointed at what he could see through the wire mesh glass. The hallway on the other side was stacked with corpses.

"All zombies. It looks like they were going in, not coming out." His voice was muffled because of the respirator. He had to nearly shout to be understood.

Justin nodded in agreement and studied them. "Any of them Mount Weather people?"

Crumby shook his head. "I don't see any I recognize."

Justin thought a moment and gave the order to exit the building. The Marines retreated outside and hustled over to the makeshift decontamination shower a couple of the other Marines had set up. They went through it and allowed the water to soak them down before moving over to a designated assembly area, pulling off their respirators, and drinking heavily from their camelbacks. Justin did the same, and then motioned for Sarah to follow him to the command Stryker.

"Mike Whiskey Actual, this is Delta Two Actual. SITREP, over," Justin said into the radio.

When he received a response, he advised them of what they'd found inside and what he intended to do next. After receiving a confirmation, he signed off and gathered his Marines.

"It's damned odd," he remarked to nobody in particular.

"It is," one of them replied. "I've only seen a few zeds; it seems like there should be more."

"Alright, listen up. Our mission hasn't changed, but it has gotten a little more challenging." He paused and took a deep breath, and then wondered if he should take deep breaths while standing so close to the labs.

"We're going to need to haul out all of those corpses, bring them outside, and we should probably burn them." He looked at the docs for confirmation.

"A wise precaution," Doctor Kincaid said.

Justin nodded. "Sergeant Crumby, along with providing security, that'll be your squad's assignment."

"Aye, sir," he replied.

"The rest of you, get your masks back on and let's get to it."

Corporal Conway raised a hand. Justin gestured at him. "Does this mean there's still people alive on the other side of those doors, sir?"

"Unknown," Justin replied.

"The first task force was equipped similar to us, a week's worth of rations and water," Sergeant Crumby said. "There's probably fresh water still available down there."

"We should have come here sooner," the corporal lamented.

"Probably, but we're here now. This is what we've got to do." Justin looked around to make sure everyone was listening. "We've got to clear out that hallway and get in there." He explained his thought process on how to do it, and everyone agreed.

CHAPTER 16 – THE HANGOVER

Melvin didn't know it, but he'd awakened right about the same time the Fort Detrick task force was beginning their mission. Looking around and ensuring they were alone, he stepped out of the truck, relieved himself, and brushed his teeth. He didn't bother waking Savannah and started the truck. She finally opened her eyes a few miles outside of Abingdon when he failed to avoid a large pothole. He hit it so hard, Savannah bounced in her seat, and the jolt caused his head to explode in hangover agony. He imagined he could even hear Peggy growling in protest.

"Where are we?" Savannah asked as she sat up and rubbed her eyes.

Melvin didn't answer. He was parched and tried to drink from his canteen, but another bump sent water sloshing all over his face.

"Shit," he muttered, drove to the side of the interstate and stopped.

"Where are we?" Savannah asked again as Melvin drank.

He responded by waving a finger in the general direction in front of him. What he'd give for a gallon of coffee right now. Savannah got out of the truck and squatted. When she stood, she fixed her pants, and then pointed.

"Hey look, there's some apartments over there. They'd be good to search, wouldn't they?"

Melvin looked to where she was pointing. There was an apartment complex backing up to the interstate. It was moderately sized, maybe a dozen or so three-story buildings.

"Yeah, probably," he said. He got out and geared up with what he called his salvaging kit.

"Stay with the truck," he said.

"But you said I could go with you," Savannah cried.

"I changed my mind. I need you to guard the truck," Melvin said and rubbed the stubble on his face. The morning was overcast and humid, and he felt like shit warmed over. The last thing he wanted was someone pestering him with questions.

"But, you said you were going to show me how to search and scavenge," she rejoined.

"Maybe later. You can talk to Miss Piggy if you get lonely."

Savannah didn't like it, that much was clear, but she did not say anything. Instead, she sulked and watched as Melvin gathered his backpack with his tools and his sword. As an afterthought, he took the key fob. He wasn't sure he fully trusted her yet and didn't want her to drive off with his only source of transportation.

He looked around again before setting out at a slow jog, each step sending miniature electrical charges of pain through his head. He climbed the interstate barrier fence and worked his way to the apartments. A sprinkle of rain started again as he approached the first apartment. He didn't mind. He was already sweating, so getting a little wet didn't bother him. He wished his headache would subside though.

The floor plans seemed to be the same generic layout of all apartments, only the façade was different. They were cheaply made with thin doors, and all of them had been pried or kicked open. In a way, this was good. The odds of zombies still trapped in an apartment were low.

The negative aspect was obvious. All of the good items, like food, firearms, and ammunition were long gone. So, he instead focused on nooks and crannies, searching for anything not taken or destroyed by humans or rodents.

The results were better than he hoped for. One apartment yielded a partial roll of toilet paper found under a couch cushion (better than gold, Melvin would declare). It was smashed, but still useable. In another apartment, he found a half-full pepper shaker, and a couple of apartments yielded small remnants of soap bars, which he dutifully collected and stored in a zip-lock bag. Later, he'd melt them down into one blob. He found one partially used tube of toothpaste, which was a rare find, and one apartment caused him to say a silent thank you to the Lord above. He pulled a bathroom drawer open and noticed a slight bulge under the drawer liner. Lifting it up, he found a cellophane package containing two extra strength aspirin. He read the label to confirm they were indeed aspirin before tearing the cellophane open and swallowing them whole. As an afterthought, he drank some water from his canteen.

The last apartment, in the back on the third floor, had obviously been occupied by a woman. The place was decorated in pastels and even had draperies, which were mildew-stained and had a rank musty smell to them.

He started in the den, which had a collection of philosophy books sitting on a makeshift shelf of planks and milk crates. Melvin took a philosophy course once when he was pursuing his Bachelor's. For his final essay, he wrote what he believed was his best paper ever, comparing and contrasting the top three Greek philosophies, and concluded by declaring philosophy was a bunch of horseshit. The professor was not amused.

Regardless of his opinion, he grabbed a few and set them by the door. The people at Weather were always looking to expand their library.

He then worked his way into the kitchen. All of the drawers had been pulled out and were scattered on the floor. There was a utility closet at the back of the tiny kitchen and the washer-dryer combo was still there. He looked in the washer and was surprised to see clothing, several pairs of white cotton socks to be exact. They were stiff from sitting in there for so long, but still useable. He grabbed them and tossed them next to the books before making his way down the short hallway and into the bathroom.

Surprisingly, there was a toothbrush still in its package lying on the floor. Someone probably found it, but it dropped out of their pack when they were leaving. He thought of Savannah as he grabbed it up.

"Now we don't have to share, you skinny little shit," he muttered.

Working his way into the solitary bedroom, he found nothing in the closet. The bed was still there. It consisted of a solitary mattress. No bed frame. The sheets were missing and the mattress itself had mildew stains, like the drapes. Lifting it up, he discovered two items; a pillowcase and a dildo.

He left the dildo behind.

Exiting the apartment, he turned and was startled by a person standing there. He instantly brought his handgun up and came close to firing before realizing who it was. Savannah was standing there, wearing his poncho, her face almost hidden, looking at him like a lost puppy dog.

"What the hell," he said in exasperation. "I almost shot you."

She stared at him. "I didn't want to be alone."

He sighed and tossed her the pillowcase.

"Alright," he said. "Keep quiet and watch my back."

Savannah nodded. He loaded up the pile of goods into his backpack and went to the next apartment. It was another one-bedroom. Melvin searched it quickly, walked back outside, and pointed at the open door.

"Let's check your skills," he said. "Go find something we can use. Use the pillow case."

Savannah looked at him with a small amount of apprehension, wondering if Melvin was tricking her somehow.

"Do I get a gun?" she asked.

Melvin shook his head.

"Are you going to run off and leave me?"

He shook his head again and impatiently pointed at the door. She hesitated a moment longer and then walked in. Melvin waited outside while she rummaged around and grimaced as something, a kitchen drawer maybe, fell to the floor with a crash. She came out a few minutes later holding an emery board and toenail clippers.

"There wasn't anything else but trash and mice turds," she said.

"You were far too noisy," Melvin admonished. "Learn to be quieter." He looked out the breezeway to see if anyone heard them and were coming to investigate. It looked like they were by themselves. "Alright, let's go."

"You're a grumpy bastard when you're hungover," she muttered.

Melvin gave her a sour look and took off jogging. She followed him as they made their way across the other side of the interstate. The sky had gotten noticeably darker in the last thirty minutes, and now the rain was coming down steadily.

Melvin jogged over to a large pine tree and squatted under it. Savannah followed suit and squatted beside him. The low-hanging limbs provided some cover, yet allowed them to observe their surroundings. He noticed she was breathing heavily and admonished himself to remember she was still weak. It took a few minutes before her breathing slowed. She looked around at the rain.

"It's coming down pretty good," Savannah said.

"I like to scavenge when it rains," he replied as he looked over the area. "Most people seek shelter and it messes with the zombies' vision."

"Are we going to search something?" Savannah asked.

Melvin nodded and pointed at a building to the west of them. "The sign says it's a health clinic. Maybe we can find medical equipment or something." He looked around. "Have you been watching for people or zombies?"

She realized she had not and did a slow three-sixty. "I don't see shit," she said with a smirk.

Melvin gave her a look.

"I do not see any threats," she amended.

"Better. Okay, see that tree over by the corner of the building?" he asked as he pointed. Savannah nodded. "We're going to jog over there and stop a second to see if we've drawn any attention. If we haven't, we're going to circle around the building and check it out." He patted the holster on his left side. "Always stay on my right side, got it?" He motioned drawing the weapon with his left hand for emphasis.

Savannah nodded.

"Okay, and if we were to somehow get separated, come back to this tree first, if you can. If you can't, find someplace to hide. Don't go back to the truck until you're sure nobody is close enough to spot you."

Savannah nodded again. He motioned for her to follow and took off. The rear of the building faced the interstate. They worked their way around to the front and Melvin paused again. He pointed at the parking lot.

"Check out those cars," he whispered. There were only two of them. They were grimy and the tires on all of them were low.

"They've been parked there a while," Savannah whispered back.

"Yeah," he agreed. "That's a good sign."

He motioned for her to follow him to the front door. It was typical of most commercial buildings, a metal doorframe of tempered glass, broken out long ago. Melvin went through his procedure: he tapped on the doorframe, whistled, and then called out.

Nothing.

"Stay behind me," he instructed and walked inside. He rounded the corner into the lobby and his foot inadvertently hit an overturned chair, causing something to fall off of it and clatter to the floor.

"You're far too noisy," Savannah whispered. "You should learn to be quieter."

Melvin glared at her. She responded by pointing at her eyes with two fingers and then pointed toward the interior of the clinic. Melvin could think of no retort, so he gave a silent grunt as he scanned the lobby.

There was a security door separating the front lobby from the examination rooms, nursing station, and the doctor's offices. It was one of those doors with a magnetic lock which was opened either with a key or by the receptionist sitting behind the counter pushing a button. One could easily hop the counter and walk on back, but someone, a previous scavenger perhaps, had decided to take an axe to the door. Now it was a mass of splintered wood.

Before the two of them could climb over the broken door, a zombie wearing soiled scrubs launched herself through from the opposite direction. She tripped and fell, giving Melvin enough time to perform a two-handed downward chop, sinking the edge of the war sword into her head.

Another one, a man this time, was close behind her. Melvin gave him the same treatment. This occurred two more times. After the last one fell, Melvin was sweating even more profusely now. Savannah started to say something, but he held up a finger. He made a similar motion with his fingers to his eyes and then pointed at the entry door.

Savannah understood. She turned back the way they had entered and scanned the parking lot and beyond.

"Nothing," she whispered as she looked back at Melvin. He nodded and held a finger over his lips. He stood still as a statue for a full three minutes. Savannah mimicked him. Finally, he motioned for her.

"Search them," he said. "But don't get any of that goo on you."

Savannah made a face and tentatively patted the pockets of the scrubs. She came up with a pack of cigarettes and a stethoscope.

"Put them in your pillow case," he directed and then motioned for her to follow him through the doorway.

The back area consisted of a nurse's station in the middle of an open area and surrounded by seven individual examination rooms. Every door except one had a number on it. He started with the unlabeled door, which he correctly deduced was the doctor's office. They diligently searched each room for zombies before searching for property.

"Okay," Savannah whispered as they started rummaging through one of the examination rooms. "How are those things still alive?"

"I don't know," Melvin responded. "Maybe the plague isn't in them anymore and they're somehow recovering. Their cognition is better than it used to be."

"Cognition?" she asked.

"They're thinking better than when they first got infected."

"Oh." She looked around. "Are we looking for anything special?"

"Medical stuff takes priority, but anything we can use or trade is good. Like those pack of cigarettes for instance."

"Got it," she said.

"You search low and I'll search high."

"Okay," she whispered and began searching the cabinets under the sink.

The place had been ransacked and was in shambles, which was not unusual. Nevertheless, Melvin was hopeful and they searched meticulously. After a solid hour, they located a couple of items overlooked or ignored by previous scavengers.

"Alright, I think we've found everything we can, let's get out of here," he said. Savannah nodded and started toward the front door, but Melvin grabbed her by the shoulder.

"Never exit a building the way you came in," he admonished and led her to a side door. The stenciled lettering on the gray metal door identified it as an emergency exit. Melvin pushed on the handle, wondering if the alarm was going to activate. Luckily, the batteries in it were dead. He led them on a roundabout jog back to the truck.

"Not a bad haul," he said as he started the truck. "Let's get on back to Weather. If the roads are still clear, I think we can make it in about three or four hours."

"Do they serve hot meals too?" Savannah asked.

"At Weather? Oh, yeah. It's a mixture of fresh food and freeze dried, but if the right cooking crew is on duty, it can be pretty good."

"Sounds wonderful," she said.

They drove in silence for a couple of miles before Savannah spoke.

"Were you bullshitting me when you said you have a Master's degree?"

"Nope."

"I dropped out of high school," she said as she opened a can of spam. "Not that it mattered. That's the year everything went to shit."

"How old are you?" Melvin asked.

"What's the date?"

Melvin checked his watch. "August ninth."

She thought for a moment. "Eighteen. How old are you?"

"Thirty-nine."

"Fuck, you're old," she said with a grin.

Melvin glanced at her. "Remember your savior vivre."

Savannah scrunched up her nose. "What's that? Some sort of weird sex act?"

Melvin sighed. "Never mind."

Savannah shrugged and took a long drink from the canteen. "I need to visit the loo," she said and then looked at him with a smirk. "Is that classier than saying I have to take a shit?"

Melvin gave her a sideways look and started looking for a dry spot. Almost three days of steady rain was starting to show. Several times they drove through standing water. Melvin used derelict automobiles as benchmarks to determine if the murky water was shallow enough to drive through. He finally spotted a fairly dry spot under an overpass, stopped, looked around, but didn't see anything threatening. He reached into the back and retrieved the partial roll of toilet paper he'd found earlier.

"Stay close," he warned as he handed it to her.

"Don't leave me," she rejoined and jumped out of the truck. Melvin decided it'd be a good time for him to go as well, number one not number two, and exited the truck on his side. He'd no sooner unzipped his fly when he heard the sound of water splashing and looked down the interstate. A zombie rounded a curve in a loping run and was heading directly toward them. A car rounded the curve right behind it, maintaining a slow pace with the zombie. It was a compact car, small and quiet. There were two men in it, laughing gleefully. One of them leaned out the window with a large barreled revolver in his hand.

Lonnie.

CHAPTER 17 – GO BOOM

It was stifling hot inside the building, which made it slow going. Most of the bodies were dead, but not all of them. As a precautionary measure, each one received either a bullet or a bayonet to the head, dead or otherwise. The last thing Justin wanted was one of his Marines to get themselves bitten and become infected.

It took them almost six hours of dragging the corpses outside, piling them up, and setting them on fire. Justin mandated several rest breaks so he wouldn't have any cases of hyperthermia.

Occasionally, he'd hear distant gunfire, followed by Rachel gleefully reporting on the radio in a mock baritone voice.

"Delta Two Actual, this is uh, Delta Two-Two. Contact has been made with a zed who appears to have once been an army colonel. Major Fowlkes has just blown the living shit out of said colonel. I repeat, she just blew the living shit out of him. Said colonel appeared to have been perpetuating lewd and lascivious acts with a friendly cow shortly before his demise."

Crumby looked at Justin. "That girl ain't right in the head."

Justin shook his head in exasperation. He motioned over to Kirby, who walked over.

"Sir?"

"You're relieved of zombie duty. Go get yourself decontaminated so you can take that gear off."

"And then what, sir?"

"Call me sexist, but I want you to get that drone operational and keep an eye on our girls."

"Aye, sir," he said before hustling over to the decontamination station.

Justin could imagine Kirby grinning beneath his mask.

After a long rest break, they reentered the hallway and gazed at the locked security doors.

"They haven't been blasted open," Crumby observed. "But, those locks have been damaged. Somebody made it so you can't use a key card to open them. Can't use key cards without power though."

"They did have a key card, but I don't know about the power."

"Maybe they're on the other side and they've locked themselves in," Justin said.

"If that's true, why ain't they answering?" Crumby rebutted. The two men had pounded on the doors repeatedly and shouted out, but they were met with silence.

"Yeah, well where the hell are they?" Corporal Conway asked rhetorically.

"They've got to be on the other side," Justin replied. "The question is, what kind of physical state are they in now?"

"Are we going to breach the doors?" the sergeant asked.

"We don't have any other type of breaching equipment, so I don't see any other way. Do you?"

Sergeant Crumby shook his head. "I've never received training on how to use C-4, have you?"

Justin looked at him with a wry grin. "Classroom training? No. On the job training? Absolutely."

Sergeant Crumby grunted in appreciation. "That's the real way to learn things. Let's get to it then, sir," he said.

When it came to Marines blowing things up, the standard protocol was to figure out how much C-4 was needed, and then multiply it times ten. Or more. Marines loved to blast the ever-loving shit out of anything in their way.

Justin was no different, but this time, he had to be delicate. After all, the lab needed to remain intact, otherwise the mission was a fail and his leadership would come into question once he returned to Mount Weather. He sat outside and configured two small, shaped charges wrapped with detonation cord, or detcord for short. Joker watched in fascination.

"That's all the C-4 you're going to use, sir?" he asked.

"We won't need much. All we want to do is blast the locks, nothing else."

"It'll still go boom, right?" Now, there was a hopeful, shit-eating grin on his face.

"Absolutely," Justin replied.

"Can I help you with it?"

Justin looked at him. It was often difficult to determine when Joker was being serious or clowning around.

"Sure," he said.

Joker's shit-eating grin got bigger. "I like it when things go boom."

They donned their NBC gear and went back in. Justin carried a roll of duct tape with him in case he needed to improvise and tape the C-4 into place, which, in fact, he ended up having to do.

After double-checking his work four times, he and Joker walked the wire outside and took cover behind one of the Strykers. Sarah and Rachel had returned and he waved them back.

"Give me a head count," he ordered Joker as he did the same.

"Eighteen," Joker said. Justin came up with the same number.

"Alright, everyone is present and accounted for," he said, and looked around.

"Take cover! Fire in the hole!" he yelled as loud as he could and then activated the detonator. A long two seconds passed before there was a concussive thump, followed by steel gray smoke billowing out.

"Awesome," Joker said.

They waited for the smoke to clear, and more importantly, to see if any infected zeds would come wandering out.

While they watched the smoke coming out in slow wisps, Briscoe and Stalling walked over.

"It took longer than we thought, but the generator is now fixed. It's ready to fire up whenever you give the word," Briscoe said. "We can't guarantee what the status is inside though. For all we know, every circuit is blown."

"Alright," Justin said. "Let's give it a few minutes."

They waited several minutes. The smoke had dissipated to nothing, and more importantly, no zeds emerged.

"Major, will you and Sergeant Benoit help Kirby provide rear security?" Justin asked.

"Certainly," Sarah said.

He nodded and looked over at Briscoe. "Alright, fire it up."

When the big generator came to life, he walked back to the main entrance. Looking back at his Marines, he shouted.

"Alright, men, stack formation, behind me."

He also used the relevant hand signal so there would be no confusion. All of them reacted instantly and lined up behind Justin.

A few lights flickered on as he led them into the building and down the hallway to the blown door.

CHAPTER 18 – THE LAB

"Oh my God."

Justin didn't know who said it, the respirators muffled and distorted everyone's voice, but it didn't matter. He was thinking the same thing. Each lab was visible from the hallway through bulletproof glass. The first lab was unoccupied. Not so with the second lab.

Sergeant Crumby pointed. "There's Sergeant Rivera."

He was a fresh one, Justin thought. His decomposing face was torn and oozing pus out of the open wounds. All of them were wearing Marine combat utilities, and all of them were now zombies.

"That's a shitty way to die, man," Joker muttered.

Justin made a count. "Looks like we have one who's unaccounted for," he said.

Sergeant Crumby did his own count and nodded in confirmation. "That scientist is missing, can't remember his name."

"Doctor Craddock," Private Burns said. "Mayo Craddock."

"Yeah, that's him," Sergeant Crumby said.

"They ain't wearing their masks," Joker observed. Justin agreed and wondered what would have made them remove their respirators in what was obviously a hot zone.

"Sir?"

Justin looked around to see who was speaking. "Yeah, Joker?"

"We ain't going to leave them like that, are we?" he asked. "They're Marines; we've got to take care of them."

"Roger that," Justin replied.

"Um, Lieutenant?"

Justin looked around. It was Doctor Kincaid. The two scientists were told to wait down at the end of the hall until the Marines had cleared the labs, but they were impatient and followed behind them.

"What is it, Doctor?"

"We can't go in there. It's a hot zone. I think it should be obvious."

"Not a problem," Joker said. "We open the door a crack and put a bullet in their heads. It's the right thing to do."

"Opening the doors, even slightly, will be releasing a toxin," Doctor Kincaid rejoined. "It may be several days before we can decontaminate."

Justin's sigh was magnified through the respirator.

"Point taken," he said. "Is there any way they can get out of that lab on their own?"

"Not without one of these keycards," he said, holding one up. "If the power goes out, the locks on the doors stay locked."

He pointed at the glass. "It's bulletproof. They won't be able to break it out."

"Roger that. Alright, will lab one work for you two?"

The two scientists looked at each other. Smeltzer shrugged.

"I'm sure it will," Kincaid said with his own shrug.

They spent the first hour testing for contamination and then the rest of the day making the lab sterile. On the morning of the second day, they started the long, meticulous process of creating a vaccine. At the end of the day, the two doctors went outside. The afternoon sun hurt their eyes. Justin waited until they went through the decontamination process before speaking.

"How's it going, guys?" he asked.

"We'll know in six weeks," Kincaid replied. "That's how long it'll take to ferment the correct proteins."

Joker overheard the conversation. "Six weeks? We're going to be stuck here for six weeks?"

Doctor Kincaid nodded patiently. Before Joker had a chance to ask why, he explained.

"There are three different methods to create a vaccine for a virus, are you aware of that?"

"Uh, I know the flu vaccine is made with chicken eggs, or something like that," Joker replied.

"Yes, that's the most common and oldest method. The virus is injected into fertilized chicken eggs and then is incubated. The virus-containing fluid is harvested, the virus itself is then killed, and it is used to create a vaccine.

"The second method is a cell-based production. I won't bother explaining it. We're going to attempt to create a vaccine using what is known as a recombinant method. It was first used in 2013 with partial success. The vaccine is produced using insect cells."

"No shit?" Private Burns asked.

"That's correct," Kincaid said. "Now, the CDC scientists made an amazing breakthrough substituting insect cells with Zach's blood cells. Our goal is to reproduce their work."

"Six fucking weeks," Burns lamented.

Justin was inclined to sigh and utter a few invectives, but then reminded himself he was the leader of these Marines and had to set a good example.

"Alright, you heard the man, we're going to be here a while. That means we've got a lot of work ahead of us. Now, the first thing we need to do is build some defensive positions."

"Wonderful," Joker said.

CHAPTER 19 – LONNIE

"Savannah, you need to hide," Melvin said urgently as he thumbed open the restraining strap on his holster. His other weapons were inside the truck, so his only option at the moment was his Glock.

Melvin watched as the zombie came closer. It was a man, probably in his twenties once. He stared directly at Melvin, and if Melvin didn't know any better, he could have sworn he saw fear and a silent plea for help in his expression. Before Melvin could react, there was a loud report of a gunshot, quickly followed by a bloody hole sprouting in the zombie's forehead. Melvin heard the sound of the bullet as it zipped by him. He instinctively ducked and drew his Glock.

The car, a burgundy Toyota Prius rolled to a stop. Lonnie was grinning from ear to ear.

"Whatta ya' say, you old goat fucker!" Lonnie shouted and looked over at his driver. "Look, Pig, it's our old buddy, Melvin."

"What the hell?" Melvin asked as Lonnie got out.

He stretched, walked over to the dead zombie, and admired his work. Melvin watched the two men warily. Lonnie was wearing a tight-fitting black tank top, his heavily muscled arms hanging like two slabs of meat. He could see the leather handle of the blackjack sticking out of the back pocket of his jeans, hence the name of his group. All of them carried blackjacks, mimicking their leader.

Lonnie admired his work a few more seconds and spit on it. Shoving the Colt into his waistband, he turned to Melvin with a smug grin.

"How the hell are you, my brother?" Lonnie asked as he walked over, ignoring the Glock in Melvin's hand and grabbed him in a bear hug. Before Melvin realized what he was doing, he reciprocated in kind.

"Oh, same old same old," Melvin replied. "I was driving along and decided to stop and take a big country crap when all of a sudden, here comes this crazy zombie running toward me. All I can say is, what the hell?"

Lonnie emitted a loud bellow of laughter and hugged Melvin again.

Pig had exited their vehicle, a sawed-off twelve gauge double barrel in hand and his own blackjack stuffed in his waistband. Melvin watched Pig carefully. He knew Lonnie was the more dangerous of the two, but Pig would probably be the first one to actually shoot. As Melvin watched, Pig walked over to the dead zed and kicked him in the side of the head. Melvin guessed it was his own way of proclaiming a job well done by his boss.

"How'd you like my shot?" Lonnie asked.

"It was a good one, but you almost got me along with him," he replied.

Lonnie laughed again.

Melvin gestured at the zombie. "What's the deal?"

"That there was an odd one," Lonnie replied. "We came up on him, and instead of trying to attack us like all the others would've done, he actually started running away like he was scared."

"I bet he was a coward back when he was alive," Pig proclaimed. "Probably one of them fudge-packing queer bastards."

Melvin nodded like Pig was lauding them with profound wisdom.

"What the hell are you up to?" Lonnie asked him.

Melvin gestured toward two abandoned tractor-trailers no more than fifty feet away from them.

"I was about to check out those two trucks over there when you two drove up."

"Doing some scavenging, huh?" Lonnie asked.

"Yeah, it's what I do. Hadn't had much luck lately though."

"You got a lot of junk in there," Pig said as he pointed in the bed of Melvin's truck.

"Yeah," Melvin replied. In fact, that's exactly what was on the upper layer, junk. Underneath was where he hid items people like Pig and Lonnie would covet. Melvin watched Pig as he started to walk around to the passenger side, presumably where Savannah was hiding.

"Careful where you step," Melvin admonished. "I dropped the kids off at the pool over there."

Pig stopped and looked at Melvin in disgust. He then looked around and pointed toward the two barrels in the back of Melvin's truck.

"I always meant to ask, what are those for? Water?" he asked.

"Nope," Melvin answered. "Those are for biodiesel fuel."

"No shit?" Lonnie asked as he walked over and looked closer. Melvin had put his Glock back in the holster, but he kept it unsnapped.

"Yeah, gas is iffy these days, so I improvised." Actually, one of the secretaries, who also happened to have two or three post-graduate degrees, wanted to experiment with biodiesel and talked Melvin into it. All Melvin did was find restaurant grease pits. He used a pump and hoses to fill up the barrels. He'd carry it back to Parvis and Parvis would convert the foul-smelling goo into biodiesel. Parvis also had a secret moonshine and hydroponics lab that Melvin helped him with.

Pig pointed at the Prius. "We found six of those. They're quiet and they get fifty miles-per-gallon."

"Nice," Melvin said.

"What do you say we help you search those trucks?" Lonnie volunteered.

"Fifty-fifty split?" Melvin asked.

"There's three of us here, partner," Lonnie said with his transparent grin. "My math says it'll be a three-way split."

Melvin knew better than to argue and gave an affable nod. "I'm cool with that, but how about Pig keeps a lookout for any friends that there zed may have nearby."

"That's a good idea," Lonnie said and pointed back down the interstate. "Go on down there about a hundred yards and keep a lookout."

"I'll be damned if I will," Pig declared.

Melvin chuckled. Pig was only about five foot eight with squat, wide hips, stubby arms, and a fat face. How he survived before Lonnie came along Melvin had no idea. He had no athletic ability, and Melvin imagined the man spent his days eating junk food and playing video games, back before.

"Go on now," Lonnie ordered.

"Aw, Lonnie, there ain't no need…"

He stopped protesting when Lonnie fixed him with a cold hard stare. He stopped arguing and began trudging down the interstate, muttering to himself as he walked.

It worked out better than Melvin had hoped. They were separated now and Pig wouldn't be wandering around his truck and stumble on Savannah by accident.

Melvin used a pair of bolt cutters on the padlocked trailers. "I'm surprised they haven't been searched already," he said.

"Yeah," Lonnie agreed.

When they opened the first one, they found it was stacked with truck tires. The second trailer was more of the same. The cabs had been previously searched and were bare.

"Nothing," Lonnie said in contempt.

"Yeah, but I found something the other day you might like," Melvin said.

When Lonnie looked at him, he made a head gesture toward Pig and held a finger to his lips. Lonnie watched warily as Melvin went to his truck and partially opened the door. He expected to see Savannah hiding in the floorboard, but she wasn't anywhere inside the truck. He masked his concern and retrieved the bottle of Jack Daniels. He showed it to Lonnie before hiding it under his shirt and gestured to Lonnie to follow him. He intentionally led Lonnie away from his truck and to the back of one of the trailers. The two men climbed in and sat. Melvin took a sip and handed it to Lonnie, who took a large swallow.

"Good shit, brother," Lonnie said. He then nodded down the road where Pig was and looked at Melvin questioningly.

Melvin shook his head. "I must insist this split is fifty-fifty only."

Lonnie let out a belly laugh and took another swallow.

"What're you two doing down there?" Pig yelled at them.

"Nothing. You better be keeping watch," Lonnie warned and grinned at Melvin.

"Well, you know anyone who needs truck tires?" he asked.

"Not off the top of my head," Melvin answered.

"Me neither," Lonnie said. "We can't use them, we don't have any semis."

Melvin nodded indifferently, but filed the information away.

"Have you seen anyone lately?"

"Nobody but some people holed up down at Oak Ridge," Melvin said.

"Oh, yeah?"

Melvin grunted. "If you're thinking of trying anything, be careful, they got a bunch of cops and military types guarding the place. They're dug in and heavily armed."

"Fucking cops," Lonnie suddenly exclaimed. "We came across a few not too long ago. They opened fire on us without any provocation and killed two of my men."

"They were cops, you say?" Melvin asked.

"Yeah."

"Where at?"

"A little town called Staunton," Lonnie said.

Melvin remembered his conversation with Savannah. "Isn't there a state police headquarters there?"

"Yep, that's where they're living," Lonnie replied. "The Blackjacks are going to get some payback, you better believe that."

"Good," Melvin said, not meaning it for a second. He sincerely doubted those state troopers fired on Lonnie and his gang for no reason. More than likely the Blackjacks were the instigators and ended up getting their asses handed to them. He reminded himself to go visit them as soon as possible.

"Dug in and heavily armed," Lonnie repeated. "You were in the military once, am I right?"

Melvin hastened a brief glance at Lonnie. He would have preferred Lonnie knew nothing about his past, but went along.

"I was, but ole Peggy over there got me kicked out."

Lonnie laughed and slapped Melvin on the back. "I knew it when I first met you. I told Snake you were military. Which was it, Army or Marines?"

"Army," Melvin replied.

Lonnie wagged a finger. "And the bitch got you kicked out. That's why you're keeping her alive, isn't it. You're tormenting her for what she did to you."

Melvin chuckled, but didn't reply. He wondered if, subconsciously, that was the real reason for keeping her alive.

"I still don't know why I didn't kill you back when we first met," Lonnie said suddenly.

"If you'd have done that, you wouldn't have any truck tires right now," Melvin deadpanned.

Lonnie laughed now. "And I wouldn't have any whiskey right now either."

The two men laughed, causing Pig to poke his head out from behind some cars.

"What're you bastards doing down there?" he yelled.

Lonnie ignored him, took a swallow, and stared out of the open trailer door.

"You and me are just alike, Melvin," Lonnie said.

Melvin nodded. "Yeah, I guess we are, in a way."

The truth was, Melvin thought nothing of the kind. He wasn't like Lonnie. If he was, he would've already raped Savannah and probably would have killed Lonnie just for shits and giggles. They swapped the bottle in silence for several minutes before Lonnie said something disconcerting.

"We've been looking for a girl."

"Oh, yeah?" Melvin asked. "You got a particular one in mind or any old gal you bump into?"

"A little whore by the name of Savannah," he said and then looked at Melvin. "She's a teenager, skinny, brown hair, small titted, freckles. We called her Stinky. Have you seen her?"

"Should I have?"

"We lost her on the outskirts of Oak Ridge a few days ago. Let's see, you said you were in Oak Ridge, when was that?"

"Yesterday," Melvin answered. That's the thing about psychopaths, Melvin thought. You never knew when they were engaging in casual conversation or if they were accusing you of something. He slowly moved his left hand a couple of millimeters closer to the Glock.

"But I didn't see any girl," Melvin said with the most apathetic tone he could. "Are you sure she's still alive?"

"No telling," he said. "But I'd like to get her back."

Melvin didn't ask why, but it seemed odd. Why did he have to have her back?

"Is she on foot? You think she made it this far north?"

"There's no telling, my friend."

Melvin grunted. "Alright, I'll keep an eye out. Is there any kind of reward?"

"My undying gratitude," Lonnie said and burst out laughing. Melvin laughed with him.

"You should join up with us, Melvin," Lonnie suggested. "We could use some military brains in our group."

"I appreciate the invite, Lonnie, I really do."

"But?" Lonnie asked.

"I'm more of a lone-wolf type. I don't get along with people all that well."

"You should consider it. We're recruiting new members and have something in the works right now, and if all goes as planned, we're going to hit a big lick."

"Oh?"

"Yeah," Lonnie said with a knowing smile. "I got Snake on it." He pointed northward. "We're on our way to meet him right now." Lonnie turned the bottle up and finished it. So much for a fifty-fifty split, Melvin thought.

He stood and worked a kink out of his back. "I guess we need to get going. If you find that girl, you look Lonnie up. I'll make it worth your while."

"Sure thing," Melvin replied.

Melvin waved as the two men drove away. When they were well out of sight, he began looking around.

"Savannah?"

There was no answer. He couldn't figure out where she went until it came to him. He crouched down and looked under the truck. She was there, lying in a mud puddle, a look of panic in her eyes and shivering uncontrollably, much like she was when he first found her.

"They're gone, come on out," he said.

He had to gently coax her before she reluctantly crawled out. When she stood, she was soaking wet and covered in mud. She eyed Melvin and looked around nervously.

"Are they coming back?"

"I don't know," Melvin answered. "But if they do, we're going to be long gone. Get in the truck."

139

He thought about what Lonnie had said. He was meeting Snake, and when he left, he was going north on 81, the direction Melvin needed to go in order to get back to Mount Weather. Sighing, he took the next exit.

"I have no idea where Lonnie and Pig are going," Melvin said to Savannah. "So, we're going to take the backroads. I want you to lean back in the seat so nobody sees you, okay?"

"Okay," she replied and reclined the seat. "Can I ask you something?"

Melvin glanced at her as he tried to jog his memory. He'd been on these back roads a few times, but not recently, and he was having a hard time remembering the route back to Weather. The whiskey certainly didn't help.

"Why didn't you kill them when you had the chance?"

It was a good question, and he was having a difficult time coming up with a good answer.

"Um, well, they're good sources of information," he rationalized. "For instance, Lonnie told me about some state police living up in Staunton. Those are good people for Mount Weather to network with. Also, he told me they were up to something big. Might be I can keep him from doing something."

She stared at him in stony silence for several minutes.

"What?" he finally asked.

"They raped me, Melvin," Savannah said quietly. He glanced over. She was lying back in the seat, muddy from head to toe, staring at him with those big doe eyes. She was crying. Not loudly sobbing, no. The tears were running down her face in silent anguish.

"Every day, at least one of them raped me, or Suzie, or one of the other girls. Sometimes it was more than one. Sometimes they'd make us do the most degrading things you can imagine. They'd laugh and make fun of us, and if we didn't go along, we'd get the hell beat out of us. And Lonnie was the ring leader of all of it." Her tone was hushed, somber, and it was tearing Melvin apart.

"It was the most awful thing you can ever imagine."

Melvin didn't know how to respond. They drove down one road and he had to stop suddenly due to flooding. When he turned his head to back up, he briefly looked over at her. She was asleep, curled in a ball. Her face was still moist.

Melvin still wasn't sure about Lonnie. Maybe he was down the interstate, waiting to follow him back to where he lived. Maybe he'd doubled back and was waiting to ambush him. Melvin didn't know, but one thing he was certain of: he couldn't lead him back home. Under no circumstances could Lonnie learn about Mount Weather, and, more importantly, that Melvin was affiliated with Mount Weather.

The flooding situation wasn't looking good. Melvin glanced at his watch and then looked around. He spotted a house up on a hill. It was a rustic, two-story farmhouse, a barn barely visible behind it. The field was not overgrown, which was the norm these days. It had either been cut or cattle had been grazing. He looked over at Savannah, who was still asleep, and decided they were going to wait out the night and see if the floodwaters receded any in the morning.

He started up the truck and found the driveway to the house. There was a gate blocking it and it was padlocked. But, whether by oversight or by design, the hinges were simple in design. They were commonly called bolt and strap hinges. Old-timers called them pintle hinges. All one had to do was lift the gate straight up and off of the bolt portions which were secured into a thick wooden post.

Melvin grabbed the gate and picked it straight up. The hinges lifted off of the bolts easily. He set the gate aside, got in his truck, and drove through. Stopping, he got out and eyed the house. There was still no movement. There was a stirring in the truck. Savannah had awakened and was watching. She started to get out, but he motioned her to stay put.

He replaced the gate back in its original position and got in.

"Where are we?" she asked.

"A little ways off of the interstate. This might be a good place to stop for the night."

He slowly started driving up the gently sloping driveway. As he approached the house, he couldn't help but wonder if someone was aiming a rifle at him. On a whim, he flashed his lights, hoping it would be interpreted as a signal of a friendly greeting.

"Hello?" Melvin called out as he knocked on the front door. There was no response. He tentatively tried the knob. It was locked, and the ground-floor windows were boarded up. He walked around to the back and spotted cattle grazing in the field. There were also three donkeys grazing with them. Melvin remembered Burt telling him that donkeys were good at protecting cattle from coyotes and other predators. The fencing had been moved so the cattle could not be seen from the roadway.

All of it added up; the place was occupied. He walked back to the front door.

"Hey, I'm not here to cause trouble, just need a place to stay for the night. I'm going to park my truck out of sight, and I'll be on my way first thing in the morning."

He waited for a response, didn't get one, and walked back to his truck. Savannah had ducked down and was peeking over the dashboard.

"Who are you talking to?" she whispered.

"There's somebody in the house," Melvin answered. "I don't think they're interested in making friends, but so far, they haven't started shooting." He started the truck and drove around beside the barn and parked. When he turned the truck off, he saw someone standing at the back door.

"Company," he said to Savannah.

CHAPTER 20 – PRISS

I'd been here four days before I found out this place had a weight room nestled away in the back of the gym. It was of moderate size, I'd guess only about ten people at a time could comfortably work out in it, but at the moment, I was the only one present. I guess there weren't many people here who were early risers.

My running buddy, Sarah, was gone, so I thought I'd change things up a little bit. The last time I'd actually worked out with weights was with Sarah back home in our barn. The reason? Life had become busy. We had a lot going on, and there was so much work requiring physical activity I didn't waste the energy on the weight pile.

Now, I found myself with spare time on my hands. I was warming up with a set of jumping jacks when the door opened.

It was Ensign Boner. He'd never gone out of his way to speak to any of us, and I guess I'd been reticent as well in not looking him up. Ever since his little tussle with Justin, he hadn't been all that sociable, or so I'd heard. His pride had definitely been wounded.

"Good morning," I said.

"You're with the group from Tennessee," he declared gruffly.

"I am. I'm Zach. Zach Gunderson."

"Yeah. I'm Ensign Lawrence Boner. I'm the OD, that's Officer of the Day, and I've got you scheduled for guard duty this morning."

Lydia, the Mount Weather taskmaster, approached us at dinner yesterday evening and doled out work assignments. She smiled warmly at Kelly and Maria as she assigned them to the daycare. She assigned the others and then came to me. She gave me a choice, guard duty or latrine duty. I tried to talk her into farming, but she didn't relent, claiming it was too risky. I chose guard duty.

"Zero-seven-hundred, correct?" I asked.

"Roger that. It goes without saying not to be late."

I didn't bother responding. After all, the man didn't know me. If he did, he'd know my punctuality would not be a cause for concern.

143

Boner didn't wait for an answer and donned a set of bright red headphones. For the next thirty minutes, the only sounds were the clanking of the weights and an occasional grunt from one of us.

I went with a CrossFit-style workout. Boner chose a more traditional routine of doing a set of heavy weights for six or eight repetitions and then resting for a minute or two before moving on to another set. Justin, Sarah, and I had talked about the various kinds of workouts and agreed any workout involving heavy cardio was optimal in a post-apocalyptic world.

By the time I finished my first revolution, I was winded and sweating heavily. I bent over with my hands on my knees and spent a minute or two recovering. When I'd gotten my breath back, I stood and wiped my face with a towel. I looked over to see Boner watching me curiously.

"I'm going to do one more revolution, you want to get in?" I asked.

His response was an apathetic grunt. I guess that meant no.

"Don't be late," he repeated and walked out, nearly bumping into a woman who was walking in. They swapped hateful stares for a second before he walked out and she walked in.

I recognized her immediately. Senator Rhinehart's daughter, the thief. She was wearing a designer gym outfit with fancy name brand running shoes. Back in the day, the ensemble probably cost more than I made in a week. When she spotted me, she glared.

"What the hell are you doing in here?" she demanded.

"Stupid question," I answered.

I could almost see her brain churning, trying to come up with a way of ordering me out. But, she came up dry. She continued glaring as she conceded she'd have to share the weight room with me and put her own set of earbuds in. I guess everyone around here preferred to cut themselves out of talking to other people, or even more important, removing their ability to hear what was going on around them. I thought it was shortsighted and naïve.

I stretched a minute, keeping a wary eye on her. She in turn pointedly ignored me, which I took as a good sign, figuring she wasn't going to try something stupid. I took a deep breath and started on round two.

I must admit, I wasn't as focused on my workout this time. The little thief with her perky tits had me on edge. She was still making a show out of ignoring me, but the two of us kept sneaking peeks at each other in the mirrors. When I was fairly certain she wasn't going to try to hit me upside the head with a dumbbell, I found my focus and finished my workout in twenty minutes.

I collapsed on the floor when I finished and lay on my back, trying to catch my breath. Priss chose that moment to walk over and stand over me. I looked up, wondering if I had the strength to handle her if she tried to get violent. From my viewpoint, the yoga pants she was wearing left little to the imagination.

I didn't want to admit it, but she was a good-looking woman. I guessed her height was about five-four, cinnamon-colored hair cut short, hazel eyes, lean but shapely legs, and a nice set of C-cups. Maybe even D, but I didn't want to stare too long. I sat up quickly.

"My ass is still bruised," she said with a petulant glare.

"Serves you right," I replied. "Your parents should have taught you long ago it's wrong to steal."

"My mother's dead," she replied with a tone suggesting I'd breached some sort of rule of etiquette.

"So is mine," I replied quickly. Grabbing my towel, I stood and wiped off my face.

"You smell like an animal," she chided.

"Yeah, most likely," I said. I guess the insults were going to continue as long as I was in the same room with her. She was looking for a fight, but I wasn't going to oblige her. She stepped closer and I prepared myself for her to try to kick me in the groin again.

"What's your name?" she demanded in a tone like I was an underling. Perhaps she thought she was going to order me to clean her toilet or something.

"Zach, and I've already been told who you are. It's Pissilla Hindfart, right?"

Her eyes burned into me. "Priss," she retorted. "Priss Rhinehart. And don't you dare call me Priscilla."

"Oh, okay."

"You were ogling me just now; what are you, some kind of pervert?"

I gave her a withering stare before walking out.

"Crazy damn woman," I muttered.

CHAPTER 21 – GUARD DUTY

I'd gotten cleaned up, put on my military gear, and found the armory. It was on the first floor behind a heavy steel two-section door. The upper section of the door was open and Ensign Boner was behind it, sitting in a chair with a bored expression on his face. When he saw me, he stood and looked me over with seeming indifference.

"Reporting for duty," I said.

He spotted my rifle. "You brought your own weapon?" he asked.

"Yep, I already have it sighted in, so I'd prefer to use it," I said.

He eyed me coolly for a moment longer and then motioned for me to hand it over. I ejected the magazine, cleared it, and handed it to him. Boner gave it a casual inspection and then handed it back.

"I assume you know how to use it."

I nodded as I reloaded it. "A couple extra magazines couldn't hurt though," I said.

"Do you have any prior military experience?" he asked.

"Nope, but, I've had some training and a lot of practical experience."

"Alright," he said slowly. "Is this your first time pulling guard duty?"

"For Mount Weather, yes," I said.

He continued with the stare for a few additional seconds before grunting. I guess that was his way of acknowledging I wasn't going to cause any problems. He turned to a metal table. It was cluttered with a mixture of tools, reloading equipment, and what not. He picked up a clipboard and turned back toward me. I noticed there were a couple of laminated pages attached as he handed it to me.

"Those are your general orders, special orders, and SOP. You're expected to know them and follow them to the letter. We have a shortage of handheld radios, but each guard post has a working field phone. Refer to your special orders sheet regarding when to call in." He paused a moment as he looked into a crate lying on the floor. Making a decision, he reached down and came up with two loaded magazines.

"Roger that," I said as I glanced at the orders. "Which post do you need me at?"

He looked at a dry erase board behind him and then a smirk slowly formed on his face.

"You'll be at post three, with Rhinehart."

"Wonderful. I'll try not to kill him," I said, looked at one of the pages showing the location of each guard post, and headed out.

Guard Post three was in the southwest section of the compound. It was a simple fortification of wood and the same earthen bastion barriers used at the main entrance. It was elevated six feet off of the ground and placed about ten feet from the fence line. It had a slightly pitched roof, a window that was propped open, and an entry door on the back. I expected something more fortified, for some reason.

There were two people waiting for me whom I had not yet met. They introduced themselves as Lois and Norman Marnix, a middle-aged married couple who had worked for FEMA in some capacity they didn't bother specifying.

"Where's the other guard?" Norman asked.

I shrugged.

"Who is it?"

"Rhinehart, I don't know which one, I assume it's the punk boy."

Norman's eyebrows arched in surprise and Lois snorted in contempt.

"A royal pain in the ass, that one is," she said. "There are people here who've been wanting to do what you did to those two for a long time now."

"There've been other thefts the past year," Norman said. "They've been suspected, but nobody has been able to prove it. Until you caught them, that is."

She chuckled. "I'm glad you did what you did, but I'm afraid you've made an enemy of the Rhineharts."

Norman looked somber now. "You watch out for that boy, Zach," he added. "There's something not quite right about him. His father is one to harbor a grudge as well."

"What about the daughter, Priss?" I asked.

"She's a spoiled little bitch," Lois said, and started to say more, but stopped when she looked back toward the main compound. "Speak of the devil."

I looked around and saw a golf cart approaching. It was being driven by someone I didn't know, but the passenger was Priss. So, she was the one I was going to be stuck with, not her brother. She was wearing a small pair of tan cargo shorts, expensive-looking hiking boots, and a tight-fitting black tank top. She had an assault weapon similar to mine, but the way she was holding it made me believe she'd had little training with it.

Norman patted me on the shoulder. "Good luck with that one," he said.

"It was very nice meeting you, Zach," Lois said with a smile. They walked past Priss without acknowledging her presence, climbed on the golf cart, and were soon out of sight. Priss walked up to within a couple of feet before stopping and staring at me in surprise.

"What are you doing here?" she demanded.

"Boner paired us up," I said. "I guess he thinks he's being cute."

"We'll see about that," she said, and stomped up the stairs and into the guard shack.

I followed behind her, which inadvertently gave me a good view of her backside. She made a beeline to a field phone mounted on one of the corner posts while I inspected the interior. There were two chairs, a pair of binoculars, and nothing else. And it smelled. Like dirty socks and sweaty armpits. At least there was a good field of view. No range cards though.

When Boner answered the phone, Priss unleashed a torrent of threats and obscenities, and even though I couldn't hear what Boner was saying, I got the opinion he was telling her too bad. She slammed the phone against the post and stared outside. After a minute, she turned toward me and glared.

"I take it he didn't give in," I said. She didn't respond. I gave a shrug. "Listen, I can handle this guard duty, you can take off."

"Oh, you'd like that, wouldn't you," she retorted. "As soon as I leave, you'll report me to Boner."

I took a breath. "Alright, we're stuck with each other for the next eight hours then. There's no reason we have to be hostile toward each other. I'll keep out of your way and you keep out of mine."

"Fine," she replied.

And, for the next hour, there wasn't a peep out of her. The only sounds were birds chirping and the occasional crow cawing. At least there was a gentle breeze, which helped with the smell.

Post three was required to phone in hourly at five minutes after the hour. I stood, stretched, and made the call. Ensign Boner sounded like he'd been sleeping.

Priss stood and stretched as well. "I have to go pee. Don't be a perv and watch me."

"As long as you have a loaded weapon in your hands, you better believe I'm going to keep an eye on you," I said. She glared at me a moment, she liked to glare, and then tossed her weapon at me. I caught it before it clattered to the floor. Her glare changed to a smirk before walking out.

Apparently, she'd only stepped immediately outside the open entrance to the shack. I heard her zipper. I glanced out the open door and saw her squatting, not five feet away. I suspected she did it on purpose to get a reaction out of me. Not rising to the bait, I turned away and focused on her assault rifle. Unloading it, I field stripped it and gave it a once over. It was filthy.

"Figures," I muttered, reached into my backpack, and retrieved my cleaning kit.

When she walked back in, she stopped and stared incredulously at her disassembled weapon.

"What the hell are you doing?" she demanded.

"Relax, I'm cleaning it."

"Why?" Her tone had changed, but she was still wary.

"Because it's dirty."

She rolled her eyes. "Big deal."

I stopped in the middle of running a cleaning rod through the barrel and looked at her.

"Answer me honestly; have you ever been in a firefight?"

"I've killed a few zombies," she answered haughtily. "I know what I'm doing."

"Okay, that's good, but have you ever been in a firefight? You know, where there are dozens of them, maybe more, and you're shooting continuously for hours? Have you ever been in something like that?"

"Have you?" she retorted.

"Yes," I replied. "A few times. The point I'm getting at is this; your life, and the life of your friends, depends on your weapon functioning properly and not jamming up at the wrong time due to it being dirty."

"I know that," she snipped.

The petulance was still there. It was getting irritating. I tried hard to be patient and gestured at her weapon. "M4s and M16s are great weapons, but they're finicky, you have to keep them clean." I showed her my dirty hands. "This one hasn't been cleaned in a while."

"Not my fault. I signed it out of the armory like that."

I gave her a look; I'm sure what she said was true, but it was a lame excuse. Instead of saying so, I kept quiet and resumed cleaning. When I was through with the upper receiver, I set it down and started on the bolt assembly. She picked up the upper receiver and looked at it.

"Hold it up to the light and see if I got the bore clean," I suggested.

She did so and then gave a look like she approved of my cleaning skills. She then watched me finish with the bolt assembly and then the lower receiver. Wiping as much grime off of my hands as I could, I then lubed everything. Priss watched quietly.

"An old Vietnam vet taught me all the tricks of the M16 and its variants. He liked to put a thick coat of oil on everything. I like a thinner coat. I guess it's a personal preference. Now, right here," I pointed at the face of the bolt, "you keep free of oil. You also keep the rifle bore dry as well, unless you're going to store it long term." I assembled the weapon, performed a function check, and handed it to her.

"Good to go," I said.

"What was that you just did?" she asked.

"It's called a function check. It lets you know your weapon is functioning properly without actually having to fire a round." I gestured for her weapon. "Here, I'll show it to you again."

She scoffed. "I got it, don't worry about it."

"Suit yourself."

After a few seconds of silence, she opted to change the subject.

"You watched me pee, didn't you?" she accused.

"You know better than that," I said.

"I bet you did, perv," she said with a smirk.

I paused momentarily, thought of a smart-assed retort, but decided it wasn't worth it. I stood, grabbed my backpack and weapon, and headed toward the door.

"I'm going to get some fresh air."

The woman sure had a way of pushing my buttons. The air was certainly fresher outside, and I decided to walk along the fence line. The concertina wire was attached securely to the regular fencing, and even back here, it was full of trash. Concertina wire was a good trap for paper and plastic being blown along by the wind. It irritated my obsessive personality. I saw a black plastic trash bag stuck in the wire, flapping in the breeze.

It gave me an idea. I reached in and fished it out and then spent the next two hours pulling trash out. I glanced up occasionally at the guard shack, and one time, I caught Priss looking at me like I was stupid. I ignored her and continued until the bag was packed full. It was kind of unusual, but the entire time, I didn't see a single zombie. I guess the Marines were telling the truth when they said they'd killed them all off around here.

Priss was standing in the doorway as I walked in and didn't move aside. She was standing so close I couldn't help but brush against her breasts as I walked by. I acted like I didn't notice she wasn't wearing a bra and sat down.

She watched me for a minute before speaking. "You had no right to beat me. My ass is still bruised."

"Yeah, you've already told me that," I replied and stared at her. "I hope you realize, I came close to killing you and your brother. Be thankful the only thing that happened to you was a bruised ass." Besides, I thought, something tells me you might've even found it somewhat enjoyable.

She didn't offer a retort, and instead sat in her chair, which I noticed had been moved closer to mine.

"You act like you've killed people before," she finally said in a dubious tone.

I didn't answer. I had a feeling if I told her the truth she wouldn't believe me anyway, but she kept pushing it.

"Well?" she asked.

I took a few seconds before responding. "What do you think? I've survived this shit storm for over three years without the protection of a place like Mount Weather and a bunch of Marines. Not only did I survive, I protected my people as well."

"Yeah, right," she retorted.

"I'm not sure why you think I'm lying to you."

"Men lie," she responded.

"Yeah, whatever."

The field phone rang. Priss answered. It was Ensign Boner wondering why we hadn't done our hourly check. Priss told him we'd been busy and hung up on him.

My stomach was growling, but I didn't particularly care to eat an MRE. Reaching into my backpack, I retrieved some hand sanitizer and a Tupperware container full of smoked venison. Priss watched me.

"Smoked venison," I said. "It's tastier than MRE food. A little on the chewy side, but it's a good source of protein. You want any?" I tore a piece off and handed it to her. She took the piece and took a tentative bite.

"It's salty," she said. "And peppery too."

"Yeah, the meat is rubbed down with salt, pepper, and some spices before the curing process. The salt acts as a preservative, the pepper repels bugs."

"Is that what you people did? To survive?"

"Yeah, among other things. Have you ever smoked meat?"

She gave me a look. "Is that meant as a double entendre?"

I chuckled now. "No, not at all."

"No, I never have," she said. "Why would I?"

I shrugged. She wasn't interested in the finer points of food preservation so I saved my breath. She stared at me thoughtfully while she chewed the rest of the venison.

"What's up with those scars?"

"They're from people who tried to kill me," I replied and pointed. "This one's a knife wound and the other one is from a gunshot."

"Tell me about it," she said.

"Nothing to tell. I lived and they died."

She waited for me to elaborate, but I was of no mind to. I finished my venison, reached for the binoculars, and scanned the wood line. Looking, I sighed.

"What?" she asked.

"I don't like this set up," I said, pointing outward. "The field of observation is crap."

"What are you talking about? I can see everything just fine."

I pointed again. "You've got a clear field of observation for only fifty yards or so, and then it's a wall of trees. Someone could easily hide out there, watching us, and we wouldn't be able to see them."

"Who the hell would want to watch us?" she asked.

I was about to explain, but when I turned toward her, she was looking in my backpack.

"Looking for something to steal?" I asked dryly. She pulled out a book.

"What's this?" she asked mockingly. "A book?" She looked at the title. "Poetry? Really? I didn't know dumb country hicks could read."

"Yep, too dumb to read," I said, not taking the bait. "I'm not nearly as smart as you."

She chortled. "I was going to go to Harvard when all of this shit started."

I did some mental arithmetic. "So, you're what, twenty-one now?"

"Yeah, how old are you?"

"Nineteen."

She did a little mental arithmetic of her own and then grinned. "So, that means you never finished high school."

"Yep."

"Yeah, that's what I thought, a dumb country hick. You don't even need this book," she said and tossed it through the open window. I still wasn't going to bite, I'd get it later, but then she started to reach inside my knapsack again. I snatched her arm and twisted it as I forced her down to her knees. She gasped in pain and stared at me with her mouth in a silent o-shape.

"What the hell is wrong with you?" I asked.

She stared back at me and then her mouth transformed into a challenging smirk.

"I like it rough," she said huskily. I let go of her then and pushed her. She rolled onto her backside with a thump.

I stared at her in annoyance, and she stared back with that same taunting smirk. She leaned back on her hands, her legs splayed out in front of me, practically daring me not to look at her crotch.

If I were a single man, I could probably see myself taking her right then and there. But, I wasn't single. Not only did I love Kelly, I liked her. She was my best friend, and I wasn't going to do anything to mess it up.

"I'm not the man for you," I said and picked up the binoculars. "Why don't you give it a go with someone like Boner? With all of those muscles, I'd bet he'd love to throw you around."

"Been there, done that," she replied with a scoff as she made a show of stretching and sticking her breasts out. "It was a waste of time."

I grunted. It figured.

"What, you've never fucked around on your wife?" she asked.

"Nope."

From the look on her face, I guessed she was thoroughly frustrated with me by now. I suspected she'd played this flirtatious game many times with other men and it probably worked almost every time.

She got up and plopped down in the chair. Propping her feet up on the open window frame, she stared out into the woods at nothing in particular while I did the same.

"The men here are lame," she finally said.

I gave her a quick glance and started to say something, but stopped. I was about to suggest she check out Cutter or Josue, but I couldn't do that to either of them. Not even Cutter.

"I haven't known you long, but I get the impression you can be difficult to handle," I finally said.

She cut her eyes at me and started to say something, but then she was quiet again. I changed the subject.

"Have you been here at Mount Weather the whole time?" I asked.

"Yep," she said. "When the balloon went up, they loaded up the senators, family, and aides into helicopters and brought us here. It's boring as hell here. Paul and I've talked about heading out and exploring the country."

"Paul, as in Paul your brother?" I asked. She gave a flippant nod. She must have sensed something.

"What?" she asked.

"It's pretty dangerous out there," I said.

The glare was back. "We can handle ourselves."

"Okay, if you say so."

If she only knew how it really was out there beyond the confines of this place, I don't think she'd be so eager to go exploring, but I wasn't going to frustrate myself by trying to explain it.

"So, you're married, huh?" she asked.

"Yeah," I answered as I used the binoculars again.

"Is she your first love?" she asked.

"Nope, but she's the one I love now."

"And you've never fucked around on her?" she asked again.

I put my binoculars down and gave her a look. "Nope, but if you ever need a switch taken to you again, I could probably manage."

"Asshole," she muttered.

I kept looking. To the casual observer, everything looked fine, serene, boring, but something was nagging at my subconscious. Priss must have sensed it.

"Why do you keep looking out there? Have you spotted a deer or something?" she asked. I didn't answer.

She scoffed. "Like I said, boring, boring, boring. The Marines killed all of the zombies within miles of here. I don't know why we have to keep up this guard duty nonsense."

I shrugged. She was probably right, but my intuition kept telling me something was not quite right out there.

CHAPTER 22 – SNAKE

The blonde-headed dude almost saw him. Snake was wearing his own homemade version of a Ghillie suit which mostly consisted of burlap bags and strips of earth tone cloth sewn on. He'd supplemented the camouflage by rubbing mud on any exposed skin. His binoculars were covered by mosquito netting and he had remained perfectly still for hours. Still, the blonde dude had paused more than once at his spot when he scanned. If not for the whore constantly distracting him, Snake was fairly certain the blonde dude might have spotted him.

He'd crawled into place several hours ago, well before dawn. It was a spot almost two hundred yards away. He was hidden in the shadow of an old pine tree and watched the guard post through a small opening between the limbs. Snake lay there all day, watching. He was certain he was hidden and undetected, but even so, he wasn't taking any chances.

He decided he had enough info and it was time to leave. The two night guards often slept during their shift and hardly stared out at the woods. The only vigilant one was the blonde-headed dude.

He was going to go back to his car, eat something, and then sleep until two the next morning. That's when he was going to make his move. The old married couple was usually asleep by then. He already had a spot picked out in the fence he was going to cut a hole in. It was then simply a matter of sneaking up on them and slit their throats while they slept. It'd be easy.

Then, it was a matter of waiting. The blonde-headed dude had a habit of walking to the post and perky tits was always late, so he'd be alone for ten minutes or so. Snake knew he'd have to be quick with that one. He'd stab him in the heart as soon as he stepped foot in the shack.

After that, he'd wait on perky tits. He'd put his knife to her throat, maybe draw a little blood, and then take her right there in the shack. Right on top of her dead friends. If she was good enough, he'd take her back and maybe share her with the rest. Otherwise, he'd amuse himself with some knife work on those nice, perky tits.

He started a slow, backwards crawl. It was already hot and muggy, and the physical exertion soon had him sweating profusely. The sweat ran down his forehead and into his eyes. He tried blinking several times, but didn't dare move a hand up to his face. Too risky. Instead, he closed his eyes and continued to slowly worm his body backwards. He'd wipe his face when he felt he was safe. The ground rubbed against his crotch, causing Snake to think about the whore in the guard shack. She was older than he preferred, but even so, he was going to have a lot of fun with her.

He paused for a minute to catch his breath before resuming slithering backwards, like a snake. His real name was Steven, but he'd gotten the nickname in juvenile lockup back when he was sixteen. One of the other juvies had rigged up a makeshift tattoo apparatus and drew a crude cobra on his forearm. It was really shitty work. Nevertheless, he embraced it and conformed himself to the persona of a cold-blooded snake, even more so after he'd hooked up with Lonnie and the Blackjacks.

Snake paused again and lay there remembering the day Lonnie had found him. He'd fallen asleep after spending a day raping and cutting on a young girl he'd found in an abandoned house. He awoke to find the huge man standing over him. His first thought was Lonnie was the girl's father or something.

"Did you do this all by yourself?" Lonnie asked him while pointing at the girl. Snake was petrified with fright and couldn't speak. He was naked and covered in the girl's blood. What was he going to say, he found her like that? So, he slowly nodded, convinced he was signing his death warrant.

To his surprise, the big man responded with a broad grin.

"I can use a man like you," he said to Snake.

The grinding of his crotch against the ground brought him back to the present. It felt good. The sensation enhanced his fantasy of the whore and what he was going to do to her. When he'd crawled back far enough, he opened his eyes and blinked several times until he could focus. He'd travelled fifty yards, well out of sight of the guard shack. He rubbed his eyes and started to stand when a voice startled him.

"Howdy," a man said quietly.

Judging by the direction and volume, he estimated the man was maybe five feet behind him. Snake had two weapons on him. His trusty knife, and a Remington model 700, chambered in seven millimeter Remington Mag. Snake had taken if off of a Pilgrim he'd sliced up a couple of months ago. He'd used the knife he had on him now. He loved the knife. It was custom-made and razor sharp.

Snake carefully moved the rifle away to the side. "Alright, be cool, man," he said as he casually reached under the burlap sacks to his knife. As Snake started to turn, the man jumped on his back. Snake struggled, but when he felt a sharp, stinging sensation to the side of his neck, his struggle turned to panic. The blade sunk in, and he could actually feel it being twisted around. Oddly, except for the initial stab, he felt no pain.

"You have about five seconds to ask Jesus for forgiveness," the man said in the same quiet tone.

"Jesus?" Snake tried to ask, but his voice wouldn't work. The man didn't answer. Everything was going dark and he was struggling to catch his breath. There was only one emotion going through Snake's mind as his consciousness faded – fear.

The man used Snake's pants to wipe the blood off of his knife, then stepped back and wiped the sweat off of his brow. As Snake lie bleeding out, the man picked up the rifle and inspected it. It was a Remington, a fine rifle, and it had a good scope mounted on it.

He then stripped Snake of his Ghillie suit and clothing, and carefully went through his pockets. In addition to the knife, he had a Bic lighter, and a key fob for a Toyota. Snake's shirt pocket held the most interesting item: a folded-up piece of paper. Fred unfolded it and looked it over thoughtfully before folding it back and placing it in his own shirt pocket.

The man gave Snake one final look, picked up the items, and began walking back to where he'd picketed his horse.

CHAPTER 23 – AN IRRITATING PRETENSE

Melvin tentatively waved. The person stood within the shadow of the open back door, not moving.

"Is that a man or a woman?" Savannah whispered.

Melvin wasn't sure. The person was wearing a heavily soiled robe of indeterminate color. Not a bathrobe, more like a robe you'd see someone wearing in a Shakespearean play. Long greasy gray hair flowed over the collar, causing more staining. The person's face was heavily wrinkled, further impairing Melvin's judgement of gender.

They didn't return Melvin's wave.

"Hello," Melvin said pleasantly. "I'm Melvin and this here is…" he started to say Savannah, but if this was a friend of Lonnie's, he'd eventually be told of this encounter.

"This is my little sister, Melvina."

Savannah glanced at him. "Melvina?" she whispered. "That's a stupid name."

"Work with me here," Melvin whispered back.

"You are intruders, an irritating pretense," the person declared in a flat, emotionless voice.

Melvin frowned and held up his right index finger, casually keeping his left hand near his Glock.

"Now, that there statement sounds real familiar." He continued frowning and then suddenly snapped his fingers. "Heart of Darkness by Arthur Clark. Am I right? No, wait, wait. Joseph Conrad wrote that one, right?"

The person stared at Melvin with dull, lifeless eyes for a moment before slowly shutting the door. Melvin could hear the distinct sound of two deadbolts being locked and a barrel bolt being slid into place.

"That's weird," Savannah whispered. "Maybe not as weird as Miss Piggy, but definitely weird."

"Alright, wait here," Melvin said and tentatively walked up to the back door. He paused a moment before knocking. There was no response, so Melvin started talking.

"I just wanted to say, we're not here to cause any problems, all we want is a safe, dry place to park our truck and get a few hours of sleep. I promise we'll be gone by sunup."

"I have nothing to give you," the person said through the door. "No food, no water."

"That's okay," Melvin replied. "We're good on that end. The flood waters are making it a little difficult for us to drive is all, but it should be better tomorrow."

Melvin waited for a response, but he was met with nothing but silence. He waited three full minutes before turning away and walking off of the porch.

"Alright, he or she may be harmless, or they may decide to fire off a couple of shots while we're sleeping. I'm not taking that chance."

"We're leaving?" Savannah asked.

"Yeah, we're not welcome here." He looked back at the house, hopeful the occupant or occupants had a change of heart, but there was nothing. He motioned to Savannah and the two of them got back into the truck. Savannah turned and watched out of the back window as they rode back down the driveway.

"See anything?" he asked.

"Nope."

At least they weren't being shot at, he thought. Savannah jumped out and opened the gate in the same manner she'd seen Melvin do it. When he drove the truck through, she replaced it and jumped back into the truck. Melvin exited the driveway and headed back toward the interstate.

"It's getting dark out," Savannah said. "Are you going to find somewhere else to park?"

Melvin thought about it. He had to be careful where they stopped for the night. If he chose the wrong location, floodwaters could engulf them while they slept. The person at the farmhouse unnerved him. It was almost like he, or she, was a harbinger of something bad.

"Alright," he said. "We're going to get back on the interstate and go back to those apartments. That apartment with the philosophy books was in decent shape, there aren't any dead bodies in it, not much water damage, and it's up on the second floor. We'll be good there until the morning. In the meantime, lay low in the seat, just in case we bump into them again."

Savannah looked at Melvin dejectedly.

"I wish you had killed them," she said. Her tone was somber, rueful, like she felt Melvin had chosen sides and it wasn't hers.

Melvin didn't answer. He couldn't.

Melvin cleared the apartment again from any possible threats, but it was the same as he'd left it. He finished at the bedroom and looked it over once more. The top side of the mattress had mildew stains on the sheets, but when he flipped it over, it was suitable.

"Okay, we'll sleep here."

Savannah looked around. "Same bed?"

"If that's okay with you. I can sleep on the floor if you insist, but I'll be stiff as hell in the morning."

"No, we'll share."

"Alright, I'm going to get some gear out of the truck. I'll be right back."

Melvin descended the stairwell, hid back in the shadows a minute, and watched. All was quiet. He loaded up a backpack and retrieved the two plastic trash bags of water bottles. When he'd gotten the bottles spread around the landing, he walked in and secured the door by moving the refrigerator up against it. When he walked into the bedroom, Savannah was hiding in the closet.

"Nobody here but us chickens," he said and beckoned her out.

They finished off the spam and used the bathroom sink to brush their teeth. Afterwards, Savannah curled up on the bed and was asleep in seconds. He lay down on the mattress next to her, checked his Glock and put it under the mattress beside him, and then went through some de-stressing exercises a psychologist had taught him back when his life was falling apart. It took a few minutes before he finally drifted off.

The sunlight woke Savannah. She had a moment of panic when she didn't see Melvin. Hurrying into the den, she stopped short when she saw Melvin sitting on a milk crate. Breathing a silent sigh of relief, she walked up to him.

"What are you doing?" she asked. He put a finger to her lips and pointed through the crack in the draperies. She looked out and gasped. The windows offered a dull view of the apartment parking lot. It was full of zombies. There were at least a dozen surrounding his truck and maybe forty or fifty more wandering around the parking lot.

"Where did they come from?" she asked.

"I don't know, but I'd rather avoid shooting our way back to the truck."

"They're all around it."

"You're observation skills are remarkable."

"So, what do we do, smartass?" she asked.

Melvin shrugged. "We're going to wait them out. So, get comfortable, we might be stuck here a while."

160

In fact, they sat there until far into the afternoon. Melvin was convinced they were going to have to spend another night in the musty apartment. He said as much to Savannah.

"Wonderful," she said. "This apartment stinks and we stink. Could it get any worse?"

"Yes, it could," Melvin replied. "Don't jinx us."

He was about to suggest they break out an MRE when Savannah grabbed his arm.

"Look," she said. As they watched through the crack in the curtains, all of them started walking across the parking lot.

"Something's drawing their attention," Melvin said. He reached out and ever so slowly moved the curtain a half inch. He could barely see the tail end of a car disappearing down the side street. It wasn't a Prius, of that he was certain, but he had no idea if it was other Blackjacks. He thought it over. If they stayed here, it was only a matter of time before the zombies returned or that car drove through the parking lot. He made a decision.

"Get ready, this might be our chance."

Their gear was already packed and ready to go. As quietly as he could, he moved the refrigerator and peeked out of the door. There was nothing.

Melvin shouldered the heavy pack and checked the magazine on his assault rifle. He then spoke in a hushed voice.

"We're going to have to leave the bottles. So, as quietly as you can, tiptoe around them, down the stairs, and jump in the truck." He handed her the key fob.

"I'll be slower because I'm hauling this rucksack, so you jump in and get it started."

"Do you want me to drive?" she asked.

"Yeah, sure. I mean, no."

"Why not?" she asked.

"If we bump into Lonnie and his boys, they'll see you right away. If you're in the passenger seat, at least you'll have the chance to hide. Okay?"

Savannah nodded. He adjusted the straps on the rucksack and nodded to her. They quietly moved the plastic bottles with their feet. Once they made it to the stairwell, they hustled to the truck. As Melvin worked the pack off of his shoulders, a short zombie leaped from between two cars and jumped on Melvin's back.

The over-stuffed rucksack is the only thing that kept the thing from sinking its teeth into Melvin's neck. He spun, causing the rucksack to fling off. The zombie lost his grip on Melvin and fell to the asphalt. Melvin did not hesitate. He ran up and stomped on its face and continued stomping until the zombie's face was nothing more than mashed goo on the asphalt. He admired his work for only a fraction of a second before tossing the rucksack in the truck. Looking over, he saw Savannah standing there, assault rifle in hand, pointing nervously.

"Quit fucking around," he said. "Let's go."

"I think Peggy attracted them," Savannah remarked as he drove.

"It's possible, I guess," Melvin said. "It's never happened before, though."

"Another reason to kill her."

Melvin gave her a frown. "Watch the road," he said.

CHAPTER 24 – I THOUGHT YOU WERE DEAD

Lydia caught us as we were walking to the cafeteria and advised me I had guard duty the rest of the week due to the manpower shortage.

"When are the Marines coming back?" I asked her.

She replied with an unknowing shrug.

"Come on, now, Miss Lydia. I think you have the inside scoop on everything going on around here. Am I right?"

She glanced at Kelly who gave her a knowing smile. Lydia actually looked conspiratorially around and then lowered her voice. "They had a hard time getting into the lab, but they've finally gotten into it. Kincaid and Smeltzer believe they'll need a minimum of six weeks for the incubation process."

I nodded thoughtfully as she spotted someone fast walking down the hall. Lydia hurried toward them, calling their name as they disappeared around a corner.

"Well, I guess you know what I'll be doing the rest of the week," I said to Kelly.

"Yeah, stuck in a small shack for eight hours a day with a woman who wears tight shorts and thin tank tops. Oh, by the way, I'm pretty sure there's some cologne stored in the trailer if you want any. I'm sure Priss would be impressed."

I glanced at her. "You're full of yourself this morning."

She smiled sweetly before entering the cafeteria.

I went to the armory, checked in, and looked at the schedule on the dry erase board. Boner had me paired up with Priss for each guard shift. I pointed at the board.

"What's up with that?" I asked.

He looked at the board and seemed perplexed for a moment, as if the question troubled him.

"That's the way it is," he finally answered. "Besides, nobody else likes working with her."

"I can certainly understand that," I muttered, got the necessary items, and walked to the kennel.

"Hi, pretty girl," I said to Zoe. She responded with a silent bark and wagging tail. "Alright, I know you hate being cooped up here, how about spending guard duty with me?"

When I opened the door, she dashed out and ran around in circles, burning off her pent-up energy. She eagerly followed while she ran back and forth, sniffing everything, and when we got to post three, she instantly became friends with Lois and Norman.

"What a beautiful dog," Lois exclaimed as she petted her.

"Yeah, she's still got a lot of puppy in her, but she won't run off, and I'd rather not keep her cooped up in the kennel."

"She'll be better company than the other bitch you'll be spending the day with," Norman quipped.

"If you don't mind my asking, why do you guys prefer the midnight shift?" I asked. "I mean, you guys have been here since the beginning, it seems like you could pick where and when you wanted to work."

Norman had a glimmer of a smile. "Just between us?"

I nodded. He gave a vague wave toward the woods.

"There's nothing going on out here. So, during the summer, we do this. It beats the hell out of mopping floors or slaving away in a hot kitchen. A little mosquito repellent, a good book, perhaps even a comfortable pillow, and we're fine."

"When the weather changes, you better believe we'll be changing jobs," Lois added. "We're not going to be freezing our asses off in this little shack again. If Lydia thinks otherwise, I'm going to wring her neck."

I would have suggested putting a small stove in the shack, but it was probably going to be something I'd end up doing myself.

"What did you guys do before?" I asked.

"We both worked in accounting," Norman said. "They're pretty much useless occupations these days, but we managed to finagle ourselves into the bunker before they shut the door."

"My wife was studying accounting, back before," I said, remembering Kelly telling me she worked in a hotel and was going to school on the side.

Norman yawned and patted me on the shoulder. "If you'd like, come by early in the morning. We'll give you the entire history about this place, but I think right now, I want to get some breakfast and then take a nap." He stopped like an idea popped up in his head.

"Say, I haven't seen you at any of the events," he remarked.

"You mean the corn-hole tournaments and what not?" I asked. Norman chuckled and nodded. I shrugged.

"I spend most evenings with my kids. Kelly spends all day with them and usually needs a break."

"Oh, well, that makes sense. A happy wife is a happy life, right?" he said as he glanced at Lois.

"Yep, absolutely," I replied.

"Well, if anything changes, on Friday nights some of the men play cards. You're welcome to join us sometime. It's a good way to get to know some of these people a little better."

"I'll see if I can get permission," I said.

Norman grinned broadly. "Excellent, hopefully you can join us."

Lois gave Zoe one last pat before they headed off. We played fetch with her tennis ball for the next ten minutes to get some of the energy out of her system and then went in the guard shack. It was cleaner today; somebody had swept the floor and knocked down the cobwebs. I checked in on the field phone and settled down.

Priss arrived twenty minutes later. She was wearing a plain tan tank top, sans bra, and some olive drab cargo shorts which actually covered her butt cheeks. Her legs were freshly shaved and I had to admit they were pleasing to the eye. I liked Kelly's legs better, but hers were nothing to criticize.

She stopped short when she walked in and spotted Zoe.

"Whose mutt?"

"Mine," I replied. "Her name's Zoe."

"She better not bite me," she retorted and plopped down in the other chair. Zoe eyed her warily. Priss looked around and spotted my oversized thermos.

"What'd you bring?" She asked.

"Iced tea. If you're nice, I'll share."

"I'm always nice," she replied. I grunted in response and poured her a cup.

"Do you have any sugar?" she asked.

"Nope. They tell me there's a shortage of it, so they save it for cooking," I said.

"Only certain people have access to it, like my father."

"Yeah, it figures."

"He doesn't care much for you," she said.

"The feeling is mutual."

"He said if it wasn't for your immunity, you and your people would have never been allowed in here."

"That's probably true," I said. "As it was, we almost didn't come."

"Why did you?"

I thought about my answer. "A couple of reasons. We had no doctors and I have my kids to think about, and if there's any validity of a vaccine being created, it would be selfish of me not to contribute." I sipped some coffee. "Have you seen the extinction model?"

She tilted her head as she stared at me. "Extinction model?"

"Yeah. They've determined unless there's some type of intervention, the human race will be gone within fifty years or so."

She frowned. "My father said something about that. If they find a cure, do you think they'll kick you out?"

"It's possible, I suppose." I picked up the binoculars and started a scan.

"If they do, where would you go?" she asked.

"Back home to Tennessee," I answered.

She scoffed. "Redneck central."

I gave her a look as I sipped some coffee. "Have you ever been there?"

She ignored my question and took the liberty of refilling her cup.

"Do you have your poetry book?" she asked.

I reached into my backpack and handed it to her. She didn't thank me. Instead, she made herself comfortable, put her earphones in, and started reading.

That was fine with me; I much preferred the silence over her snide remarks. I made another scan of the wood line and then got another book out. After a few minutes, she asked me what I was reading. I held it up so she could see the title. It was a mystery thriller I'd checked out of the library.

"Looks stupid," she said with a roll of her eyes to accentuate her remark. Honestly, I was having difficulty enjoying it, but if I voiced my agreement with her opinion, I'm sure she'd respond with some kind of smart-assed response.

An hour later, she did her usual restroom break and actually waited until she got back in the guard shack before zipping up her shorts. I waited until she was finished before standing and pulling the used trash bag out of my backpack.

"I'm going to stretch my legs," I said. Zoe jumped up quickly and followed me out. She stopped to sniff a spot on the ground, presumably the spot where Priss had urinated. Zoe squatted and pissed on top of it. She then caught up with me and dropped her tennis ball at my feet. I gave it a throw and then worked on getting trash out of the wire. I'd made significant progress yesterday and there wasn't much left.

After an hour, I went back to the shack. Priss was asleep. I tried not to wake her; she was a lot more pleasant to be around when she was asleep, but Zoe ruined it by sniffing her crotch. Priss awoke with a start, and of course glared at me.

When our relief came, she practically pushed me aside getting out of the guard shack. I chose to walk instead of riding in the cart. It was an overcast day, but the temperature was not too bad, low eighties I'd guess. I felt like I'd wasted an entire day doing nothing, but I guess guard duty was a necessary evil. As I neared the main buildings, I spotted Burt riding toward post three on one of the carts. I waved. He turned and made a beeline toward me.

"What's up, Burt?" I asked.

"There's a man at the main gate claiming to know you and Kelly. Hop on."

As we got closer to the main gate, I saw a man sitting on a horse, one leg wrapped around the pommel, his head angled down, like the fatigue of being in the saddle too long was wearing on him. The Stetson hat covered his face, but I would've known who it was if I was blind in one eye and nearsighted in the other.

Even so, as we got nearer, I realized I couldn't feel anything from the neck down, and I think I was actually trembling a little. I jumped off of the cart before it came to a stop and jogged up. My mouth had suddenly become dry and I could barely croak out his name.

"Fred?"

He looked at me a long moment before responding. "I would've been here sooner, but those damned zombies made things a little hard on me."

I nodded in understanding. He looked like he'd aged ten years. Though he had a thick gray beard, I could tell he'd lost weight. His features were drawn into an older, meaner version of the Fred I'd met not so long ago. A lifetime ago.

He handed me the reins before stiffly getting off of his horse and then offered his hand. We shook and then embraced in a hug.

"It's good to see you, son," he said huskily.

"I thought you were dead," I replied, my voice breaking.

"I thought I was too for a while," he replied. He pulled back and looked at me. "Damn, it's good to see you."

"What are you doing here?" I asked.

"You and the kids," he answered. I knew he wasn't going to say much without me prying it out of him, and even then, he most likely wasn't going to talk in front of strangers. I gave him a look of understanding. We'd talk more when we were alone.

"The kids have grown so much I don't think you'll recognize them."

Fred actually smiled now. It was a tired smile all the same. "That's good," he said quietly. "That's good."

Burt cleared his throat and introduced himself. "If you're a friend of Zach's, you must be a good man, and I see you know your way around a horse."

"That I do," Fred said.

Burt slapped his side. "Hot damn, we got us another cowboy on the payroll." He then looked the two of us over and his grin was tempered somewhat. "Well, I imagine you two have a lot of catching up to do."

I laughed. "That's an understatement." I hugged Fred again, not noticing him flinch slightly. "I must have a million questions to ask you."

"Alright," Burt responded and looked at me. "You know he's got to be tested, so I'll get that expedited, and maybe I can even talk my contrary wife into fixing him a plate of hot food while he waits for the docs to do their thing."

I looked at him in appreciation. "Thanks, Burt."

"So, what the heck happened?" I asked. Everyone had gone inside, leaving Fred and me sitting on the ground several feet away from the guard post. Doctor Salisbury had come out, introduced herself, and then drew a couple of vials of blood. Fred waited until she was out of earshot before speaking.

"A sniper shot me," he said plainly.

"Yeah, that's what I was told. I looked for you, but it wasn't until several days later." I briefly told him of the abduction, the escape, and how Kelly and I found each other. I paused and cleared my throat.

"Did you see the pile of burned bodies?" I asked.

"I was told about it," Fred replied.

"A Marine colonel was behind it all. He's dead now; Janet cut his throat."

Fred gave me a look and I was about to explain, but we stopped talking when we saw a golf cart barreling down the road. It was Kelly and the kids; Kelly had Macie in her lap and Sammy was holding Frederick tight as Kelly drove. Zoe was running close behind and Anne was in a second golf cart.

Fred got to his feet and waited. It was then I saw him favoring his left side. He gave Kelly a hug and looked at the kids. "Holy cow, they have grown."

"Yes, they have," I said. "We stopped calling him Rick."

He looked at me questioningly. "When we thought you were gone, we reverted to his formal name." I looked at my son and rubbed his head. "Now, he's Frederick."

"I like that," he said and looked over at Kelly and me as Zoe checked him out. "So, you two?"

"Yep," I said.

He nodded slowly, reached down, and scratched Zoe behind her ears. "That's good."

He looked at the kids again, and then focused on Sammy. Fred sized him up and then offered his hand.

"I don't believe we've met, I'm Fred McCoy."

"I'm Sam Hunter," Sammy replied. He looked Fred squarely in the eyes, like I'd taught him, and shook Fred's hand.

"Zach said you were the fastest man with a gun he'd ever seen."

"Well, I don't know about that. How about this, when everything settles down a might, maybe the three of us can do some shooting. Maybe I'll show you a trick or two."

Now Sammy was wide-eyed, and all he could do was nod his head.

We sat back down and made small talk while he ate, but I got the impression Fred didn't want to talk in front of the others. Kelly asked a couple of questions, but I gave her a subtle shake of the head. She understood. Soon, the small talk dried up. The phone to the guard post chimed and there was a small conversation.

"The doc said you're good to go," the guard yelled out.

"Thanks," I replied. We all stood and brushed off our pants.

"As soon as we get inside, I'm going to find Lydia and insist Fred gets a room," Kelly said.

"Good. You go ahead and we'll be in shortly."

Kelly nodded at me and took off in the golf cart with the kids. The rest of us walked to the barn. Burt had stripped his horse down, brushed him, and neatly stacked his gear. Fred didn't have much, a bedroll and saddlebags, but Sammy carried them proudly.

We'd barely got to the door when Kelly met us.

"Piece of cake," she said with a grin. "Lydia likes me. Follow me."

"Alright, I'm going to deal with the kids," she said and gave Fred another hug before leaving.

Fred walked in his new room and gave it a cursory once over. "It's going to be a little strange sleeping in a real bed."

I chuckled. "I think you'll get used to it."

Fred looked around some more, and then focused on Sammy. "Mister Sam, I'd like to speak with Zach in private. I hope you understand."

"Yes, sir," Sammy responded and quickly left, closing the door behind him.

Fred walked over and sat on the edge of the bed. "I suppose I should take a shower before getting in between these clean sheets."

I nodded and waited. I knew he wanted to talk, but Fred wasn't one to speak casually. When he had something he wanted to say, he'd chew on it a minute and form it in his head before his mouth moved.

"So, I'm out there in the corn field, just hoeing out the weeds, and all of a sudden, I'm lying on the ground and in a world of pain." He unbuttoned his shirt and spread it open. There was an ugly puckered scar on the upper left side of his chest.

"I'd say he aimed center mass, but his aim was off a might," he said. "It went clean through, nicked the scapula, maybe did a little nerve damage. It's still healing up."

"What'd you do?"

"I played dead for a while. When I was sure nobody was going to walk up and finish the job, I managed to get my handkerchief into the front hole. My back was caked in mud, so it probably staunched the blood. Then I started crawling through the rows of corn. Bo had been out fishing. He laid low and found me the next day."

"Bo's alive?" I asked.

Fred nodded. "He was. Penny was too. She gave birth to a little girl."

"Yeah, we went to Bo's place, but nobody was there."

"We had a spot of trouble one day. Bo had to kill a few boys, but they had friends. Bo was a proud new daddy and was worried, so we went to a little cabin out in Hickman County."

"I think I know why, but why didn't y'all go back to the school?"

"None of us liked those people, and we weren't certain whether or not they were involved in the murders."

"Okay, so what happened?"

Fred's features darkened. "We were doing okay. It was only us three and the baby, but we were doing okay. Then, Bo came home from hunting one evening and complained of a headache. He'd somehow got infected. He turned sometime during the night and attacked Penny. I had to kill them both."

I shook my head sadly. Bo was a good man and a good friend to Fred. I knew it must have been hard on him. "What happened to the little girl?"

"I came across a group of people led by an overly large man who I had a conversation with once on the CB radio. They said they knew you."

My eyes widened. "Big Country?" I asked.

Fred nodded again. "Big Country, his wife and sister, and a man with a bad arm."

"Floyd," I said.

"Yeah. They told me about the rendezvous and how you were still alive."

"Wow," I said. "So they're doing okay?"

Fred nodded.

"How long ago was that?"

"About a month ago. When they told me you were still alive, I left the little girl with them and went back to the school. Marc, Ward, and Tonya were there."

I frowned in puzzlement. "What about the rest?"

"Murdered," Fred answered. He paused to take his boots off. "Some marauders hit them in the middle of the night. They managed to fight them off, but everyone was killed except those three. I guess it happened not too long after you guys had left."

"Even the kids?" I asked.

Fred nodded somberly. "All but three; Brittany and the two twins." He scratched his ear. "I guess I'm getting old, I can't remember the names of those twins for the life of me."

"Melinda and Melissa. They were Gus's kids. Brittany was an orphan girl they picked up along the way."

"Yeah, that sounds right. So, Tonya, Marc, and Ward sat me down and told me everything that'd happened since I got shot. Then they told me about Mount Weather and gave me the map you'd left with Tonya."

I sat in the lone chair and held my face in my hands. It was sad news. I barely knew some of the people who'd recently come from the CDC, but I liked Rhonda. I even liked the kids. It was going to be tough telling Kelly.

Fred stretched his feet out and wiggled his toes. His socks were heavily soiled and had holes in them.

"Okay, I have to ask, why didn't you use a car? You could have gotten here a lot sooner."

Fred shook his head slightly. "Cars are too undependable these days. I'm better on a horse. It's slower, but I can see and hear things on a horse that I wouldn't be able to in a car."

It made sense. Fred was an outdoorsman, through and through. Riding all day on a horse and sleeping on a bedroll under the stars was no problem for a man like him.

"You run into any trouble?" I asked.

"A couple of hordes. I managed to avoid them. Oh, I bumped into some people in Bristol. They talked about y'all, but I didn't let on that I knew you."

"Ah, that had to be Joe and his two kids," I said.

"Yeah, I met Riley, never saw the son, but I knew he was there." He scratched his head. "I got an odd feeling about them. I didn't stick around."

"Yeah, same with me, but they treated us well enough."

"How's Sarah?" Fred casually asked. I looked at him, realizing I had not mentioned her.

"She's good," I said. "She's currently out on a mission to Fort Detrick. They're attempting to get a lab up and running and create a vaccine."

He looked at me for a moment. "They've found a cure?"

"Right now, it's a definite maybe." I explained how it all came about and how it turned into Colonel Coltrane deciding he needed to abduct us. Fred listened quietly.

When I was finished, he was quiet for a minute before speaking again. "Tonya said Sarah has gone and hooked up with somebody."

"Yeah, Rachel Benoit. She's a sergeant in the Army. She came up from the CDC. She's nice. Has a zany sense of humor. You'd like her."

Fred took the news in silence and looked at his toes sticking out of his socks.

"I've got extras back in the room," I said. "I'll get you a couple of pairs."

"Appreciate it," he replied and stood. "I think I'll take a long shower and hit the sack. What time do you roll out of bed in the morning?"

"How about five? I have guard duty at seven, so we'll have a little time to get a cup of coffee, and I'll get Burt to show you around and get you acquainted." I grinned. "I have a feeling you and him are going to become fast friends. He's a little bit, uh, loquacious though."

"Loquacious?"

"He's a talker," I said.

When I walked in our room, Kelly had Macie and Frederick tucked in and was reading them a bedtime story.

"Contrariwise, continued Tweedle-Dee, if it was so, it might be, and if it were so, it would be; but as it isn't, it ain't. That's logic!"

Frederick laughed gleefully while Macie looked confused. She could barely keep her eyes open, but little Frederick looked wide awake and could stay up all night. He looked up and saw me.

"Hi, Daddy," he said with a big smile.

I walked over to the bed and sat on the edge. "Hi yourself, big guy," and gave him a hug. Macie did not want to be left out, and although she was too tired to sit up, she held her arms out expectantly. I leaned over and gave her a hug too.

After we had gotten them to sleep, I told Kelly about the deaths of the others. I then held her in my arms while she sobbed quietly.

"There's so much death in this world now," she lamented. "Will it ever change?"

I held her tightly. "I don't know, sweetheart."

Fred was awake and waiting for me the next morning when I knocked on his door.

"Fresh socks," I said with a grin and handed them over. "I got fresh jeans and a couple of shirts too." He gave one of his famous micro expressions, letting me know he was immensely grateful before he set everything on the bed, took the pair of socks, and walked over to a nearby chair.

"I believe my feet will be pleasantly surprised," he said as he sat down and put them on. He wiggled his toes in satisfaction before putting his boots on.

"I'm pretty sure I can scrounge up a new pair of boots too," I said as the two of us walked down the hallway.

172

"How did Kelly take the news?" he asked.

"About like what you'd expect. First, there was grief, then she started feeling guilty for us not being there for them."

"Yeah," he said in understanding. After a moment, he changed the subject.

"Tell me the layout of this place," he requested.

"There's some good people here, but I swear to goodness, they should have left the politicians back in DC. They think the best way to solve a problem is to talk about it for hours, weeks even. The people who do the real work around here put up with them for some reason."

We'd barely made it to our table when Burt burst through the door. He spotted us and quickly walked over. I already had a cup of coffee poured for him.

"Hot damn, I can tell this is going to be a good day already. Are you men ready to do some good old-fashioned farm work?"

"I'm afraid it's only going to be you two. I'm relegated to guard duty." I looked at my watch. "I report in an hour."

Burt looked crestfallen for a moment, but then his grin returned. "Alright," he said. "Let's get some breakfast and then we'll get started."

CHAPTER 25 – MELVIN'S RETURN

"Mount Weather," Melvin announced as they drove up to the main gate. Those zombies had held them at bay for hours before they could get back on the road and didn't roll in until eighteen hundred hours.

He parked his truck off to the side and killed the engine.

"We're not going in?" Savannah asked.

"I have to keep my truck parked outside of the compound because of Peggy."

"Let me guess, nobody wants a zombie inside the fence," she surmised.

"You'd be correct; they take a dim view of her."

"I wonder why?" she asked sarcastically.

Melvin gave her a look. "C'mon," he said and got out of the truck.

"Howdy, Slim," Melvin greeted the man in the shack. Slim was a skinny twenty year old with a constant grin who could eat all day and not gain a single pound.

There was always supposed to be a minimum of two guards at all times. Melvin started to ask where his partner was, but then decided he didn't care. He was tired from the road and hungry.

"Well, well, well," Slim said. "You've been gone a while this time."

"Did you miss me?" Melvin asked.

Slim responded with a boyish grin. "I missed Peggy."

Melvin chuckled. He liked Slim.

"Anything going on?" he asked.

"We got some new people the other day," Slim said. "All the way from Tennessee. One of the dudes caught Paul and Priss breaking into his trailer and beat the hell out of them."

Melvin chuckled. "Sorry I missed that one. Paul is a smart-mouthed punk."

"Yep, so is his sister."

"Well, we're going to hustle to the cafeteria before they shut it down for the night. Keep an eye on my stuff, will ya?"

"Sure, Melvin," he said. "I'll take real good care of Peggy," he chuckled and then focused on Savannah for the first time as the two of them walked off.

174

"Hey, wait, Melvin. Who's that? She can't go in 'til she's been tested!"

Melvin gave a flippant wave and kept walking. Savannah looked back questioningly before hurrying to keep up with Melvin.

"Holy shit," Savannah muttered when they walked into the cafeteria. She stopped to take everything in and then followed the crowd to the buffet line. Her appearance, raggedy clothes with dried mud, got her more than a couple of suspicious looks, but she only had eyes for the food and began loading up a tray. Melvin watched her in amusement before spotting Fosswell, Stark, and some others sitting at their usual table. He walked over.

"Good evening, sirs and-or ma'am's," Melvin said to the table and then focused on Stark. "You want a report now, or in the morning?"

Stark took a drink from a glass of water and eyed Melvin coolly. "Considering you've let an individual into the compound who I would guess hasn't yet been tested, perhaps you should do it now," he said.

Melvin sat, but before he got started, Savannah slapped the tray down on the table and sat beside him. "I got enough for both of us," she said, and gave Melvin a sarcastic look as she daintily unfolded a napkin and placed it in her lap. She then picked up a knife and fork and with the same daintiness cut into the hamburger steak.

"This is Savannah. We met in Oak Ridge," Melvin explained. Savannah glanced at them shyly before concentrating on her food.

"Have you vetted her?" one of them asked.

"Of course," Melvin answered and started to speak, but Savannah interrupted him.

"What's vetting?" she asked.

"It's where I check you out and make sure you're not a spy or some crazy chick whose intention is to cause problems."

"Oh," she said and looked back at the person, who was one of Stark's aides. "I'm not crazy," she said plainly.

"You see? There you go," Melvin said. "Properly vetted."

Savannah held up a fork with a piece of meat on it in front of Melvin. He stuck it in his mouth and chewed.

"Not bad at all," he said.

"Sergeant Clark, if you please," General Fosswell said.

"Y-12 is occupied. They wouldn't let us in, but they seem to have a really sweet operation going. They have power, water, food, advanced fortifications, you name it. I spoke to a man who was presumably their leader, but he only identified himself as Doc Kries."

Stark nodded at one of his aides, who opened a laptop and started tapping on the keyboard, presumably doing a name search.

"How is their health?" Stark asked. "They appeared to be in good shape," Melvin answered. "I didn't see all of them, but the men were

175

healthy, nourished, clean-shaven. They had gardens, crops, and some cattle. I'd say they've done alright for themselves."

"Weaponry?" Seth asked.

"All were armed with Heckler and Koch MP5s. Each man also had a handgun as a backup weapon, and all of them had level two holsters. None of that stuck in their waistband nonsense, and each had pouches for extra magazines. It gave me the impression they were disciplined. I didn't see anything heavier, no tanks, artillery, or mortar pits."

"Are they nuclear?" he asked.

Melvin nodded. "The cooling tower had water vapor coming out of it. They have plenty of power."

"They have little kids," Savannah said. "I saw a bunch of them. Maybe ten or twelve. And they looked healthy, and clean, and they were running around playing and having fun, and that kind of tells you they ain't starving. They wouldn't be having fun if they were starving."

She looked around to see everyone at the table staring at her, suddenly causing her to become embarrassed. "I took pictures," she added, her voice trailing off.

Secretary Stark regarded her thoughtfully while General Fosswell's expression was anything but thoughtful. He seemed irritated at her mere presence and it showed.

Stark focused back on Melvin. "Thank you both for your input. I'll expect a full report from you ASAP, Sergeant. In the meantime, I'm sure you two want to enjoy your dinner."

Melvin recognized he was being dismissed. "You'll have it, sir," he said, stood, and motioned Savannah to follow him.

"Why'd we change tables?" Savannah asked as they sat.

"They don't know you, so they weren't comfortable talking about things with you present."

"Oh." She drank some water and then looked at Melvin again.

"So, you report to a general, that's pretty cool. Is he the head motherfucker in charge?"

"Language?" Melvin chided. Savannah rolled her eyes. "In answer to your question, that was the secretary of defense I was speaking to. The other guy is a general, but no, they're not the head honcho, the president is." He gestured. "He's sitting right over there."

Savannah looked over. "He looks older in real life," she said and then continued eating.

Melvin had only gotten a couple of bites of the hamburger steak when he felt a presence. He looked up to see Doctor Salisbury standing over him. She was an African American woman in her mid-forties who had been stranded and trapped within the confines of Georgetown hospital for over a year.

"Hi, Doc, what's cooking?" Melvin asked.

"It would appear that once again you have brought someone into Mount Weather without allowing for the testing protocol to take place first."

"Are you talking about me?" Savannah asked.

"Yes, I am, young lady," Doctor Salisbury said and again looked pointedly at Melvin.

Melvin gestured with his fork. "Doctor Salisbury, meet Savannah Stratton. Doctor Salisbury is my personal proctologist."

Doctor Salisbury emitted a sigh as she frowned and cast a brief glance heavenward. "Melvin, could we please dispense with your callous brand of humor? This is a serious matter."

"What is she talking about?" Savannah asked.

Melvin chewed and swallowed before answering. "Before anyone is allowed into Mount Weather, they have to be tested first to see if they're infected."

"Oh." She looked at Doctor Salisbury. "I'm not infected," she declared.

Doctor Salisbury continued frowning. "Be that as it may, we have protocols in place. I'm going to have to bring this matter to the attention of General Fosswell and have this young lady quarantined until she is tested."

"What kind of tests?" Savannah asked.

"Blood tests," Doctor Salisbury replied as she eyed Savannah's skinny torso. "When is the last time you've had a full checkup, dear?"

Savannah shrugged. "I guess maybe back when I was thirteen or fourteen. Back before, you know?"

The doctor appraised Savannah and was about to speak, but Melvin interrupted.

"Now, Doc, General Fosswell has already met her. He has enough on his plate already. You don't need to be bothering him with trivial matters."

"This is not a trivial matter, Mister Clark."

He sighed. "I understand," he replied and fished into his shirt pocket. As he did so, he caught sight of a particular woman sitting at a table on the far end of the cafeteria, giving him a hard stare. The fact that she was sitting next to her husband did not seem to dissuade her. Melvin quickly turned away and refocused on the doctor.

"I brought you a present, Doc," he said.

Doctor Salisbury looked down at a small strip of paper Melvin was holding.

"You know what it is, right?" he asked.

She took it out of his hand and inspected it.

"Of course, it's a test strip for a blood coagulation test meter."

Melvin nodded. "Yep, you're exactly right. On our way back here, Savannah and I happened upon one of those health clinics. It was mostly empty, you know how it goes, but Savannah found a box of about a thousand of these little rascals sitting in a drawer."

"Very nice, Melvin, but they're worthless without a meter, and we don't have any." Doctor Salisbury pointed at Savannah. "Now, I must insist you escort Savannah out of the compound until she can be tested."

Melvin once again nodded in seeming agreement. "You say you don't have a meter?" he asked.

Now, Doctor Salisbury arched an eyebrow. "Melvin Clark, what are you up to?"

Melvin helped himself to a forkful of green beans before answering. "I've got two," he said casually.

"Two? Two testing meters?"

"Yep, found them still hooked up to their chargers, and they look like they've hardly been used."

Doctor Salisbury folded her arms as she stared at Melvin, watching him eat. "Alright, I'm listening."

Melvin pointed his fork at Savannah. "I've been with her for a couple of days now. If memory serves me correctly, you and those other smart people gave us a lecture about infected people and you yourself said the symptoms will manifest itself no later than twenty-four hours after being exposed. Right?"

He waited for Doctor Salisbury to respond, but she merely kept staring at Melvin.

"So, with that in mind, I've not seen any kind of zombie symptoms. Besides, you won't be bothered to do tests until in the morning anyway. Let's do this; how about I keep her with me for the night? I'll keep her locked up in my room and, first thing in the morning, I'll bring her to medical."

"Don't I have a say-so in this?" Savannah asked with a touch of indignation.

"No," Melvin replied curtly and then looked at the doctor expectantly.

Doctor Salisbury stared hard at Melvin, as if he were hatching some evil plot to infect Mount Weather for nefarious purposes. She then eyed Savannah up and down, looking for any telltale signs of infection.

"Alright, but she better be secured in your room, away from other people." She then looked at Savannah. "I'll see you promptly at eight."

"You got it, Doc," Melvin said.

"And bring those meters," she said before walking off.

After eating, the two of them went to Melvin's truck and gathered some gear.

"What do you do with Peggy?" Savannah asked.

"If I think it's going to be bad weather, I'll throw a tarp over her. Otherwise, I leave her like she is."

"Are you ever going to kill her?"

"Hell, I don't know," Melvin answered. He thought about it as they walked back. He knew she was never going to get back to normal, and yet, he couldn't bring himself to putting a bullet in her head. Someone once commented, he couldn't remember who, but they said it was the best way to give mercy to people who were no longer human.

Melvin had been lucky enough to be assigned a room. It was so small it reminded him of a prison cell, but he was grateful all the same. There were about a dozen people who still slept in the dorm, but Melvin was a light sleeper and listening to other people snoring and farting all night was not his idea of fun. Besides, the guys who lived in the dorm loved to get high. They'd smoke until the late hours of the night. Melvin didn't care, but the smoke was overwhelming and he never cared for marijuana.

"Uh, this place could use some cleaning," Savannah said when they walked in. He looked around. She was right; his room was filthy.

"Yeah, well, I've been meaning to get around to it."

"Where's the bathroom?"

"Down the hall," Melvin answered. "There's a male and female locker room. The luxury suites have their own restrooms, but not us."

"I'd really like to take a hot shower," she said. "I haven't had one of those in I don't know how long."

"Yeah, go ahead," Melvin said. He dug in a drawer for a couple of towels and a fresh pullover shirt for her to wear. "I think I'm going to do the same. I'll leave the door unlocked; just make yourself at home if I'm not here when you get through."

"Okay."

Melvin unlaced his boots and tossed them in a corner. He looked around. Savannah was right; his room was filthy. If he didn't have a work detail tomorrow, maybe he'd work on it a little.

But, there was an urgent issue he had to attend to right away. He grabbed his toiletry kit, a towel, and hustled down the hallway. He heard someone in one of the shower stalls, singing off-key. He set his stuff on a bench and then hurried into a toilet stall. He dropped his pants and sat.

That was the thing about MREs. They stopped you up. There was nothing like some fresh vegetables to loosen things up. He closed his eyes in relaxation as nature took its course. Whoever was showering was finished now. Melvin could hear them drying off and dressing, then he heard the sound of the locker room door. He was alone now, which certainly helped with his current activity.

Oh, this one is going to be a double-flusher, he thought, but that was okay. Get it all out now, he thought. His thoughts were interrupted by the sound of the locker room door opening.

"Melvin?" Savannah asked.

Damn, he thought, can't a man have a little private time?

"I'm a little busy at the moment," he said.

"Okay," she said. He kept waiting for the sound of the door, but he never heard it.

"Go back to the room," he ordered. "I'll see you in a few minutes."

Finally, he heard the door. He flushed, opened the door, and peeked out. Satisfied she was gone, he walked across the locker room to the showers.

She was sitting on the bed wrapped in a towel waiting for him.

"That was wonderful," she said with a smile.

"Yeah." He opened a dresser drawer, found a hairbrush, and handed it to her. She could see the mirror from where she sat and began brushing her hair out. He couldn't help but noticed how much better it looked once she'd washed it with real shampoo.

Once finished, she slipped on the shirt and then crawled under the covers. Melvin put on a fresh T-shirt and a raggedy pair of sweatpants.

"Alright, sleep good. I'm going to crash out in the dorm," he said.

"You're leaving?"

Melvin nodded.

"Stay here," she requested.

Melvin insisted he was going to sleep in the dorm; Savannah argued she wasn't going to steal his bed and would, therefore, join him in the dorm. After arguing the point back and forth, Melvin gave up and found himself in the bed with her.

"This is nice," Savannah cooed as she snuggled close. "But your sheets smell like a monkey's ass."

CHAPTER 26 – SAVANNAH'S PHYSICAL

"I have good news and not so good news," Doctor Salisbury said and looked at Savannah with what she hoped was a reassuring smile. "You aren't infected."

"Okay, I knew that already," Savannah replied.

Melvin had surprised her the next morning. He'd awoken early and washed her only set of clothes. Although they were clean now, she still looked like a ragamuffin. Doctor Salisbury continued.

"The not-so-good news. You're suffering from malnourishment. I'm sure it has to do with how you were living and not something like anorexia, correct?"

"Yes, ma'am. I mean, no ma'am. I'm not anorexic. I've been through a rough time recently is all, but it's all good now, and I had a big dinner last night."

"Okay, good. And now, for some more unpleasant news; you have chlamydia. Based on my examination, you also have what is commonly referred to as pelvic inflammatory disease."

She waited for a response, but Savannah remained quiet and slowly folded her arms around her. "You may have noticed some symptoms. Painful urination? Perhaps an unpleasant odor?"

Savannah reluctantly nodded as she stared at a spot on the tile floor.

"Okay, I'm going to prescribe you some antibiotics. Take all of them, and do not engage in sexual activity until you've completed your dosage. The symptoms should clear up, but I want you back here in two weeks for a follow-up. In the meantime, eat."

"Okay," Savannah answered, wondering if she was still going to be around in two weeks.

"Have you and Melvin been engaging in any type of sexual acts?"

"No, ma'am," Savannah answered. "I mean, he's nice to me, but there's been no sex. I don't think he's interested in me like that." Probably because my ribs poke out like a skeleton and up until recently I was a whore for a group of scumbags, she thought.

Doctor Salisbury eyed her, as if wondering if she were telling the truth or not. "There is one other thing," she said.

Savannah looked at her expectantly.

"The PID has caused issues. You will most likely be unable to have children."

"Okay," Savannah said in almost a whisper. She stared off into space as she wondered why God had been so cruel to her.

Doctor Salisbury sat beside her. "Tell me what happened to you, dear."

Savannah hugged herself tighter with her arms and remained stubbornly silent. The doctor waited for a few minutes before relenting and giving Savannah a reassuring pat on the leg.

"Well, if you ever need someone to talk to, I'm here, okay?"

"Can I go now?"

Doctor Salisbury stood and gave her a motherly expression. "Of course. Be sure to follow my instructions. The dentist is next door."

She waited until Savannah had left before getting on the phone and calling General Fosswell. In an uncharacteristic move for a doctor, she gave a full recounting of Savannah's health issues.

"So, she's putting Weather at risk of spreading STDs," he surmised.

"I don't think so," Doctor Salisbury responded. "She's obviously been traumatized; I'd guess there's been at least one incident of rape. The good news, if it's good news, she's formed an attachment to Melvin. I don't see her sleeping around. The only person at risk of contracting an STD from her would be him."

"Let's hope you're right, Doctor."

General Fosswell drummed his fingers in silent thought. He glanced over at his desk to a framed photograph. It was a picture of him in his twenties, arm around a pretty blonde who was close to his age. They were dressed in formal attire. It was his wife. The venue was a soiree at her parent's country club.

Happier times.

General Harlan Fosswell thought of himself as a good Christian, Catholic to be precise. His wife was the first person he knew who became infected. He and his son buried her in the backyard before loading up their belongings in his government-assigned Lincoln Navigator and driving directly to Mount Weather.

Harlan looked at his Bible. It was lying beside the photo and opened to the book of Revelations. Verse 16:21 to be exact. He'd read it so many times he had memorized it long ago. He believed the Lord was using the plague to punishing mankind. And, it wouldn't do for a couple of crazy scientists to create a vaccine so the unjust could continue living.

Gunderson. Zachariah Gunderson. The young man had some sort of immunity. Even if he sabotaged the second mission like he did the first, Gunderson was an endless supply of untainted blood.

He had no idea what happened to the soldiers in the first mission. The original plan was simple. He cozied up to his scientist friend and converted him. Craddock. Mayo Craddock. He talked him into taking a vial of the plague and surreptitiously breaking it inside one of the labs. The ensuing tests would identify it as a hot zone, the mission would be aborted, and everyone would come back home.

Nobody came back. Something went wrong. Logic dictated they were now dead or zombified. He certainly did not mean for anyone to die needlessly. But, so be it. It was the will of the Lord.

Untainted blood.

Harlan was convinced this was contrary to the Lord's will. He picked up the phone and dialed three numbers.

"Get in here," he ordered. He was already scheming. He knew what people did in those guard shacks to while away the boredom; that's why he got Melvin paired up with the senator's wife. That one worked out splendidly. Melvin didn't know it, but Senator Duckworth was all too aware of his wife's illicit affair.

That's also why he put Zach and Priss together. He was sure Rhinehart's whore of a daughter would successfully seduce Zach, but somehow it did not work. Priss was probably too much of an arrogant bitch for the hayseed, but a whore closer to his own age would work. He was sure of it. Once he caught an STD and passed it along to his wife, his value to Mount Weather would come to an end. He'd either have to leave or, better yet, Melvin would kill him. He smiled smugly at himself as his plan formulated in his mind.

"You don't have any cavities, but your teeth could stand a good cleaning," the dentist said. He was a thin waspish-looking man who didn't bother introducing himself. "You'll have to schedule an appointment for later. I have other things to do today." With that, he shooed Savannah out of the office.

Savannah aimlessly wandered around the main facility looking for Melvin, and, not finding him inside, went outside to the main gate. His truck was gone. She felt a knot in her stomach and walked over to the guard shack.

"Have you seen Melvin?" she asked them.

"Yeah, he left out this morning," one of the guards replied. "I haven't seen you around here."

"Are you new?" the other one asked.

"Yeah," she answered. "I got here yesterday evening."

"Uh, have you been checked out?" he asked.

Savannah nodded. "I met with Doctor Salisbury this morning."

She could see the two men visibly relax. "So, do you guys know where Melvin went?" she asked.

"Ole crazy Melvin comes and goes," the first one said. "Anyone leaving is supposed to let us know where they're going and how long they'll be gone, but he never follows protocol. Are you a friend or something?"

"Yeah," she answered. She wasn't a relative, but she wasn't sure how to label her relationship with Melvin.

"Well, I wouldn't worry," the first one said. "Melvin can handle himself. He'll be back for dinner, guaranteed."

"Thanks," Savannah said and walked back inside.

She found herself aimlessly wandering and found herself staring into an open room of what was obviously the children's day care. There were several kids of various ages being tended to by four women. One of them was standing in front of a dry erase board trying to teach some simple math. Another one of them saw Savannah and walked over.

"Hi," she said. "I'm Kelly. I'm new here and haven't met everyone yet."

"I'm Savannah; I'm new too."

"I'm happy to meet you, Savannah."

"Is this a school or something?"

"A combination of a day care and school, yes. Do you have any kids?" Kelly asked.

Savannah found herself biting her lip as she shook her head. Kelly noticed it as well.

"Well, those three are mine," she said, pointing. "The older one is Sammy. He's an orphan from Oklahoma. The younger boy is Frederick, and the little girl is Macie."

Savannah looked at her as Kelly smiled.

"They're a handful. Well, Sammy isn't. He's quiet and adores Zach, but Frederick is full of energy and is constantly getting into everything." She smiled again. "And Macie is a typical girl, she loves attention."

Kelly expected some type of reaction or response, she usually got one when she talked about the kids, but Savannah remained quiet and continued to stare at the children. Kelly opted to change the subject.

"So, I thought I saw you with Melvin at dinner yesterday."

Savannah nodded. "Yeah, we met out on the road. I, um, well, my family was killed and Melvin found me. He brought me here."

Kelly nodded in seeming understanding. "He seems to be a unique person."

"Everyone thinks he's crazy, but he ain't," Savannah replied quickly with a trace of defensiveness. "On account of his zombie wife, I guess."

"It's definitely not something a person would normally do," Kelly reasoned.

"Yeah. I told him he should kill her."

Kelly paused a long moment before speaking. "Sweetie, are those the only clothes you have? I mean, I couldn't help but notice you were wearing them last night and they look a little rough."

Savannah dropped her head but didn't say anything. Wonderful, she thought. First, a stranger tells her she has STDs and now, another stranger is making fun of her clothing.

Kelly realized she'd hit a sore spot and tried to smooth it over.

"Well, okay," she said. "It's none of my business, but if you're interested, I have more clothes than I know what to do with stored in our trailer outside. If you want, we can find some for you."

Now, Savannah looked up. "You'd do that?" she asked.

Savannah walked in Melvin's room an hour later carrying an armful of clothing.

"Honey, I'm home," she said cheerfully. There was no response. She dropped the clothes on the bed and looked around. No Melvin, no note. Realizing she didn't even know what time it was, she spotted a clock on the nightstand, but it wasn't working. Changing into a fresh pair of jeans and a polo shirt, she checked herself in the mirror. The clothes, the smallest size Kelly had, hung a little loosely on her.

"I'll grow into them," she murmured and again wondered where Melvin was. She stuck her head out of the door and looked down the hallway, but nobody was in sight. Sighing, she focused on sorting and folding her new clothing. There was a generic dresser in the small room, and she decided to use one of the drawers, hoping Melvin wouldn't mind. But, there was a problem. Melvin's clothing was carelessly stuffed into each drawer. She did a sniff test and wrinkled her nose.

"Men," she exclaimed and proceeded to dump each drawer onto the bed. She spent the next two hours in the laundry room. When everything was dry, she made two trips back to the room with arms full of clothing and began the task of sorting and folding.

She was deep in thought of what she was going to do with her life when she was startled by a soft knock on the door. When she opened it, there was a woman standing there whom she had not met.

"Um, I'm looking for Melvin," she said as she looked over Savannah's shoulder.

"He's not here."

"Where is he?" she asked. The woman was an attractive strawberry-blonde in her mid-thirties. The way she was staring at Savannah hit her wrong and she was immediately suspicious.

"I don't know where he is," she said. "Who are you?"

She stared at Savannah a moment longer before turning on her heel and walking away. She passed Kelly and another woman walking in the opposite direction. The two exchanged glances, Kelly said hello, but the woman ignored her and kept walking.

"Hi again," Kelly said with a smile when they'd walked up. "This is Maria. She came from Tennessee with us."

"Hi," Maria said with a quiet smile. "How are the clothes? Do they fit?"

"A little loose, but I'll grow into them." Savannah felt the need to explain. "I went through a rough time recently and didn't get much to eat."

"Oh, well, you'll have your weight back in no time," Kelly replied. "Speaking of eating, we're meeting everyone for lunch and we were coming to invite you."

"Sure," Savannah said, wondering if she should instead wait in the room for Melvin. Her growling stomach won out. She shut the door and joined the two women.

"Do you know that woman who walked by you just now?" she asked.

"Yeah," Kelly answered. "Angela Duckworth."

"Do you know anything about her?"

"Not really," Kelly answered. "She's pleasant enough, but kind of aloof. Oh, her husband is Bob Duckworth, he's a senator from Utah, I believe. Has she done something?"

"Oh, no. She was looking for Melvin. I'm sure he'll turn up for lunch." She looked down the hall as they walked. "Where are the kids?"

"They're with Janet," Kelly said. "I guess I need to go ahead and warn you about her." Kelly filled her in as they walked and were soon nearing the cafeteria.

"So, let me get this straight, Janet is Zach's mother-in-law from his first wife and the kids aren't really yours."

"They may not be my biological children, but they're mine," Kelly replied. "I love 'em to death."

"And Janet is a bitch," Maria said with emphasis.

"With a capital B," Kelly added.

The two women laughed and Savannah smiled uncertainly as they walked into the cafeteria. When they walked through the double doors, the cooking aromas caused her stomach to growl, which she took as a good sign. She refrained from running to get in line and forced herself to walk casually with the rest of them.

"Looks like today's special is shit on a shingle," a man in front of her joked. Savannah didn't care what it was; she was ravenous. She looked around for Melvin, but not seeing him, followed Kelly.

186

"Everyone, this is Savannah," Kelly said when they got seated and introduced everyone individually.

"Where's Melvin?" one of them asked. Savannah looked up to see the one who called himself Shooter doing the asking. For some reason, she had taken an instant disliking to him. Whenever he looked at her, he stared longer than was necessary. An attractive woman his age was sitting beside him.

"I don't know," Savannah answered.

"He's probably having a romantic picnic with his wife,"

The woman sitting beside him snickered. The other one, the one who called himself Cutter, laughed gleefully.

"That's messed up, man," a young Hispanic man said. He'd walked up as Shooter was making the disparaging remarks and sat down across from her. Savannah glanced at him for a quick second. She thought he was cute, but he needed to shave off the pencil-thin moustache. It made him look stupid.

"What're you doing with him anyway? He's old enough to be your father," Cutter remarked.

Savannah didn't respond and concentrated on her food. She'd already done the math; Melvin was thirty-nine and she was eighteen. Technically, Cutter was right, but for him to point it out angered her all the same.

"You never did say where you're from," Shooter pressed.

Savannah was about to put a forkful of food in her mouth, but paused momentarily and fixed Shooter with a stare. "I'm from a small town called Gofuckyourselfville. I'm sure you've heard of it."

Kelly and a couple others burst out in laughter while Shooter glowered.

"Don't mind those two," the Hispanic man said. "They grow on you after a while. My name's Jorge, I'm Maria's brother."

"It's nice to meet you, Jorge," Savannah responded and tried to mind her manners as she ate.

"So, where are the men?" Janet asked.

"Zach, Josue, and Burt are showing Fred the farms," Kelly answered.

"He doesn't have guard duty again?" Jorge asked.

Kelly shook her head. "He reported in this morning and was told he'd been reassigned to the midnight shift."

"Why?" Jorge asked.

"According to Ensign Boner, somebody was pissed because they felt they had seniority over Zach and yet was stuck on midnight shift while Zach got to work the day shift."

Jorge scoffed. "Figures. At least he won't be stuck with the senator's daughter. I tried to say hello to her yesterday and she turned her nose up at me."

"Speaking of job assignments," Janet said in a low voice. They turned and saw Lydia making her way toward them. She smiled warmly at Kelly.

"Hi, Lydia," Kelly said sweetly.

"Hi, Kelly," she replied. "How are you liking your job assignment?"

"It's wonderful, thanks for taking care of us. Right, Janet?" Kelly pointedly asked.

Janet gave her a look before responding. "Yes, you've been very gracious."

"Yes, well, I need to speak with Melvin, have any of you seen him?" she asked. She received several shakes of the head. Lydia then looked at Savannah.

"Do I understand correctly, you're Melvin's girlfriend?"

"This is Savannah," Kelly said quickly. "She and Melvin are good friends."

"Yes," Lydia said as she glanced at her tablet. "You're scheduled for guard duty tonight."

"But, I'm supposed to stick with Melvin," she said, fighting to keep a quaver out of her voice.

Lydia smiled condescendingly. "Orders are orders. Captain Fosswell is the Officer of the Day. He advised me you are to report directly to the main guard post no later than twenty-three hundred hours. Let's see," she paused a moment and looked on her screen. When she did, her smile faltered.

"It looks like you'll be working with Mister Gunderson," she said, and then looked at Kelly.

Kelly was not to be put off. "Perfect," she said.

"Are you sure?" Lydia asked, her expression uncertain.

"Of course," Kelly said and looked at Savannah with a reassuring smile. "Don't worry, Zach will take care of you."

Janet snorted. "At least he won't be stuck with that Rhinehart bitch," she said.

Savannah almost finished her plate of food before she thought she was going to bust. She excused herself and went back to the room. Melvin still was not there. The ordeal of the physical and a full belly made her sleepy. She didn't remember even lying down. She awoke suddenly with a fright before she realized it was Melvin who had sat on the bed beside her.

"How're you doing, sleepyhead?" he asked with a smile.

Savannah sat up and stretched. "What time is it?" she asked.

Melvin looked at his watch. "About twenty minutes before your guard shift," he said.

"You knew?" she asked.

His expression tightened. "I got told about ten minutes ago."

"Can't you do anything about it?" she asked.

Melvin shook his head. "Somebody's pulling some shenanigans. I've got guard duty too, but I'm the acting sergeant-of-the-guard." He stood and worked a kink out of his back before he realized he was doing exactly what Lonnie had done. He stopped himself.

"What's that?" Savannah asked.

"Sergeant-of-the-guard? It means I've got to keep an eye on the whole compound and can't stay with you the whole time. I'll get to the bottom of it tomorrow, but tonight we're stuck."

She sat up in the bed, looking at Melvin.

"What?" he asked.

"Your girlfriend came looking for you earlier. Is that where you've been all day?"

Melvin stared at her. "She told you?"

"She didn't have to."

Melvin inhaled and let out a sigh. "I was helping Burt at one of the farms. She was waiting for me when I got back."

"Did you do her?" Savannah asked.

"No," he replied quickly. "I'd told her it was over before I left. She seemed to think after a few days on the road, I'd come to my senses. I made it clear she was mistaken."

Savannah wrapped her arm in his and put her head against his shoulder.

"And here I am, getting in the middle of things."

Melvin patted her on the leg. "It's not your fault. Alright, get cleaned up for guard duty."

She would have liked to have taken a fresh shower, but she only had time to brush her teeth. Shortly after walking back to their room, there was a knock on the door.

CHAPTER 27 — ANOTHER SHADE OF GUARD DUTY

Kelly told me how Savannah had reacted when she was told she'd been assigned guard duty and now she was absent from dinner.

"Zach, she looked scared to death," she said. "I'm not sure what's happened to her, but the thought of being away from Melvin and stuck in a little shack with a strange man has unnerved her."

"I'm not strange."

She gave me a lighthearted punch in the arm. "You know what I mean."

So, I got an idea. I raided the cafeteria, made a fresh urn of coffee, fixed a couple of dozen sausage biscuits, and loaded it all up on one of the pushcarts. I rolled it to the elevator and down the hallway to Melvin's room. Zoe was with me, and she acted like we were on a great adventure which was going to culminate with me feeding her all of the sausages.

"Alright," I said to her. "Let's see what kind of reception I'm going to get." I then knocked softly on the door. Melvin opened the door almost immediately.

"Hello," I said. "I'm Zach Gunderson."

"I'm glad to meet you," Melvin said. "In fact, I believe we've met before, out on the road."

"Yeah," I said. "Outside of Roanoke."

"Where are my manners, come on in," Melvin said. "We were just getting ready to go report in."

"Oh, I just wanted to stop by and introduce myself before guard duty. I took the liberty of raiding the cafeteria, so we're going to have hot coffee and some real food to snack on," I said. I then unslung one of the assault rifles I had with me.

"I also went ahead and signed out a rifle for Savannah." I looked at Melvin and explained. "Whoever is running the armory isn't making people clean their weapons before turning them in. So, I checked one out and gave it a quick once over." I then patted the buttstock of the one still slung over my shoulder. "This one is mine. It's good to go."

"What, you didn't bring me one?" Melvin asked questioningly.

I chuckled. "I've heard about you, Sergeant, and I strongly suspect you have your own personal weapon you're going to use."

He responded with a wry grin and retrieved a rifle from behind the open door.

"Yep," he said. He took the rifle I brought for Savannah and handed it to her.

"Check it," he directed. I watched as Savannah ejected the magazine, inspected the bolt, performed a flawless function check, looked over the loaded magazine, and then inserted it, charged the handle, and put it on the safety. She then looked at Melvin expectantly.

"Atta girl," Melvin said. "C'mon, let's get up top."

Melvin drove us to the main post and we relieved the evening shift guards ten minutes early. They showed their gratitude by helping themselves to a couple of the biscuits before leaving.

"I take it you know this guard duty procedure," he said to me.

"Yeah, a little bit," I replied.

He nodded and then focused on Savannah. "Alright, I have other duties to attend to. If there's any issues, get on the field phone. I have someone constantly monitoring it if I'm out and about."

"Okay," she said.

"If anyone comes wandering up, they aren't allowed inside the compound under any circumstances." He saw her looking at him questioningly. "Yeah, I know, we broke that rule, but anyone coming inside the compound has to be tested first.

"I'll be back in an hour, so if you need to go the restroom, I can run you back to the main building."

"Okay," she said again. The nervousness was apparent.

Melvin gave her a reassuring look and then motioned to me. "Zach, can I have a word with you?"

I followed him over to his truck, which was parked about fifty feet down the road. His zombie wife sensed our approach and a hissing noise came out from beneath her helmet.

"Savannah is a little nervous around strangers, especially men," he said in a quiet voice. "She's had a hard time lately."

"Not a problem," I said, remembering Kelly's same admonishment. "I'll be on my best behavior."

"Oh, and she's just now getting her strength back, so she may nod off."

"I'll let her sleep. In fact, if you want, you can send her back to the room. I can take care of it."

Melvin shook his head. "As much as I'd like to, I can't show favoritism."

"Okay," I said in understanding.

"Hmm, let's see," he said and scratched his chin. "Oh, that zombie over there is what's left of my wife. If she starts snarling and raising hell, it means there's zombies nearby."

"Okay, good to know. My dog is a pretty good zombie alarm too," I said, gesturing at Zoe, who had taken a sniff of Peggy and was now growling.

"Well, alright then," Melvin said. "I need to make sure the other guard posts are properly relieved and all of that bullshit."

"She'll be fine, Melvin," I said. "I promise."

He looked at me and nodded. "Alright then."

"What did Melvin say?" Savannah asked after Melvin had ridden away on the golf cart.

"Not much," I said and smiled. "He's just worrying over you." I poured myself a cup of coffee. "Would you like some?" I asked. Savannah tentatively nodded. I poured her a cup and handed it to her.

"I'd love to have some fresh coffee one day," I said. "None of this freeze dried stuff. When I'm free again, I'm going in search of coffee plants."

"Free?" Savannah asked.

I nodded and explained about my immunity and how they were keeping me out of harm's way.

"So, until they've created a vaccine, I'm not allowed to do anything risky. They apparently think guard duty is harmless, which I guess is true enough."

"You're a prisoner then," Savannah said.

"No, it's not like that. I made an agreement with them. I can leave at any time, but this is the best place for my kids to grow up. We have doctors here, a formal education system in place, a fortified location, and don't forget about the Marines. So, I'm trying to conform. What about you? What's your long-term plans?"

"I don't know," she said. "I've been thinking about it, but, I don't know."

We were getting along, but my last two questions seemed to have struck a nerve or something, so I backed off and changed the subject.

"Anyway, Kelly and the kids really like it here. Personally, I'd rather be back home on my farm, but don't tell them that," I said with a small chuckle.

She did not respond and had become quiet. I guess my attempt at light conversation had run its course.

I looked around in the shack and saw a thermal imaging sight. I pulled it out of the case and tried it out. One of the lenses was scratched, but I had no problem seeing objects in the dark. The only thing outside at the moment were trees.

"Have you ever been to the ocean?" Savannah suddenly asked.

I turned the night-sight off and looked at her in the dim red light.

"No, I haven't."

"I did once, when I was a little kid. I remember standing on the beach at the edge of the water. I was too afraid to go in, but the surf felt wonderful on my feet. Every time a wave would come in, my feet would sink a little further in the sand. My uncle told me if I stood there long enough, I'd sink all the way to China."

I chuckled. "Sounds like he liked to joke around."

"I'd like to see the beach again one day," she said softly.

"Maybe one day we can get up a big road trip and all go together," I suggested. "That'd be pretty cool."

"Yeah," Savannah agreed.

I was about to say we'd need to find some fresh fuel somehow before doing something like that, but I didn't want to be a Debbie Downer.

We talked throughout the night. Unlike Priss, Savannah was a pleasant person with a little bit of smartass to her. She reminded me of Andie. I told her so.

"Was she an old girlfriend?" she asked.

I chuckled. "No, she started out as an adversary, but we eventually became good friends. In fact, she saved my life once or twice." I absently rubbed the knife scar on my cheek.

"I take it she's dead."

"Yeah," I replied. "A lot of good people have died and a lot of evil people are out there, still alive."

"Yeah," Savannah replied. There was some anger in her tone and I looked over at her. The dim red light barely illuminated the interior of the guard shack. Even so, I could see pain in her expression.

"People that have lived out there, not these people here at Weather, people like you and me who had no protection of an underground bunker, we've had it rough, but we survived. Andie was petite, but she was tough as nails. I bet you are too."

There was a long pause before she spoke. "Thanks, Zach." She said it so quietly I almost missed it.

Before I knew it, the sky was turning a light gray. I looked at my watch. "Only one hour to go," I said. "Man, this night flew by. Maybe our relief will come early. I don't know about you, but I'm heading straight to bed. Kelly will have the kids in daycare and I'll have a nice, quiet room all to myself."

"This is the first time in a while I've stayed awake for eight hours straight."

I looked at her in understanding. It confirmed what I suspected; she'd been suffering from starvation recently.

"That's a good sign. You're getting stronger." I looked at my watch again. "Time to call in." I started to reach for the phone but Savannah stopped me.

"Let me," she said. She picked up the phone. "Post one, negative SITREP."

I smiled at her as she hung up the phone, but then Zoe awoke suddenly and gave a small bark.

Savannah looked at me in concern. "I heard something too," she said.

My hearing wasn't as good, so I utilized the binoculars. As I watched, a car slowly came into view. When it came to within fifty feet, Savannah gasped. I looked over.

"Do you recognize the car?" I asked.

Savannah looked frightened and tried to answer, but all she could do was stutter.

"Okay, get back on the field phone and call Melvin."

The car, it was a Prius, approached quietly. The driver stopped near the barricade and made a point of showing his hands before getting out. He was an oafish-looking man with a fat face. The passengers, there were two of them, also got out of the car, but lingered back and stood behind the open doors like they were using them as shields. The driver took a long hard look at Melvin's truck, and when he turned back around, he had a goofy grin on his face.

"What can I do for you, gentlemen?" I asked when the piggish-looking man had walked closer.

"Hello," he said and his grin increased in size. "We're friends with Melvin," he said, hooking a thumb back toward Melvin's truck. "We don't..."

He stopped in mid-sentence as he looked at Savannah. His mouth dropped open before turning into a leer. He turned back to his friends.

"Hey, look guys, it's Stinky," he said joyously and then turned back to Savannah with a lascivious grin. "How've you been, Stinky, we've missed you."

Savannah emitted a moan from deep within her throat. I looked back at her. She was holding the phone halfway up to her head in a death grip, her face ashen and fixed in an expression of sheer terror.

When I looked back at the man, he was still grinning, like there was a big joke and Savannah was the punchline. His teeth, the ones he still had, were the color of old corn, making him look even uglier, more sinister. As he continued to leer at Savannah, it dawned on me. Call it an epiphany, a revelation, whatever you wanted. I understood.

I didn't know who he was, but I knew what he was, and I knew what he'd done to Savannah. He and his friends. I took one last look at Savannah, and the decision was crystal clear. The kinder, gentler,

Zachariah Gunderson decided it was time to take a coffee break and let the other Zach take over for a while.

My thumb flicked off the safety with practiced ease as I brought my M4 up to my shoulder. The piggish-looking man's jaw dropped open about a microsecond before the 5.56 full metal jacket entered his skull between his eyes. It was an excellent shot. I could already see Fred giving one of his micro nods of approval.

The oafish one hadn't even hit the pavement before I started shooting at the next one. He already had his weapon out; it looked like an M1. An M1 was a wonderful rifle, but it was heavy. He was still trying to aim it when he caught two rounds, one in the chest, the second one in the neck. I moved on to the third one. He had taken cover behind the car and was now shooting back. I managed to squeeze off one shot before a round hit the wood framing inches from my face.

I ducked down and saw Savannah, still standing there, frozen, staring out like she'd zoned out. I grabbed an arm and pulled her down.

"Look at me!" I yelled. When she did so, I spoke in a calm voice.

"Stay down and wait for Melvin. I'm sure he's heard the gunfire and is on his way."

There was a lull in gunfire. I peeked my head up at about the time I saw the third one disappear into the wood line. I exited the guard shack and it took far too long for me to open up the heavy gate. Once I did so, I took only a second to insert a full magazine before taking off at a run. I entered the woods at the spot where I saw him go in and took up a position behind a tree.

It was a cat-and-mouse game now. I saw a slight amount of ground disturbance and a couple of blood drops. Good, I'd hit him. Probably nothing more than a grazing wound judging from the scant amount of blood, but that was okay. I moved from tree to tree, deeper into the forest. His trail was easy to follow at first because he was blindly running and leaving a trail a blind man could follow. When he finally slowed to a walk, it became harder, but I was not deterred. I continued onward, and kept my eyes open. Suddenly, I heard something behind me. I turned sharply, rifle ready to fire.

It was Zoe. In the heat of the moment, I'd forgotten all about her. She looked up at me with one of those dog expressions wondering why I'd left her. I squatted down and gave her a pat. It was as good a time to test her training as any. I pointed.

"*Such,*" I commanded in a stern voice barely above a whisper. It was the German command for track and was pronounced *Sook.* Zoe hesitated at first. I repeated the command and she started walking, back and forth at first, sniffing the air, but then she took off at a lope.

I ran to keep up and she stopped at a tree a hundred yards ahead. There was a blood smear on the tree trunk and several drops on the ground. He'd stopped here to catch his breath and his wound was bleeding faster now. There was also a Ruger Mini-14 lying on the ground, the fore stock broken. I tapped the ground where the blood spot was.

"*Such,*" I commanded again. Zoe took off at a dead run now. Within seconds, she was barking furiously. I sprinted through the bushes to catch up, crossed a small glade, and approached a thicket of briars where Zoe was standing, the fur on her back standing up.

The man had drug himself into the middle of a briar patch. The briars had scratched his face up and he stared at us both, his face bloody and fixed in a mixture of hatred and fear.

"*Ruhig,*" I commanded. Zoe stopped barking and stood beside me, anxiously waiting for me to give the command to attack.

"Crawl out of there," I ordered.

"Fuck you," he growled.

I coolly appraised him. He wasn't much older than me, but shorter and far skinnier. His acne-covered face was intermixed with blood, sweat, and oil, and he generally appeared as if he wasn't worried much about hygiene. I'd run into his type before and I'd never been impressed.

"Suit yourself," I said and raised my rifle. "The first shot's going in your gut. Then I'll leave you for the zombies."

"Wait!" he cried.

As I held the rifle on him, he slowly crawled out and then worked himself into a sitting position. He cradled a bloody left arm.

"How bad is it?" I asked.

"You shot me through my arm, you sonofabitch," he said. His tone was hateful, threatening. "Wait 'til Lonnie and my boys get ahold of you."

"Who's Lonnie?" I asked.

He cackled now. "He's the leader of the Blackjacks."

"Blackjacks?" I asked.

"Yeah, we're nobody to fuck with." He then snickered. "We're the ones who made Stinky one of our whores. Maybe we'll do the same to you."

I'd had enough. I put the safety on and placed my rifle on the ground. He watched me cautiously. He was on edge, waiting for an opportunity to pounce.

"What's your name?" I asked.

"Ask your mom," he said. "She was screaming it last night."

I chuckled. "Good one."

He thought he was being sneaky as he casually reached behind his back with his good arm. I obliged him and appeared to be distracted by Zoe. He sprang from the ground suddenly and lunged, swinging wildly with a blackjack. I easily stepped out of the way. He was momentarily off balance, which was all I needed.

Or should I say, it was all Zoe needed. She latched on to his arm and bit down. The punk howled in pain. I grabbed the blackjack, wrenched it from his grip, and then put a hard right into his nose. He landed on his back with Zoe still working on the arm. I commanded her to stop her attack and stood there, waiting. He was winded and gasping for breath, but when he looked up at me, the hatred was still there.

"I'm going to kill you real slow," he threatened between breaths.

I smiled. "Ooh, you sound ominous." I put a boot in his nose this time and blood exploded out.

"Any other threats you want to make?" I asked.

He stayed quiet now and stared at me sullenly.

"Part of me wants to take you back because there will be some people who'd like to ask you some questions, but there's a problem."

"What's that?" he asked.

"Savannah," I answered and raised the blackjack.

I eventually found my way out of the forest and onto Morgan's Mill Road. Within minutes, I heard the sound of horses cantering up. It was Fred and Burt.

"Zoe and I could use some water," I said. Fred tossed me a canteen as Burt pulled out his handheld radio and informed them they'd found me.

I knelt and slowly poured water into my cupped hand as Zoe lapped it up. When she was sated, I took a few gulps before handing the canteen back.

"Did you get him?" Burt asked. I nodded. He relayed the information and listened to the response.

"They're sending a vehicle to come get you."

I shook my head. "No, cancel that ride. I'd rather walk back with you two."

Burt nodded and spoke into the radio again. "Okay, done. There's going to be a lot of questions."

"Yep, I imagine so. How's Savannah?"

"She's pretty shook up," Burt said. "Melvin wouldn't let anyone speak to her and locked her in his room."

I nodded. She was in no condition to be peppered with questions by uncaring people. "That's good. She doesn't need any further trauma."

My response caused Fred to look at me oddly; it was more like his right eyebrow twitched a little, but he didn't question it.

Burt was puzzled as well. "Did something happen to her?" he asked. "She didn't look injured."

I shook my head. "It's nothing. Let's get going."

Fred motioned. "Hop on," he said to me. "There's something I want to show you two."

Burt and Zoe followed as Fred led off. He led us to a spot on the road and pointed. Zoe spotted it first and loped up to it. It was an abandoned car, hidden by a lot of tree limbs and brush stacked against it. Zoe sniffed it over as we stared at it.

"Look familiar?" Fred asked.

"Looks just like the car those three fellas were in," Burt said.

He was right. It was a Prius too, and it was even the same color.

Fred motioned for me to dismount and he did the same. "Let's picket the horses here. They'll be okay for a while."

Fred led us deeper into the woods. Eventually, we came upon a dead body. I walked closer and knelt beside it. It was a man, nude except for underwear, and it looked like he'd been chewed on extensively by coyotes and other critters, indicating he'd never been a zombie. The man's clothing, including a crudely made ghillie suit, were lying nearby.

"Yep, he's dead," I said.

"You think?" Burt asked facetiously.

"Did you shoot him?" I asked.

"Knife," Fred replied. "I didn't want to waste a bullet."

"So you snuck up on him and knifed him?" Burt asked.

"Yeah," Fred answered. "He was too focused on you and that girl in the guard shack. He never saw me and he didn't have any backup."

Burt whistled in appreciation.

"I'm not following," I said.

He pointed. "Go that way a little bit and you'll come up on the perimeter fence. He was spying on you people. I'd say he was planning on doing something nasty."

"So, why'd you strip him down to his panties?" Burt asked.

"Makes it easier for the critters. They need to eat too."

Burt nodded like it made perfect sense. "Too bad his face is all chewed up; it'd be nice if I could've seen what he looked like. Could've been I might've knowed him."

Fred pointed at what was left of his right forearm. "He had a tattoo of a snake. I think it was supposed to be a cobra, but it was crudely drawn. Probably a jailhouse tat, and his tongue was split."

Burt frowned. "Doesn't sound familiar."

"He was scouting the place out?" I asked, although Fred had already said as much. He nodded patiently.

"Him and those other three driving the exact same kind of car, that's too much of a coincidence," Burt said. I agreed.

I searched through his pants. Fred must have read my mind.

"He had a fob for that car. I put it behind the driver's side tire. He didn't have anything else but a rifle, knife, a Bic lighter, and this." Fred pulled out a folded-up piece of paper. When I unfolded it, I felt the hair on the back of my neck stand up. Burt looked at it over my shoulder and whistled again.

We went back to the car. I knew Fred had already searched it, but he remained quiet while I searched it again. The interior was filthy and smelled like BO. There was some dirty clothing, a blanket, a couple of jugs of water, a can of chili, and a toiletry kit, but nothing of significance. It started easily.

"Let's take it back," I said. The men agreed. Zoe reluctantly jumped in and rode with me.

I parked beside the other Prius, which had been moved to the side of the road. Zoe growled at Peggy as we walked by her.

The mess had been cleaned up, and it even looked like someone had spread fresh dirt on the bloodstains. There were two new guards present.

"Has anyone seen Melvin?" I asked.

"Not lately," one of them said and pointed at an approaching golf cart. Captain Fosswell was driving. "I was ordered to call as soon as you showed up."

I waited for the captain to stop and walked up to him. "Do you know where Melvin is?"

He ignored my question. "Come with me," he ordered.

"Where are we going?"

"You don't ask me questions. Now turn over your weapon and get in the cart."

I stared at him for a moment and then stepped forward so that we were only inches apart. I spoke in a low voice so the guards couldn't hear me.

"I'm not in the mood for attitude from anybody at the moment. Either change your tone or piss off."

To my surprise, his hand started drifting toward the handgun holstered on his hip.

"Go ahead and try it," I challenged as I adjusted the grip on my M4.

He tried to give me a hard stare, couldn't do it, and put his hand back on the steering wheel.

"Do you want me to tell the command staff you are refusing to meet with them?" he asked. The arrogance was still there, not as significant, but it was still there.

"I want you to get rid of the attitude," I replied. "I've been through enough bullshit for one day, it sounds like I'm about to go through some more bullshit, and I haven't had any sleep in about," I looked at my watch, "twenty hours now."

He gave me a look and then stared straight ahead. "My orders are to escort you to the conference room for a debriefing."

I sighed, walked around to the passenger side of the golf cart, and got in.

"Make a detour over to the kennels and I'll put Zoe up."

CHAPTER 28 – THE INTERROGATION

We walked to the main conference room. The big one. They should put a sign on the door, "The Big Room," or something like that. It was full of people.

There was POTUS, Raymond and Earl, Secretary Stark, his aides, General Fosswell, and an assortment of politicians and their lackeys. If I had to guess, I'd say every politician was present. Sheila was sitting by the president. She was wearing a rather short dress that showed a little bit of cleavage. I usually got a smile from her, but today, she was overly preoccupied with her laptop.

Judging from some of the looks I was getting, a few folks considered me trouble. That's trouble with a capital T which rhymes with Z and that stands for Zach.

There was a singular chair placed in the middle, separate from everyone else. I took my cue and sat.

Seth walked over to me. "I'll need to secure your weapon," he whispered. "I promise I'll get it back to you when this is over."

I gave him a long look before handing over my rifle. Everybody watched as Seth took it out of my hands and then there seemed to be a collective sigh of relief. It was obvious none of these people ever thought about carrying a backup weapon. It was a trait my old buddy Rick instilled in me, and especially after the abduction incident, I always carried a hideout gun hidden in my crotch. It was a little uncomfortable at times, but so what.

After the tension subsided, a few people started having hushed side discussions while others seemed to be reviewing a report or something on their laptops. Hell, for all I knew, they could be playing solitaire.

"Can we get this meeting going?" I asked, although I wasn't asking. "I've got things to do, like sleep."

"Mister Gunderson," President Richmond said. "We are on our timetable now."

"I suggest you get your ass on my timetable, sir. My patience is somewhat limited at the moment."

I saw a flash of anger cross his face, but being a true politician, it passed quickly and was replaced with a patient smile.

"Very well, why don't you start by giving us a synopsis of this morning's events?"

"Certainly. I was on guard duty. Three men approached our facility with nefarious intent. I killed them. End of synopsis."

While the president stared in disbelief, Secretary Stark leaned forward in his chair.

"Son, we're going to need far more detail. You know that."

I took a deep breath. I was not sure of how much detail I wanted to go into. One thing was certain: there were certain facets of my life none of these limp-wristed people needed to know.

"A few minutes before the end of my guard shift was due to end, three men drove up in a Prius."

"A Prius?" one of them asked.

"Yes. One of..."

"Why a Prius?" the same one asked.

"My guess is because a Prius gets excellent gas mileage and it runs quiet. It's an excellent post-apocalyptic vehicle. May I continue now?"

POTUS gave me an impatient nod.

"Alright, so they drive up and stop. One of them, the driver, got out and approached the guard shack while the other two stayed back and took up cover by their car."

"How do you know they were taking cover?" another one asked.

"For the reasons I just articulated," I replied. "I attempted to engage the lead man in friendly conversation. He made a threatening gesture. I took action."

"What type of threatening gesture?" General Fosswell asked.

I replied with an ambiguous shrug. "I'm so tired, I can't recall specifically."

Senator Polacek partially raised her hand. "One of the relief guards stated the man near the guard shack was unarmed."

Her aide quickly whispered to her. She acknowledged her and amended her proclamation. "He was only armed with," she looked at her aide again. "What did you call it?"

"A blackjack."

"Yes, a blackjack," she said. "He had a blackjack in his back pocket, which would indicate he was not holding it in a threatening manner."

I shrugged again. She was undeterred and eyed me shrewdly.

"Would you care to explain why you shot a man who was not posing a threat, Mister Gunderson?"

"I disagree. He *was* a threat. His friends were a threat. I responded to the threat."

She frowned. "Oh, yes, I'd almost forgotten. One of them ran away and you chased after him."

"Correct," I said.

"Did you find him?"

"Yes."

"And?" she pressed.

"And now, he's dead." I leaned forward. "But, since you abhor firearms, you'll be pleased to know, I didn't shoot him." In fact, I bashed his head in with his own blackjack.

Senator Polacek looked at me in befuddlement. I didn't know if she was amused or appalled, but, truth be told, I didn't care. Her expression then turned into an accusing stare.

"You chased him down and killed him," she exclaimed.

"Correct."

"Why?"

"Because he was a threat," I said.

"I think I can fill in some of the blanks," a voice said behind me. I turned. It was Melvin. He'd quietly slipped in while I was talking.

"By all means," Secretary Stark said.

Melvin walked up and stood beside me.

"The three men in question are called Pig, Scooter, and Crash. They're members of the Blackjacks."

"Ah, the Blackjacks," the president said. "I've read a report on them. If I remember correctly, you described them as a roving band of marauders."

"That'd be correct, sir," Melvin said. "They're led by a big, mean brute by the name of Lonnie. They're the ones who've been terrorizing the southern part of Virginia for the past year or so."

"Could you be more specific?" Senator Polacek asked. "How have they been terrorizing?"

"You've seen the young lady with me, right?" he asked.

The senator nodded with a hint of distaste in her expression. Melvin acted as though he didn't notice.

"That's Savannah. The Blackjacks murdered her entire family. She'd previously told Zach how her family was brutally murdered and then recognized them as soon as Pig had walked up. Now, Zach is no naïve little schoolboy. When he was made aware of who, and what they were, he knew they were up to no good and he knew he had to protect Mount Weather."

He looked at me. "Right?"

"Yes."

"Interesting," President Richmond said. There were a few nods of agreement.

"There's more," Melvin said. "I just spoke with Burt and he introduced me to Mister Fred McCoy. He's a recent arrival. Mister McCoy said he caught a man scouting out Mount Weather. He told me about a tattoo on the man's forearm, which I immediately recognized. That man went by the name of Snake. He was a psychopathic SOB, and also a member of the Blackjacks."

"What do you mean, *was*?" Senator Polacek asked.

"Because he's no longer an is. He's a was." Melvin saw the senator's blank expression and explained. "That means he's dead."

Melvin knew he had their attention and wagged a finger.

"Snake always deferred to their leader, Lonnie. So, if Snake was here, Lonnie ordered it. The Blackjacks are close by and they're up to something."

"Interesting," the president said again. "Where is Mister McCoy?" he asked.

"He's right outside, sir," Melvin answered.

"I understand he's somewhat of a cowboy."

"Yes, sir," Melvin said.

The president nodded. "Why don't we get him in here so we can hear it straight from the horse's mouth?" He then gave a small smile as he glanced at me.

"That's called a colloquialism, I believe."

Sheila giggled before catching herself.

Melvin nodded and escorted Fred in the room and had him stand beside me. Nobody thought to offer him a chair and he didn't ask for one. The room was silent with the exception of someone typing on a keyboard.

Fred was wearing a plain brown T-shirt, jeans that had a couple of old stains, and of course, boots. He must have left his gun in his room. He was a nondescript man to the untrained eye.

He stood there, staring at them stoically. The silence continued for a full minute. If they were waiting for Fred to introduce himself or something, they were going to be waiting a long time, and I was tired.

"Everyone, this is my friend, Mister Frederick McCoy. He's also from Tennessee. For those of you who know me, you know my son is named Frederick. This is the man he was named after." And most of you would have to sit on your mother's shoulders to kiss his ass, I thought.

"Very nice," the president said. "If you don't mind, would you explain the circumstances which led to you killing a man, let's see..." He looked at Sheila's laptop. "A man identified as Snake. Would you tell us what happened?"

"I caught a man spying on your facilities. It looked like he was going to be a problem, so I took care of it."

A full thirty seconds passed before one of them grasped Fred was a man of few words.

"Explain," General Fosswell directed. "Start from the beginning."

"Alright. Back when I was in Tennessee, we all ran into a spot of trouble. I thought Zach was dead and he thought I was dead. When I found out Zach and his family were still alive and had relocated up here, I hopped on my horse and came up," Fred began.

"You rode a horse all the way from Tennessee?" one of Stark's aides asked in surprise and looked at me to see if we were playing some kind of asinine joke.

"Yes," Fred replied.

"Why?" the same man asked.

Fred stared at him. "It's the way I do things."

Nobody else could see it, but I could see he was getting irritated, so I spoke up.

"You people sure do like interrupting a man when he's trying to tell a story."

"And it's taking up a considerable amount of time," President Richmond admonished as he looked at everyone to make his point. "Please continue, Mister McCoy."

"Like I said, I rode up here to be with Zach and his family. When I got here, I decided to look things over before coming in. I spotted a man hidden in the woods, looking things over his own self. He was using a scoped rifle to do his looking. He was up to no good. So, I took care of it."

Everyone waited for Fred to continue, but I guess it was General Fosswell who first realized Fred had finished his story.

"So, you killed him?" he asked.

Fred gave one of his micro nods.

"Alright, where is he?" the general asked.

"About two hundred yards in the woods from the fence on the southwest side. There's a guard shack he was watching at that particular moment when I decided it was time to send him to Jesus."

He glanced over at me momentarily. I understood better now what he said back in the woods. He was surveilling post three, and I had missed it.

"He was watching post three?" General Fosswell asked.

"He was watching everything," Fred said. "On the first day, he watched the main entrance for about four hours. Then he started moving clockwise, ending up on the southwest side of the perimeter. At sunset, he went back to his car, which was parked on down the road and hidden. He woke up an hour before sunrise and went back to the same spot and watched the rest of the day. He sure did like post three. There was a girl on guard duty with Zach. I suspect that had something to do with it."

Fred then fished into his breast pocket and took out the folded-up piece of paper he showed us earlier.

"He had this with him."

He handed it to Seth who unfolded it and looked it over. I saw his brow crease as he realized what he was looking at. He then walked it over to General Fosswell.

"What is it?" one of the politicians asked.

Seth spoke up. "It's a hand-drawn map of Mount Weather. He has detailing of the fence line, the location of the guard posts, and the building placements. He's even identified dead spots along the perimeter."

He looked at the audience. "It's a fairly accurate drawing," he remarked before handing the map over and it began being slowly passed around the room.

Somebody cursed under their breath. Fred walked over to an urn sitting on one of the tables and helped himself to a cup of coffee.

"So, these people were planning to do something," Senator Polacek surmised.

"Yep," Melvin answered. "Just like I said."

The senator frowned at Melvin. She didn't believe him. She didn't believe Fred, she didn't believe me. She honestly believed she had a grasp of how it was out there, all the while never leaving her ivory tower.

"What were they planning, Sergeant?" General Fosswell asked.

Melvin rubbed his face. "Snake was conducting the recon and they lost him. Since they didn't find the body, they either figure he got himself killed, or turned into a zombie, or something, so Lonnie sent Pig and his boys in to test the waters."

"And you believe they are planning some type of action against us?" Senator Duckworth asked before Melvin could continue. He'd been mostly quiet the whole time, but I sensed now he was finally seeing things for what they were.

Melvin nodded. "A couple of months ago, Lonnie had twelve men with him. He's lost a few since then, but might've recruited replacements. I'm betting they're planning on a snatch-and-grab raid or an ambush."

"For what purpose?" Duckworth asked. "We'd give them food. We've given food to people before."

"Food? Sure, but you wouldn't have given them weapons, or your women," Melvin bluntly replied. That shut everyone up.

"I'm curious, Melvin, how do you know all of this about the Blackjacks?" Senator Polacek asked.

"I've met them," Melvin replied.

"You're friends with them?" Senator Duckworth asked.

"They think so," Melvin said.

I'd like to think the majority of the crowd was moving over to our side now. However, General Fosswell seemed a little frustrated. I wondered why. I stood.

"I'm sure you people have a lot to talk about. I'm going to get some rest. Check back with me in eight hours if you have any further questions." I looked at Fred. "Captain Kitchens, that's the man seated over there, he has my rifle. Get it back from him before you leave, okay?"

Fred gave a small nod as he stared at Seth.

Secretary Stark cleared his throat. "We're not through, Mister Gunderson."

Melvin interjected before I spouted off. "Sir, Zach needs some personal time to decompress. Let him get caught up on his sleep. I've spoken with Savannah, and I believe I can fill in some of the blanks and answer any questions you might have for him."

"Why isn't she here, Sergeant?" Fosswell pointedly asked.

"She's extremely traumatized, sir. You don't want her to come in here and have a nervous breakdown right in front of you, do you?"

The three people who seemed to be running things were the president, Stark, and Fosswell. I watched their expressions as they took it all in. I spotted Parvis. He'd been sitting in the back of the room with a couple of other secretaries. None of them had said a word the whole time.

Stark finally glanced at the president, who gave a singular nod. I walked out without waiting for a formal dismissal.

I started to open the door to our suite, but I hesitated a moment and made a decision. I turned, walked down to the end of the hall, and turned the corner. Coming to the correct room, I gave a soft knock on the door.

"It's Zach," I announced. The room was quiet and there wasn't a response, but about the time I started walking off, the door opened a crack. Savannah was standing there, peering out. She looked awful.

"Hi. I won't keep you long, but I have something I want to tell you," I said.

"Okay." Her voice was quiet with an undertone of anxiety.

"I knew someone a while back. This person was younger than me. A great kid, but innocent and vulnerable. One day, something terrible happened to this person. I killed the people who did this despicable thing, and I promised this person I'd never tell anyone what had happened to them. I have kept that secret to this day. The only person who suspects anything is my friend, Fred, but I didn't tell him the details and he didn't ask."

"You figured out what happened to me," she said as fresh tears streamed down her cheeks. "That's why you killed them."

"I killed them because they were a threat to Mount Weather. As far as I'm concerned, that's all anyone ever needs to know."

"Did you hear Pig calling me Stinky?" she asked as she choked back a sob. "That was their pet name for me."

"Are you sure? My hearing is dodgy at times. I never heard such a thing."

Savannah didn't respond.

"So, anyway, that's what I wanted to tell you." I dipped my head and started to walk away. Suddenly, the door swung open and Savannah rushed out. She grabbed me in a tight hug. After a moment, she let go.

"Thank you for everything, Zach." She then hurried back into their room and shut the door quietly.

I heard the deadbolt being turned as I walked back down the hall. I turned the corner and bumped into Kelly. I could tell instantly by the look on her face she'd been there long enough to have heard everything.

"Maria's covering for me," she explained. "I thought I'd sneak back and check on you."

"I'm fine. A few scratches from running around in the forest, but nothing serious."

"You sound tired."

"Dead tired," I said. "No pun intended."

"Maybe you should get to bed then."

"Yeah, I'd like that."

Kelly followed me back to the room and pulled the blankets back while I took my boots off and stripped.

"Please tell me everything is going to be alright," she said.

I plopped into bed and yawned heavily. "I'm pretty sure everything's going to be fine," I said. "Some people are definitely under the opinion I acted in an irrational manner, but I think it'll be okay."

Kelly pulled the blankets over me and stroked my cheek. "I overheard you talking to Savannah."

"Yeah, I figured."

"We're you talking about Tommy?" she asked. I didn't answer, but it didn't matter, Kelly could read me like the back of her hand. Probably better.

"Why didn't you say anything?"

"I made a promise," I said.

"So, those men…"

"Deserved to die," I said. "If you saw the look on Savannah's face, you'd understand."

"I do understand."

She looked at me deeply. "Every time I think I know you, I learn something new. You're a complex man, Zachariah Gunderson."

I looked up at her and gave a small smile. She returned it as she worked her hand under the sheets.

"Maria isn't expecting me back for a while; how tired did you say you were?"

CHAPTER 29 – ZACH HAS A DREAM

I was awakened by the bedroom door opening, followed by the pitter-patter of little feet as my son ran in and climbed up on the bed.

"Daddy, why are you in bed?" he asked. I rubbed my eyes and looked at my watch. I was confused until I realized it was four in the afternoon.

"I was taking a nap," I said and gave him a hug. "How was your day?"

"It was fun. Bobby went poo-poo in his pants and it was stinky."

"Oh, how nice," I said, laughing. Kelly and Macie then came in the bedroom.

"Who's Bobby?" I asked her.

"One of the kids. He's the son of Becky Hardin, who is an aide to Senator Nelson. Rumor has it he's the father."

"I thought he was married?"

"He is, but, not to Becky," she said with a scoff. "This place is a regular soap opera."

"Yeah, I can believe that." I absently rubbed the side of my head.

"Were you hurt earlier?" she asked.

"Nah, just a few scratches."

"You keep rubbing your head."

I forced my hand down. "Oh, the way I slept made it itch, I guess."

What I didn't say was I'd had an intense dream. One of those dreams.

"Let me shower and we'll go eat dinner."

"Okay."

"I wonder what kind of reception I'll get," I questioned.

"About sixty-forty," Kelly said. I looked at her questioningly. She smiled sweetly. "All the moms come in the school and they gossip. Like I said, this place is a soap opera."

"Figures," I mumbled and headed to the restroom. Kelly came in a couple of minutes later and put some fresh clothes out for me.

"Thanks, sweetheart, but I'll have to change for guard duty later."

"No, you won't. You've been relieved of guard duty."

"Oh? When did that happen?" I asked.

"While you were asleep. Lydia came by and told me. They don't want you to expose yourself to danger."

I would've argued, but frankly, I hated guard duty. It was boring.

When we walked in the cafeteria, there were some friendly smiles and a few cool stares as well. I didn't care either way.

"May we join you guys?" I turned to the voice. It was Melvin and Savannah. Both of them were freshly bathed and their hair was still wet.

"Of course," I said. "We've kind of taken over this table, but you two are always welcome."

"Thanks, Zach," Melvin said. The two of them sat as Josue and Sammy came in.

"I'm glad you're here," I said. "I wanted to thank you for what you did in the meeting earlier."

Melvin fixed me with a stare. "It's the other way around, Zach. I can never thank you enough for what you did for, well, you know."

"Did you really kill three men, Zach?" Sammy asked with big wide eyes.

Janet had come in and sat as Sammy asked the question. Both she and Kelly were giving me a look, wondering how I was going to explain the incident to a kid who was not yet eleven.

I took a deep breath, wondering exactly what I was going to say. Melvin spoke up.

"There's an old saying, Sammy. People sleep peaceably in their beds at night only because rough men stand ready to do violence on their behalf. Big Zach here was standing guard, protecting this place." Melvin waved a hand around and began speaking little louder so others could hear. "Some of these people don't understand, but those men meant to do harm. Zach realized it and stopped them."

Sammy was still wide-eyed. "You took on three men all by yourself and killed them."

"Yes, he did," Melvin said.

I glanced away and saw Priss looking at me curiously. But, sitting right beside her was her idiot brother, Paul. He was mean-mugging me. I guess he thought if he looked mean enough, it meant he was the toughest kid on the block. I'd already proven him wrong. His crooked nose should have served as a reminder, but he apparently had a hard time accepting it. I ignored them and turned back to Sammy.

"Sammy, we're going to have a man-to-man talk later on, and one of the things we're going to talk about is killing, and that when you take someone's life, you never brag about it. Okay?"

"Yes, sir," he said and looked worriedly at Fred. Fred responded by giving him a small, somber nod.

"You're a smart young man, Sam," Fred said. "I could tell that from the first time I talked to you."

"Zach taught me a lot," Sammy said. He was interrupted by a girl walking up to him. She was carrying a computer tablet.

"Hi, Sam," she said. She was a cute little girl about Sam's age, hair as blonde as Macie's with baby blue eyes. Sam seemed suddenly embarrassed and refused to acknowledge her.

"Hi," I said. "I'm Zach. I don't believe I've ever met you."

"I'm Serena," she said and perfunctorily held out her hand.

"I'm pleased to meet you, Serena," I said as we shook.

She pointed to another table. "Those are my parents." I looked over at a table full of people engrossed in a conversation and oblivious to Serena's whereabouts. One of them was an attractive blonde who I assumed was the mom. She was maybe in her early thirties. I'd seen her before. She was an aide to Senator Polacek.

"Miss Kelly said I should help Sam with his homework."

I looked over at Kelly who smiled and winked.

"I don't need any help," Sammy retorted.

"Well now, I think you should ask Mister Fred what he thinks," I said.

Sammy looked at Fred questioningly. Fred leaned forward in his chair and motioned him to do the same. When Sammy leaned closer, Fred spoke in a low voice.

"Never, ever, turn down a pretty girl," he said, leaned back, and gave Sammy another somber nod.

"Come with me, Sam," Serena said. It wasn't a request, it was more like an order that Sammy did not dare disobey. I fought hard not to laugh as Sammy got up and dutifully followed her to a table at the far end of the cafeteria.

"He's hooked and he doesn't even know it," Fred said. Melvin busted out laughing as Kelly and Maria giggled.

In spite of recent events, we had a pleasant dinner. A couple of people even came by and voiced their appreciation for what I had done, but only a couple. I guess most wanted to see which way the wind was blowing before they came out and either sided with me or against me. I scratched my scar again and turned my attention to Melvin.

"Say, Melvin, Fred, and I have been admiring your truck."

"Oh, yeah? I've modified it a little bit here and there. It looks rough, but actually it runs like a top."

"We'd like to look it over, maybe get some ideas, if you don't mind," I said.

"Sure, whenever you want."

"How about now?" I suggested. "No time like the present."

Melvin shrugged. "Yeah, sure. Okay." He looked at Savannah. "We'll be back in a little bit."

"We'll keep you company," Kelly said with a smile. Savannah looked a little anxious. Melvin gave her a wink.

"Save some dessert for me."

"I have a little bit of an ulterior motive," I said to Melvin as we walked.

"I've been wanting to talk to you as well," Melvin said. "If you don't mind, let me go first."

"Alright," I said.

"Okay, so it goes like this. The Blackjacks are the ones who murdered Savannah's family and friends, but you two already know that."

"Uh, huh."

"She told me what you said, so I guess you've figured out the rest."

I glanced at him as I walked. "I meant every word."

"Yeah, I know she appreciates what you've done for her. I do too. It could've got you into a pickle though."

"How's that?" I asked.

"If you had told them everything, everyone would've understood why you killed those bastards. By not telling, it made you look like a cold-blooded murderer," he said.

"You got it straightened out."

Melvin scoffed. "I hope so, but some of those people get into a certain mindset and even something as simple as logic can't change them."

"If it was so, it might be, and if it were so, it would be; but as it isn't, it ain't. That's logic."

Melvin looked at me funny. "I've heard that before, where's it from?"

I chuckled. "Through the Looking Glass. I figure a man who quotes Orwell can appreciate Lewis Carroll."

"Ah," Melvin said in understanding, and then stopped. "Who the hell is that?" he said.

We were at the gate, maybe fifty feet from his truck. There was someone standing close to Peggy. They had their back to us.

"If I didn't know any better, I'd guess they were having a conversation," I said.

"Yeah," Melvin muttered.

He started walking again, faster now, and I could feel the tenseness emanating off of him. Fred and I glanced at each other as we followed him. As we exited the gate, I glanced in and saw two people who appeared to be playing cards. They barely acknowledged us as we walked by.

"Who is that down there with Peggy?" I asked, pointing. They paused with their cards and looked down the road toward Peggy. The look of confusion on their face was obvious.

"Who is that, Melvin?" one of them asked. So much for keeping vigilant, I thought. Melvin ignored them and kept walking.

The person, it appeared to be a man, was wearing heavily soiled and torn combat utilities. He seemed to either not be aware of our approach or was simply ignoring us as he continued to stare at Peggy.

I guess we got to within twenty feet when the three of us realized the man was a zombie. Melvin pulled a camp knife out of a sheath on his belt, walked up to it, and tapped him on the shoulder. When it turned, Melvin looked momentarily startled before stabbing him through the eye and twisted the handle, ensuring the blade destroyed enough brain matter to end its life.

"Shit," Melvin muttered as the person fell to the ground.

"What?" I asked. "Do you know him or something?"

"Yeah. He used to be one of us." Melvin stepped over the now lifeless zombie and raised the visor on Peggy's helmet. She hissed at him.

"Yeah, that's my girl," he said sarcastically before putting the visor back down.

One of the guards came running up. When he stopped and looked down at the zombie, his jaw dropped open.

"Holy shit," He drawled. "Is that who I think it is?"

"Yep," Melvin replied and pointed at the zombie with a bloody knife. "That used to be Lieutenant William Morris of the glorious United States Marine Corps," he explained.

"Oh, man. He was a good dude," the guard said.

"Yes, he was, Slim. Yes, he was," Melvin replied and explained to us. "Morris and a few others went missing last year during a long-range patrol up into Pittsburgh."

"I always thought they found some horny women somewhere and decided not to come back home," Slim remarked and then sighed. "I'll go call it in."

I waited until Slim had walked out of earshot before speaking. "This is kind of what I wanted to talk to you about."

Melvin gave me a puzzled look.

"Now this is going to sound a little bit crazy, but I have these dreams and sometimes they come true."

Melvin nodded somberly and looked at Fred, tacitly asking if I was being serious. Fred didn't react.

"Yep," he said. "That does indeed sound crazy; I guess that's why we seem to get along."

He nudged the late Lieutenant Morris and spotted a bulge in one of his cargo pockets. He squatted down and opened it. It held a topographic map.

"Damn, I can use this," Melvin said to himself, and then looked up at me. Standing, he unfolded the map and showed it to us. "Topo map of the area."

I looked at it and nodded. "Yeah." I waited as Melvin started alternating between staring at Peggy and the dead lieutenant. After a moment, he refocused.

"Okay, you were saying something about dreams coming true."

"Yeah, not all of them, but sometimes I'll have a dream and I seem to know it's the real deal."

"Have you had one recently?" he asked.

I nodded.

"Okay. Uh, in your dream, are there a couple of twenty-year-old twin sisters with big titties asking you to ride them like a Shetland pony? I keep having that dream, but it don't ever come true."

"No, nothing like that."

"Oh." Melvin sounded disappointed. "Well, what'd you dream of?"

"I dreamt Peggy is communicating with other zombies telepathically, and any day now, there's going to be an attack on Mount Weather."

Melvin nodded. "We should tell the bosses, I suppose. I do have a question though." He looked me directly in the eye. "Why'd you come to me first?"

"Because Peggy needs to be killed. She's putting Mount Weather in danger."

Melvin gave me another long stare, wondering again if I was bullshitting him. Deciding I was not, he took a look around in the growing darkness and rubbed his face.

"Fellas, I won't go into the reasons I've kept her alive, but I will say this. I'll know when it's the right time to kill her." He stared at the two of us, almost pleadingly.

"Either one of you could sneak out here and kill her while I'm sleeping or doing whatever, but I'm asking you to leave her alone."

Slim stopped our conversation when he came jogging up. "They said since he used to be one of ours, we'll use the crematorium in the morning. We're going to leave him right here for the night.

"Alright," Melvin said.

"Speaking of which," he said. "Are you guys going to be out here much longer? I need to lock it down for the night."

"Let's get back in," Fred said.

So, that settled it. My intention was to kill Peggy, but I didn't. I hoped it wasn't a decision that'd come back and bite me in the butt.

CHAPTER 30 – THE ASSASSINATION

Fred was waiting on me when I emerged from my room. I glanced at my watch and wondered how long he'd been awake.

"Coffee?" I asked. He gave me a nod.

I'd classified his nods now. There was the micro nod. It was his most common reaction. Sometimes, he substituted it for a slight arch of an eyebrow, the right one, never the left one.

Next was the somber nod. He used it only when there was something serious being discussed.

And, finally, there was the death nod. That was the one where whoever he gave it to better be careful.

The nod he gave me was a micro. We both knew breakfast wasn't ready, but there would be coffee. Burt and Josue usually joined us. Sarah was also an early riser and liked to join the coffee club as well. I'd told Fred she'd be back any day now. He didn't respond this time, not even with a micro.

Surprisingly, when we walked in, there were other people present. About a dozen. There were never this many people in here this early. I saw Jim talking quietly to a couple of them. His expression was tense. When he saw us, he broke away from them and walked over.

"The president is dead," he said.

"What?" I implored. "What happened?"

"They found him about thirty minutes ago," he replied. "Apparently, somebody stabbed him."

I looked around and saw his cooking crew. All of them were sitting at a table, somberness etched on their faces.

"Does anyone know who did it?" I asked.

He shook his head. "They're investigating." He made air quotes when he said investigating. "Every fucking politician in this place is investigating." His tone was caustic, which was uncharacteristic of him. He got up and fixed us two cups of coffee before sitting back down.

Jim stood there, staring at nothing, seemingly lost in thought.

"Uh, Jim?" I asked. He was broken out of his reverie and looked at me.

"Yes, Zach?"

"With the vice president long dead, aren't you next in line for succession?"

He chuckled without humor. "Yep, and that probably makes me the number one suspect." Jim looked at the two of us forlornly. "We're in for some difficult times, gentlemen."

Some other people walked in.

"Excuse me," Jim said and walked off.

"I never kept up with politics a lot," Fred said. "So explain to me why he's next in line to be president."

"Jim was the Speaker of the House. The VP is assumed dead, so he's next in line."

"Got it," Fred replied, saving me from having to explain any further.

Before I could comment on the matter, the intercom system came on. There was a slight amount of feedback before someone started speaking.

"Attention, all Mount Weather personnel. I say again, attention, all Mount Weather personnel, report immediately to the cafeteria. There are no exceptions; all personnel are to report immediately to the cafeteria."

"That was Secretary Stark," I said.

"And Stark is the Secretary of Defense," Fred said.

"Yep," I replied. "This ought to be interesting."

The cafeteria began filling quickly. Everyone was talking, and soon it escalated to a very loud din of overlapping chatter. Fred, Burt, Josue, and I sat quietly, listening to everyone else's conversations. There were a lot of armchair experts and a lot of speculation being thrown back and forth.

Kelly and Janet came in about twenty minutes later, each of them with one of the kids. Kelly's hair was still wet and freshly combed. I thought it was sexy. I even saw a few men turn their heads when she walked by. Janet's hair was still damp too, but all I saw when I looked at her was a sour woman with damp hair.

"They're doing room-to-room searches," Kelly said as she sat down. "I had barely got the kids dressed when they were at the door and ordered us out. What do you think they're doing?"

"I would guess they're looking for evidence, like a knife or bloody clothes," I said. I doubted anyone here had any law enforcement experience, so they were looking for the obvious. Still, I resented anyone searching our room.

The front doors opened and five people led by Captain Fosswell walked in. After our terse encounter yesterday, I asked around about him. He was the adult son of General Harlan Fosswell. Coincidentally, his name was Harlan Fosswell Junior. Officially, he was the general's aide. Some people liked him; others thought he was a moron.

He made a show out of putting his hands on his hips and sweeping the room with a severe gaze. When he spotted us, he walked over and made a show of dropping a knife on the table. It was custom made in the Bowie style, about ten inches long. The steel had a beautifully layered design, and I happened to know personally that it was razor sharp.

"Care to explain this?" he demanded.

I made a show of studying it. "It's a knife," I said. "It's used for whittling and stuff."

"Not you, smartass, him," he said and pointed a chubby finger at Fred.

"It's mine," Fred said in his usual quiet tone.

"It has blood on it."

"Thanks for reminding me. I need to clean it."

"Who the hell are you?" he demanded.

Fred set his coffee cup down and slowly looked up at the captain.

"You'll get that disrespectful tone out of your voice when you speak to me, or you're going to be in a lot of pain in a minute."

The captain looked incredulous for a moment, but then his expression turned to an arrogant glare. He bent forward slightly so that his face was close to Fred.

"Be advised, old man, when you're in my house, I'll speak to you however you…"

He never had a chance to finish his sentence. If you weren't watching closely, you would've never seen Fred's right hand dart out and jab his fingers into the captain's throat.

The younger Fosswell grabbed at his throat, emitted a sound like a dying frog, and fell to his knees. Fred wiggled his fingers a little bit, and then reached for his knife. He unsheathed it and turned toward Captain Fosswell, who was now in the fetal position on the floor, grasping his throat and trying desperately to breathe. There was a ripple in the crowd and everyone became quiet. I carefully put a hand out.

"Fred," I whispered.

Fred cut his eyes at me and I saw something in him I'd never seen before. His eyes were cold, like a killer. It was only there a moment, and then he seemed to calm down. I reached for the knife and put it back in the sheath.

"What's the meaning of this?" It was General Fosswell. He had come into the cafeteria, saw his son lying on the floor, and purposely walked over.

A soldier with an assault rifle was right behind him. She was a young African American woman, mid-to-late twenties, medium-skinned, athletic, attractive. She looked like she was almost six feet tall, making me think she'd be more at home playing sports rather than soldiering.

Fred stared at the general with cold hard eyes. Before I could say something, Kelly stood and spoke up.

"That soldier was being disrespectful," she said, pointing at the captain.

"Ma'am, we're investigating the murder of the president," General Fosswell declared.

"No, you listen," she rejoined. "I don't know why some of you so-called soldiers think you can treat people like lowlifes." She pointed at Fred. "You don't know this man, but I do."

"Oh, do please enlighten us," some sarcastic ass said from the back of the cafeteria. Kelly was not deterred and stared toward the voice.

"Okay, I will. In the first year of this fiasco, Fred travelled from Tennessee to California and back, through zombie-infested lands, in search of his daughter. That's about four thousand miles, people. He did it practically by himself. I seriously doubt you could've done it, smartass. And it doesn't end there. Back last September, he was shot through the chest by a sniper."

She looked pointedly at General Fosswell. "A soldier shot him. So, if some asshole in a uniform treats him disrespectfully and he warns them to back off, they better back off."

Burt cleared his throat and stared at the general. "There's something else he did. When he heard his family was up here, he hopped on a horse and rode up. That's a ride of over six hundred miles. I know every one of you people, and there isn't a damn one of you that could do something like that." He stared pointedly at General Fosswell. "Especially any of you soldier boys. He don't deserve to be talked down to by anyone here."

You could have heard a pin drop in the cafeteria. Well, with the exception of Captain Fosswell's coughing. General Fosswell had been staring at Fred, who in turn had sat, staring at nothing, his face a cold, silent mask. There was a hint of the death nod forming, and I hoped nobody did anything stupid. Fosswell stabbed a finger at Fred.

"You shouldn't have done that," he said.

Fred glanced over at Captain Fosswell, who was sitting on the floor, tenderly rubbing his throat.

"He'll live," he said quietly.

The general looked down at the captain and then motioned toward the soldier. She bent down to help Captain Fosswell up.

"Here, let me help you out, Stretch."

I turned to see who said that. It was Cutter. He was grinning broadly at the soldier as he helped get Captain Fosswell to his feet. If it wasn't such a tense situation at the moment, I would've chuckled, and maybe even given him an encouraging thumbs up.

"Explain," General Fosswell ordered.

Captain Fosswell pointed a little bit too forcibly at Fred. "We found that knife in his room, it has blood on it," he croaked. "He murdered President Richmond."

There was a collective gasp in the crowd followed by nervous murmuring. I stood.

"Fred did not kill the president." I said it loudly so everyone could here.

General Fosswell looked at me, looked at Fred, and looked at the sheathed knife, which was lying on the table. He held his hand out. I looked at Fred, who gave a micro. I picked it up and handed it to the general. He unsheathed it and inspected it closely.

"It certainly appears to be blood," he remarked.

"It is," Fred said. "Human blood, in fact." He looked at his empty cup of coffee. "Janet, would you mind getting me a fresh cup? I'd get it myself, but one of these soldiers will think I'm trying to escape and do something stupid."

Janet frowned, but she stood and took his cup.

"Would you care to explain yourself, Fred McCoy?" the general said. His tone was nothing like the younger Captain Fosswell, but it was spoken in a tone from a man who was accustomed to giving orders.

I spoke up. "General."

The general cut his eyes at me, but when I gestured toward my kids who were staring at us in rapt attention, his expression softened slightly.

"Let's go to Secretary Stark's conference room," he said and looked over at Captain Fosswell a moment. I thought I detected a hint of shame, or maybe disdain

Janet handed both Fred and me a fresh cup. She gave me a look, which I knew all too well. She was tacitly telling me I owed her.

"Thanks," I said before we followed the general out.

"How are you two related?" Fred asked the general as we walked down the hall.

"He's my son."

"He could use a lesson in manners," Fred said dryly.

The general did not respond and continued walking. When we walked in, the room was full. Raymond was standing beside Seth. They both looked stressed. Raymond waved us in.

"It was Earl," he said before they had even taken a seat. "It didn't take much to figure out."

"How so?" General Fosswell asked.

"He was still in his bloody clothes when we found him hanging from a belt in his closet," Raymond replied. "The knife was lying on the table, along with a note." He gestured at Seth and himself.

"We took some pictures to document it, if that even matters, and then locked the room. We were in the middle of discussing what to do next."

"How's Sheila?" I asked. General Fosswell looked at me sharply, as if I should not ask questions and instead should keep my mouth shut.

"Physically, okay," Raymond replied. "Emotionally, a damn mess. We've got her in hiding at the moment." He gestured toward Senator Polacek. "We were on our way to the cafeteria to inform everyone."

"We won't keep you," General Fosswell said and walked over to the conference table. Secretary Stark motioned him to a chair.

Raymond and the senator walked out and closed the door. I'm not sure if we were still needed or not; we'd suddenly seemed to have become invisible. I walked over to a woman standing along the side wall.

"Does anyone know why he did it?" I asked in almost a whisper.

She glanced nervously at the table of people, realized they weren't paying attention, and leaned closer to me.

"Sheila and the president were having an affair," she whispered. "Apparently, Earl found out. He made some less than flattering remarks about her in his suicide note."

She said it like everyone knew about the affair but Earl. Hell, I didn't know about it. I wondered if Kelly did.

Everyone at the table was now engaged in an intense conversation. While I listened, they alternated between discussing who was now in charge to what kind of funeral they were going to have for the president. Stark was fine with cremating both bodies, but a couple of the politicians disagreed. They wanted instead to have a traditional presidential funeral with all of the pomp and protocol.

I probably could have listened to their nonsense for a while, maybe get an idea of who the true leaders were around here, but Fred caught my eye. He made a subtle motion toward the door. Reluctantly, I agreed, and the two of us quietly walked out. I don't think anyone even saw us leave.

"I'm not so sure I like this place," he said as we walked back toward the cafeteria.

CHAPTER 31 – THE VIGIL

Fred had intentionally skipped dinner the evening before. The recent death of President Richmond had everyone in a titter. Conversations usually began with the lamentations over his death, which lasted for maybe ten seconds before it segued into heated political debates. Fred wanted nothing to do with them.

It had absolutely nothing to do with seeing Sarah, or so he kept telling himself. Zach told him she had been recalled from Fort Detrick. He made a point of working in a garden at the far corner of Weather, but still within eyesight of the front gate.

He saw her when she arrived. She looked tired. Her girlfriend looked tired as well. He waited a full hour, when he was certain they'd be in the cafeteria before walking in. He bumped into Janet in the elevator and told her to tell Zach he was tired and wouldn't be joining them.

He awoke at a little before four, crawled out of bed, and quietly walked down the hall to the men's locker room. He started this morning's ritual by pulling a straight razor out of his toilet kit. He shaved carefully, trying to avoid cutting himself. He was fine with a beard, but when he'd hugged little Macie the other morning, she grimaced at its roughness.

Finishing, he checked his face in the mirror for any missing spots and then looked over his wound. Both the entrance and exit were angry-looking pink puckers of scar tissue. It was a smaller caliber bullet, 5.56 most likely. Anything larger would have killed him straight away. Still, how he escaped death was beyond him, but here he was.

"Yeah, here I am," he muttered. He turned away from the mirror and was about to step into a shower stall when the door opened. He looked to see who in the world was also awake at four in the morning. Zach, probably.

It wasn't Zach.

"You missed dinner last night," Sarah said. She was wearing running shorts and a T-shirt. He spotted the outline of an athletic bra under the shirt. She was probably going for a morning run. She looked the same, maybe a little older, but to him, she was still beautiful.

"Yeah, I wasn't hungry." He then gestured at her clothing. "You were wearing pretty much the same thing the first time I met you."

She stepped forward and touched the spot on his chest. Fred instinctively reached for the towel wrapped around his waist and held tighter.

"I finally got over my stubborn streak and came to Tennessee," she said.

"Yeah."

"Zach told me you had been killed."

"Yeah."

She continued staring at the scar while softly caressing his chest. "You've lost weight. You need to stop skipping meals."

"You need to stop doing that before I embarrass myself," Fred said.

Sarah looked up and made eye contact. She then reached a hand around behind his neck and pulled him close. She kissed him tenderly before slowly pulling away.

"I have so much I want to say to you," Sarah said.

Fred gave a small nod, but didn't respond.

"But the first thing I want to say is how sorry I am for not going with you when you left Oklahoma. It's a mistake I'll always regret."

"No worries," Fred replied.

She looked at him a long moment and kissed him once more. This time it was a little longer, a little more passionately. She caressed his face lightly and smiled.

"I hope I see you at breakfast," she said and walked out.

Fred watched her leave and then hurried into a shower stall. He turned the cold water on full blast and stepped under it before someone else walked in and spotted his turgid state.

Fred dressed and walked around Mount Weather until six. He'd considered hitching up a horse and going for a ride; it would have made things a lot easier if he mounted up and kept riding, but hunger won out. He walked in the cafeteria and looked over at the Tennessee table, that's what they called it. Sarah was the only one sitting there. She was dressed in some military utilities now.

"Sit down," she said, patting the chair beside her and stood. "I'm going to get you a tray."

She walked away before waiting for a response. He took the chair across from her. She came back with two trays, one of which was overfilled with food. She took note of where Fred sat and returned to her seat.

"Afraid I might bite you?" she asked teasingly as she set the overloaded tray in front of him.

"No, but your girlfriend might," Fred answered.

She looked at him a moment. "Her name is Rachel Benoit. She'll be here in a minute. She has a rather zany personality. You'll either like her or you'll think she's a nut. I'm going to get us coffee."

One of the double doors opened and a woman walked in a moment later. She paused momentarily as she spotted Fred before walking up and sitting down in the seat Sarah had intended for him to sit in. She was pretty, Fred thought. Strawberry hair, lots of freckles. What struck Fred more than anything was her age. She was young, much younger than Sarah.

"Good morning," he said.

"Hi yourself, cowboy," she said with a smile. "You have to be Fred."

"I am."

"I'm Rachel," she said and held out her hand.

"I'm pleased to meet you, Rachel," Fred said and shook her hand. Rachel held it with both her hands and turned his palm face up.

"Wow, you have a lot of callouses," she said as she stroked his hand. "I hooked up with a rodeo star once. Even he didn't have callouses like this. He didn't last longer than eight seconds either."

Fred pulled his hand away while Rachel grinned mischievously. He was saved from further discomfort when Sarah rejoined them, or so he thought.

"I see you two have met," she said.

"We have," Rachel answered. "He's handsome. I can see why you jumped his bones."

"Rachel!" Sarah scolded. Rachel responded by giggling. She gave Sarah a peck on the cheek, stood, and walked toward the buffet.

"Sorry," Sarah said. "She likes to do that."

"I noticed," Fred said and put a fork full of sausage into his mouth.

"Oh, I forgot to mention, they have milk today."

"I'll get some in a minute," Fred said.

Rachel came back with a plate and sat. "Have you two had time to catch up?" she asked.

"No," Fred said. He looked at Sarah. "Zach said you two had gone to Fort Detrick with a group of Marines."

"Yeah, it was a bitch," Rachel said. "We had to kill a bunch of zombies and secure a lab so a couple of scientists could create a vaccine."

Fred looked at Sarah for confirmation. She nodded.

"They seemed to think they were on to something. We would have stayed there longer, but four of us were ordered back after President Richmond was killed. The Marines are still there, guarding the scientists."

Sarah and Rachel continued talking to Fred, telling him about everything regarding Mount Weather as people started trickling into the cafeteria. Soon, the room was packed and noisy. People were talking loudly, arguing politics and what was the proper course for the government of Mount Weather. Raymond was making his way around to different tables and finally reached theirs.

"How is everyone doing this morning?" he asked.

There was a murmuring of answers. He smiled in understanding, answered a couple of questions, and then excused himself. He walked to the front of the cafeteria, stood on a chair, and let out a loud whistle.

"I hope everyone is coping with our recent tragedy."

There were a few responses. He waited until they died down before continuing.

"There will be a vigil held today at eleven. All work duties are being suspended, with the exception of Congressman Hassburg and his kitchen crew, who have graciously volunteered to ensure we don't go hungry today."

"Can you tell us what's going on?" somebody from the back asked.

"All I can say is, even as we speak, there are meetings being held over the best course of action for the future of Mount Weather and the United States."

"It's a no-brainer," the same one said. He was speaking a little louder now. "Jim Hassburg is next in line. He's now the president."

This statement immediately started everyone talking. Raymond held up a hand and once again whistled loudly. "All I can tell you is these matters, and others, are being discussed. I'm sure there will be a meeting held soon where everyone will be informed. Thank you."

"Damn," Rachel said. "I hope it turns out okay, I was just starting to like this place." She casually looked around when the double doors opened. Her eyes lit up in recognition.

"Hey, isn't that crazy Melvin?" she asked.

Sarah looked over. "Yep, I believe you're right." She then explained to Fred. "We bumped into him and his zombie wife out on the road when we were coming up here." Sarah continued looking at them. "I have no idea who the girl is, though."

"Oh, my God," Rachel said in feigned shock. "He's cheating on Peggy."

Even Fred chuckled.

*****

I was approached by Parvis on my way to breakfast.

"You want to see the crematorium in action?" he asked. "We can eat after, if you still have your appetite." He was grinning when he said it, almost like he was challenging me.

"Sure," I answered and turned to Kelly. "I'll see you in a little while." She gave me a kiss and guided my two little monsters to the cafeteria.

"I've read about you extensively," he said as we rode the elevator down a couple of floors. We stepped out onto a floor filled with pipes, conduits, and electrical panels. Parvis made a sweeping gesture with his hand.

"The bowels of Mount Weather," he said.

I followed him as he walked down the hallway. Soon, he turned into a side room. There was a body wrapped in a plain paper blanket. The blanket had bloodstains in the chest area of the corpse. Parvis gestured.

"The president in his final repose," he said.

He pointed at the crematorium. "When this place was originally designed, it was acknowledged people may die during lockdown. We decided this was the most expedient method of disposing of their remains. The only problem is we never expected mass casualties."

"How is it powered?" I asked.

"Propane. As you can imagine, it is in limited supply." He pointed at a gauge. "We have enough left for maybe a couple dozen more burns."

"You can probably find a propane truck and a supply somewhere," I suggested.

"It's on one of those long lists," Parvis said. "You were right, you know." I looked at him. "On the first day, you pointed out how more could have been done."

I shrugged. "It was an observation, nothing more."

He smiled tightly. "Let me show you how to properly burn a body."

The cremation process took a little under three hours. The remains of the president, or cremains as they're called, were poured out of a tray into something that looked a lot like a brass flower vase. The kind where you pour water in it and stick a few roses in. Parvis confirmed my suspicions.

"Don't tell anyone," he said with a conspiratorial wink.

"What's going to happen around here?" I asked.

"I can't tell you," he said as he admired his work. "But, I can say this, there will be changes. I'd like to think they're going to be positive changes. You see, the president and a lot of these politicians were perfectly fine with being isolationists. The male-to-female ratio is a little low here, but they didn't care because most of them have a wife or an aide who slept with them. Eventually, it was agreed the Marines needed to be sent out and eradicate the zombies in and around Mount Weather."

"It seemed to work, for the most part," I said.

"Yeah, for the most part. Captain Jones was in charge of the Marines at that time, and you know Marines, they love to kill."

"Yeah," I agreed, thinking of the massacre.

"We eventually came up with the extinction model and used it to convince these politicians that we needed to reach out and make contact with other survivors."

"It's my understanding there were problems."

He ran a hand through his graying hair in seeming frustration. "Three delegations went out, only one came back. Don't you know the armchair experts had a hay day criticizing me for that plan. We lost some good people, not to mention the equipment."

"It was your idea?"

"Yep," he said with a nod. "They started to come around, albeit reluctantly. Polacek was convinced we'd bring in nothing but rapists and murderers." He scoffed. "Like anyone would rape her old ugly ass."

"I'm sensing some animosity," I said.

"Yeah, you might say that. Even before the president's death, two political camps have formed and are constantly battling against each other. Verbally, of course, nothing physical." He gave a flippant wave.

"It gave the isolationists ammunition for their argument. The president was on our side, but a majority of the politicians were beginning to side against him. There is now a movement to have an election."

"You're against it," I said.

He sneered slightly. "I was, and still am. An election at this time will change nothing. In fact, I believe it'll cause even more problems than we already have."

"Why are you telling me this?"

He gave an offhanded smile. "There are going to be changes, young Zach. Now, I think I know you well enough to believe when these changes occur, you and your people will pack up and leave."

I eyed him, wondering what he was saying. "Should we?"

He looked at me pointedly. "Not yet. In fact, I think the coming changes will be positive."

His smile returned and he held up the vase. "C'mon, the president has a vigil to attend."

Mount Weather had a chapel, but it was far too small to hold a hundred people, so they held the vigil outside. Each politician felt it necessary to speak, and each one lauded praises upon President Richmond while finding their way to interject themselves into any of his successes. It lasted over two hours, but everyone was respectful, and finally the Marines rendered a twenty-one gun salute and they cast his ashes into the wind.

I couldn't wait to leave.

CHAPTER 32 – HORSESHOES

Fred hit another ringer. "Damn, you won again," Burt said loudly. He picked up the horseshoes and banged the dirt off of them.

"So, Parvis said there are changes coming," Burt remarked, this time in a much lower voice. "But he wasn't specific."

"Nope," I said. "I believe he was giving us a heads up, but didn't want to go into detail."

"I've asked around as discretely as I could," Burt said. "I didn't get much. There's a lot of arguing and stuff going on, behind closed doors of course."

"What about?" Josue asked.

Burt threw his second shoe. It was a leaner. Josue picked them up and took aim.

"All I know is there's a power struggle going on," he said. "Some people are good with Hassburg becoming president, other people want an outright election."

"There's something else going on too," I said. The men paused and looked at me. "One of the women told Kelly there's something else, a third path, if you will."

"Like what?" Josue asked.

"Head's up," Fred muttered before I could answer. We all looked over at once, not a great way to act casual, and saw Senator Nelson walking our way.

"I should've known Tennessee folks liked horseshoes," he said with a broad grin.

"None of us can beat Fred," Burt said. "He's a horseshoe savant."

"Well, I'd sure like to give it a shot," he said in a good-natured tone.

Burt handed him two horseshoes. "I'm done anyway. My battle-axe is probably wondering where the heck I'm at. I'll see you men tomorrow."

The senator glanced at Burt as he walked away. "I didn't run him off, I hope?"

"Nah, he just hates losing," I said. "How've you been, Senator?"

"Please call me Conrad, or Connie," he said while taking aim. He threw a shoe and it landed three feet short of the stake.

"How've you been, Connie?" I asked again.

"Not too bad up until just now." He chuckled at his own joke and threw again. This one landed closer, but was still short by a foot. He stepped back and appeared to be evaluating his throws.

"It's more difficult than it looks," he said. "I guess it's a good thing I don't have some kind of bet going."

"True," I said.

"What do you gentlemen think about the recent events here at Mount Weather?" he asked. I wondered how long it was going to take for him to reveal his real reason for joining us.

"Why hasn't Jim Hassburg been installed as president yet?" I countered. "I mean, the president has been dead for two days now, what's the holdup?"

"It's a complicated issue," he said as he watched Fred throw another ringer. "There has been a lot of discussion about it."

Josue scoffed. "Política," he muttered.

Conrad looked at him in puzzlement, wondering if he'd been insulted.

"I don't see how," I said. "I looked up the law last night. The Presidential Succession Act. It was clearly written."

Josue picked up the horseshoes and threw a ringer. "Ha!"

Fred responded by giving him a micro.

"So, am I the only one who has read the law?" I asked, somewhat facetiously.

"The problem is, President Richmond never appointed a VP after the death of Puckett," Conrad said. "This has caused an enormous amount of complexity in the proper line of succession."

After Josue finished his turn, Fred picked up the shoes, squared himself, and aimed for maybe a second before throwing. He made a ringer.

"Did you see that, Connie?" I asked.

"Yes, I did," he replied. "He threw another ringer."

"But, did you see what he did there?" I asked again. "He didn't stand there and have an endless discussion with the horseshoe. He knew what needed to be done and he simply did it. What's so complicated?"

Conrad pursed his lips. "If only running a government was as easy as throwing horseshoes." He held up a hand before I could respond. "I understand your analogy. Let me throw in my own analogy, right now there are too many cooks in the kitchen."

It didn't seem to fit, but I went along with it. "What do you think is the best course of action?" I asked him. Josue was about to throw, but paused and waited for the senator's answer.

"I think the best course of action is to have an election," he said. Josue scoffed again and threw.

"Excellent," I said. "Tomorrow morning at breakfast make the announcement and have everyone vote. Lydia has a list of everyone living here; we can set up a voting booth at the end of the buffet line and have the results by lunch."

The senator chuckled, perhaps a little condescendingly. "Oh, it's more complex than having a simple election. Whoever is running needs time to tell everyone how they stand on the issues."

Now it was my turn to respond with a condescending chuckle. "You people have been living in a fishbowl for almost four years now. Everyone knows everyone else inside and out, I suspect."

"Perhaps you have a point," he conceded.

"Are you running?" Josue asked.

Conrad smiled. "It has been discussed."

Josue made a face. "You people need to learn how to say yes or no."

Suddenly, a shot rang out, causing us to stop our conversation.

"That came from somewhere around post three," I said. Another shot rang out. All of us were armed with handguns, well, with the exception of Senator Nelson, but we ran together toward post three. It was occupied by Shooter and Kate.

"There's somebody out there!" he shouted to us as he pointed toward the wood line.

I climbed into the guard shack and grabbed the binoculars as the field phone rang. The sun was setting, which caused the forest to be cast into deep shadows. Short answer, I didn't see shit. I handed down the binoculars to Fred.

"Did you see anything?" the senator asked.

I shook my head. "Lots of shadows. Whoever it was is either long gone or they're out there dead. Or hiding."

We each took turns with the binoculars as Captain Fosswell rode up in a cart. Even though there was now four of us in the small guard shack, he climbed the steps and wedged himself in. I had to squeeze between him and the wall to get out. Fred did the same. He scanned the woods with the binoculars for around twenty seconds or so before setting them down and giving a tremendous sigh.

"Somebody has an overactive imagination and is wasting ammo," he declared.

"Dude, I'm telling you, somebody was out there," Shooter retorted.

Fosswell gave him a harsh stare. "It's not dude. You will address me either as sir or by my rank."

"Shooter, come on out here," I said. The last thing we needed was for another one of us to put our hands on Fosswell. Shooter clambered down the steps and walked over to where we were standing. His expression showed both frustration and agitation.

"I'm not making this shit up, man. There was somebody out there."

"I believe you," I said. He looked at me a little bit in surprise and realized I was taking him seriously.

"Yeah," he said.

"Was it a person or a zed?" Fred asked.

Shooter looked at Fred, and after a moment, shrugged. "I don't know."

"Tell us what you did see," I suggested.

He yelled up at Kate. "Hey, come down here."

He waited for her to exit the guard shack. Junior Fosswell was now in the shack by himself, so he followed her out.

"So, Kate was looking around with the binoculars. She said she thought she saw something and pointed." He pointed at a gnarly oak tree about seventy-five yards back in the woods.

"So, I take the binoculars and have a look-see. Sure enough, there was someone peeking out from behind the tree." He looked at everyone, wondering if one of us was going to call bullshit.

"Keep going," I said. "What'd you do next?"

"I told Kate to get on the phone and report it, just like we're supposed to, right?"

Kate nodded in agreement.

"So, I holler out at him, but he doesn't do anything."

"What made you think it was a male?" Fred asked. The question seemed to confuse Shooter. He stared at Fred, but didn't answer.

"Was it tall or short?" I asked.

"Um," he responded. He was searching his brain, but was coming up dry.

"He was tall," Kate said. "About Fred's size, but not as tall as you. So, it was either a man or a tall woman."

"Fair enough, so what happened next?" Fred asked.

Shooter's jaw tightened, so Kate nudged him.

"Alright, so he's not answering when I holler at him, so I shot above his head into the tree. He ducked back behind the tree and then I saw two of them take off running. I might have clipped one of them, I don't know."

"Let me get this straight, they were running away and you shot at them?" Captain Fosswell asked. Shooter reluctantly nodded. The captain stood there a moment, looking at Shooter like he was the proverbial redheaded stepchild.

"Un-fucking-believable," Fosswell muttered.

"He didn't do anything wrong," I contended. I pointed out at the woods. "Why is someone sneaking around out there? If they were friendly, they would've come to the front gate and introduced themselves."

He looked at all of us sourly, with the exception of Fred, who he pointedly ignored. He walked over to his cart and got on. He took one last look at us.

"You know what I think? I think you Tennessee people have more bullets than brains."

With that proclamation, he drove off.

"I didn't do anything wrong," Shooter reasserted.

"Don't worry about it," I said. "He's got his panties in a wad, but I bet nothing will come of it."

"They're too worried about who is going to be the next el presidente," Josue said. He gestured around. "See? Nobody else even came out to see what was up."

I looked at the senator to see if he had a comment. He saw me looking and only offered a slight smile.

Captain Fosswell did not feel it was necessary to inspect the area where Kate and Shooter saw the two people, so we did. Senator Nelson was visibly nervous about going out, but even so, he joined us.

Shooter, who remained at the guard post, guided us to the spot. Josue pointed at a spot behind a tree.

"Looks a little trampled down, man," Jorge said.

We all agreed. I went up to the spot and looked things over. I even pantomimed peeking out from behind the tree toward the guard post.

"Yeah, it's a good spot to spy on post three," I said and looked at Fred. "Where was that man you spotted scoping things out?"

He pointed at another tree, about twenty yards over and a little deeper in the wood line.

"So, people are watching the place," Senator Nelson remarked.

"It would appear so," I agreed and looked at the sun. "Well, it's getting dark; I suppose we should get back inside.'

"Yes, by all means," Senator Nelson said and looked at us anxiously.

After reentering the gate, Jorge motioned for Fred and me to hang back while the others walked inside.

"Me and pops have been talking," Jorge said. Josue nodded.

Fred and I looked at him, waiting for him to explain.

"Things are getting weird around here," he continued. "And we were wondering if we should stay here or maybe leave."

"And go back to Tennessee?" I asked.

Josue nodded again. "What do you think?" he asked.

I looked at Fred. I knew he wasn't sure about this place, but he remained quiet.

"I understand the sentiment, and I'm inclined to go along."

"But?" Josue asked.

232

"I'd like to see how this is all going to play out," I said. "We have doctors here, a dentist, a vet, and when we go to bed at night, we're sleeping in a secure location." I looked at them and took a deep breath.

"If you're asking my opinion, I'd say let's give it until the spring. If things become drastic within the next week or two, we'll leave before then. Kelly, Janet, and I have already discussed it and that's what we've agreed to."

"What do you think Shooter and Cutter will do?" Jorge asked.

"I'm pretty sure they'll stay. Cutter has started messing around with that soldier, Stretch, or whatever her name is, so unless she dumps him, he's happy here, and I honestly don't care what Shooter does."

The father and son looked at each other and spoke in Spanish. I only understood a word or two, but I could've swore Joker's name was mentioned. The spoke for a couple of minutes before Jorge spoke to me.

"Maria says one of the Marines has been flirting with her," he said.

"Let me guess: Joker."

Josue nodded.

"I've gotten to know him a little bit. He's a little bit of a clown, but he seems like a good guy. But, if he's causing problems, I'll tell him to back off if you want," I offered.

The two men looked at each other again. Josue shrugged.

"Nah, man, it's okay. I think she likes him. She gets a big stupid smile on her face whenever his name is brought up."

CHAPTER 33 – THE ATTACK

Fred, Jorge, Josue, and I had spent most of the day at the armory reloading ammunition. It was tedious work, but it was better than sitting in a guard shack or cleaning the latrines.

"We done good, but I'm getting hungry," Josue said.

I looked at my watch. "Yeah, let's go eat."

The field phone rang, waking Boner up. After a moment of an intense, heated conversation, he hung up and hit the alarm. The four of us looked at each other for maybe half a second. I hopped the half door into the armory and started tossing weapons and magazines out to my eagerly waiting friends.

"Holy shit," Jorge exclaimed as we exited the front door. The two guards in the main post were firing as quickly as they could, but they weren't taking the time to aim and the sheer numbers were overwhelming them. There were hundreds of them, maybe even more. It was hard to tell at the moment.

We took up positions and began firing. Slowly, methodically, making our shots count. Within seconds I heard additional gunfire coming from my right. I paused only a moment to see it was the reactionary force being led by Captain Fosswell. Unfortunately, they too were rushing their shots, resulting in low hit rates.

The front gate was open for some unknown reason and the zeds were pouring through. We were losing ground, there were too many of them. Whoever was in the guard shack had stopped firing. They were probably either dead or they'd closed the shutters before they got killed. I was about to yell for everyone to fall back when someone shouted behind me.

"Coming up!" I briefly turned to see Seth running up with another Marine. He knelt beside me and grinned.

"What's up, Zach?" he asked lightheartedly as he began firing.

"Where've you been?" I shouted back over the noise of gunfire.

"Meetings, lots of meetings," he said. "I've got Stretch with a group flanking around the left."

It sounded like a plan. I hoped it worked, and I hoped the members of the reactionary force didn't shoot any of them by mistake.

It seemed to take forever, but after only a few minutes, I heard the eruption of gunfire on the west flank. I looked that way and caught a glimpse of Stretch. She was standing behind a group of four people, shouting orders and directing their fire. In short order, they were firing into the flank of the horde and cutting them down rapidly.

"There's my girl!" Seth shouted. "Alright, let's get this shit over with." He stood. "Everyone, get on line with me and start walking forward! Make your shots count, people!"

Within seconds, we began gaining an advantage. And more people started joining us. I strongly suspect they were cowering inside the buildings until they saw us winning, then they wanted to join in and try their hand at killing zombies. Seth gave me a look when a few of them ran up to us. I nodded knowingly. Whatever he thought about them, he kept to himself and hustled them on line. We slowly worked forward, firing as we went.

As we moved forward, Lois and Norman jogged up beside me. Both were carrying a bags full of magazines.

"Who needs ammo?" she shouted, and without waiting for answers, started going down the line handing out full magazines and picking up the empty ones.

I didn't stop to count, but I figured there were a couple of dozen of us firing in concert now and the zombies were dropping like sacks of fetid shit.

We worked our way up to the main guard post and everyone stood in a loose line. As the zeds continued falling, their numbers began thinning and the rate of firing diminished.

We'd stopped their advance, and in fact were pushing them back toward the main gate. A year ago, they would have continued charging forward, but now, some of them seemed to have more of a survival instinct. Some still charged toward us, some stood there awaiting the inevitable, while others turned and began running away. After approximately five minutes, I yelled out.

"Cease fire! Cease fire! Only shoot if you have a good target, don't waste ammo!"

"Look," Josue said, pointing at a dozen or so who had broken off the attack and were fleeing toward the woods. I caught Fred's attention and grinned before bringing up my M4 and picked off two.

Fred gave me the arched eyebrow, handed Josue his assault rifle, and drew his pistol. He took casual aim and picked off two more before the rest disappeared into the woods.

"Holy shit!" Jorge shouted. "Those fuckers were over a hundred yards away. That's some awesome shooting, old man."

Fred's only response was to reload and holster his weapon.

I walked over to the side of the guard shack and pulled open the door. The small shack was full of zombies. Some of them were dead, others were chewing on one of the guards. A zombie was making a meal out of his face, but even so, I recognized him immediately. It was Paul. I took aim and shot them in the head. Including Paul. Jorge and Josue ran up and stood by me, guns at the ready.

"What's up, man?" Jorge asked. I didn't need to answer. One look inside and they understood.

"Cover me," I said, leaned my rifle against the wall, and began dragging them out.

Some of them were still active; I would have said they were still alive, but who the hell knew what they were anymore. In any event, Jorge and Josue took turns putting bullets in their heads as I drug them out of the small confines of the shack. I drug out seven before I found the other guard.

It was Priss. She was still alive, a look of sheer terror on her face. She gazed at me when I'd dragged the zombie corpse off of her with one of those thousand yard stares.

"Priss," I said. She continued staring and started to bring her rifle up. I stepped forward quickly and snatched it out of her hands. I looked back and handed it to Josue before focusing back on Priss.

"Priss, it's me, Zach."

It took her several seconds before responding. "Zach?" she asked.

"Yeah, it's me, Zach."

I held a hand out. After a moment, she reached out and grabbed my hand. I helped her up and then began checking her for bites. She was covered in blood and zombie goo, but otherwise, I did not see any injuries.

"Zach?" she asked again.

I held her by her hands. "It's okay, Priss, it's okay."

It took a moment, but then she saw her brother lying on the ground. A low, sorrowful moan erupted from her. I looked around, spotted Stretch, and motioned her over.

"Please do me a favor and take her to medical."

Stretch looked her over. I could sense from the expression on her face she did not like Priss, but to her credit, she kept those feelings to herself and reached out, taking her hand.

"Come on, baby girl. Walk with me."

As I watched Stretch lead Priss away, Josue walked up and held up her assault rifle.

"Empty," he said and pointed at all of the cartridge casings lying on the floor of the guard shack. "She put up a hell of a fight."

I looked over and saw another assault rifle lying on the floor. Thinking this one must have been Paul's, I picked it up and inspected it. The magazine had seventeen rounds left in it and there was a stovepipe in the chamber. Frowning, I popped the back pin and broke it open. The weapon was hideously dirty. I cursed under my breath as I showed it to Jorge, Josue, and Fred.

"This is ridiculous," I said. "Nobody is cleaning their weapons."

Everyone had gathered around the carnage now. Some of them were even giving themselves high-fives and congratulating themselves.

"Listen up, everyone!" I shouted angrily. When I had their attention, I continued.

"This was Paul's weapon. It malfunctioned because it was filthy." I looked around for emphasis.

"All of you know I didn't like Paul, but Jesus, people, being eaten alive is no way to die. Clean your fucking weapons!"

Nobody said a word. No arguments, nothing. Fred gave me a micro.

"Coordinated attack," Captain Fosswell said. I turned toward the voice. He was with his father, and both of them had M4s slung across their shoulders. Captain Fosswell was leading the reactionary squad during the attack, but I never saw the general. He must have had more important matters to attend to. The younger Fosswell hooked a thumb behind him.

"Post three and four were also attacked, but not as many. Good thing I was OD," he said, looking expectantly at his father, who ignored him and stared at the slew of dead zombies.

There was an expression on Captain Fosswell's face, and it took me a minute to understand. He was seeking his father's approval. In that moment, I realized young Fosswell had spent his entire life seeking his father's approval and had never quite succeeded in getting it.

"Not much different from the attack on the CDC," Rachel said. I had not seen her at all during the attack, but I had no doubt she was in the thick of it. "The only difference is the numbers; the CDC was attacked by over fifty thousand."

"Their numbers must be diminishing," Captain Fosswell opined.

The general nodded thoughtfully and then looked at Rachel. "Do you think they followed you here from Fort Detrick?"

"It's possible, sir. After the first day, we had intermittent contact with hordes. Most of the time, it was only like three to ten in a group. A couple of strays here and there, but nothing significant. We'd wondered where they went to."

The general nodded again and then seemed to notice his son for the first time. "What are you doing, Captain?"

"Sir?" Captain Fosswell asked.

"Don't just stand there with your head in the clouds, Captain. Get your reactionary squad together and conduct a recon of the perimeter. Make certain there are no breaches."

"Yes, sir," Captain Fosswell said. He looked dejected, wondering why he was being chastised instead of praised for his work.

"And double the guards, muster up some of those damn senators if you have to."

"Yes, sir," he answered, rendered a salute, and walked over to his reactionary force, which was comprised mostly of civilians.

"I'll give him a hand," Rachel said and hurried after him, ignoring the required protocol to give the general a salute.

General Fosswell then turned to me. "Sergeant Clark advised me you predicted this attack. How'd you know?"

"I dreamt it," I responded.

He looked at me in puzzlement. "A premonition?"

"I guess so."

"Have you had other premonitions?" he asked. This time, I didn't answer. He looked thoughtfully a moment before pointing at all of us.

"Let's get a body count."

"Three hundred and seven," Norman said when we'd finished counting. "In technical parlance, that's a shit load."

"Yep," I said as I looked them over. There was nothing discernible about the demographics of the things. They were mostly younger; I didn't spot any of them that appeared over sixty, although it was hard to tell due to the scarring. I ripped a few shirts open and looked them over.

"What are you seeing, Gunderson?" General Fosswell asked. I pointed at the one I was currently looking at.

"The scarring is old and healed. These aren't fresh; they've been zombies for a while now."

"I understand you people have had similar attacks in the past," the general remarked.

"We did."

"I also read where you and your crew organized and conducted a large killing operation."

"Yeah, there'd been a buildup north of where we lived. They hampered our scavenging, and it was only a matter of time before they were going to drift toward our neck of the woods. So, we took a proactive approach and eradicated a sizeable proportion. It was mostly effective."

"And, you did it with civilians," he remarked.

"We had one soldier with us, but yeah, the rest of us were civilians."

"Nice. We're going to have the Marines go on more missions, so they will be absent frequently. I need to find a way of training these civilians so they may be able to perform a similar operation without depending on military personnel. I think you people could be instrumental in that endeavor."

"Yeah, good luck with that," I said. "You have too many chiefs and not enough Indians. I'm sure it's hard getting them to listen to orders."

He didn't respond, and instead changed the subject. "What did you do with all of the corpses after you'd killed them?"

"We used a bulldozer to pile them up and then burned them." I pointed at the corpses. "The longer they lay here, the worse the smell is going to get. If you want, I can organize a work crew and get started on them. How about you guys? How'd you handle the corpses?"

"We've been dumping them in a local landfill, but it's caused side effects," the general said.

"Flies," Norman said. "Millions of flies. And, there's no telling what those rotting bastards are doing to the groundwater."

"We have a crematorium down below," Lois said. "It would make things a lot easier."

Parvis, who had been listening to our conversation, cleared his throat. "It's only large enough to cremate three at a time. It was only meant to dispose of anyone who died while in lock-down, not for larger numbers like this." He gestured at the corpses again. "As you can imagine, it'd be problematic to transport all of these things down into the bunker."

"So, we dump them in the landfill," I said.

Parvis grinned. "Maybe not. I rigged up something in Bluemont that I've been dying to try out."

And that's how it worked out to where we were tasked with cleaning up the mess. It took most of the day to load up the corpses into dump trucks, and then we followed Captain Fosswell and Parvis into the small town of Bluemont. When we stopped, his reactionary force casually exited and formed a loose defensive perimeter. Parvis led the caravan to four dumpsters that appeared attached together with pipes.

We stopped and got out. I walked over and looked it over. There were a series of two-inch holes drilled in the base of the dumpsters, which I presumed enhanced airflow. Each dumpster also had a pipe running into it. I followed the pipe back to a nearby propane tank. He even had regulators attached. I looked inside. It looked like he'd attached stainless burner tubes to the pipes.

"What do you think?" Parvis asked. "It won't get as hot as a crematorium, but I believe it'll do the job."

"If there's enough propane in that tank, it should work," I said.

Parvis grinned and started tinkering with the gauges.

He eventually got it going, and we spent the rest of the day tossing the bodies into the dumpsters. We'd toss a few in, add a little stale diesel fuel, wait for them to burn, and then toss in a few more. It was nasty, stinking work.

It was sundown by the time we'd burned the last dead zombie and I'll have to say, I was tired and I smelled. We all smelled. We stood around talking about the day's events.

"Well, all in all, this was a success," General Fosswell said.

"Yes, it was," Parvis agreed.

"Who needs those Marines anyway, right, General?" Lois said with a nervous laugh. General Fosswell ignored her comment and motioned for his son, who jogged over.

"Yes, sir?" he asked.

"Get everyone loaded up and back to camp. Zach and I are going to ride back together."

The younger Fosswell gave me a look. "Do you want me to ride with you?"

"That won't be necessary. I need to have a private conversation with Mister Gunderson."

"Roger that, sir," he said, saluted, and jogged off before his father had a chance to return his salute.

"I'd like for Fred to stay," I said. The general looked over at Fred and nodded. We watched as the younger Fosswell got everyone loaded up.

"Your son has a lot of respect for you," I commented.

The general did not immediately respond. Instead, he watched as Captain Fosswell took one last look at him, perhaps waiting for a signal or something. General Fosswell merely nodded. His son hopped in the last truck and they drove off.

"He was a graduate of West Point, just like me," he suddenly said. "Only, unlike me, he was last in his class. He was going to be Special Forces, just like me, but he barely made through jump school and was cut from Ranger school. Twice."

"There are worse things a son could do," I said. The general glanced at me and gave a clipped chuckle.

"Yes, I suppose so. How were you with your father?"

"My parents died when I was young. I was raised by my grandmother." I gestured at Fred. "This man is my father, as far as I'm concerned."

"I see." He continued staring out in the distance. "Are either of you a religious man?" he asked. I was trying to figure the man out; he kept jumping from subject to subject.

"I am," Fred said quietly.

"My grandmother was. She carried me to church every Sunday and Wednesday night. When I started high school, I was on the track team and had a job, so I more or less quit going."

He turned to me. "What religion?"

"Presbyterian," I answered. Fred nodded in agreement.

"Ah," he said as he turned back toward the street the trucks were on. They'd already disappeared from view.

"I'm Catholic. The Catholics have a slightly different religious perspective than the Protestants." He then held his arm out and made a slow, sweeping gesture with it.

"The quaint little town of Bluemont, Virginia. Have either of you ever been here?"

"Nope, this is my first visit," I said. Fred gave a small nod in agreement.

"Not much to it," he said. "A typical sleepy town. A few of the Mount Weather employees lived here."

He pointed. "That road will lead you to Route 7, which is commonly known as Harry Byrd Highway. He was a Virginia senator, among other things. If you continue to travel east, you'll come to Round Hill, then Purcellville, and then Leesburg. All nice Virginia towns, back in the day. Eventually, you'll come to the Dulles airport."

"Okay," I said. "Where are you going with this?"

"We are wanting to eradicate all zombie presence through that pipeline, all the way to Dulles."

"I understand the need to reestablish air flight, but without fuel, that'd be a dead end, wouldn't it?"

He gave me a look and pointed toward the northwest. "That way, about two hundred miles, are refineries."

He let that sink in for a few seconds before continuing.

"You two should be a part of it. You're adventurers. Neither of you should be kept pent up within the confines of Mount Weather. We need leaders out here in the wilderness." He pointed in the general direction of Mount Weather.

"Those people only have an inkling of what it's like out here. Even me. Wouldn't you agree?"

"Yeah, probably," I said. "With the exception of Melvin."

"Ah, yes. Melvin is definitely an exception. Perhaps one or two others. The Marines would fare well, I would think. The rest, well..." He didn't finish the sentence, and instead changed the subject once more.

"The sinners and non-believers are feeling God's wrath. They are being purged from the earth. We must let it take its course."

I looked at him questioningly, wondering where he was going with the line of thought. He looked out into the distance, but I had no idea at what. I glanced over at Fred, who seemed to be lost in thought.

"Did you hear? Doctors Smeltzer and Kincaid believe they have created a vaccine."

241

"That's good news," I said.

"You would think so, wouldn't you?"

"Is there any reason why it wouldn't be?" Fred asked.

He kept staring off into the distance as a small knowing smile crept across his face. I continued watching him, wondering if I was seeing a side of General Fosswell he kept hidden from most other folks. I glanced over at Fred again, who gave me an arched eyebrow.

As we stood there, silent, wondering what the hell was going on, we heard the distinct snarling of zombies. The general pointed them out. If was six of them, they were maybe a hundred yards off, walking up the road.

"They're never too far away, are they?"

"We should get back," I suggested.

He stared at me queerly, the small smile still there. "Yes, I suppose you're right."

The ride back was quiet. I tried to engage him in casual conversation, but his responses were short, if he responded at all. I finally gave up, glanced over at Fred who still seemed to be lost in his own thoughts, and watched for threats. When we reached the front gate, he paused only long enough for the guards to open the gate and then parked in the parking lot.

CHAPTER 34 – COUP D'ÉTAT

The klaxon alarm sounded promptly at six. Sammy, Fred, and I were outside walking the dogs and chatting lightheartedly. I frowned as I looked around. I didn't hear any gunfire or anything else. I looked at Fred who gave a small shrug. I jogged over to the main guard post.

"What's going on?" I asked.

"Damned if I know," the guard replied. "We didn't do anything."

The klaxon continued for a full minute before shutting off. A woman's voice then came over the speaker.

"All personnel report to the cafeteria. Repeat, all personnel report to the cafeteria. This is not a drill."

The first thing I did was jog to our room and bumped into Kelly as I opened the door.

"What's going on?" she asked.

"I don't know," I said. For some reason, I was suddenly concerned. "Are you armed?"

She looked around to make sure nobody was nearby and patted her crotch. "Of course."

Janet exited the room next door.

"What's going on?" she asked, mimicking Kelly.

"We're about to find out. Are you armed?"

"Should I be?" she asked.

"Yes," I said. "Absolutely, but keep it hidden."

She gave me a look and disappeared back into her room. I watched through the open door as she opened a lock box and retrieved a derringer. She stuck in the pocket of her jeans, came out, and gave me a nod.

We walked together to the cafeteria. Everyone in our group, filtered in, along with almost everyone else who lived here. I saw a lot of familiar faces. They all looked tense, worried. But, what stuck out most was who I didn't see. Jim Hassburg, an almost ever-present person in the cafeteria, wasn't here.

Fifteen long minutes went by, with a couple of reminders over the intercom for everyone to get their asses to the cafeteria. Finally, a group of people walked in. The late arrivals included the Fosswells, Seth,

Raymond, a couple of civilians, and two soldiers I hardly ever saw. They were surrounding the Secretary of Defense, Abraham Stark. He raised a hand.

"May I have everyone's attention?" he asked in a loud voice. He waited until everyone had stopped chattering before continuing.

"I want to thank all of you for being here," Secretary Stark said. "I won't even attempt to manipulate you with political nonsense, there seems to be too much of that lately, so I'll make it short and sweet. I am now in charge."

I expected a massive collective gasp, but there was none. It was almost like everyone expected this to happen, and well, oh shucks, whatever.

I raised my hand. Secretary Stark looked at me impassively.

"Yes, Mister Gunderson?"

"A coup d'état?" I asked.

"Congressman Hassburg, the former speaker of the house, has formally declined to assume the role of presidency, as well as Senator Polacek, the former speaker pro tem."

"That leaves you," I remarked. He responded with a small nod.

"What exactly does this mean for all of us?" I asked.

"Status quo, Mister Gunderson." He looked around the room. "We are going to continue growing Mount Weather and moving forward with rebuilding this once great society." He looked around at his captive audience. "However, some of you will may want to reassess your value here at Mount Weather. Some of you seem to feel entitled to be here. Quite frankly, whoever does not pull their weight around here will find themselves being invited to leave Mount Weather."

I narrowed my eyes at him. "The way you phrased that last sentence implies some of us will be forced to leave."

"You are either with us or against us, Mister Gunderson. There is no in-between."

"That's a hell of an ultimatum," I said as I casually looked around. We were getting sidelong stares from a lot of people. I caught a look from Fred. Now was not the time for a confrontation, he was telling me. I understood.

"We're not against you, Mister Secretary," I said. "But, don't expect me to agree with everything you say or do."

Secretary Stark, or should I say President Stark, smiled easily now. "Oh, I expect you will find yourself agreeing more than disagreeing, Mister Gunderson. Excuse me."

He then walked away and approached a table full of politicians and their aides. They all looked tense. Hell, everyone looked tense.

"What does this mean for us?" Janet quietly asked.

I saw Cutter about to say something, but I cut him off by clearing my throat. When he looked at me, I made a subtle gesture toward a table near us. At least two of them heard Janet's question and were obviously listening.

"It's a nice day outside," Josue said. When he had everyone's attention, he made a subtle gesture toward the door. Everyone seemed to understand.

We walked outside and I led everyone to our parked trailer. Everyone was present except one.

"Where's Kyra?" I asked her sister, who shrugged indifferently.

"Alright, the big question, how will this affect us and what are we going to do?" I posed both questions for everyone and then waited for someone to respond.

"Will they impose martial law or something?" Kate asked.

"Technically, we've been under martial law since the outbreak," I answered. "So, the answer is no."

"What do you think, Zach?" Janet asked.

"I think it'll be status quo for the most part. I think the only people who will suffer will be these politicians. They are going to find themselves obsolete."

"What'll happen to them?" Jorge asked.

"If I have a good read on Stark, he'll relegate their status down to common laborers. They'll put up a fuss and try to resist, but the only way they know how to fight is with words and manipulation of people's own personal interests. Those tactics won't work anymore, I'm thinking."

"And then what?" Kelly asked.

"At first, you'll see a subtle change. Things will be run more efficiently, but without the power of the vote and individual rights, it'll eventually become a totalitarian type of government around here."

"What do you think, Fred?" Josue asked.

"All I know is I don't care much for some of these people."

"So, it begs the question, what do we do?" Kelly asked.

I looked them all over. "Alright, here's what I think. They have a pretty good set up here. Plenty of livestock, good gardens, electricity, a functioning water supply and sewer system, a couple of doctors, a dentist, a veterinarian, a structured education system for the kids. These are things we didn't have back in Tennessee. With the politicians out of the way, I foresee improvements continuing."

"Like what?" Maria asked. She'd been quiet the whole time, as usual, but now I could see genuine concern in her expression.

"They're going to expand. Once they're sure the vaccine works, the word will get out, more people will be coming here. Parvis has already told me they're expecting this to happen. They have two major goals. The

245

first one is expanding the power grid into Bluemont, resettling people there, and then to expand eastward to Dulles airport."

"Why Dulles?" Janet asked.

"That's where Sarah plays a major part. Once they get fuel, they're going to get the airport up and running again. It's a long-range plan. They have a ten-year model all written up. It's pretty impressive."

"What's the downside?" Fred asked.

"The political dynamics are going to change dramatically. I'm guessing about all of this, but I foresee a lot of rules being created in the next few weeks or so. And, if you don't follow the rules, they'll instate some type of punishment, banishment probably. It's not much of an ultimatum for us; we can simply go back to Nolensville. But, for a lot of these people who've been accustomed to their elite status, they're not going to fare so well."

CHAPTER 35 — PEGGY

Melvin walked into the conference room to an audience of eight people.

"Good morning, Sergeant," Stark said.

"Back at you, sir," Melvin replied. "You know, I think this is the first time I've walked into a meeting in this conference room when it wasn't full. It's a rather stark contrast, don't you think?" Melvin arched an eye, wondering if anyone caught the pun. Stark responded with a tight smile.

"We've come to the conclusion large meetings with a bunch of gas bags is no longer and efficient means to operate at Mount Weather," an aide said.

"You'll get no argument from me," Melvin replied and cocked his head. "Say, how do I address you now?"

"President Stark, or Mister President," the same aide quickly replied.

Melvin nodded, grabbed a chair, and made himself comfortable. "Well, Mister President, what's cookin'?"

Melvin was hiding his apprehension. He assumed he was getting a new mission, but something in Stark's body language suggested something more was brewing.

"Sergeant, how do you like Mount Weather?" President Stark asked.

"Oh, I like it okay. The people here are decent, for the most part. There are some who don't care too much for me, but that's alright. Why do you ask?"

"We want to begin implementing outposts around the area, and with your experience and knowledge, we want you to start setting them up. What do you think of that?" General Fosswell said.

Melvin rubbed his face. "Sure, that sounds fine. Who are the personnel for this, if I may ask?"

"I think you will agree there are certain people who have not pulled their weight around here. They will be given the option of manning these new outposts," Fosswell said. "In time, it is hoped they will become self-sufficient."

"What if they refuse?" Melvin asked.

"That is their choice, of course," President Stark said. "But they will be summarily evicted from the Mount Weather community and receive no other assistance from us."

"We'd prefer not to exercise the latter option," an aide said. "So, if we can provide them with relatively safe locations and get them set up, it would go a long way to achieving our long-term goals."

Melvin nodded slowly. He knew who was going to be kicked out: most, if not all, of the politicians who have skated by ever since the evacuation from D.C.

"Alright, I can do it. A couple of questions: how many locations, how far apart, and when do you want me to start?"

The aide stood, picked his laptop up, and carried it over to Melvin. He pointed at the screen.

"We think a reachable goal is to have at least five, and maybe ten, before the first snowfall. We'd like them focused starting in Bluemont and then various locations southeast along the 734 corridor. Our goal is to eventually establish an outpost at Dulles. You should try to find structures that can be fortified and hold ten or more people."

Melvin nodded as he looked at the computer screen.

"Do you see this?" The aide pointed at an overly of a blue line running along Highway 734. There were occasional symbols along the line.

"Yeah, what is that?"

"That's a power line," President Stark said. "Parvis and a couple of others are going to go with you and assess it, see how damaged it is, and if it can be repaired."

Melvin nodded in understanding. "You want these new homes to have power."

"Yes," President Stark said.

Melvin grunted. "The further east you go toward the larger cities, the more zeds you'll encounter. Not to mention damage to the infrastructures."

He thought about it as he looked at the computer. "Yeah, I already have a few places in mind." He looked up at President Stark. "You're going to evict a hundred folks? There's only a hundred and thirty here."

"As soon as your mission gets underway, we are going to initiate radio broadcasts inviting people to come live up here. Having a working power grid will be a major selling point, we believe."

"Yeah, okay. When do you want me to get started?

"How about tomorrow morning?" General Fosswell replied with a tight expression. "We already have a family who is ready to relocate."

Melvin listened as they explained. His mood grew somber. It sounded like a certain politician was being railroaded, but he kept his opinion to himself. When they were finished, Melvin stood.

"Well, I better get going. I have a lot of stuff to do before tomorrow."

"There is one other item we need to discuss, Sergeant," President Stark said. Melvin slowly sat back down.

"We've had complaints about Peggy," he began.

"She isn't bothering anyone," Melvin retorted.

"There was an incident yesterday in which some curious children got a little too close to her before one of the guards manning the front gate intervened."

"I'm wondering how that guard allowed those kids to get out of the gate unattended in the first place," Melvin mused.

"Probably because the guard was not paying attention," General Fosswell said. "It happens and kids will be kids. Let's not beat around the bush, Sergeant. You need to find somewhere else to keep Peggy when you are in garrison. It's nothing personal, but it is a serious safety issue." Captain Fosswell leaned over and whispered to his father a moment.

"It's my understanding Mister Gunderson's intuitions indicate she's a threat to Mount Weather."

"He was only speculating," Melvin replied.

"He speculated about an imminent attack as well, and it seemed to be well founded," the general rejoined.

"She can't be kept anywhere close to Mount Weather," President Stark said.

Melvin stood again. "I understand. I'll take care of it." He turned around and left.

"We should follow-up on it," the aide said. "Maybe we should direct someone to kill her tonight. Gunderson maybe."

"No," Stark said. "Sergeant Clark is a man of his word. He said he'll take care of it and he will."

Savannah was waiting for Melvin outside of the conference room. He didn't say anything and walked directly outside. She followed and the two of them walked toward the main gate.

"How's it going, Melvin? Hi, Savannah," Slim said as they approached the gate.

"Guard duty again?" Melvin asked.

"Yeah," Slim replied. "As long at the Marines are gone, I'm going to have it every day. You'd think certain people would step up and start volunteering to do more, give us peons a break once in a while."

Slim was a maintenance man with Mount Weather. He had no political pull and no specialty skills other than knowing little things like how to unstop a toilet. He'd never even fired a weapon until Melvin taught him.

"Yeah," Melvin said. Melvin had a feeling there would be a lot more volunteering once word got out of Stark's plan to evict some of them.

"I'm going to check on Peggy," he told Slim.

"Alright, buddy," Slim said and helped with opening the gate.

Savannah wondered what he meant and kept following him. She watched as Melvin stopped in front of Peggy and carefully took her helmet off, which he normally only did when he was going to feed her. "Do you have something to feed her?" Savannah asked.

"No," Melvin replied. "It won't matter." He moved closer to Peggy.

"Careful," she admonished.

Melvin ignored her and dropped the helmet to the ground. Peggy usually took the opportunity to gnash at Melvin whenever he took the helmet off, but this time, she stared at him silently. He faced her, his face only a couple of feet away from hers.

"Hello, Peggy," he said. She stared back at him with her black eyes.

"Maybe she's thirsty," Savannah suggested.

Melvin thought about it and then retrieved a canteen out of the truck. He held it while Peggy drank sloppily.

"C'mon, let's take a ride," he said to Savannah and then yelled up to Slim. "We'll be back in a little while!"

Slim acknowledged with a wave and the two of them got in the truck.

"I'm heading out on a mission tomorrow," he said to Savannah as he drove down a fire road southeast of the compound. Savannah looked at him questioningly.

"What kind of mission?" she asked.

Melvin didn't answer immediately and stopped deep in the woods. He turned off the truck and got out. Savannah followed him to the front of the truck. He stood there, staring at his wife.

"*Melvin.*"

It came out as a guttural rasp, barely understandable, but Savannah jumped in surprise.

"Oh, my God, she just said your name!" she exclaimed. Melvin didn't say anything.

"Has she ever done that before? I mean, since she became infected?"

Melvin shook his head.

"*Melvin,*" Peggy said again.

Melvin stared intently into his wife's eyes, trying to get a reading on her. As he watched, a single tear fell down her scarred cheek. He looked over at Savannah, who was standing behind him. He turned back to Peggy.

"It's time, sweetheart," he whispered. She smelled bad, like roadkill simmering on hot asphalt. He'd never gotten used to it. He stepped back, drew his Glock, and fired. The bullet entered an inch above her right ear and exploded out of the other side in a mist of brain tissue and black goo. Savannah yelped as she jumped back in surprise.

Melvin holstered his handgun, pulled out his knife, and began cutting through the duct tape holding his late wife to the chair. When he finished, he picked her up and laid her down on the side of the road before getting a shovel out of the back of the truck. He found a spot that looked free of roots and rocks, but before he could stick it in the ground, a chorus of unhuman screams emanated from within the woods. Both of them instinctively crouched partially and drew their respective handguns.

"What the fuck was that?" Savannah asked under her breath.

Melvin wasn't sure. His first thought was zombies, but he'd never heard zombies make blood-curdling screams like that.

Savannah gasped. "Oh shit, look!"

She was pointing down the fire road. Zombies started emerging from the woods, dozens of them, and started walking toward them.

"Get in the truck," Melvin urged. He need not have bothered; Savannah had jumped in the truck and locked her door before he'd even had a chance to close his mouth. He was right behind her.

"Where the hell did they come from?" she asked.

Melvin had no answer. They'd patrolled all around Mount Weather and thought they had eradicated all of the infected. Even though the last patrol was back in June, he had a hard time understanding why the things would move back in.

"What are they doing?" Savannah asked.

"I don't know." There were probably thirty of them. They'd stopped and were now standing together, motionless, less than twenty feet away from them. Savannah gripped her handgun tightly. Melvin noticed.

"Easy now," Melvin said. "They aren't attacking us. Let's not waste bullets. Something else is going on here."

They sat there and watched six of them walk forward and surrounded Peggy. They then picked her up and carried her back to the main group.

"What the fuck?" Savannah whispered as they watched the zombies carrying her. Within a minute, they disappeared into the woods.

They sat there for several minutes, but they were gone. Gone back to wherever they'd come from. Melvin started the truck and drove back to Mount Weather. He parked at the decontamination station this time, and the two of them began washing down his truck. Slim exited the guard shack and walked down to them.

"Where's my girl at?" he asked lightheartedly. Savannah waited for Melvin to answer. When he did not, she answered for him.

"He put her down," she said. Slim's grin disappeared.

"What do you mean? He killed her?"

Savannah nodded her head. Both of them looked at Melvin uncertainly. He ignored them and continued scrubbing his truck.

"What'd y'all do with her?" Slim asked.

"We were going to bury her, but a bunch of zombies came out of the woods and carried her off."

Slim looked at her dumbly. "C'mon now, don't bullshit me with something like that."

He kept staring at the two of them but neither responded. Savannah shrugged apathetically.

"I'm going to call it in," he said and jogged back to the guard shack.

Melvin finished washing his truck and drove it through the gate, absently thinking it was the first time he'd brought his truck inside the Mount Weather compound in over three years. He parked it in the parking near the main building and looked over at Savannah.

"Why don't you go get something to eat? I'm going to prep the truck for tomorrow."

"Aren't you going to join me?" she asked.

He gripped the steering wheel tightly, not looking at her. "I need to be alone for a while."

"I can wait, I'm not that hungry right now —"

Melvin cut her off. "Damn it, Savannah, is it too much to ask for some alone time? You're up my ass constantly for Christ's sake. I just want some fucking space."

Savannah looked at him as he continued staring straight ahead, gripping the steering wheel.

"Okay," she said quietly, fighting the tears welling up in her eyes. She got out and walked inside.

Savannah made a detour to the women's locker room. She locked herself inside one of the stalls, sat, and cried silently. Other women walked in and were chatting about nothing important. She waited for them to leave before exiting the stall. She washed up at the sink, retrieved Melvin's comb out of her back pocket and fixed herself up in front of the mirror before going to the cafeteria.

She put on a pleasant face and walked to the cafeteria. Most of the Tennessee people were present. Maria saw her first, smiled, and waved her over. She got halfway through her meal when she felt a presence looming over her. It was Captain Fosswell and Ensign Boner.

"Where's Clark?" Captain Fosswell asked gruffly.

"I don't know," Savannah replied.

"Don't hand me that shit, where is he?" he demanded.

Kelly jumped to her feet. "She said she doesn't know. Stop being an asshole!" She literally shouted it, causing everyone to stop talking and turn to the commotion.

Ensign Boner stepped closer. "Sweetie, tell us what happened with Peggy."

"Her name is not Sweetie!" Maria shouted. She was standing with Kelly. "Her name is Savannah. Either call her Savannah or ma'am, you sexist pigs!"

The rest of the Tennessee crew stood now, even Shooter.

"You know, if Zach or Fred were here, you two would already be flat on your asses," he said.

Boner held his hands up and backed off. "I'll go check the armory," he said and quickly left. Captain Fosswell looked uncomfortable now and left soon behind him.

Everyone sat down then.

"Holy shit, I've never heard you yell before," Cutter said to Maria.

"Me neither," Kelly said. "You go, girl."

Maria actually blushed a little.

"So," Shooter said. "What the hell were those two bozos wanting to know? Boner said something about Peggy."

Savannah drank some water, her hand trembling slightly but nobody said anything.

"Melvin took her out in the woods and killed her," she said.

"What?" Jorge asked. "He killed his wife?"

"Well, she wasn't his wife anymore, she was a zombie," she said.

"Yeah, yeah, I meant to say that," Jorge said.

"What'd he do with the body?" Cutter asked.

"He was going to bury her, but a bunch of zombies came out of the woods and carried her off."

Now there was a collective gasp. Savannah told them the details.

Melvin walked in a little before midnight. Savannah was already in bed, but she couldn't sleep. The dim light in the hallway illuminated the room when he opened the door. He closed it quickly and moved toward the bed. There was enough light coming through the crack at the bottom of the door where she could watch as Melvin stripped to his underwear and then crawled in bed with her.

"Hey," she said quietly.

"Hey." He was silent for a long ten seconds. "I'm sorry about earlier."

"It's okay," she said.

"I can go sleep in the dorm if I'm making you uncomfortable."

He was lying on his back. Savannah rolled over, draped an arm across his chest, and snuggled into his shoulder.

"I want you here, with me," she said.

"Okay," he said.

"Are you okay?" she asked.

Melvin sighed before answering. "I knew this day would come; it just hit me a little funny. I shouldn't have taken it out on you."

"It's okay."

He sighed again. "How was your day otherwise?"

"It was okay. Oh, I went to my follow-up with Doctor Salisbury after lunch."

"Oh yeah, everything okay?" he asked.

She snuggled a little closer. "She gave me a clean bill of health." She was silent for a minute before speaking again.

"So, if you want to, you know, we can."

Melvin was silent. After a moment, he turned toward her and kissed her on the top of her head. Savannah started stroking his chest and waited. And kept waiting.

He was quiet for so long she thought he'd gone to sleep, but then he kissed her again. And again. He worked his way down to her mouth and kissed her passionately. He then helped her out of her T-shirt.

Melvin awoke at his usual time and lay there, trying to clear his head. He'd dreamt about Peggy all night. Mostly bad dreams. He arose quietly and went straight to the locker room. He hoped a long hot shower would put him in a better mood. He heard the shower curtain opening behind him and turned to see Savannah. She removed her towel and hung it on the hook, self-consciously folding her arms over her breasts. He looked around nervously, wondering if there was anyone else in the locker room.

"Get in," he said and pulled the shower curtain closed behind her.

"Oh, shit, you've really got it hot," Savannah said as she stepped under the water.

He looked at her as she closed her eyes and turned her face up, letting the water spray her face. He found himself reaching for the shampoo bottle and lathering up her hair. She murmured in contentment and leaned back against him.

"You've gained weight," he said. "I noticed last night."

"Doctor Salisbury weighed me. Ninety-eight pounds. She said my target weight should be one-twenty by Thanksgiving."

"Good," he said and rinsed off. "Maybe you should start lifting weights, build up your muscles."

"Will you work out with me?" she asked.

"Sure." He watched as she rinsed off, fighting the urge to get frisky. "There's something I have to get off my chest," he said.

Savannah rinsed the soap off of her face and looked up at him with her big brown eyes. She knew better, but somewhere in her brain, she suddenly worried he was about to dump her.

"There've been a couple of women since Peggy," he said. "But, they weren't anything serious. Casual flings, friends with benefits, whatever you want to call it, they weren't anything serious."

"Okay," Savannah said.

"I kept it that way on purpose so when it was time to end it, there'd be no emotional attachment, at least not on my end." Melvin searched for the right words, even putting his face under the showerhead, momentarily hoping the hot water would get his brain moving.

"So, anyway, I wanted you to know that. And, I want you to know that I don't think of you in the same way. I laid there last night trying to think up something to say to end our relationship. I thought of a few of reasons, but ultimately I realized it was the last thing I wanted. I want you, and not for just a casual fling. I want more than that. Is that okay?"

Savannah stared at him deeply. "You'd have me?" she asked.

"Absolutely."

She hugged him tightly and then kissed him. "You won't be sorry," she said.

Melvin smiled. "Good. Let's get out of here."

He peeked through the curtain. Nobody else was currently in the locker room.

"C'mon." They hurriedly dried off, wrapped the towels around themselves, and went back to their room.

CHAPTER 36 – JIM

"Alright, start it up," I directed to Savannah.

Savannah dutifully cranked the ignition, and after a moment, the engine roared to life. Jim nodded in somewhat sad gratefulness.

"I appreciate it," he said.

I removed the jumper cables and closed the hood as Melvin did the same to his truck. Savannah exited the car, a Subaru Outback, and joined the rest of us.

"Are you sure this is what you want to do?" Parvis asked him.

Jim looked at his wife, Linda, and nodded.

Parvis looked solemn, but did not argue with him. He reached into his pocket and handed Jim a set of keys.

"All of the entry doors on the house use the same key. The barn and tool shed have different keys. These are the ones," Parvis said and pointed them out.

"And another thing," he continued. "As soon as you get settled in, give us a shout on the radio. If we don't hear from you in two hours, we're sending out a search party."

"I will do so," Jim said and held out his hand. "I appreciate everything," he said and looked over at Linda. "Are you ready, honey?"

Linda, Jim's wife of thirty years, was a statuesque blonde who carried herself like a beauty pageant contestant, which she once was. She nodded once, trying hard to maintain her composure. He nodded at his two girls, two younger versions of their mother in their late twenties.

The four of them got into the car and quietly drove away from Mount Weather.

Melvin gestured at his truck, which was loaded down. "I'm going to follow along, help them get settled in, and then I'm going to check on some stuff. I'll be back in a couple of days." He gave Savannah a long hug.

"I want to go with you," she begged in a low whisper.

"We've talked about this," he said. "As long as Lonnie and his boys are in the area, it's not safe."

She continued holding him. "I still want to go," she said.

"You'll be fine here. I check in every day on the radio, and I'm only going to be gone a few days. Besides, you need to start socializing, get some female friends. If you have any problems with anyone, you go tell Kelly and she'll sic Zach on them," he said, looked over at me, and winked.

"Okay," she said and reluctantly let go of him.

Everyone else had walked in, with the exception of Savannah and me. We waved at Melvin as he left.

"Well, I don't have anything to do until three. Lydia finally stuck me with the evening shift maintenance duties. I think I'll go pester Kelly 'til lunch." I paused, waiting for her to say something. She looked a little apprehensive. She'd been looking that way since Melvin drove off.

"You got any plans?" I asked. She shook her head. "You want to come with me?"

Kelly had a group at one side of the room, teaching them math. Maria had the younger kids, including mine, in a separate room. She was reading them a story both in English and in Spanish. Savannah and I found a chair in the back of Kelly's room, sat and watched.

She really seemed to be enjoying herself, and the kids were being attentive. One kid raised his hand.

"Yes, Billy?" Kelly asked.

"Why do you need to know what square foots are?"

She seemed at a loss for words for a moment, then she looked back at me and smiled.

"Well, why don't we let Mister Zach explain? What do you kids think, should we let Mister Zach explain?"

There was a chorus of yesses. I stood, reluctantly, and walked to the front of the class, thinking along the way. When I got to the front, I saw a ruler.

"Oh, here we go," I said. I used the ruler and a marker to draw an almost perfect square foot on the board.

"So, this is one square foot, right?" I asked. I was met with silence. "Yes, that's right, I'm glad you kids agree. Now, answer me this, if this were one square foot of earth outside, how much wheat could you grow in it?"

There was more silence, but at least I had their undivided attention.

"Let's say you can grow one wheat plant in that square foot of earth, so how many plants would a one-acre field yield?" More silence. "Okay, hold on, let me give you guys some information."

I turned back to the chalkboard and wrote out the number of square feet to an acre.

"43,560, that's how many square feet are in an acre. So, how many wheat plants can you grow in an acre?"

Sammy tentatively raised his hand. I pointed at him.

"43,560?" he asked.

"Yep, you nailed it. So, now that you know how many wheat plants will grow in an acre, you get a pretty good idea of how much wheat you can harvest and how many people you can feed."

I paused, looking to see if any lightbulbs were going off in their young brains. But, honestly, I didn't see shit. I tried again.

"Here's another example. Say you want to build a house and you need to know how much concrete to pour for the foundation. The first measurement you take is the square footage, oh and how thick it's going to be, then you know how much concrete you'll need. See?"

After a moment, a little girl raised her hand. I pointed at her with a smile.

"Are we going to build a house?"

"Um, no, not right now."

"Why not?" another one asked.

I looked over at Kelly. "Okay, I give up."

She giggled at my efforts and looked at the clock on the wall. "Okay, everyone. Put your things away and line up to go to lunch."

CHAPTER 37 — RETURN FROM FORT DETRICK

"Alright, men, five miles to go," Justin said over the radio. He was in in the lead vehicle and was standing in the open hatch. In addition to the second Stryker they brought with them, they were bringing the two abandoned Strykers back home with them. If the vaccine works, it was going to be a successful mission. He might even pester General Fosswell for a promotion, he thought with a smile. He keyed the microphone.

"I want to tell you I'm proud of all of you. Nobody died, nobody got infected, and we accomplished the mission. You done good, men, you done good."

"I've never been so glad to see this place in my life," Joker said as the grounds of Mount Weather came into view.

"Yeah," Kirby agreed.

They parked the four Strykers at the decontamination station. Everyone got out and stretched. One of the guards exited the post and started walking toward them, but Justin waved them off.

"Gather around, everyone," Justin ordered. He waited until everyone was together in a loose formation. The two scientists awkwardly stood off to the side. Justin motioned toward them.

"Why don't you two go on inside. We'll bring your equipment in shortly."

Justin waited until they walked away before speaking in a low voice.

"First, I want to commend you Marines. Everyone's performance was top notch; you made my job easier. We'll have a more detailed debriefing at a later time, but for now, I just wanted to say I'm proud to be a part of you hard chargers."

"Thank you, sir," Sergeant Crumby replied.

"Second, we're going to go ahead and get these vehicles decontaminated before we do anything else."

He got a few hard looks, but nobody said anything.

"We'll worry about the rest later, but I must insist all of you shower before evening chow. We all smell awful."

There were a couple of guffaws now.

"Now, for the final thing I need to tell you men: I owe you Marines an apology. There are some things that have happened here while we were at Fort Detrick and I kept the information from you."

"What happened, sir?" Joker asked.

"The president was murdered," Justin replied. The Marines erupted with sounds of disbelief followed by a barrage of questions. He waited for the noise to die down and then explained.

"What are we going to do?" Corporal Conway asked.

Justin saw two carts approaching, each being driven by a Fosswell. He lowered his voice and spoke quickly.

"For now, we'll obey our chain-of-command. We'll talk more about all of this later when we know more details. Whatever we do, we do together, and we only talk about this amongst ourselves. Oo-rah?"

"Oo-rah!" the Marines said in unison.

"Alright, let's get this equipment cleaned up."

They started up the pressure washer and quickly began spraying down the Strykers. Justin helped out, but watched out of the corner of his eye as the two Fosswells spoke with the two scientists for several minutes. The scientists got on one of the carts with General Fosswell and they made a U-turn. A guard opened the gate and Captain Fosswell drove out. He made his way down the roadway and parked a few feet away. Justin walked over and rendered a salute to the captain.

"I need you to load up the doctor's equipment," the captain said. He hadn't even bothered getting out of the cart and made it clear he had no intention of assisting with the manual labor.

Justin recruited Joker to help him with the equipment. When they got it loaded, Captain Fosswell stared pointedly at Justin. "This stuff isn't going to get unloaded by itself, Lieutenant."

Justin held back a sigh and looked at Joker. "Give him a hand, will you?"

"Absolutely, sir," Joker said and jumped in the passenger seat. He then stretched, letting his left armpit get close to the captain's face.

Captain Fosswell looked at him briefly in annoyance before focusing back on Justin.

"There'll be a briefing in thirty minutes in Secretary Stark's conference room. Your presence will be required, but don't bring any of these smelly soldiers with you."

"Aye, sir," Justin replied and then lowered his voice. "Can you give me any additional info, sir?"

"All in due time, Lieutenant."

"Yes, sir," Justin said and rendered a salute. Captain Fosswell returned the salute casually and started to drive off, but paused momentarily.

"Since you've been gone, General Fosswell took the liberty of appointing Corporal Bullington as his administrative assistant. You didn't hear it from me, but she's anxious to see you, and she may even have some answers to your questions."

"Aye, sir," Justin said. Even though he'd been going on only four hours of sleep a night for the past two weeks, he had a feeling Ruth was going to keep him up half the night telling him everything that had been going on.

They got the armored vehicles hosed down in no time and double-timed to the locker room. Justin caught Ruth in the hallway on the way to the cafeteria and pulled her into an unoccupied side room. He kissed her and hugged her tightly.

"Easy, big guy," she said, smiling. "I'm pregnant you know. Besides, you need to take a long shower, you smell."

"Maybe you can scrub my back," he said with a grin.

"Maybe," she agreed, still smiling. "I have a lot to tell you."

"Okay, you can tell us all during dinner."

Ruth pushed away and shook her head. "No, half the stuff I have to tell you is secret. You're not going to believe some of it."

Justin looked at her questioningly. "Okay, but the boys are dying to know what the hell is going on."

Ruth gave him a pat on the cheek. "Alright." She was interrupted by the sound of the klaxon, followed by an announcement over the intercom.

"We have zombies approaching the main gate! Repeat, we have zombies approaching the main gate!"

"Damn it," Justin growled and sprinted back outside. He heard the sound of automatic weapons fire, and by the time he made it to the front gate, it was all over. Conway and Jenkins were standing in the open hatches of two of the Strykers, the barrels of their machine guns smoking.

Justin jogged up and saw fifteen zombies lying dead in the roadway. Conway looked over.

"What're you doing out here, sir?" he asked.

Justin stood there, catching his breath and looking at the carnage. "That's a good question," he said. The other Marines broke out in laughter.

CHAPTER 38 – THE VACCINE

"So, tell me, what's the next step with the vaccine?" I asked Parvis. He was watching Senator Nelson and I play chess. The senator took my rook with his queen. I quickly moved my remaining knight.

"Check," I casually mentioned. His king was hemmed in by other pieces, so his only move was to take my knight with his queen. He did so, and I took his queen with a pawn.

"Damn," he muttered.

I waited quietly as he worked it out and realized he was going to be mated in three moves. He sighed as he pushed over his king.

"Well played, sir," he said and stood. "I'm going to take a break and stretch my legs."

"Fancy a game?" Parvis asked after he'd walked off. I looked up and motioned toward the empty chair.

Parvis smiled and took his place. "Your game is good, but not perfect," he said as he began resetting the pieces.

"Human trials," he said as I advanced a pawn and he quickly advanced one of his own. I looked at him in puzzlement until I realized he was answering my question.

"When?" I asked and moved a piece. He responded by quickly moving another man, like we were under the clock, which we weren't.

"Tomorrow morning. Two people have volunteered."

"That's not very many," I remarked.

"Nope, it isn't. A few people are going to be voluntold," he said, moved a piece and lowered his voice. "The Marines."

"All of them?" I asked.

"Half. The pregnant one, Bullington, is exempt, but, we're going to need some women to volunteer as well, eventually."

Each of us was silent for the next few minutes as we developed our men. There was a quick trade off of pieces, leaving each of us down one knight and a pawn. The appearance of the board looked like I had better development, but I caught a small smirk on his face, which made me slow down a little and reassess the board. I almost missed it, but he was setting me up for a trap. The obvious move was for me to push my king's bishop pawn into a fork which would threaten a bishop and his remaining knight, but it was exactly what he wanted me to do. If I did it, he'd move his knight, I'd take the bishop, and he'd move his knight again, trapping my queen.

"Are there any side effects?" I asked, wondering if he would answer honestly.

"Shouldn't be," he said as he watched me move a pawn, freeing up my queen and queen's bishop. He was no longer smirking.

Yeah, no issues. It was easy to state there were no issues when you haven't done anything.

Our first game ended in a stalemate.

"I have a question for you," I said as we set up the board again.

"Shoot," he said.

"You have an intimate knowledge of this place and the protocol, correct?"

"Yep."

I was black in the first game. Now I was white and moved a pawn.

"What happened to the rest of the people on Capitol Hill? The Marines said not all of them were brought to Mount Weather."

"For continuity of government purposes, they were divided up into three groups, Alpha, Bravo, and Charlie. Mount Weather is designated for Alpha group. Bravo and Charlie were to be located in other bunkers similar to Weather."

He paused a moment while each of us took turns making moves and swapping pieces.

"So, originally, Alpha group was to be made up of POTUS, certain members of the cabinet, and all of SCOTUS."

"I sense something went wrong," I said and attempted to trap a bishop. Parvis immediately saw through my ruse and countered.

"Murphy's Law took charge. And, certain people insisted on being in the same bunker with POTUS. The entire Supreme Court judges were moved to Charlie. You can thank the esteemed Senator Polacek for that move."

"What happened to Bravo and Charlie?" I asked.

Parvis shrugged. "Dead, most likely. Hell, we were almost killed off by people who were locked down with us and were already infected. We were lucky enough to contain it."

Parvis won the second game and I was ready for bed, but he insisted on a third game. We played well into the night, even after everyone else had gone to bed.

"We think the first mission to Detrick was sabotaged," he said offhandedly during the middle of the third game. I'd managed to take a knight and had his queen pinned.

"Are you making that up?" I asked. "Trying to throw me off balance?"

He smiled tightly. "Is it working?"

"Nope. I think I may have you this game."

He grimaced as he stared at the board. "I do seem to be in a pickle at the moment." He pushed a pawn.

"Do you know who and how?" I asked.

"What do you think about the Fosswells?" he asked offhandedly.

I gave him a look. "The Fosswells? Are you sure?"

He glanced around. "Call it a suspicion," he said. I nodded in semi-understanding.

"The general is a highly decorated soldier," he said. "He finished first in his class at West Point and almost every specialty school after. As a young lieutenant, he received a Silver Star in Operation Desert Storm. A definite type-A personality."

"He doesn't seem to think much of his son," I said.

Parvis chuckled. "Harlan junior would have been better off as a civilian. He's no soldier. He's an intelligent man, but he's always been a type-B. He blindly follows his father."

After a series of moves, I was up three pieces. Parvis capitulated and yawned.

"Well now, that was a difficult match," he said. "By the way, everything we've talked about tonight should remain between the two of us."

"Of course."

I watched the next morning at breakfast as the Marines were given the news. They reacted about like how I expected them to. Then, Justin finished his breakfast, wiped his mouth, and stood.

"Alright, Marines. Let's see what this vaccine is all about."

Without saying another word, he walked out of the cafeteria. I gave Kelly a look, stood, and caught up with him in the hallway.

"What's the word?" I asked.

"Heading to medical," he said.

I heard the cafeteria doors open and looked behind us. The rest of the Marines were exiting the cafeteria and catching up to us.

"You're going to let them stick you, sir?" Sergeant Crumby asked.

"That's affirmative, Sergeant," Justin replied.

Sergeant Crumby got close to Justin and lowered his voice. "We don't have to be guinea pigs, sir. We got the firepower, they don't."

"Not necessary, Sergeant," Justin said, and then he stopped momentarily. "If any of you do not want to be inoculated, that's fine. I'll square away anyone who objects." He began walking again.

"But, they haven't done proper tests on that stuff," Joker said and he looked at me. "Right, Zach?"

"They've done some testing," I answered. "But I couldn't say whether or not it's good enough."

"You hear that, sir?" Joker cried. "They ain't done enough testing."

"Well then, there's one way to find out," Justin replied. He stopped again. "Men, without a vaccine, my unborn child won't stand a chance in this world. Nobody's children will."

"But, it might fuck you up," Joker lamented.

Justin looked at him and gave a small smile. "Yes, it might."

He resumed walking toward medical.

CHAPTER 39 – ISOLATION

After the announcement at breakfast, everyone's conversation was somewhat hushed, subdued. After Justin had gone into medical, two other Marines went with him. The others refused, or as Sergeant Crumby told General Fosswell, they were declining the request, and if he didn't like it, he could go fuck himself. Fosswell stared steadily at him for a few seconds before ordering the Marines to relieve the midnight guard shift.

I returned to the cafeteria and sat beside Kelly.

"Did he do it?" Kelly asked.

"Yeah, him and two others. The rest refused."

"I don't blame them," Cutter said.

I looked over at him and was about to say something harsh, but I paused and thought about it. If I weren't immune and was asked to be a test subject, what would I have done? Chances were, I would have refused as well. I refreshed my coffee and looked over at Fred, who'd been quiet the entire time.

"What've you got planned today?" I asked.

He made a small gesture toward another table. "Burt and I have farm work, but first thing in the morning, we're going to take a ride up to Bluemont."

"What for?" Shooter asked.

"We're going to check on Jim and his people," he said.

"Alright," I said. "I'll ride along."

"Zach," Kelly said. I looked at her and she shook her head slightly. I knew what she was implying.

"Yeah, I know, you don't have to spell it out," I said and looked at Fred. "Guess I'm not going."

"I'd like to go," Cutter said.

"Yeah, me too," Shooter added.

I caught Kate giving him a look, but she didn't say anything. I'm sure the brothers' desire to go visit had absolutely nothing to do with Jim's attractive daughters, but then again, I was the king of sarcasm.

Burt had apparently overheard the conversation and walked over.

"We're riding on horseback. Do you think you two can ride all day on a horse?"

"Horseback? Why horseback?" Shooter asked. "Let's take one of those Humvees."

Fred ignored both of them and handed me a piece of paper. "Here's the address where they're staying. It's a straight shot from here. We're leaving at sun up and should only be gone for two days at the most."

I looked it over before putting it in my pocket. "Alright, you two old men try not to terrorize the countryside."

Burt chuckled and Fred gave me a micro.

Jorge and I ended up in the armory and continued the never-ending task of reloading ammo. Surprisingly, Ensign Boner pitched in and helped out. It was slow, tedious work. I grew bored after three hours and stretched.

"I need a break," I said and stood. "I think I want to go see how it's going in medical."

"I thought it was quarantined?" Jorge asked.

"Not for me," I replied. I started to explain, but he waved me off with a grin.

"Yeah, go ahead," Jorge said. "I'm going to lunch in about an hour."

"Alright, I'll see you there."

"Tell Smithson he better not die before he gives me a rematch," Boner said.

I smirked as I walked out.

In medical, they'd fashioned a makeshift isolation ward. There were a total of six people in it, including Justin. Since I was immune, and I use that label loosely, I did not have to wear a mask or anything. I walked in and looked around. A couple were playing cards, a couple were sleeping. Justin had his bed adjusted so he could sit up, but he had a couple of blankets wrapped around him.

"How's it going?" I asked him.

He pointed over at a bed. There was a figure lying under a sheet. I thought it was someone who was sleeping.

"Who is it?" I asked.

"Grippentrog," he said.

Grippentrog. Everyone called him Grip; he was one of Justin's Marines. He was quiet, kept to himself mostly, but seemed like a decent guy.

"It sucks man," Joker said. He was in the next bed over, sitting up looking bored.

"What happened?"

"He went into anaphylactic shock about thirty minutes after being dosed," Justin said. He reached under the blanket and pulled out a used epi-pen.

"They tried this, but it didn't work. Check the expiration date."

I looked. It expired almost two years ago. I looked back up at him and then over to the covered corpse. Standing, I walked over and slowly pulled the sheet off of Grippentrog's head. I didn't see anything, but that didn't mean anything. I pulled my knife out and looked questioningly at Justin. He nodded somberly.

I shoved my knife deep into Grippentrog's left eye socket, wiggled the blade around to cause as much destruction to the brain that I could, and then cleaned the blade off with the sheet before covering him back up.

I walked back over to them. Joker looked okay, bored in fact. Justin was shivering and his brow had beads of sweat.

"I believe they call it ague," he said, answering my unasked question. "I'm running a fever, but I have chills. I can't get warm." He emphasized it by wrapping the blankets tighter around him. I looked around the room. Out of the seven left still alive, all of them except Joker seemed to have the same symptoms.

"Yeah, that happened to me," I said to them. "Don't be surprised if you get delirious. Well, if you get delirious, you won't realize what's happening, but anyway, it could happen."

"What do you recommend?" he asked.

"You need fluid intake and someone to watch you. My wife did it for me. My first wife. I was locked in a cage, but she took care of me. I'll go get Ruth, if you want."

"No," he instantly said while shaking his head. "She's pregnant. I don't want her anywhere near this room."

"No worries then," I said. "I'll stay with you."

He looked at me. "Are you sure, Zach?"

I scoffed. "I'm immune, remember?"

"No," Joker suddenly said. "I'll take care of them. You take care of Grip."

"I can cremate him, if that's what you guys want."

Joker glanced at Justin, who nodded.

"Yeah, man, but don't do anything with the ashes. We'll be wanting to give him a proper Marine funeral."

I nodded in understanding and looked at him.

"You know, I'm surprised you agreed to be a part of this."

He shrugged, but didn't comment. I nodded at him and pushed his friend out of medical.

I rolled the gurney down the hallway to the elevator and pushed the down button. A couple of people walked out of a room, saw me and the remains of Grip, and beat a hasty exit.

The bottom level was unoccupied. I pushed the gurney toward the crematorium, and remembering the process, fired up the oven, and moved the body off of the gurney and onto the table in front of the oven door. As I pushed Grip into the oven, I heard the elevator open and soon Parvis appeared. He pointed up at the surveillance camera in explanation.

"Grippentrog," I said, pointing at the corpse before I shut the door.

"I heard," he said. "It's a shame. We need trained soldiers more than anything else."

I stood there watching him work.

"I'm sensing you have something on your mind," Parvis said without looking at me.

"Congressman Hassburg," I said.

He turned and faced me. "Jim Hassburg is a good man," he said.

"I'm sensing a but in there somewhere."

"But, he lacks vision. He's the kind of man who believes he's serving his constituency by cooking for them." He gestured with a wave of a hand. "He was opposed to our future plans, but surprisingly, volunteered to occupy our first outpost."

"What about the esteemed senator?" I asked.

Parvis chuckled. "Senator Esther Polacek. You know, back in the day, she was one of the most powerful people in the nation. She believed she still held that power and went against us, or tried to. It didn't work."

"So, you're fine with Stark being sole ruler?" I asked.

He shrugged. "I was a tenured professor at MIT, did you know that?"

"Yeah, I read your bio."

"Yes, well, they offered me the job here. I had a wife, three kids, and two grandkids. I was looking for a laid-back retirement job."

"How'd your wife take it?"

"At first, she was all for it. I was tired of the big city life, and I assumed she was as well. We moved to Bluemont, which was a bit of a culture shock to her. She left me three months later and moved back to Boston."

"How about your kids?"

"You've met two of them, Garrett and Grace."

"Oh, yeah, the computer geeks."

Parvis chuckled. "Yeah, that's them. The other one, Grayson, he's the big brother. He ran an engineering firm in Boston. He had a pretty wife and two beautiful kids. I don't think they made it."

His face darkened at the memory. I made myself busy by looking at the temperature gauges.

"Anyway, here I am. The twins were students at MIT and were visiting me for Thanksgiving when the balloon went up."

"Funny how things work out," I said.

"Yes indeed. I would've liked my whole family here, even my wife, who had filed divorce and was trying to take everything I owned, but it is what it is."

"So, you're good with the current status quo?" I asked.

"Let's be frank, Zach. The politicians were dragging us down. We're behind the curve. Israel is back up and running. There are other countries as well. North Korea, for example. And we're mostly unchanged. Can you believe it? We've been here, languishing in a quagmire of political rhetoric ever since we went into lockdown."

He stared pointedly at me now. "All that is about to change. The winter is going to slow things down a bit, but you'll see some significant progress by this time next year."

He looked at me with a gleam in his eye. "It'll start with the vaccine. Soon, we'll expand the power grid, reestablish air transport, we'll get a refinery up and running again, and soon we'll have factories back online."

"Lofty goals," I said.

"Obtainable goals," Parvis countered.

I nodded thoughtfully.

Parvis folded his arms and used one hand to rub his chin.

"Zach," he said. "I've been thinking about this ever since you arrived. I'd like to mentor you."

"You want me to be your protégé?" I asked.

"Think about it. You don't even have a high school education and you have a tenured professor from one of the most prestigious universities in the world with more formal education than I have time to spell out offering to mentor you."

I let out a brief chuckle. "The first thing that comes to mind is, what's the catch?"

He looked out into space. "Well, if I was a good liar, I'd say there is no catch. I was simply identifying an intelligent young man who has a lot of potential and only needs guidance."

"But, you're not a good liar."

"No, I am not." He looked at me with a serious expression. "My kids are brilliant, but they're not leaders. They never will be. I'm thinking of the future. Our nation's future, Zach. My plan is to groom you to take over one day."

I snorted. "Take over? Did I hear you correctly?"

"Yes. One day."

"Parvis, what do you know about me?"

"I've read your bio, what you've bothered to divulge about yourself anyway. I imagine there's a lot you've not told about yourself."

"Here's one for you, that's probably not in my bio. This is my first time out of Tennessee. I've never even seen an ocean."

Parvis laughed.

"How are they?" Kelly asked. After leaving Parvis, I met all of the crew in the cafeteria and when Kelly asked, everyone stopped talking and waited for my response.

"One died. One of the Marines. Grip. When he was dosed, he went into anaphylactic shock."

"Man, that sucks," Jorge lamented. I heard someone at another table mutter an obscenity and looked over. It was the Marines.

"Yeah."

"How're the others?" Cutter asked.

I looked around at everyone at the table.

"Back when I got exposed, I ran a high fever for a little bit and was even delirious. There are a few who are experiencing the same symptoms." I looked at Kelly. "Justin included."

She looked worried and glanced over at the Marine table. They too were listening to my every word, including Ruth.

"That could be a good sign," I hurriedly said. "Like I said, it happened to me too. I worked through it and I'm fine now."

"How's Joker?" Sergeant Crumby asked.

"He's fine," I said. "No symptoms or anything."

"He's like a fucking cockroach," one of the Marines said with a clipped laugh. "You can't kill him."

Sergeant Crumby got up and walked over to our table. He stood in front of me and stared hard. "What are they going to do with Grip?" he asked.

"He's being cremated," I replied and looked at my watch. "The process should be finished in another hour."

We watched as Sergeant Crumby looked back at his Marines.

"We'll take it from here," he said. I nodded in understanding. They all stood and started walking toward the door. Crumby paused a moment.

"They won't let us in medical," he said. "You let us know how it goes, okay?"

"Yeah, you got it, Sergeant," I said. He stuck out his hand and we did a fist bump before he walked out.

CHAPTER 40 – PARTY TIME

The ague only lasted two hours before disappearing completely. Joker never showed any deleterious effects or discomfort. When the docs started checking on him, he jumped out of bed and knocked out fifty push-ups, jumped back up, and stared at them defiantly. Even so, the docs drew blood from everyone, checked their vitals at least four times, and finally declared them infection free. They were released in time for dinner.

They got a standing applause when they walked into the cafeteria. There was a lot of congratulatory conversation, and it was decided to have an impromptu party in the dorm room at twenty hundred hours.

Certain residents of Mount Weather, that is, kids and anyone under the age of forty, were not invited. When Kelly and I arrived, there were already several jugs of homemade wine being passed around. It was going to be one of those parties. It was fine with me. Everyone was in a good mood, even Priss, who I noticed was wearing her usual ensemble and had freshly shaven legs.

Heck, I even helped myself to a glass of wine. Before it got too loud, Justin emitted a loud whistle. Everyone became quiet. Justin nodded to Sergeant Crumby. The sergeant was holding an urn. He held it out and raised his glass with the other hand.

"This is for Grip, a damn good Marine." Everyone raised their glass in salute.

A little later in the evening, the weed came out. It was a stoner's heaven, and soon the dorm was full of smoke. I didn't partake, but my lovely wife loved the stuff. To my surprise, I saw her and Priss smoking a bong together.

"So, what do you think is next, Zach?" Joker asked. He'd gone around asking everyone the same question and he eventually got to me.

"Like Justin said, voluntary vaccinations for now, but eventually everyone will be required to get it," I said. "Well, except for me."

He put his arm around my shoulder and hugged me tightly. "Man, if this shit works, you'll be like a god around here."

"Well, I don't know about that," I said.

He hugged me again and then lowered his voice. "Hey, man, there's something I need to talk to you about."

"What's up?" I asked.

"Uh, well, I've kind of been seeing Maria on the sly," he said. "And I want to take it to the next level."

"You're going to propose?" I asked.

Joker laughed. "No man. I want to get with her, you know what I'm saying?"

He spotted Maria at the other end of the room. She was talking with Melvin and Savannah. When he caught her attention, he blew a kiss at her. Maria pretended not to notice, but I could see her struggling to hide a smile.

"I don't know, Joker, she's pretty conservative," I said. "And traditional."

"Man, I really like her."

"Have you gotten to know her brother and father?"

"No, man. Jorge I can handle, but the old man looks at me like he'd like to sneak up on me one night and cut my throat. I bet he was Mexican Mafia or something back in the day."

I chuckled. That sounded like Josue.

"I don't know, Joker. When it comes to women, I'm not all that smart, but I think Maria isn't the type to jump in the sack with you unless she's in love with you and she's sure you're in love with her."

Joker frowned and took a large gulp of wine. "Yeah, you're probably right. I'm going to have to properly court her, ain't I?"

"Yep, probably so," I said with a grin. He spotted Cutter and Stretch and wandered over to them.

Justin walked up to me and gave me a fist bump.

"Still feeling okay?" I asked.

He shrugged. "I have a headache, but it might be from all of this smoke."

I laughed. "Okay. I have another question. Somehow, none of these people have any kind of work duties until tomorrow afternoon. Did you have something to do with that?"

He grinned. "I called in a favor. They owed it to me."

He nodded over to a group of his Marines. "They need this. They've been underappreciated for so long they were all ready to bug out. Especially after Grip died."

"You got that right," somebody said.

I turned toward the voice to see Sergeant Crumby who had walked up behind us. He gave us each a fist bump.

Justin focused back on me. "The Sarge here is going to keep an eye on our boys. I'm going to sneak out of here and spend some time with my wife." He paused for a moment and then suddenly gave me a hug.

"I'm glad we're friends, Zach," he said and walked out before it got all gushy.

"He's a good man," Crumby said.

"Yeah, I believe you're right."

I mingled around, talking with everyone before I started yawning. I looked at my watch and realized it was a couple of hours past my normal bedtime. I spotted Kelly, still sitting in the same chair. There were others around her now. All of them were laughing and carrying on. I walked over, trying to figure out how to subtly get her out of here so I could go to bed.

Kelly saw me and motioned me closer with a finger. When I bent over, she put her arms around my neck and whispered in my ear.

"I am so fucking horny," she drawled out and punctuated it by briefly sucking on my earlobe.

"Let's get out of here," I whispered back.

As I was helping her out of the chair, I noticed Priss smiling at me. She'd never done that before, which was weird.

We said our goodbyes and made our way down the hall.

"Where are we going?" Kelly asked as she grabbed my butt and giggled.

It was a good question. It was difficult to get frisky in our room with the kids so close, and Janet was babysitting as well. Also, there were surveillance cameras almost everywhere...the key word being almost.

"I know where we can go," I said and grabbed Kelly's hand.

We ended up in the tack room of the horse barn. I had barely gotten some blankets on the ground when Kelly jumped me. It'd been a long time since she'd been so aggressive and I reacted in kind. When we were finally spent, we lay there, sweating and breathing heavily.

"I think all of that screaming scared the horses," I said to her. She giggled.

"I got hit on tonight," she said.

I scowled in darkness. "Oh, yeah, by who?"

"Priss."

I turned to her. "No shit?"

"Oh yeah. All she wanted to do was talk about sex. She first suggested she and I do it, then she suggested we have a three-way."

"Oh, hell no," I said quickly.

Kelly pulled me back on top of her. "You're damn right, now fuck me," she said huskily.

CHAPTER 41 – BLUEMONT

Fred frowned at the horse blankets lying on the ground. He had neatly stacked them the day before, and he was pretty sure Burt hadn't thrown them down there.

"Damn kids," he muttered as he picked them up.

He had gotten as far as feeding and brushing the horses when Burt walked into the barn.

"There's been a slight change in plans," he informed him. Fred stopped what he was doing and looked at Burt questioningly.

"Uh, well, it goes like this. My wife insists on going with us."

"I'll get another horse ready," Fred said.

"Yeah, about that. She also insists on taking a motor vehicle. She's wanting to take some supplies to them. They haven't gotten themselves sorted out yet."

"Alright," Fred said.

"I got a nice Chevy crew cab we can ride in," Burt said. "I bought it a few months before it all went bad, so it's still in good shape."

Fred gave Burt a micro. "Sounds good."

"Oh, and there's something else," Burt said. Fred waited. "There's somebody else who wants to go with us."

Burt motioned toward the open barn doors. As Fred watched, Sarah walked in. And she wasn't alone.

Rachel waved cheerfully as the four of them exited the main gate.

"You kids have fun!" she yelled as they drove by.

"Is she always like that?" Burt asked Sarah, who was sitting in the backseat along with Fred and Senator Esther Polacek.

"I'm afraid so," she replied.

They'd driven only a couple of miles down 601 before Fred spoke.

"They didn't have a problem with you tagging along, I take it."

"Who? Fosswell and Stark?" she asked. Fred nodded. "Rachel's going to tell them in about an hour."

"She certainly didn't seem to mind," he said.

"She encouraged me to go."

Fred glanced at her. Sarah responded with a shrug and a slight smile.

The road from Mount Weather to Bluemont had been cleared over a year ago, and a lot of the potholes had even been filled in with asphalt. This resulted in a drive of approximately ten minutes.

"It would've been a nice day for a horseback ride," Burt remarked. His wife gave him a look.

"Just saying," he muttered.

They continued on 601 past Bluemont proper for a mile and then turned right onto a long driveway. The house was a large modern two-story rambler. As the house came into view, Burt slammed on the breaks.

"Oh, dear God," Anne exclaimed.

The house was surrounded by zombies. Fred did a quick count and estimated there were at least thirty of them of various sizes and genders.

"It's a good thing we're loaded for bear," Burt said as he put the truck in park. Anne had two rifles resting barrel down between her legs. She handed one to her husband without being asked and took the other one for herself. Fred noticed it was a Winchester model 9422 lever action rifle.

"We can't shoot at them without taking a chance of hitting the house," Burt said.

Fred opened the back door. "No problem. I'm going to draw them away. Be ready."

"That's too dangerous," Sarah warned.

He gestured at the M4 she was holding. "Not if you cover me."

He hopped out of the truck before she could argue and began jogging toward an open field to the left of the house. As he did so, he drew his pistol and fired six times in rapid succession. Six of the zombies dropped immediately.

The others turned toward the sound of gunfire. Fred stopped and calmly reloaded. Most of them were drawn toward Fred now and started making their way toward him. Two more ran ahead of the pack. Fred palmed the hammer and fired, but as he fired the second shot, he heard a gunshot to his right. Anne was out of the truck and had been running toward Fred, but stopped to shoot. She cycled the lever and jogged over to Fred.

"You're going to need a hand," she explained and shot three rapid-fire shots, dropping three more. Fred paused only long enough to arch an eyebrow before refocusing.

Burt and Sarah stuck their rifles out of the open windows and joined in. Fred watched Anne out of the corner of his eye. She'd only take a second to aim, fired, and worked the lever in a fluid motion. All of her shots were headshots. It was over within minutes.

"Ain't she something?" Burt said with a grin as he walked up.

"That was some fine shooting," Fred admitted.

"My daddy taught me," Anne said, blushing slightly.

As they stood there admiring their work, there was a sound of the front door being opened. They all watched as Jim Hassburg emerged, a handgun at his side. Upon recognition, he holstered his weapon and waved.

"Good morning, Congressman," Burt said as the four of them picked their way through the corpses and joined Jim on the front porch.

"I think I'd rather be simply known as Jim from now on," he replied as fist bumped Burt. The rest did the same as others emerged from the house.

There was Jim's wife, Linda, and their two adult daughters, Cynthia and Caroline. Sensing it was now safe to exit the truck, Senator Polacek opened the door, stepped out.

"Hello, Senator," Linda greeted with as much cordiality as she could manage. Burt and Tom nodded to her.

"Where in the world did they come from?" Esther asked. "I thought the Marines had killed them all."

"The cities, probably," Sarah said. "They start migrating when they run out of food sources."

"Well, that's totally unacceptable," Esther said.

Fred saw one of Jim's daughters roll her eyes.

"And you wanted to ride horses up here, smack dab into the middle of all of those things," Anne said with a reproachful look to her husband. Burt acted like there was something interesting in the sky to look at.

"I'm glad you came along when you did," Jim said. "We have a few guns, but we weren't quite sure how to deal with them. I guess it's something we need to work out."

"What are we going to do with this mess?" Esther asked nobody in particular.

Burt gave a sour expression. "What the senator means is what are *we* going to do with this mess while she watches and does nothing."

The two daughters laughed while the senator scowled at him.

"Well, there's no time like the present," Burt said, looked over at a nearby barn and pointed. "You got a trailer parked in there?"

They did indeed have a trailer, along with several canvas work gloves. Fred, Burt, Sarah, and Jim's daughters had the arduous task of removing the bodies, which they took down the road to the repurposed dumpsters. They had to kill four more zombies who, for some reason, were drawn to the dumpsters.

"I didn't think they could smell any worse," Caroline commented as the first few started to crackle and burn.

"You get used to it, sort of," Burt replied.

Sarah scoffed. "Yeah, right."

They ate dinner in the dining room, all formal settings with expensive china and fancy silverware.

"May as well use it," Jim said. He had taken venison and an assortment of vegetables and made an appetizing meal out of the confection. He got several compliments, even from Esther.

"How are things going around here?" Burt asked.

Jim shrugged. "None of the water pipes have busted, Parvis made sure of that. We don't have electricity yet, but Parvis seems to think he can get the powerlines repaired before it gets cold. Even so, we have a generator."

"That you hardly use," Cynthia said.

"Don't be cynical," her mother chided.

Cynthia responded by smiling sweetly.

"Fuel usage is a concern," Jim explained. "Plus, at the moment, we only have one generator. If it breaks down..." he finished the sentence with a shrug. "So, we use it sparingly. I had it on for the oven and stove, and I'll fire it up again after dinner so we can have hot water for showers."

"That sounds wonderful," Anne said and looked at the women. "How are you gals doing?"

"Well..." Caroline started to say but was cut off by Senator Polacek.

"We are suffering from a terrible injustice," she declared. She then stared pointedly at Sarah and Fred.

"Ever since the Tennessee contingent arrived, the dynamic at Mount Weather has taken a destructive downward track."

"Now, Esther," Linda chided. "These people came to visit out of the goodness of their hearts; they don't want to hear criticisms."

"I do," Sarah said. "Please, tell me, Senator, how have my friends from Tennessee caused all of the issues Mount Weather is currently going through?"

Esther made a display of a frowning. "Let me refresh your memory, young lady; we had a democratic process in place, and then you people show up and stirred things up. Why, on the first day, Zach brutally assaulted two of our children."

Burt saw Fred frown and explained. "The two children she's referring to are grown adults. Zach caught them breaking into his trailer. He took a switch to them." Burt cackled. "Those two Cranston idiots had a hard time sitting for a week."

Fred gave a micro and then stared pointedly at Esther. "Sounds like they got what was coming to them," he said.

"Perhaps you weren't paying attention, Mister McCoy; we had a democratic process in place. People don't go off willy-nilly and administer their own justice."

"That's twice I heard you say that," Sarah said. Esther looked at her. "Democratic process, you've said it twice."

"Yes," Esther replied. "The representatives of the country, that would be people like Jim and myself, address issues, discuss, vote, and come to a resolution that is for the betterment of all."

"Correct me if I'm wrong, but I was led to believe the congressmen and senators from Tennessee are dead," Sarah said.

"That would be correct," Jim said.

"So, when Tennessee residents arrived at Mount Weather, why wasn't one of them appointed as a state representative or senator?" Sarah asked as she looked pointedly at Esther, whose lips were pressed together.

"Hell, for that matter, there is no representative from Oklahoma, so why was I not appointed? I'll tell you why, because it would have diminished your perceived power base." Sarah shook her head and continued.

"You've got it wrong, Senator; you people caused this and it had been brewing for a while. The president's death acted as an impetus to the upheaval, us new arrivals had nothing to do with it."

There was a long moment of silence before Jim cleared his throat.

"Well, now, that is certainly an interesting perspective of the Mount Weather events. Why don't I get the generator going again and everyone can enjoy a hot shower?"

The rest of the evening was spent with everyone taking turns with the showers before Jim shut the generator off for the night. The house had five bedrooms and Fred was assigned one of them. After showering, he wrapped himself in a towel and went immediately to his room. It was hot and stuffy and he broke out in a sweat immediately. He opened the windows and was hit with a soft breeze. It felt good and he stood there letting it wash over him. He heard the door softly open and close behind him. Turning, he saw Sarah.

"Do you really think I'm going to share a room with the esteemed senator?" she asked. She dropped her bag and walked over to him. She was wearing a pair of shorts, a T-shirt, and nothing else.

"I'm not sure Rachel would approve," Fred said.

"Rachel is the one who encouraged it, remember?" she reminded him as she stared at him deeply. "I've missed you."

"Yeah, I've missed you too," Fred admitted. "Why did the senator come?"

"Apparently, she and Stark butted heads over something and he banished her. So, she came here. But, I'm not here to talk about the senator."

Sarah stepped forward and pulled her T-shirt over her head. Fred hesitated only a moment before embracing her and kissed her passionately. At some point, his towel fell to the floor.

"I think Rachel knew this was coming before I did," she said. The two of them were lying on their backs, the blankets pulled aside. In spite of the breeze, they'd worked up quite a sweat and the sheets were soaked.

"And she's fine with it?" Fred asked.

"Oh, we've not been intimate in a while. I mean, we're still close, but I think we've both come to realize our relationship began because of nothing more than loneliness and lust rather than a true emotional bond. Besides, sometimes I feel like I'm more of her big sister than her lover."

Fred grunted quietly. "I haven't been with anyone since you," he said.

Sarah turned her head and looked at him in the dark. She then reached out and interlaced her fingers with his.

"I'm going to tell her when we go back," she said.

"Tell her what?"

"I've got my man back and I'm not going to let him slip away again."

"I believe I'd like that," Fred said.

CHAPTER 42 – THE GREENHOUSE

Sarah caught Fred looking at her as everyone ate breakfast. He actually broke into a smile. It was a small smile, but a smile nonetheless. She felt blood rushing to her face and hurriedly sipped some coffee. Fred sipped some of his own coffee and looked away.

"Jim," Fred said.

"Yes, Fred?"

"I couldn't help but notice there are parts to a greenhouse stacked in the barn."

"Are you referring to that stack of aluminum and Plexiglas?"

"Yes."

"Well, I'll be. I wondered what all of that stuff was. I've been waiting for Parvis to pay us a visit and ask him about it."

"How do you know it's a greenhouse?" Caroline asked.

"Because it's one of mine," Fred replied.

"What do you mean, one of yours?" Linda asked.

"Back before, I had a manufacturing company that built greenhouses. That one is one of mine."

"So, that thing has been sitting in the barn for a few years now," Jim said. "Do you think all of the parts are still there?"

"They appear to be. If not, we can improvise. Parvis has that barn full of doo-dads."

"My my," Sarah said. "Not only are you a cowboy, you're an entrepreneur too. I'm impressed." She extended a booted foot under the table and rubbed against his shin. He didn't smile this time, but Sarah noticed a slight twitch at the corner of his mouth as he tried to fight it.

"Well, life is certainly full of surprises," Jim said with a big grin. "Is it easy to assemble?"

"It will be with me supervising," Fred replied. "I think we should put it right there," Fred said, pointing out the back window.

"Right off the back patio?" Esther Polacek asked incredulously. "Why, that'll ruin this scenic view. That's one of the only good things we have around here."

"When can we start?" Jim asked, ignoring the senator.

"How about after breakfast?"

The den had a set of French doors which opened to the large back patio. It was pea gravel which glistened from being professionally sealed. There was also a high-end stainless barbeque grill to one side, a couple of concrete planters with dead plants, and a rectangular lap pool which was currently full of leaves and stagnant water.

They looked around and discussed the location for the greenhouse and ultimately agreed on a spot which would offset the greenhouse from the main house so the view wouldn't be obscured. Fred didn't say how he wanted it to be hidden from the road and went along. After all, he had other things on his mind and found himself looking at Sarah again.

"I think my contrary wife should stand guard," Burt said. "In case those zombies have friends out there somewhere."

Everyone readily agreed.

It took most of the day, but they had installed the last Plexiglas panel a few minutes before sundown. When Fred put the final screw in, everyone exchanged congratulatory fist bumps.

"This is great, Fred," Jim said with a grin. "I have all kinds of ideas of what to grow."

"Find something to repurpose into small wood stoves," Fred said. "Put one at each end and you can keep it warm enough to grow throughout the winter."

"I'll certainly do that," Jim said.

Fred looked over at Sarah, who was smiling at him again. Fred fought it, but could not help himself and grinned as well. He was still grinning when Sarah's chest exploded.

CHAPTER 43 – SNIPER

"Take cover!" Fred shouted. Another gunshot punctuated his command, jarring everyone out of their momentary paralysis. The Hassburg women were standing on the back patio and quickly ran inside. The rest ducked for cover.

Fred quickly determined the direction of the gunshot and put the greenhouse in between himself and the hidden sniper. He made a quick peek at Sarah. She was on her back, staring back at Fred. She was still alive, but looked bad. He crouched and started to sprint toward her, but she shook her head violently.

"No!" she croaked. She had a coughing fit and blood spurted from her mouth. Then she went limp.

Fred continued staring before a bullet struck the aluminum frame of the greenhouse no less than an inch from his head. He ducked back and looked for the rest. Anne and Burt were hugging the ground grimacing in a mixture of surprise and anger. Jim was hunkered down behind a large concrete planter. He was obviously frightened, but keeping a cool head.

The only one who was losing it was the esteemed Senator Esther Polacek, who was standing motionless, staring at Sarah with saucers for eyes.

"Get down, Senator!" he yelled. She slowly turned toward him and stared, but Fred could tell she was in sensory meltdown. She did not even appear to recognize him.

No matter. Another gunshot rang out. It hit her in the back and came out of her chest in a furious eruption of blood and tissue, much like it had with Sarah only seconds before. She fell face forward without saying a word.

Fred saw Sarah's M4 leaning up against the greenhouse, no more than ten feet from him. He took a chance and darted to it. More gunshots rang out as he grabbed it and dived back around the corner of the greenhouse. Several blew large holes in the Plexiglas, but they missed Fred by several feet.

"What do we do?" Jim asked nervously.

Fred hastened another peek. As he watched, another round hit the planter, blasting out a chunk of concrete the size of his fist. The sniper was using a large caliber rifle. Fred could only hope his shoulder was aching from the recoil.

"Alright, when I start shooting, I want you to run inside as fast as you can," Fred directed.

"What about you?" Burt shouted from inside.

"I'm fine, as long as I stay put. I'm guessing there's more than one and they're probably circling around to the front of the house. Burt?"

"Yeah, Fred?" Burt shouted back from inside the house.

"You and Anne cover the front. Kill anyone you see, no questions asked."

"But, they may be friendly."

Fred looked around to see who said it. It was one of Jim's daughters. Caroline, he believed.

"There aren't any friendlies out there. Alright, get ready."

"What about Sarah and Esther?" Jim asked.

"They're dead," Fred answered. "Now shut up and get ready to move."

He checked the magazine on the M4, flipped the selector from safe to semi, and took a deep breath. He lunged around the corner, firing multiple times toward the wood line where he thought the sniper was. He emptied the magazine as Jim jumped up and ran toward the back door.

His tactic worked. There was a singular return gunshot, but it only succeeded in striking the flower planter.

"What now, partner?" Burt yelled from somewhere inside.

"Go to a window and give me some covering fire," Fred said. "But be careful." He didn't want to tell Burt that maybe Anne was best suited for the job and hoped he figured it out for himself.

It took less than a minute before he heard the sound of gunfire coming from a window at the far end of the house. Fred crouched and ran for the back door. He ducked to one side and someone slammed the door shut behind him.

"Don't show yourselves in front of the windows, but get all of the drapes closed," he ordered. Cynthia and Caroline hurried to make it so as he began pushing furniture up against the French doors.

"Alright, you two girls, get upstairs and keep a look out, but stay back from the windows. Burt and Annie, take each end of the house. Jim, watch the front. Linda, watch the back."

Nobody argued; they knew they were under attack and Fred's directives made sense.

"I wonder who it is," Jim said to nobody in particular.

"Marauders, maybe," Fred replied.

They waited. There was no additional gunfire, but fifteen minutes later, Jim shouted out.

"There's someone walking up the driveway!" he nervously shouted.

Fred walked forward and looked through a crack in the draperies. He was a younger man, maybe in his late teens, every bit as tall as Zach. But, unlike Zach, this one was skinny as a rail and had a face full of acne. His hair was a greasy tangle of dog shit brown, and his clothes looked like they hadn't been washed in a while. He whistled while he walked. Fred didn't know what irritated him more, the man's casual attitude or the off-note tune he was whistling.

"I got a couple of men crouching down behind some trees on the other side of the road," Burt said.

The man walked up to the front porch and knocked on the door.

"Hello? Anybody home?"

Fred walked over and watched him through the peephole. The young man peeped back.

"I know you're in there," he said in a singsong voice.

"Shouldn't we talk to him?" Jim whispered.

"No need to," Fred replied. "They ain't looking to palaver."

Fred stepped back and looked at the door. It was a standard entry door, a metal shell with a hollow inside. Probably filled with some type of Styrofoam product, Fred surmised. He drew his pistol, unloaded the forty-four hollow points, and replaced them with full metal jacket rounds.

He looked back through the peephole at about the same time the young man knocked again. Louder and more forcibly this time.

"You people need to open the door, or else there will be consequences!" he yelled.

Fred moved over to the other side of the door and responded with a soft knock. He watched as the young man pressed his eye against the peephole. Fred stepped back, leveled the barrel where he estimated the man's belly button was, and fired twice.

The man screamed in agony as he fell in a heap to the porch.

"Get back," Fred admonished and quickly led Jim back into the kitchen. As he suspected, once the man regained his wits, he fired several times through the door with his own handgun. His friends joined him and fired several rounds through the windows. Fred turned up the walnut dining table and pulled Jim down behind it. They hunkered down behind the table and waited as the gunfire continued. After a couple of minutes, the gunfire died down until it was only an occasional shot or two. He then yelled out so everyone in the house could hear him.

"Alright, everyone, they're going to lay siege, take pot shots, and hope we do something foolish."

They lay there behind the table and listened to the man moaning in pain and calling out to his friends.

"Are we going to help him?" somebody yelled down from upstairs.

Jim looked at Fred questioningly. Fred gave a slight shake of his head.

"No, honey," Jim said. "If anyone goes outside, they'll shoot us."

The man groaned again and called for help. His voice was weaker this time. It won't be long now, Fred thought.

"Do you think they'll come for him?" Jim asked.

Fred gave another slight shake of his head. "He was expendable, that's why they sent him. They wanted to see if we have guns and if we would use them."

"So, we're going to let him die an agonizing death, huh?"

Fred did not bother with an answer.

"So, what do we do now?" Jim asked. Fred reloaded as he looked over at Jim. He could see the anxiety etched on his face. Fred reloaded his pistol and looked outside. He could only see Sarah's legs from his position, but it was enough to steel his resolve. He looked up at the setting sun. Complete darkness was not for another two hours.

"What do we do?" Jim asked again.

"We wait 'til dark."

He looked out one of the back windows. He could see more of Sarah now. He was going to cry, he knew he would, but that would have to wait. He hoped whoever shot her didn't get bored and leave.

CHAPTER 44 – TIME TO HUNT

"Jim, what size shoe do you wear?" Fred asked him as he looked at the Nikes Jim was wearing.

"Size ten, why?" he asked.

Fred nodded. "Same as me. Are those comfortable?"

"Yes, they're Nikes."

Fred began taking off his cowboy boots and motioned for Jim to swap with him.

"Uh, I'm not much of a cowboy boots kind of guy, Fred," he said.

"I'll give 'em back in the morning, the good Lord willing," Fred replied.

Jim looked at Fred warily before taking them off. "These are two hundred dollar shoes," he muttered as he handed them over.

Fred nodded and put them on.

"Anything else you want?" he asked.

"I need something to camouflage my face, like charcoal, or something similar."

Jim thought for a moment. "The girls have their makeup sitting in the bathroom closet."

"It'll have to do," Fred replied.

Jim low crawled up the stairs to his daughter's bathroom. He came back a minute later carrying a metal case.

"Are you going to do what I think you're going to do?" Jim asked as he began streaking Fred's face with dark eye shadow.

"They ain't going away," Fred replied. "This is our best chance." He saw Jim looking at him like he was having a hard time understanding. He tried to explain.

"My guess is they'll try some type of attack after dark. If they're not hurting for provisions, they'll probably set the house on fire to draw everyone out. If they're hurting for food, they'll try a different tactic."

"Like what?" Jim asked, the nervousness in his voice growing.

"Either a direct attack, or they'll try to sneak in, or put up harassing fire all night, wear us down, and then try to get us to surrender."

"Is that not a viable option?" Jim asked.

"No," Fred answered. "They'll kill everyone. Maybe not your daughters. They're pretty girls and still young."

"I see," Jim said. "Is there anything I can do?"

"Yeah. I'm going to need you to stay up all night and stay alert. If you hear anyone messing around the doors or windows, get ready to shoot. If it's me, I'm going to say," he paused a minute. It was possible whoever was out there knew Fred's name. He looked down and noticed the shoes.

"I'm going to say Nike. Got it?"

"Nike," Jim repeated.

"Yeah. If you don't hear that, even if someone says something like, 'hey, it's me, Fred,' I want you to shoot, okay?"

"Yeah, okay."

It was almost dark now, and Fred used the time to determine which door or window would be the best manner to exit the house. It was then he remembered the garage. There was one bay door still open. His plan was to slip out through the utility room door and out through the garage. He only hoped there was nobody in the garage lying in wait.

"Alright," Fred said quietly. "It's time."

Jim stared at him and after a second held his hand out. "Good luck, Fred McCoy."

Fred shook his hand and gave him a nod. A somber nod.

Fred crawled over to the door in the utility room that led to the garage. He spit on the hinges so they wouldn't squeak, but even so, he expected gunfire to ring out as soon as he opened the door. As soon as he turned the doorknob, he moved out of the way and used the handle of a broom to push it the rest of the way. He waited for five full minutes, occasionally waving the broom back and forth in an effort to draw fire.

Nothing but silence.

Fred moved out quickly and ducked down behind the Subaru Outback Jim and his family left Mount Weather in. There was a hint of a moon peeking out from behind clouds and there was fog starting to roll in. It wasn't much light, but it was all Fred needed.

He waited.

Fred had his six-shooter, eighteen rounds of ammo left, and his knife. The same one he killed Snake with. He didn't bring a rifle with him. He needed his hands free for what he had in mind.

It took thirty more minutes before he heard a soft footfall and a shadow appeared from behind a large elm tree in the front yard.

The person was armed with some type of long gun. He made a beeline toward the garage and thought it'd be a great idea to hide beside the Subaru where Fred was crouched down. Fred met him with his knife.

The point of it went up under the chin, through the epiglottis, and sunk deep enough to pierce the vertebrae. Fred didn't know it, but he'd stabbed the newest member of the Blackjacks, T-Dawg. T-Dawg was twenty-nine and was living with a group in Riverton, West Virginia before being kicked out for stealing. They gave him a shotgun and the clothes on his back. He had not eaten in five days when the Blackjacks found him.

Fred caught the weapon before it clambered onto the concrete floor and watched the man drop. He emitted a gurgling noise for a few seconds before becoming silent. He felt the long gun in the dark and determined it was a pump action shotgun. Fred stuck his finger in the open end of the tubular magazine. It was full of rounds.

He searched the man and felt something sticking out of his back pocket. Feeling it in the dark, he realized it was a blackjack. Fred now knew who was attacking them.

He knew they were making a move now and wondered where the rest of them were. He did not have to wait long. He heard a gunshot ring out from the back of the house.

"Take that, you cocksuckers!" someone yelled and fired again.

Fred moved now. He worked his way out of the garage and around to the side of the house. The fog was limiting the ambient, but it also worked to Fred's advantage. He hugged the side of the house and peeked toward the back.

The man fired again. The flash of the burning gunpowder momentarily lit up his face as he shouted another obscenity. It was all Fred needed. He aimed the shotgun, and fired once before ducking back. He heard the satisfying sounds of a person falling and racked another round.

After a moment, several gunshots rang out, chewing up the brickwork on the corner of the house where his face was a second ago. Fred was sure his shot was true, so there must have been someone else with him. He backed away and moved toward the big elm tree in the front yard. He hoped if any of the marauders saw his outline, they'd assume it was one of their comrades and not shoot. He only hoped nobody inside the house would take a potshot at him.

While he waited for his next move, he heard more shouting of obscenities from the back of the house. But, the yelling stopped immediately after a small caliber gunshot rang out from the house. It had to be Anne and that twenty-two rifle of hers. She was probably posted at a window and patiently waited for the opportunity to kill one of them.

Including the man lying dead on the front porch, they'd killed four of them now. He remembered Melvin stating there were twelve at one time, but Snake was dead and Zach had killed three more. If Anne's shot was a good one, which he did not doubt, that'd make a total of eight of them dead and maybe four left.

If they hadn't increased their ranks. Yeah, that was a big if.

No matter, Fred had an appointment with a sniper and he had no intention of missing it. He'd already determined the general location of where said sniper was and started low crawling.

The night was cool. Even so, Fred was sweating profusely and he was parched. He hadn't thought to take a canteen with him. He ignored his discomfort and kept crawling through the high grass. After an hour, he made it to the wood line.

He reached a couple of trees growing close together and took a moment to rest. His hands, elbows, and knees were scraped up and his healing gunshot wound was aching terribly. It did not deter him though. Fred had no illusions. He knew the odds were against him, but before he died, he was going to kill the man who murdered Sarah.

He stood and started walking slowly toward the spot where he believed the sniper was posted up. If he was gone, he'd wait until sunup and attempt a track. He'd taken no more than a few steps when someone less than twenty feet away fired a rifle.

"Damn it, Hot-Shot, tell me before you shoot again, my ears are ringing."

"Sorry, dude," another voice said a little louder than normal. He must have been wearing hearing protection.

A moment later, one of them turned on a flashlight. It had a red lens on it, but it put out enough light so Fred could see his two adversaries.

Fred didn't know it, but Hot-Shot was the self-proclaimed sniper for the Blackjacks, and coincidentally, Lonnie's little brother.

None of it mattered to Fred. Only one thing mattered. He worked his way closer.

"Alright, it's been thirty minutes, time for another one."

"Roger that," Hot-Shot said and fixed his earmuffs. He levered the action and laid back down in a prone position.

He didn't like wasting ammunition, but Lonnie's orders were clear. Shoot into the house sporadically throughout the night so whoever was inside wouldn't get any sleep. They were going to make entry through the back door before sunup, and Lonnie told him to keep them off balance. The house was dark, but he could see the glint of windows. He took aim at one he'd not yet shot out and fired.

Immediately after firing, he felt his buddy stumble across his legs. He moved one of the earmuffs aside and looked behind him; he could make out the shape of his friend sitting there.

"Mako, what the hell are you doing?" he asked.

Mako fell forward, his face hitting the dirt inches from him. It was at that moment Hot-Shot saw the man standing immediately behind Mako's body.

"What the fuck?" he said as he tried to bring the rifle around.

Fred jumped on top of him, bringing a knee into his gut. Hot-Shot expelled air out of his lungs in a painful gasp, but before he could react, Fred slit his throat.

As the man began having spasms, Fred found the flashlight and turned it on.

"That was for Sarah, you piece of shit," Fred growled as he watched the sniper bleed out.

Once Hot-Shot stopped twitching, he inspected the two men closely. One of them had a water bottle. It only had a few swallows left, but Fred wiped the top off and gulped it down. He then inspected the rifle. It was a Marlin 444, lever action. A nice, western-style rifle meant for large game. More than enough to obliterate a human. The heavy weight of the bullet the large caliber bullet limited its range to around two hundred yards, but they were only a hundred yards from the house.

He looked out toward the house, imagining Sarah's lifeless body lying on the ground and looked at the rifle again. He gently set the rifle down and then slowly, deliberately, jammed his knife through the eye socket of each man to ensure there would be no zombie resurrection, and then did something else with his knife.

CHAPTER 45 – THE DEATH NOD

"That's the last of the coffee," Topsy said as he handed Lonnie a cup. Lonnie eyed him cynically.

Topsy shrugged apologetically. He'd been on the receiving end of a beating from Lonnie before, and he wasn't in the mood for another one. Standing only five and a half feet tall and barely a hundred and thirty pounds, he needed the safety of Lonnie and the Blackjacks.

"Maybe those people will have some," he said, hoping to calm Lonnie.

Lonnie was a cruel-natured man with a hair-trigger temper, but these past couple of days he'd been even worse than normal. First, Snake went missing. He sent Pig, Scooter, and Crash to that Mount Weather place and they haven't heard from them since. Lonnie thought they'd been killed, which was probably true.

Yesterday, Hot-Shot had found the house the Blackjacks currently had under siege. When told about it, it was the first time Topsy had seen Lonnie smile in a week.

"They have a couple of young split-tails," Lonnie said, referring to Jim's daughters as he watched them through the binoculars. "This is good, boys. Real good."

Topsy's job was to set up camp out of sight of the house and guard the whores while the rest of them took care of business. He didn't like the woods at night, so he kept the truck and camper parked in the middle of the road. Who the hell was going to make them move, the police?

He heard a lot of gunshots while he set up a fire and began to cook some dinner.

"Sucks to be them," he mumbled.

They came back an hour later and nobody was smiling.

"What happened?" Topsy asked Freak.

"One of those bastards shot Tank," he said.

Topsy gasped as Lonnie walked over and looked at the food.

"What's this shit?" he asked.

"It's the rest of the chicken soup," he said. He was about to tell Lonnie they were almost out of food, but the look on his face made Topsy decide the best thing to do was keep his mouth shut, or else he might get backhanded.

Lonnie ladled most of it into a bowl. "Alright, listen up. Mako and Hot-Shot are going to throw some rounds into the back of the house off and on all night. I want you fuckers to occasionally sneak down the road and put some rounds in the front of the house. In the morning, they'll either surrender or we're going to charge the house."

"What about Tank?" Freak asked.

Lonnie paused and looked back. Freak lived up to his nickname. He had multiple tattoos, including three on his face, and two piercings in each eyebrow.

"Feel free to go get him if you want. I doubt you'd live through it." He then looked at Topsy. "Wake me before sunup."

With that, he walked into the trailer. "Hello, girls," he said before slamming the door shut.

The rest of them split what was left of the soup.

"Man, we need to get in that house," Freak said in a low voice. "I need fresh food and fresh pussy, and not necessarily in that order."

He chortled at his own joke. Topsy laughed along with him.

"They got guns," Crank said quietly. "They already killed Tank."

Crank was a meth head. In fact, anyone with street smarts would've taken one look at him and knew immediately he was a meth head. Even so, he was often the voice of reason among the group.

"We're a hell of a lot meaner than them," Freak retorted. "They don't stand a chance."

"Yeah," Crank replied, keeping the uncertainty out of his tone.

When the sky started turning gray, Topsy dutifully knocked on the camper door and woke Lonnie. He walked out wearing only a pair of blue jeans and some sneakers. Topsy dutifully handed Lonnie back his handgun while staring at his muscled chest.

"Alright," he said as he jammed the handgun into his waistband. He worked a kink out of his neck. "Damn, the girls were insatiable last night. I hardly got any sleep."

Topsy cast a quick forlorn glance at him. It seemed like to him Lonnie could've been a team player and let them take turns with the girls. At least for an hour or so. But he didn't and they were relegated to taking turns keeping guard and sleeping on the hard asphalt.

Lonnie glanced over and he quickly looked away.

"Say, it's quiet. When's the last time you heard a gunshot?" Lonnie asked.

"A couple of hours now," Topsy said and looked over at Crank.

"Yeah, a couple of hours now," he said in agreement and spit between the gap where two of his front teeth used to be.

Lonnie looked at Freak, who nodded apathetically.

"Fuck 'em, they're probably sleeping. Are we gonna do this or what?" he asked.

Lonnie was about to reply with a derogatory retort, but he was interrupted by a man's voice.

"Hello, boys."

The four men looked up suddenly at the direction of the voice. They saw a visage of a man standing down the road about thirty feet away in the swirling fog. Lonnie stood slowly and looked the man over. He was tall, lanky, and dirty as hell. The knees on his jeans were torn and green from grass stains. And, it looked like some kid had been coloring on his face. In spite of it, Lonnie could see a hardness underneath.

"Where did he come from?" Topsy asked under his breath.

"Who the hell are you?" Lonnie asked.

"The name's Fred. Fred McCoy."

Lonnie spat. "Never heard of you."

"Oh, I'm not surprised, I'm a nobody. May I ask your names?"

Lonnie smirked. "Certainly." He pointed. "That's Topsy, Crank, Freak, and I'm Lonnie. We're the Blackjacks. Now, I'm betting you've heard of us."

"I have," Fred said.

Lonnie nodded at the perceived compliment.

"Well now, you certainly have some balls, sneaking up on us."

"I apologize if I've upset you."

Lonnie chuckled. "So, what the hell do you want, Fred McCoy?"

"Those are my friends in that house up the road a ways," Fred said.

Freak had stood and began moving off to the side.

"Don't do that," Fred said.

"Why not?" Freak replied with a taunting smile.

"Because then you may not be able to hear the story I'm about to tell."

Lonnie chuckled again. "And why would we want to hear your story, old man?"

"It's a good one. It's a story about how a race of Indians was wiped out because they pissed off the wrong people."

Lonnie chuckled again. "Well hell, old man. I'm game. Tell me your story and then I'll decide if I'm going to kill you or not."

"I appreciate it, sir. Well, it goes like this. Back in 1634 or so, the Puritans were running the Massachusetts Bay Colony. I'm sure you've heard of it. They teach it in grade school."

"Yeah, I remember that," Topsy said. Lonnie glared at him. Topsy shut up.

"Anyway, they had a truce with the local tribes and everything seemed to be fine and dandy, but one tribe, they called themselves the Pequots, they got into a disagreement with the crew of a Puritan ship and a couple of people were killed."

"I like killing," Freak said and grinned, showing Fred his two missing front teeth.

"Good. You'll really like what happens next. The Puritans became angry and wanted revenge. So, they declared war on the Pequots and put a bounty on their heads. Now, there were other tribes of Indians living around the area and they didn't like the Pequots too much, so they started killing them. For the bounties, you understand."

Fred paused a minute and looked them over. All of their rifles were leaned up against their truck, which had a camper hooked up to the back of it. But, all of them had a handgun of various makes and models. Two of them had holsters, and the other two had them jammed into their waistbands.

"Is that it?" Lonnie asked.

"Oh, no," Fred answered. "Here comes the best part of all. The local Indians started killing the Pequots, cut their heads off, and turned them in for the rewards. But, the heads were cumbersome and got to stinking after a few hours, so they came up with the nifty idea of scalping their kills instead of taking the whole head. This is how Indians started the tradition of scalping their conquered enemies."

"That's a real nice story, Fred, but I'm wondering why the hell you're telling it to us," Lonnie said. He was growing bored and was ready to kill the old man and move on to the house.

"Well, sir, I brought you boys a present, and I thought the story would help explain the present," Fred said.

They watched as Fred slowly reached behind him with his left hand. He came out with what looked like a clump of fur and tossed it. It landed at Topsy's feet. Topsy squatted down and looked at it before gasping and jumping back.

"Those are scalps!" he shouted at Lonnie. Lonnie looked down at them and then looked back at Fred with a look of incredulity.

"Those are two of your friends," Fred said. "Mako and Hot-Shot. I didn't catch the names of the others, but they're dead too."

They didn't know the proper terminology, but they watched as Fred gave them the death nod.

"I see you boys are armed. That's good. You might have a chance."

Fred spread his feet slightly. His right hand dangled beside his pistol.

Freak went for his gun first, but if he'd ever seen Fred shoot, he would've known he would have been better off dropping to his knees and begging for mercy.

Fred shot all four men in under a second. Even though he had two additional rounds in the chamber, he reloaded quickly as he scanned the area.

After reloading, he walked up to Lonnie, who was still alive. He'd managed to get his handgun out of his holster, but he couldn't seem to hold onto it. Fred kicked it away.

"Looks like I missed your heart by an inch or so. My aim isn't as good as it once was. No matter, you'll be dead in a few minutes."

Lonnie looked up at him. "Who are you?" he choked out.

"I told you, my name is Fred McCoy. When you show up in hell, be sure to tell everyone you met me."

Fred stared at him for a moment longer and then went around to the rest of them, ensuring they were dead and retrieving their handguns.

There was a small fire someone had made in the middle of the road and circled with rocks. A coffee pot sat on one of those rocks with a cup beside it. He helped himself. He only took a swallow and dumped the rest. It was awful.

Looking at the camper, he realized there might be someone hiding out in it, waiting for the opportunity to take a pot shot at him. He approached it warily and then stood to the side as he flung the door open. He did a quick peek and saw movement. He backed away, holding his pistol at the ready.

"Come out of there," he demanded.

It took a long minute, but then three women slowly exited. They saw the dead bodies and looked at Fred with sheer fright etched into their expressions.

Fred eyed them suspiciously. They were pitiful looking. Dirty, emaciated, wearing nothing but tattered underclothes.

"Anybody else in there? Don't lie," he warned.

"No, sir," one of them stammered. The other two shook their heads.

Their clothing left little to the imagination. Fred was worried about weapons, but it was obvious they weren't armed.

He peered in, ignoring the rank smell and, finding nobody left inside, focused back on the women. He holstered his pistol.

"It's going to be okay, ladies."

CHAPTER 46 – JOURNAL ENTRY

This journal entry is being recorded on September 25th, three years into this living apocalypse, fifty days since we first arrived at Mount Weather, Virginia.

As I am writing this, it is coming up on two in the morning. I couldn't sleep, so I volunteered to relieve the guards at the main post. They thanked me tiredly and hurried inside before I changed my mind.

Yesterday, we were attacked yet again by a horde of approximately a hundred of the infected. The Marines kicked ass, as usual, but some of the civilians here are really starting to shine when it comes to fire discipline and killing zombies. Most importantly, we had a (mostly) coordinated firefight and nobody was injured or killed.

It was a long day, but everyone pitched in, even President Stark. Unfortunately, as I'm writing, I am looking at a dump truck full of dead corpses. The truck ran fine for about a minute before dying. Now, it's sitting on the roadway, and when the breeze hits, I get a good whiff. Maybe we can get it running tomorrow.

Where do I begin? There has been so much that has happened since our arrival here. First, a man who I thought was dead turned out to be alive. Fred was shot during the Nolensville massacre, but he's too tough to kill. When he found out we were up here, he didn't think twice. He hopped on a horse and rode six hundred miles to join us. Six hundred miles on horseback. That tells you everything you need to know about the kind of man Fred McCoy is.

He's changed though. I'll try to explain in more detail at a later time.

Once I was here, there was an attempt to cultivate a vaccine. Sarah and Justin led a contingent to Fort Detrick with two scientists and an Igloo cooler with several vials of my blood. I was told the place was full of zombies, but they managed to eradicate most of them and get a lab running. They were up there for almost six weeks before coming back home. The scientists believe they've successfully created a vaccine, but only time will tell. The important thing is, all of them made it back alive. They also experimented with an antidote. We captured a few zombies using control poles the dogcatchers used to use and tried it out them.

There were mixed results. Two of them displayed no changes whatsoever, but one of them actually started trying to talk. They are uncertain how best to proceed, but I bet we'll be tasked with catching more zombies for testing.

The scientists, and a couple of others, suggested releasing the zombies we'd caught rather than killing them. I told them I'd take care of it. Fred, Jorge, Josue, and a couple of Marines helped me walked them out about a mile down the road and then we killed them. History may paint me as a bad person, but as far as I'm concerned, the only good zombie is a dead zombie.

Another notable incident, not too long after our arrival, the president was murdered by a jealous husband. President Richmond had apparently been having an affair with Sheila Hunter. Her husband, Earl, took offense and killed him. Then he hung himself.

Since then, Abraham Stark, the former Secretary of Defense, has assumed command. He usurped two other individuals who were ahead of him in the line of succession. Those two being the speaker of the house, Jim Hassburg, and the president pro tempore of the senate, Senator Esther Polacek.

I will say this, since Stark took over, there has been a noticeable improvement in the efficiency of operations around this place. There has also been talk of starting outposts around the area of Mount Weather. Jim Hassburg volunteered to be the first and moved into Parvis Anderson's house in nearby Bluemont. Senator Esther Polacek's acerbic personality soon made her persona non grata, so she was voluntold to move in with the Hassburgs.

They'd not been living there long when they were attacked by a gang of marauders known as the Blackjacks. Sadly, Major Sarah Fowkes and Senator Esther Polacek were both murdered.

This was a terrible mistake on behalf of the Blackjacks. Fred McCoy took grievous offense to this action, hunted them down, and killed them all. Burt later confided in me that Fred scalped a couple of those boys.

The day-to-day activities of Mount Weather have undergone several subtle changes. There have been more improvement projects, and people who once considered themselves too good for manual labor have found themselves being voluntold to participate in work crews. Like I said, so far, it's going pretty good.

Among the major projects, there has been a concerted effort to restore the power grid into Bluemont. Parvis is adamant the hydroelectric dam that powers Mount Weather cranks out more than enough wattage for Bluemont and beyond.

There are several things I don't agree with, no surprise there, but I have to look at the positive side. We have health care for my family, they're safe, and they're happy. That made my decision rather easy.

*****

I heard a door shut, looked toward the main building, and saw Parvis. He was wearing a backpack, which I knew held his laptop, and he also had his ever-present Yeti mug. I closed my journal, put it away in my own backpack, and checked my watch. It was three in the morning. I stood, stretched, and made the mandatory call.

"Post one, negative SITREP," I said into the field phone.

"Roger, out," a woman's voice replied. It was Sheila Hunter. Ever since the murder of the president, she kept a low profile and did not socialize with anyone.

"How's it going?" Parvis asked as he walked into the shack.

"All is quiet," I replied. "Why are you awake?"

"Couldn't sleep," he said. "I went into the armory and chatted with Sheila a little bit and she told me you were out here, so I thought we'd do a lesson." He looked at me with a grin as he booted up his laptop. "So, what do you say, my young Padawan? Shall we continue discussing Philpott damn and how we're going to rebuild the power grid?"

I smiled at him. "Sure."

Parvis took a sip of coffee and grinned again. "If I haven't said it, I'm pleased you decided to become my apprentice. This is a win-win for everyone."

I hoped he was right.

CHAPTER 47 – THE BEACH

"It's more of a greenish blue," Savannah said. "I don't remember that. I always remembered it being a deep blue, you know?"

She looked at Melvin and grinned as the waves lapped against her bare feet. She wiggled her toes in the wet sand.

"Careful, you might sink all the way to China," Melvin said. When Savannah giggled, he couldn't help but smile.

They'd arrived at Virginia Beach less than ten minutes ago. Savannah was driving and she made a beeline to the seashore. Parking in the sand, she looked at Melvin expectantly. Melvin used binoculars to scan up and down the beach. There wasn't a soul in sight. He smiled at Savannah and got out.

"It looks clean," Melvin said. "I thought it'd be polluted."

"It's beautiful," Savannah said. "I want to get in."

"Sure, go ahead."

Savannah grinned mischievously and pulled her shirt off. She tossed it to Melvin, who wasn't surprised she wasn't wearing a bra, and did the same with her jeans before trotting into the surf. A wave knocked her off of her feet. She stood back up, flipped her hair out of her face, and looked back to see if he was watching.

Melvin was indeed watching. The sunlight glistened off of her wet skin. When the two of them first met, she was skin and bones. She might have weighed eighty pounds, if that. She'd filled out nicely since then; he guessed she was around a buck twenty, and all of it in the right places. Melvin thought she was beautiful.

He looked around. There were numerous hotels, most of them still intact. He wondered if any of them were occupied; perhaps they were being spied upon at this very moment. He decided he didn't care, stripped, and ran out to join her.

After a few minutes of frolicking in the surf, they walked out together. She had goosebumps.

"It's cold," she said, the grin still on her face.

"C'mon," he said, grabbed their clothes, and the two of them walked back to the truck. He found a towel and began drying her off. At one point, there was a pause and they made eye contact. Melvin bent down and kissed her deeply. Savannah put her arms around his shoulders and pulled him down into the sand.

Please enjoy a sneak peek into book six of the Zombie Rules series: True.

CHAPTER 1 – TRUE

Nimrod Abraxas True. That's me. Named after my father, or so my mama claimed. Truth was, I had no idea who my father was. He was African American though, which wasn't a good thing for my mother. Her family disowned her the moment I was born, or so she said.

I guess I was around fourteen or so when I told people to stop calling me by my given name. I hated it. Being named after a man who took no interest in me was hard, so I'd tell people just to call me True.

I was the oldest of seven. My momma was what you'd call a wanton woman. Each of my siblings had a different father, so there you have it. Life growing up for me was about what you'd expect under those circumstances. I was constantly doing stupid shit and getting in trouble.

When I was seventeen, I got caught breaking into a home, the home belonging to my history teacher. He was an old crusty-looking white man. Rumor had it he was a veteran of both Korea and Vietnam and had lots of medals. He visited me in juvie and told me if I enlisted, he wouldn't press charges.

It wasn't a hard decision. I'd been arrested so many times, the District Attorney said she was going to get me tried as an adult. Make an example of me, she said.

Besides, the only thing waiting for me was an apartment in government housing I shared with my siblings, my mother, and whoever she was sleeping with at the moment. The place had a permanent odor of badly cooked food and dirty clothes.

So, Mister Johnson drove me to the recruiting office. It was at one of those commercial strip malls. They had the Army, Navy, Air Force, Marines, and National Guard all jammed together. Everyone had gone home for the day, except for a National Guard Sergeant who was playing solitaire on his computer. Mister Johnson had a long, private talk with him, and the next thing I knew, I was signing papers as a full time member of the National Guard. After basic training, they assigned me to Houston Barracks, Nashville, Tennessee.

It was fine with me. Once I got out of basic, I actually got a room with only one other roommate, a wormy little white boy who spent all of his free time in his own world, sitting on his bunk in nothing but his underwear, wearing a headset, and playing video games. I didn't complain; it was a hell of a lot better than where I used to live.

And then, it all went to hell. That was nine hundred and eighty-one days ago. I kept track of the day the world ended by starting on the day I first saw a zombie. Actually, I saw about a thousand of them. That's the day I started my life over, the day everything changed. Nine hundred and eighty-one days ago.

It don't matter what all I got into during that time. Not much to tell. Chaos, people going crazy, the National Guard being called upon to restore order. Hah! What a fucking joke.

Anyway, here I was, standing outside in the middle of the night with three white men who'd become my friends.

"The truck is a good one," Zach said as he handed the keys to me. It was a red dually four-by-four diesel. The man had modified it all kinds of ways. He had those big redneck tires on it, a huge bumper with a winch so you could either push things or drag them out of the way, a light bar on top, and he'd even put some fencing over the windows so the zombies couldn't get to you. We found a camper top that fit on the back so we always had a place to sleep.

"There's an M60 in the back with five hundred rounds," he told us. "It's all I could spare."

"You are fucking awesome, Zach," Blake said.

Zach was Zachariah Gunderson. That name alone screamed, "*White Boy!*" but, he was a good dude. Smart too.

"Are you guys sure I can't talk you into coming with us?" he asked.

I shook my head. We'd talked about it many times, and a few days ago, we made the decision. Me and my two friends, Blake Mann and Brandon Caswell. We decided we were tired of being in the military and tired of taking orders. We were going to strike out on our own. I wanted us to keep it a secret, but Brandon decided to get advice from Zach.

I'm glad he did. Zach planned it all out, thinking of things I would've never thought about. He said if we decided to leave while everyone else was there, one or two of the military officers might raise a stink, so he suggested we leave in the middle of the night. We agreed. And, he gave us the truck and the M60.

Yeah, Zach was a good dude.

THE END

CHECK OUT OTHER GREAT ZOMBIE NOVELS

DEAD ASCENT
by Jason McPhearson

The dead have risen and they are hungry...

Grizzled war veteran turned game warden, Brayden James and a small group of survivors, fight their way through the rugged wilderness of southern Appalachia to an isolated cabin in the hope of finding sanctuary. Every terrifying step they make they are stalked by a growing mass of staggering corpses, and a raging forest fire, set by the government in hopes of containing the virus.

As all logical routes off the mountain are cut off from them, they seek the higher ground, but they soon realize there is little hope of escape when the dead walk and the world burns.

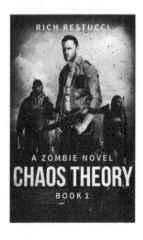

CHAOS THEORY
by Rich Restucci

The world has fallen to a relentless enemy beyond reason or mercy. With no remorse they rend the planet with tooth and nail.

One man stands against the scourge of death that consumes all.

Teamed with a genius survivalist and a teenage girl, he must flee the teeming dead, the evils of humans left unchecked, and those that would seek to use him. His best weapon to stave off the horrors of this new world? His wit.

CHECK OUT OTHER GREAT ZOMBIE NOVELS

RUN
by **Rich Restucci**

The dead have risen, and they are hungry.

Slow and plodding, they are Legion. The undead hunt the living. Stop and they will catch you. Hide and they will find you. If you have a heartbeat you do the only thing you can: You run.

Survivors escape to an island stronghold: A cop and his daughter, a computer nerd, a garbage man with a piece of rebar, and an escapee from a mental hospital with a life-saving secret. After reaching Alcatraz, the ever expanding group of survivors realize that the infected are not the only threat.

Caught between the viciousness of the undead, and the heartlessness of the living, what choice is there? Run.

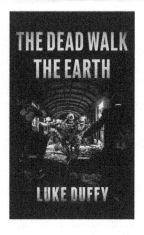

THE DEAD WALK THE EARTH
by Luke Duffy

As the flames of war threaten to engulf the globe, a new threat emerges.

A 'deadly flu', the like of which no one has ever seen or imagined, relentlessly spreads, gripping the world by the throat and slowly squeezing the life from humanity.

Eight soldiers, accustomed to operating below the radar, carrying out the dirty work of a modern democracy, become trapped within the carnage of a new and terrifying world.

Deniable and completely expendable. That is how their government considers them, and as the dead begin to walk, Stan and his men must fight to survive.

CHECK OUT OTHER GREAT ZOMBIE NOVELS

DEAD PULSE RISING
by K. Michael Gibson

Slavering hordes of the walking dead rule the streets of Baltimore, their decaying forms shambling across the ruined city, voracious and unstoppable. The remaining survivors hide desperately, for all hope seems lost... until an armored fortress on wheels plows through the ghouls, crushing bones and decayed flesh. The vehicle stops and two men emerge from its doors, armed to the teeth and ready to cancel the apocalypse.

TOWER OF THE DEAD
by J.V. Roberts

Markus is a hardworking man that just wants a better life for his family. But when a virus sweeps through the halls of his high-rise apartment complex, those plans are put on hold. Trapped on the sixteenth floor with no hope of rescue, Markus must fight his way down to safety with his wife and young daughter in tow.

Floor by bloody floor they must battle through hordes of the hungry dead on a terrifying mission to survive the TOWER OF THE DEAD.

Made in the USA
Monee, IL
25 March 2024

55745345R00184